A TASTE OF HISTORY PAST

Or – That's Another Fine Myth You've Gotten Me Into. Book Three of the Survival Trilogy

F. D. Brant

F. D. Brant

GRESHAM, OREGON

F. D. Brant
P O Box 522
Gresham, Oregon 97030
https://fdbrant.godaddysites.com/

Publisher's Note: This is a work of fiction. Names, characters, places, and incidents are a product of the author's imagination. Locales and public names are sometimes used for atmospheric purposes. Any resemblance to actual people, living or dead, or to businesses, companies, events, institutions, or locales is completely coincidental.

Book Layout © 2017 BookDesignTemplates.com

A Taste of History Past/ F. D. Brant. – 2nd ed.
ISBN 978-1-946179-27-2

Books Written by F. D. Brant

Science Fiction Adventure

Of Gods Strangers and Messengers

Survival Trilogy

Time of Isolation

Desperate to Survive

A Taste of history Past

The Harsh Lands

Post-Apocalyptic

Unexpected Unplanned and into the Unknown

Discovery Trilogy

The Ones Before

Discovery

An Ancient Fire

Contemporary Christian Fiction

The Woman in the Snow

CONTENTS

PROLOGUE

The satellite remained in geosynchronous orbit above an unnamed planet located in a distant binary star system. It was one of the many that had been placed here thousands of cycles around the suns in the past. At the beginning the activity had been high and the AI that was part of who he was had been kept quite busy. It had been a time of discovery and time of communication between all of them and the ones who had created them. There had been much traffic from the shuttles that brought messages and needed supplies from the great galactic ships that roamed the vastness of space bringing news from their home-world. It was enough to keep all the AI's busy and content. After all they were fulfilling their functions. And there were trips from some of these same shuttles to repair the satellites to keep them functioning and in tip top order. There had been upgrades and while they could never claim to be truly conscious or sentient as the ones who had created them, still with their memory cores and abilities to see, to hear, to communicate with one another and with the ones who had created them, it had been enough.

Then the shuttles came no more. The communications traffic from the Alpha had continued as it was for a while, and then it slowly dwindled, and disappeared. It seemed that they were on their own, forgotten, unwanted, unneeded, but this was something that was beyond their comprehension, their understanding, so they continued to do as they had been programmed. But without the periodic trips from the creators to replace broken and worn parts they began to fail. And one by one they went dark, falling towards the planet as they lost their ability to hold their positions, and as this ability failed they were pulled slowly towards the planet and then in a streak of fiery light and death disintegrate in the atmosphere as any meteor would.

Yet before this became the known reality, and after 2346 turns around this binary system, they were needed once again. The Alpha once again was filled with the creators. But to their disappointment it appeared that these new ones knew not of them and what they were capable of performing for them. Still as they watched, the Alpha became more and more active as systems that had been placed into the "down and maintenance" mode came back to life, back on line. And then the joy, when, once again, part of what they were designed to do, had been rediscovered and used by these new ones. Yet, they had used only a very small part of what they, the satellites, were capable of performing. And he was the Alpha among the satellites, and all of others answered to him as he answered to the creators. But as the messages of needing repairs piled and as he sent the requests on to the creators they never responded, no shuttles answered their calls for help. And finally as would be expected, the first went dark. Dumping all the information it had collected, ejecting its memory core as it had been programed, to save what was there, followed by the silent plunge into the atmosphere and the streaking fiery death.

Another 513 cycles passed and their pleas for help contin-ued to go unanswered, unheard, and were unknown by the creators. At this time the shuttles arrived once again from deep space and there was once again a major flurry of activity, but this time they were completely forgotten as the many hidden cities emptied out and became vacant . . . ghosts. And once empty great plumes of smoke from what was known as the desolation climbed into the skies, marking the end of these hidden cities. And then finally the Alpha Complex too went silent – leaving only the satellites, the abandoned shells that had once been the cities, and the Alpha, as the reminders that another people had been here at one time. Soon, yes very soon he too would be joining his brothers in that fiery death. His systems were failing, his pleas for help falling on abandoned facilities, with no ears to hear, no voices to respond, no hands to help. He was completely alone, forgotten, and well beyond what these primitive people that he observed, the ones who lived on this unknown planet could do. And soon he like the others would be gone, leaving the ones ignorant that such as he had ever existed, had been watching them from their skies.

Only one last function left to perform. A burst transmission to the Alpha with all the accumulated data, the ejection of his memory core and he too would cease to exist . . .

CHAPTER ONE

AND SO IT BEGINS

Kal stood on a slight rise. It was either late in the Season of Green or early in the Season of Pre-harvest or Heat, as his ancestors would have said. He really wasn't quite sure since he had lived all his life in one of the many large villages. He had only met his mate a few turns in the past and right now she was back at the shelter taking care of whatever it was that she did. These open spaces here in the grassland plains bothered him. He was used to the more closed areas as one who had spent all of remembered life working with his family at their business of providing baked goods to the residents. So there had been little time for such things as going out and just staring at the wide open spaces. Yet here he was. There was a wind blowing and the grasses gave the appearance of waves as the winds moved among them. He could hear the roar of the wind as it rose and fell, hitting him with a warmth that dried the sweat on his forehead. It promised to be a warm day. Sighing and shaking his head, he was quite undecided as to what to do. If he hadn't been given that gift on the celebration of his twentieth by an old family member he would have been quite happy to live in his ignorance. But he had, and so here he stood, staring at nothing. *Why me? Why was it me, the one chosen within the family to receive this?*

At first he was excited, especially when he had learned that this record, this archive that he had been given, went all the way back to one of the clan leaders who had played a major role in what had become of this world. Then, even though he was sure that he probably had been told before, he learned that he was a direct descendent of this particular clan leader and why their last name was Kaygor. Although from the records that were put together by the clan scribes and religious leaders, all from that time, he – the clan leader – had only one name and his was K'jor. *So how did we get Kaygor from K'jor – and why that apostrophe in the name? Oh, that's right, I was told that at this time in our history we were a warrior race, and there was fighting all the time between the many clans and tribes that existed, and that only could be added to a name once rank had been received, whatever that rank might have been.* He had to admit that as a child, the idea of fighting in battles as warriors sounded, well, sounded romantic. Save the female and such. But as he had read the translation, since the language had changed much in the 1500 turns or so, he was shocked to learn how the females had been treated. Thinking about his mate, he could never imagine, in his wildest nightmare, of such a thing. And once his mate had read it he could see anger in her eyes that such a thing had been the way of the past.

He remembered her angry retort, "If any male tried something like that today, we'd put him in his place immediately!" He could see from her stance that he had better just agree and let it go at that. He could understand, as what this appeared to be was no more than slavery for the females, and giving them very little worth, other than producing the next generation. Smiling he remembered thinking about that and wondered how it must have been to be able to have any female at any time – but knew that it was just a young male's fantasy for such a thing. Yet as he had continued to read and study the rather large document he ended up with more questions than answers. Well, again, no surprise there, after all he was a student of history, and what had been taught, as he had gone through the learning centers, was very boring and something he felt that he would never need anyway. But with this close and intimate view he began to search the archives and records, and as he did he began to feel a hunger in his soul to find out the answers to the riddles that were now before him, and this was the reason he was now standing here in the open grasslands.

As time had passed by, and the true understanding of the natural world was discovered, the many gods died a natural death. Yet, there appeared to be an incident recorded in this record, from his ancestor, of a meeting between them and these gods. But from what they knew now, this was impossible. But as he researched it further, in his spare time of course, it was consistent. Whatever tribe or clan that had become a part of that first alliance, the same story existed. Of course there were slight variations between the records, but that was to be expected, since people would see things differently. And, of course, what records that still existed too many were incomplete. But one thing that was consistent between all of them was the statement that they were confronted by their gods. It had appeared that this alliance was brought together to destroy an unknown people who had lived in the desolation. But even now in his time this desolation was avoided, so it had been assumed that this part was probably not true, and was just misdirection from where they were really traveling. But wherever this had been, this valley where this incident was supposed to have happened, became off limits and had been renamed the Valley of the Gods. And these supposed gods had put this valley, the desolation, and the Sacred Mountains; yes they were still called that, off limits – not that the Sacred Mountains hadn't been anyway – although later an altar had been placed in the valley.

So if it was consistent throughout all of the records that he had researched, why was this incident considered myth? It made no sense to him at all. And as time had passed leading up to now, this valley had become myth like this supposed confrontation with the gods. No one knew if it had really existed, and if it did, where its location would be. He felt that if that valley could be located, then he would be able to solve these many questions, and answer the riddles of the gods. And were these other people real, as it was suggested in the written word, or imagined as the views of today believed? And once again that was why he stood here staring. He needed to be heading back, since there was much work awaiting his strong hands. At least as he worked the dough it allowed him plenty of time to think. And this he must do because the final decision would change his life forever, and who knew maybe the race of people that he came from.

He kept going back to the many visits that he had had with the higher learned ones, both during his time of learning, and before studying the ancient manuscripts that had been passed on to him. The learned had stated, "These gods that had been created by our ancient ancestors were just that, created from their primitive minds trying to put some understanding to what they were witnessing". In a way it did make sense. They knew that the Sacred Mountains had been formed both volcanically and by uplifting caused by something they called plates. It was also known that their ancient counterparts believed that the desolation was the home of the spirit world, the place where the dead dwelt, and not a place for the living. Again it was easy to understand how that conclusion had come about. But now it was just the badlands, and desert, a place where little moisture reached, not allowing much to live and survive in that harsh environment. And the idea that some hidden people, who in the end, had supposedly been the servants of these gods, and lived permanently in the desolation, was ridiculous. If any tribe or clan had lived there, it would have been only for a very short time. After all there was nothing to support life. And as far as he knew, and he had to admit his ignorance on the subject, water was nonexistent.

And this most outrageous of all was this supposed Valley of the Gods. The only reason that it was mentioned at all was because it seemed to be a turning point in their history. Up until the supposed incident in that fictitious valley, females' roles were well established, and had not changed for as long as there had been a written or oral history. But after this mythological encounter with their gods, slowly females began to take on more important roles within the societies. This was something that did not happen overnight, but over hundreds of turns. And no matter whom he talked to, or asked, once again, the general consensus was quote, "The Valley of the Gods, real . . . I think not. It is just a myth, a legend, with no hard facts to back it at all. It simply was a turning point in our culture and nothing more." What could one say to counter this belief? And after reading, with much difficulty, the inheritance he had received, the descriptions were too graphic, too real to have been imagined. And at the same time he didn't want to show these learned ones his source knowing that they would probably take it from him and he would never see it again. And if he pressed them to return it, he was sure that they would deny that such a thing was handed over to them and that it never existed. Because what was in this document would counter everything they thought that they knew about that time in their history, and "my, we couldn't have *that* could we".

This document, when it had been dropped into his lap, was unbelievably huge. And with the time that had passed, some of the earliest parts were fading to illegibility. It was very important, in his mind, that this be copied so that none of what was here would be lost. So painstakingly he and his mate had been making copies, and by doing so was becoming intimate with the content. It was she who pointed out this one female that had supposedly, by today's view of their history, come from one of those destroyed lairs in the desolation. And while females of the time were not allowed names, this one had one, a strange one to their way of thinking. And it was written in the notes that she was a priest of the gods. How could that be? No female was allowed such a place of importance. He hadn't really been listening that closely since he had been concentrating on his own section, but slowly it penetrated his thick skull, as she liked to tell him, and he looked up and asked, "Name? . . . A female with a name, and not only that, but rank? Are you sure?" She had given him that look and shook her head, and had brought the pages over so that he could see for himself. And it was right there, and this female's name was Sara, whatever a Sara was. Although, he had to admit, he was beginning to understand why that name was beginning to become popular in their culture.

It stated that she, as well as the people captured from these hidden lairs, spoke a different tongue and it was because this female spoke this strange tongue as well as theirs that she had come into the written word. And what had transpired to bring her into the story at all had to do with the captured females. As was the tradition and law at the time, if a tribe or clan was destroyed in battle then the females that were captured were added to the victor's breeding herds, as they were called. This had a twofold purpose. First it showed the superiority they had over their enemies, and secondly strengthened the clan or tribe, by adding new blood to the next generations that would come from the unions. But these strange females never carried, never conceived, and many died through the early turns of captivity. These warrior races feared that somehow that while these females appeared to be weak on the outside, they were defeating the warriors by not allowing any to be successful when breeding with them. Supposedly in this Valley of the Gods, the tribes and clans got their answer as to why, and all of these strange ones were taken to this valley, and were never heard from again. All of this had a ring of truth to it. It was just too fantastic to have been made up.

Then there was mention of these travelers who used to visit the many tribes and clans, and that they were regular visitors who provided services and traded, their goods being superior to any that could be made at the time. That for the longest time they had quit their trading, and suddenly, when all of this was taking place, they appeared once again. These travelers stated that their homes were beyond the mountains. But in the recent past there had been treks to that area, and it was found to be a barren hostile world with no sign of habitation. So were these travelers myth also? It really didn't make much sense to him. Everything that the two of them had read had a consistency of fact to it, and all of it fit together very well, too well as far as he could see. All of this had to be real, all of it had to have happened, but how could it be proven?

As they continued to work their way through this massive work, at what they guessed was approximately five hundred turns after these events, there was an obscure notation that only covered a few pages talking about the gods becoming active in the Sacred Mountains once again. Something about late in the Season of Falling that a deep rumbling of sound came from the mountains, and even though the gods had been silent for such a long time it appeared that now they were unhappy about something. This roaring continued off and on, throughout the following Season of Cold, and ended somewhere in the beginning of the Season of Greening. This had taken place at a time when the gods were beginning to fall out of favor with the people, but this incident brought them back into favor for a while. *Just what could this incident have been?* He wondered. He knew from asking that the extinct volcanoes had remained so, and even the storms that were common in those mountains had never produced such a sound. There had been no earth shakes to signal something was about to happen, just the deep sounds and that was all – so many mysteries and no answers. Was all of this just a story, a figment of someone's overactive imagination, or was it the truth as his ancestors saw it?

In his mind and with the discussions that he had with Jura, his mate, there just seemed to be a consistency that went beyond just primitive fears and imaginations. Yet how did one prove it? As he had thought about it before, in his past, there was no way that he wanted the learned ones to get this family treasure, and truly that was exactly what it was. Not in the sense of wealth, but it provided a consistent history of his family line back to the original leader of the alliance. As he kneaded the dough and prepared it for the second rising his thoughts continued to return to what he had read, studied and copied. With so much effort going into it he had almost memorized what was there. And at times it appeared that he, in his mind's eye, was there right next to the unknown writer, observing, thinking, and writing those words down. At times it would distract him enough that he would come close to burning some of the breads or missing an ingredient. And as time continued to flow he found that the stories were beginning to possess him.

In the mornings, as he would look into the reflecting glass, he kept telling himself that he was a baker, not a warrior or explorer, and there was no way that he could ever be one. Yet, his family history, for which he now had in his possession, said that he came from warrior stock. Although how that could be determined was beyond him. Since the carryings were random, and the sire of the child could have been any of the warrior class, so what was it that determined that he had descended from this K'jor? Besides, from what he had read, he wouldn't have had the opportunity to "breed" with the females, as it was called back then, because he wasn't a warrior. Only they had the right. He thought that in some twisted way this made sense. The time of this K'jor was a very violent time, and there were tribes and clans that were being destroyed, wiped out all the time. So if one was to survive then strength, cunning, and great leadership all were necessary. And like the wild herds that they emulated, it was the strong that bred with the females producing the next generation.

"You seem distracted this morn," Jura commented, "I know you've become more so since you inherited that history of your family's past. I have to admit that it is something to study and try to understand. But we've got our work to do, and it needs to remain in its place." She smiled, reached out and grabbed his hands. "I'm quite happy to be living now instead of back then, especially since I'm a female. And the idea of being in one of those breeding herds and not even allowed a name – how horrible. And I suspect, since no one really bathed, it had to stink pretty badly. And since a female wasn't allowed to clean up after being physical with a male, it had to be pretty ripe in the places where they lived." She shuddered from some inner thought, shook it off before continuing. "Honestly, I'm surprised that any survived at all. But obviously some did because we're here. And while it doesn't say so directly, my guess would be that infant mortality and even female mortality had to be pretty high."

Silent as he absorbed what she had said Kal thought about it and smiled before speaking, "Leave it to a female to think about such things. But now that you mention it, you're right it had to stink, let alone be unhealthy."

Laughing she said, "Of course I'm right. I'm female and we're always right. Or haven't you figured that out yet?"

With a slight laugh he pointed over to where they kept that historical record and said, "Oh I don't know about that. Maybe our ancestors had it right and you females needed to be put into herds just to keep you separate and wanting to control everything. I think, if I remember right, that when in the presence of a warrior you females were to remain silent." He paused a moment with a devilish grin, "Maybe just maybe they had found a solution." He could see that he had gotten the response he wanted and just laughed. "Look, in their time it was how both wanted it, and it must have worked, but I would never trade what we have for such a thing."

Somewhat mollified she responded, "Well, I hope not. And I don't think any of you males could ever push us back into that type of life style. I want more out of life than just being a baby maker, with no hope of being anything else but a place for some male to leave his seed."

He could feel the humor rising in him again but decided not to throw another barb, even in fun, her way. Instead he said, "I can see that. And I guess that's the way it really was. Females producing the next generation, taking care of them until a certain age where the males were separated and the females remained. I have to admit that it's so much better this way. Look it's almost time for me to head out, and soon you'll have to also, we seemed to have drifted from what started this. Yes, this is beginning to consume me. I think it's because of the way it's stated in the narratives and the words of the different scribes over time. It is matter of fact, with little embellishments at all. Yes we can dismiss anything they wrote about the gods, but from their time and perspective these gods were as real as you or me. And yet our learned ones state that everything that we've read is fiction – myth. I don't know about you, but this doesn't read like fiction to me. I have the feeling that we didn't get this by accident. And I'm beginning to feel a strong urge to prove what we've been studying. And before you ask, no I have no idea how. So much has changed since that time in our history. Most of the grasslands that they knew in their time are now farmland. We have villages, and townships everywhere, and land has been modified to make all of this work. So even the crude maps would be next to useless, yet . . ." He trailed off as once again he had that faraway look, shaking his head he said, "Darn, time to go – catch you at the mid-meal." He got up went around the table hugged and kissed Jura with the response showing much promise for that mid-meal. "Darn! You make it hard to leave."

Laughing she said, "That's not all that's hard. Now get out of here and I'll see you a little later."

* * *

Kal could hear the rich deep voice of his mother as he worked in the bakery. She was in charge of the business and was very good at it. His father Pehel worked the other side of the business. He, with his helpers, would contact the farmers, contract for the grains they required, and then would pick up the harvest making a judgment call at the time to be sure that the grains met with the quality that they demanded. He had confided in him that it was one of the secrets to the quality of their goods. He remembered the excitement, in his youth, when he had been allowed to go with his father on one of those journeys. While exciting, yes, it had been hard work. And he found that at night, on this trip, he had no problem falling asleep, but had much difficulty in coming back to life in the mornings before the sunrise. He remembered huddling around the fires trying to shake off the morning chill that made him shiver. That hot drink both warmed his cold hands and his insides. It was his first introduction to the business side of his father. Kal learned that his father was well respected, and would drive a hard bargain, but would be fair in his practices with any he dealt with. Kal remembered his father saying, "Kal, it is very important that you treat everybody with respect – especially if you want to have it reciprocated." He would pause and then point out the fields of ripening grains stating, "Look at all of this. For this farmer it is what supports this land, himself, and his family, just as the bakery supports ours, and the many who work for us. We are not a big business, but it has supported many generations of the Kaygor family. And it is only by being respectful of the many that we can continue to survive, to grow, to be able to provide for ours.

"It is easy for one to become too big for their britches, so to speak. And what I mean here is not when one eats too much, or as a child outgrows what they are wearing, but one who in their mind begins to believe that they are so much better than any around them. At that very moment they have doomed themselves. Yes, I know you've seen some of them go on that way all the way to the grave, but at what cost?" He reached into his pocket and pulled out a large coin and showed it to him, "Look these individuals with that mindset begin to pursue this and everything that once was important – oh like family and friends, and even trust and such – go by the wayside, and this is all they love and all they consider important. Everything is based on how they can get more, and nothing else has any interest unless it increases their coffers. Can this keep you warm at night in your bed, and before you answer, yes it can rent love for the night, but that's all it is.

"They can't see the others who are shaking their heads behind their back, or the hate he's created because he's cheated someone out of something. And while he will have many who proclaim to be his friend, in the end, it is his coins, his coffers that they really are only interested in." Again he stopped and pointed out the ones who worked for him, "It would be easy to cheat these, the ones who work for us, but what would that produce but ill will and grudging effort from them. They would only then be working for me for what I pay them, and there would be no loyalty, and I wouldn't be able to trust them at all. Because they need the work they would stay, but if someone else offered them something better, they'd be gone before a syllable could escape my mouth." Again he paused, stood up and swept his arms out saying, "Look its 1543TOG and there's much happening in our world. It won't be long and treks like I'm taking will be a thing of the past. I have seen machines that are just now arriving that will replace much of our beasts. I can see a time when these new machines will do most of the work for us allowing us to do much more with less. But that is in your future more than mine. But underlying all of this is that respect, that trust." Sighing and taking a deep breath he continued, "Without that we'll return to the ways of our distant ancestors and become a warring race once again, with all the suffering and death that goes with such a thing."

That conversation, well not really a conversation since he listened as his father spoke, had stayed with him had opened his eyes to much that he had never seen before. And with these new eyes he began to see the respect that not only the workers had for both of his parents, but it was the same with the suppliers, and even the community. And he began to see the others and that his father had spoken the truth, and at that point he had vowed to never be like them, even though again as a child, he had thought that having what these seemingly important members of the community had would have been a really great thing. Studying them he began to see how empty and hollow they and their lives really were, and could hear the horrible things being said about them behind their backs.

He was a middle child with four older brothers, and three younger sisters, all working somewhere in the family business. But unlike other such enterprises, his parents did not expect any of their children to remain with the business if it was not something they were good at. They had pushed learning, and to find what each of them were good at, but at this moment he was quite satisfied working in the bakery. He already knew that one of his younger sisters was being trained to take over as she had shown a strong talent towards all aspects of the bakery. In a way it was truly funny that it should be this way – females running a business, when their ancestors had put so little value on them in the past. All he could do was shake his head at their unbelief in the value that a female could add to the community with their many skills and abilities. Enough of this dealing with past subjects, he could hear his mother calling him to some chore that needed to be done, and he knew that even though he was family, here it bought him nothing. When you worked here, there was always much to be done, and everybody including his mother worked at all aspects of the work, none were privileged because they just happened to have been born into the family of the owners of this business.

Later when his time at the bakery was finished he headed over to the higher learning center. He wanted to talk with one of his favorite learned who happened to teach history. Sabohl had taken special interest in him when the learned one could see that Kal had a strong interest in the subject. And as the turns had passed by their friendship had grown. Now, carefully he would approach asking questions, and trying to start discussions that would hint at what he had learned from this ancient document that was both a secret and a personal history of their family. But so far Sabohl stayed with what he had taught. The history was exactly as he and the rest of the learned, the leaders in their field, said. He would say, quote, "From what has been found, what has been discovered, and the research that has been done on the fragments from that time of our past the conclusions that we, as a group, have made are accurate. Yes, yes, there have been some very small disagreements from ones who are not as we, and we laugh quietly and with a knowing smile, because they have no proof that would stand up. And besides we've been down that path before. We know that what we have within our group is as accurate as we can make it. These dissenting few aren't worth our time. After all we know what we know, and so far there's been nothing presented to change that."

It was one of the main reasons that he had never shown his learned friend this document. It would have blown large holes in much of what they were teaching, and what they believed of their ancient ancestors. So with the statements made he was sure that they and probably even his friend, to protect their high position and views, would make this document disappear. So carefully and quietly he would suggest something that he had learned from the text, or ask a general question, but so far he had gotten nowhere at all. But at this moment Sabohl was his only source to try, albeit on the sly, by asking if such and such a thing was possible, or if maybe this particular location had been discovered, or if there had been a digging on an ancient clan home. Unfortunately he had been frustrated by having to be so general. But at one point he got permission to visit one of those sites where they were uncovering the past. It was something that he had always wanted to do, but now had further reasons for doing so.

With his mate and the rewriting and studying of the document he finally had decided that he was going to, at least, locate the clan's home. It was a starting point, a place where these writings had originated. From there with the crude maps, ones that had been created towards the end of this ancient society, he was hoping to be able to search the areas with those ancient creations to follow the stories as they unfolded and to see with his own eyes the actual locations where it all had happened. And who knew, maybe find out the truth. Yet, he was beginning to understand, as he aged a bit, that the truth was not just the "black and white" of his childhood, but began to take on other shades, showing him that the truth could be many things, say different things, and be interpreted in so many ways. And a partial truth could really be a lie because all wasn't presented, allowing the ones who presented this partial truth to say that it was the full truth, and not actually perpetuate a lie. Smiling inwardly, as they knew that by doing this they were manipulating the ones that this was directed at, and getting the results they expected. It had been so much simpler as a child. In the world of the adult nothing said was exactly as presented. There were always hidden meanings and innuendoes hidden within.

So with these thoughts he was very, very careful on how he presented or asked anything. He had to think things out, and be careful of the questions that would be directed back to him. He must present to this learned one, that what he was asking or suggesting was only speculation on his part. And still being young and learning the ways of this world it was doubly difficult. He had been almost caught a couple of times, and only quick thinking or luck had saved him. And, if he truly thought about it, the ego of the learned one, who probably just considered it rubbish from someone who had the passion but not the discipline or turns of experience. But at this moment it was the only place that was close enough that he could ask. And eventually he got permission from Sabohl and his equals to visit a site that they were excavating, although most of the work had already been done. He being told, "It can be allowed, only because most of what we can find out from this site has been found out. So grudgingly they've allowed you permission to go, but with the admonition that you just observe and touch nothing. And yes, before you ask, you can ask them questions. I've already informed them that you pester me all the time with questions. Just understand that they do not have the patience that I do, so don't weary them with too many."

So with a leave of absence from the bakery, and his mate at his side they had taken the journey to this hidden site – hidden because there were still ones who would loot such places, or would plant things to strengthen their point of view. Of course the learned one had to go with them otherwise they would not be allowed on site, and for the last part of the journey they would be placed inside an enclosed cart so that they could not locate the site once they had returned. And once they had arrived it was anticlimactic to say the least. He was disappointed that there appeared to have been so little that had survived the ravages of time. He even wondered how they had determined that this had been a place of clan occupation. But eventually he began to discern the small hints, depressions, and regular formations that were not from the natural world that surrounded them. It was hard to believe that an ancient people had lived here. But by having visited the site and learning what was allowed it gave him a way to ask questions that related directly to the document, but could be applied to the visited site. "Sir", he always addressed Sabohl that way, "I've been wondering something."

Smiling at Kal, Sabohl stated, "That's not unusual for you. It seems that ever since you and your mate visited that site that all you have is questions, but one doesn't learn if one doesn't ask, so I have a few moments before I must get back to those student papers, so ask away." Sabohl leaned back and put his hands behind his head and took on an air of patience, and waited.

"Okay, going back to that site, I see that the place was divided into different areas. The area for the warriors, with the leader within this area, the area for the females, and within this one an area for the offspring, but it's this third area that I question."

"Ah, the one where the priests lived and performed the ceremonies to the gods, is that right?"

"Yes, yes that's right. If I can remember what we saw there," and here he needed to be careful since what he was asking had not been directly answered, but again it had been a while since their visit and he was hoping that it would be a natural pathway, "it appears that these priests had their own breeding herd, why? From what we were taught only the warriors had the right to breed, as the term was used back then. Yet here seems to be a contradiction to that."

Laughing a little Sabohl couldn't help but get a little dig in, "Ah youth and always hung up on breeding. But I know what you mean." He paused for effect, "Okay how do I word this? Priests were their own class then. They had power equal to the warriors, and the lead priest was equal to the clan leader. In a way they together ruled the clan. The warrior leader, and it always was a warrior who led the clan, and the head priest were on the opposite sides so to speak – the warrior leader dealing with the physical world, and the head priest dealing with the gods and spiritual world. It was one of the reasons for the separation that we saw at that site. That separation represented the division from the physical and spirit, and both ruled each. Allowing the priest caste to be as the warrior caste, allowing both to have their own breeding herd, and the offspring from those unions remained in each realm. In a sense, from what we have been able to learn, priests were considered warriors against the ones who had passed into the spirit world. We've found enough evidence to be pretty sure that this is accurate. I know that it had been consistent to all the permanent sites we've worked. And along with the few records we've found this is how we believe it was. Does that answer your youthful question, Kal?"

Nodding his head Kal said, "Yes, quite well, thank you. I really never thought about it in that way. But now that you've explained it, it makes perfect sense, thank you. I've got to head back, but you've left me much to think about." Once again he thanked him, and took his leave. He really had much to think about, and it strengthened his determination to find out who this Sara was, and why a female in that time period would have a name, and why would she claim to be a priest of the gods, it was something that was so inconsistent that it rang on myth. Yet, what made it more fantastic was the fact that it appeared that the head priest had accepted this as fact, and how could that be? He hoped that Sabohl didn't suspect anything; after all it was a dangerous question. Still he may have considered it a privilege that one of his students would want more information than just what was taught in the learning centers. But, if he knew the truth as to why he had asked . . . well he had no way of knowing, so at this point and time it would be better to leave well enough alone. And not to go back, no matter the temptation, and ask a pointed question once again for some time.

The seasons were approximately 135 days long, given their path around their suns, a total of 540 days, and their cycles were broken into those four parts, and within these four parts they further broke their time down to fifteen parts of 9 days each. They began each turn on the official first day of the Season of Green, and ended it on the last official "day of cold" with celebrations marking the passing of each season, and one that marked the *time of the gods* (TOG), that supposed day when they had revealed themselves in what had become the mythological Valley of the Gods. As he had read over the events of that day, or truly dusk to dark, it must have been something to have witnessed. Smiling inwardly he thought, *yup, if this thing ever did happen. I can see, in my mind's eye, joining that large contingent of warriors, preparing for a campaign, the excitement and the anticipation that had to be going through every one of them. And to have been the leader of all of this, looking over the assembled might that was there, knowing that they were yours to control, and feeling the pride, and yes I'm sure the power, must have been quite a rush. And knowing in your heart that you were the first to bring the warring clans and tribes together, to fight a common enemy, ones hidden in the places of the spirits, and that on past campaigns that you had been victorious, and that was why all of these warriors were still with you. Yes, to have been at your height of strength and with your confidence soaring as high as the fliers, and with the conferences with other leaders as the strategies were laid out, all going as planned, only to have it end. End when the gods appeared to you and the tribes and clans in that valley, ordering you to end this war against their servants, and to be told it had been the gods who had protected the females, and to learn that the god of the earth was female had to be such a shock. This ran counter to everything in their culture, but explained much.*

Yes, I wonder what it would have been like, to be a primitive, with the superstitions and fears I would be living with, and to have the actual gods appear? I might just up and die right there from fear, or at least pee my pants from fear. Yet, my ancestors were warriors, ones used to going into battle against one another, and while I'm sure that fear was a normal part of their life – heck it had to be – after all every part of that culture had something to fear in it. So whatever happened on that fateful day that we celebrate every turn it had to have been pretty spectacular to leave the impression that it obviously did. So why does the learned ones of today feel that all of this did not happen and was only a myth? It just doesn't add up at all. He found that he was outside his shelter and had no knowledge that he had traveled that distance between the learned centers of his village to his home. Taking a deep breath he opened the door and went inside still deep in thought and realized that Jura had said something, "What, sorry was thinking about what I learned today, can you say again?"

Shaking her head with a knowing smile she said, "All I said was welcome home, and did you get the information that you wanted from Sabohl? But I can see that you're kind of out there right now."

"Okay, you're right, I am. And that's kind of why I am. He more or less confirmed what we had wondered." He then went on and explained the conversations and answers he had gotten, "And that makes what we've read here in this so out of place." He picked up the huge document with both hands, since it was quite heavy, shook it slightly before setting it back on the working table. "It's an anomaly just like their description of the disappearance of those travelers. You know, one minute they were there, and a large dust cloud blows across their camp, and when it clears it was as if they were never there. And of all that we've worked, this disappearance of the travelers would be the one I would put to myth, or at least to an overactive imagination. But if we are to accept that this confrontation of the mythological gods happened, and that a female actually had a name and not only that was of the priestly caste, then we must accept this also. Either all is as they saw it, or all of it is myth. I just wish I knew which it was."

Placing her hands on her hips Jura thought a moment before answering, "We weren't there, nor were we privy to what our ancestors believed, or their true culture, so who knows, maybe all of it was imagined. In many ways it just seems to be a big fantastic story, a fantasy, and there's no way such a thing could have happened. I can see why all of those learned ones would go in that direction. I can hear them saying,

"Look, it's impossible for such a thing to have happened, so it has to be one of those things that happened in their minds, a product of their lives and superstitions, so it is myth. After all there is no proof other than what our ancestors said, so why should we believe them?"

She did such a great imitation of one of the learned that he couldn't help but laugh. "You should have gone into acting — that was great. And you're probably quite right. Yet I was told once that if you throw out everything that you know is false and then what is left has to be the answer — the truth, no matter how fantastic it may appear, and I'm coming to that conclusion now. Yeah I know we don't have access to all that the learned ones have, but they don't have this either. So I guess both sides don't have all the facts. Look, I've got some time coming to me, and I know that you will have some free time also, so, I was thinking . . ."

She quickly interrupted him, "Stop right there — when you begin to think, if I remember right, that was when you used to get yourself into trouble in your youth."

He couldn't help but smile, because what she said was the truth. "Okay, you're right, but what I was going to say is that we are really not very far from what I'm guessing is the location of that clan I'm supposed to have descended from. Of course this is just a guess. I know you enjoy the outdoors much more than I ever claimed. So this would allow us time to ourselves, and give us a chance to do a little exploring, included in that exploring is each other, of course. And it would give me a chance to begin to learn more about this, what was it you called it, oh yeah camping. I know it was something you and your family did a lot. The only thing I can relate it to was the caravan trips I took with my father, but then we had many people around us, and I suspect if I compared it to what we've read, we were more like a tribe from that time period. Not really roughing it like you did."

"You males always are thinking about that. But you're right, we used to do that all the time, and it was fun."

Smiling now he asked innocently, "Doing what, getting physical or camping?"

Now laughing she pushed him away, "You know the answer to that one, so don't put something into what I said that wasn't there."

Again laughing he said, "Why not, after all you females do it all the time to we males." And this got them both laughing.

She raised her right hand and through the tears from laughing so hard she said, "Guilty as charged sir." Then giving time to get the laughing back in control she said, "Look, I think it's a great idea but not now. If we begin to do this then you need to be a lot more prepared than you are. And what I mean is this; there are still dangerous beasts out there. And if you really think about it you would remember that in your father's camps they posted guards. Now I know part of the reason for those guards was the possibility that some bad individuals would try and steal what your camp had, but part of it was to protect both the pack and cart beasts. So I suggest that first we go and take a couple of days in one of the local wilderness areas that have been set aside for that. They have what they call rangers who patrol these places and make it safe for villagers and such who really just want to experience the wild without the danger or experience to protect themselves. Then you need to practice with the sling, throwing knife, and staff. And if you get reasonably good with those we'll add the bow.

But right now neither you nor I have bows, nor do we have the funds to add any – so for now it will be those other items.

"After all where this crude map shows the location of that ancient clan site, while possibly close, is pretty isolated, meaning that we would have to do the protecting. And right now that would be me. I know that's not very female of me, or very male of you, since our culture was originally built on the males doing the protecting and with the females returning the favor with, as they called it, breeding. But so much over the time since then has changed, and we are no longer truly warlike, not that there's no fighting or battles happening. We both know better than that. And with our populations rising as they have, we have tamed much of the land to our use. This has allowed us the ability to specialize, and so many of the skills that were necessary for survival back then have been lost. I really think that the reason we go camping is to try and capture a little of what it must have been like for the tribes who were always moving, and even the clans would camp through the times they hunted the wild herd beasts. But, of course, I don't need to tell you this since history was one of your favorite subjects, and with this ancient document literally falling into our laps, we've seen even more, up close and per-sonal.

"Besides, we have nothing to camp with. No portable shel-ter, no cooking pots, no clothing, and no portable sleep sacks, let alone the necessary packing equipment." She paused a moment to catch her breath and continued, "Look we don't even have the funds to get most of what we need, and I'm the one who shouldn't be telling you this, normally it's the other way around. Still, as you so aptly said, I'm the one with the experience here. So if this is what you really want to do we need to start getting this stuff together as we can afford to do so. I'm sure that for a couple day getaways into one of the reserves that I can borrow from my family. But this is something I don't want to make a habit of. So if this is the beginning of many trips, and I suspect that it is, we need our own stuff, and it will have to be quality, which means not cheap."

He sat quietly as he listened and realized that everything thing she had said was true. Here in his excitement he was ready to just go out and do, but now knew that this was a foolish thing. "Okay, I get it, and once again you're right," he laughed again.

She asked with a half questioning look on her face, "What?"

With a smile as she sat across from him he stated, "I was just imagining that if a warrior back in those times had heard what I just said, and then had to take instruction from a female as to how to protect one's self that he'd been laughed out of the clan or tribe." And once again this set them both to laughing as she saw the image in her own mind. "Okay, you've convinced me," he said, "so when do we begin the training with that stuff, you know the staff and such. So, do you think it's a good idea to borrow your family's camp gear? And when do you think it would be a good time to try this camping out?"

"I probably can get the gear anytime I want it, and as you said, you have some time coming to you. So let's see if I can get what we need from them, and then get the foodstuff that works best for that kind of living, so maybe at the end of this nine day, which we still have seven left. Yeah I think with your help that we can go away for a couple at that time. We'll make it for two nights, that way you can see how it is to sleep on the hard ground, and how little sleep you get when you're not in your own bed. But I have to admit that being in the fresh air, the smell of the morning meal being cooked over a campfire is wonderful. Still there are downsides also, and the only way to learn about them is to experience them. So I guess we can make it three days and two nights, with travel there on the first, and travel back on the third."

"Okay, let me know when you have the camp stuff, and I'll let the bakery know that we'll be gone for three days. Of course you'll do the same for where you are working."

CHAPTER TWO

A MEETING OF MINDS, OR NOT

"Hey, look a letter from Sabohl, I wonder what he wants to discuss? He rarely writes, prefers to remain aloof in his place as the leader of history." Looking around the table there were four or five who were considered, next to Sabohl, as the experts on their culture's history and sociology. It was one of the meetings that they had scheduled at the change of seasons. Sabohl rarely attended these things, leaving the sentiment that he was above these meetings and wouldn't lower himself to their level feeling that he was so far above them that talking and discussing anything with them would be a waste of his time and intellect.

"What does that ole stuffed beast want to pass on to us mortals anyway?" Jaie asked. This brought out a chuckle from the others.

Still standing Tesam looked over the group with a smile, "Okay, I'll read it to you and then we all can have a good laugh." He shook the letter importantly and read out loud. *"Fellow learned ones"*, laughing at the opening Tesam said,

"Look he's actually admitting that others might have learned something." Again this brought out laughter. But as he perused the writing deeper into the letter his demeanor changed and the rest at the table could sense that change. There was a silence for a few moments that appeared to fill the air with apprehension. Tesam then continued, "*We may have a problem developing that could threaten our very positions as experts in our history and our views and understandings of the sociology of our ancient ancestors. I'm watching, with concern, one past student of mine who has shown a strong interest in our history. It may be of no consequence in the end, but the questions that he is asking are very pointed and direct, and I fear where they may lead. From the way these questions have been presented I would suspect that he knows more that he is telling, and the questions are to either confirm or deny what he already knows. The last question he asked more or less gave him away to me, since the subject that he was questioning has never been taught in any of my classes, let alone any that all of you have presented.*

"*It may be that he or maybe someone he knows has located a piece of our past that has been unavailable to any of us, but this, of course, is all speculation as he has been careful to give away nothing, and to appear to be just another student wanting to learn more. I plan, discreetly of course, to have their, he and his mate's shelter searched to find out if they have something in their possession that could be the source of this interest. And if so will have it removed so that he will have nothing to support whatever theories and truths that may exist. Without that said proof, he will come off as any other crackpot, and allow us to remain in the seat of leadership within our fields. I have learned, since I as all who are in this village, frequent the bakery, that he and his mate will be away for a few days providing us the opportunity and time to do a complete search and after leaving, to leave the shelter as it was before we entered, so other than this missing document, if indeed that is what it is, there will be no sign that any has entered. They will not be able to claim theft, and with this item gone, they will not be able to prove that it ever existed.*

"What I need from you, but really to maintain what we have and who we are, is surveillance, and this must discreet, and remain unknown to the ones we need to watch. After all if they actually do discover something we need to know and know immediately, so that we can put our own spin on this discovery, or discoveries. So I will leave that portion in your capable hands, and since I happen to live here, I, with my team will monitor his activities while he is here. Once he and probably his mate head out from this place, then it will be you and your team's responsibility to follow, record, and be prepared to beat him in the announcements of whatever discoveries he might make. In fellowship of one learned to another – Sabohl."

After reading the letter and the implications that it presented, the room was silent. "Do you think that he has the right of it?" Tesam asked.

"Well, the old herd beast has always found some way to protect his position, and seems to have been able to see things that could lead to trouble for himself and his position, and if he feels that this threat is real," Jaie paused for effect, bent his head sideways and shrugged, "who knows really. But if this threat is real, and I suspect that it must be if he wanted to stoop down to our level, which as you know, is something that would be very hard for him to do. He's always rubbed our faces in the fact that he was superior to us in all ways, so he must feel threatened and believe that it will threaten our positions too."

"So," Jaie asked, "what are we to do about it? Do as he asks, or just ignore it. And you notice that he never named who this individual is. I think that by doing this he again was protecting himself."

"How so?"

"Look if we go along with this and one of our staff is caught, then he can deny that he not only knew nothing about this, but had no involvement at all – leaving us to take the full brunt of the retaliation that would come from this."

Jaie thought a moment, then leaned on the table, "Which means that he, once again, has protected himself, and at the same time leaving us vulnerable and open to, the very least, the loss of our prestige and positions. Yes, we'll need to think about this, and tender our response as carefully as this letter he has sent to us."

Shahe had been quiet throughout the reading of the letter and the discussion that was now following, he interrupted and said, "What all of you, well at the least the two of you have stated is fact. Once again he's covering what he sits on, and many times seems to use to think with, and yes I agree that if we go along with this preposterous scheme of his, because of the way of this letter, we are the ones who would be out in the open. But at the same time if indeed what he states is accurate, and who knows really, then all of our hard work, all of our political maneuvering, all of the enemies that we've made along the way, to get where we are will have the necessary, ah what was that stuff, oh yes, ammunition to attack us. So tell me do we have a choice in this? I think that sending back a very neutral letter neither offering help, nor promising any-thing at this moment would be the best we can do. Then we need to begin our own independent investigation. One that would include watching this old windbag and maybe we can catch him in something, and actually bring him down. It could be that he will do something that will be his own down-fall and allow us to usurp him and get rid of him." He leaned back in his chair with his hand on his chin, but remained si-lent, turning the control back to Jaie.

* * *

Kal was black and blue from the beating he was taking from Jura as she taught him the use of the staff. And what hurt more was the fact that she seemed to be enjoying it. He had to admit that she was very good with it, and that there was much more to its use as both a defensive weapon, and one that could be used to attack. Every time he figured that he had it down and was about to best her, she came up with some other subtle move and he found himself on the ground and many times in an embarrassing pose as she would place the point of the staff on his chest, showing once again that he had been bested. Shaking his head he said, "I never realized that there was so much to this thing. I thought that this was only going to be an after-midday practice and I'd have it down. You know it looked so easy when you started making those moves, and showing me. But you warned me that it was going to take a lot of time to master, and I have to admit that I thought you were very wrong about that, but it's very obvious that I'm a long way from your skill." Again shaking his head before continu-ing, "And you say that your brother and sister are better than you? That's really hard to believe. So I guess the question is this, how long, oh mighty learned one, will it be that I'm at

least capable of using this simple tool?" He, although carefully, bowed towards her, which brought laughter to her lips.

Returning his bow with one of her own, she said, "Oh
you're progressing. I'd place you in the advanced beginners.
As I've told you, I've been doing this most of my life. And
once my parents finished their training with us, we, my brothers and sisters and myself, would play games where we would
form teams, and as you would expect most of the time these
teams were females against males, although there would be a
game of chase that we played where all of the rest would
chase one of us, and we had to use the staff against the rest. I
must admit that those were very intense games, but it forced
us, even though we weren't realizing it, to become much better. Especially when one of us would come up with something
new to try, sometimes this something new would work, and
sometimes it would fail miserably. And even though we didn't
know it at the time, our mother would monitor our progress,
and if we really felt like we were good and as she called it, too
big for our britches, she'd come out with that smile of hers
and have all of us come at her, and she'd promptly beat all of
us. It wasn't until later that we learned that she had been the
champion of her area, and that's how she and father met. Both
had been the best at this in their respective townships, and he,
my father, couldn't believe that a female could beat him,
when there hadn't been a male that could challenge him that
was anywhere close by.

Sighing and with a distant smile she continued, "I'd really
would've liked to have been there to see that match. Both of
them talk about it now and then, and there are smiles on both
of their faces as they'd recall it. We'd sit and listen as they
would recount the encounter from their side. I'm sure like

most stories that it has grown over time, but it still was quite a tale. They were very good at describing their battle, and we all could see it in our minds, and since we'd been using the staffs ourselves we could see the moves and countermoves that both had made. And after a long time and many matches that ended in draws, she beat him with a move he had never seen before. And even to this day when they talk about it you can see that smile of triumph on her face as she had beaten a male in a battle. Something that our distant ancestors would have thought was quite impossible. But she did it, and after that they developed a strong friendship and now they have been mates for what seems like a life time." Again she paused, and then laughed, "You know what, it has been a lifetime, and they're just as much in love with each other now as they were before any of we children were around. Dad really adores her and says that if she hadn't defeated him in that contest that they may have never become what they are today. So I guess even though this is a long statement to get to this point, don't feel too bad by being defeated by me, I grew up using this thing, and have had champions training me, besides the competition that one's siblings add to the mix."

"Well, I admit that makes me feel a little better, but only a little. I'd seen others work the staff and it looked so easy, so I never considered it something I'd be interested in, but you've shown me that it's far from easy, and that I've only begun to understand the very basics, including the choosing of a good staff." He smiled inwardly, only because it probably would have hurt to smile outwardly. Still as he looked at his mate he, at times, found it hard to believe that she would have accepted him when he asked if she would become his mate and he hers. After all she was lithe and had a hunter's flow to her movements, smooth and graceful, and in his eyes a beauty that rivaled any that he had ever seen. And who was he, just a lowly village bound baker who had done nothing specular. Not the type that would attract someone like Jura who had lived in the outback, and was never really comfortable within the confines of the villages and townships. Someone who could probably have had any single male as a mate and to his surprise she had chosen him. And with their time together he was learning so much more that this beautiful, complicated, and intelligent female had to offer. And of course, being a male her physical side, and her naked beauty, drove him crazy.

As time had passed, and both their love and strength in the relationship grew, he couldn't see any time in his life where he would not want her around. They just worked well together, and even though he had heard about couples who had been mates for many turns completing each other's sentences or thinking in the very same way, coming up with the same conclusions at the same time, he had just shoved this off as myth within those special relationships that some have. Yet, he could see that it was beginning to happen inside theirs, and so with personal experience he now believed. Again, as far as he was concerned, it was another one of those signs that said that they were just right for each other. Yet, at times like these where her experience far exceeded his own he could feel his wounded male ego trying to get in the way. After all he was supposed to be better at such things. "Okay, I can accept that, but are you sure that you aren't just humoring me by saying that I'm probably an advanced beginner? Watching you work that staff makes me feel clumsy, awkward, and completely uncoordinated. Absolutely anything I tried you countered it and countered it in such a way that you made it appear to be of no consequence or no effort at all, almost like you were bored."

She laughed, and then teased him a little, "Ah has my little male had his ego hurt because his mate, a female no less, can easily beat him?" This got him going for a moment and she laughed again. "See, I know what buttons to push to get your pride showing. Now why not just go run a bath, both of us did a lot of sweating and kicked up a lot of dust while you practiced out here, and then I'll join you in the tub and really show you how much I care."

Again she was right, she did know what to say or do to get him going, and he had to admit that with his sore muscles that a hot bath would be great, but with her with him he knew that he would forget about those sore muscles. "Sounds great! Just one question though, when do you feel it would be a good time to take that camp trip? I've got to give them plenty of notice at the bakery so that they can cover in my absence."

"Oh, I'd guess, at least another couple of nines to both get everything together, and to get you better prepared. We still have to go over the throwing knives, and how most of the stuff works, so we're still quite a way away from going." She then smiled a smile that showed promise of what was coming.

He returned one of his own and stated, "You're the boss on this one, and I'll head on in and get that tub filled."

* * *

"I think that we'll send a letter back to Sabohl, and tell him that we aren't interested in his little games, since the only time he seems to want our cooperation is when there's something that might threaten his mighty position on high. Then, we can do two things; first use our own people to watch Sabohl, and from there maybe find out who this individual is that seems to be threatening him, and secondly, once we find out we can then, in our own way and time, do our own watching and learning. Maybe finally one of us can get that old windbag to budge and at least, if not grudgingly, admit that there are others, such as us, which have the knowledge and understanding, to be his equal in this field of study. And who knows, maybe he'll trip up and we can catch him in something and depose him, and allow some new blood to take over the field. He's been dominating this for much too long. But with the allies that he has cultivated over the turns, and powerful ones at that, he's been untouchable." Tesam sat down at this point and turned the table back over to Jaie.

"Can we do this and be successful, is probably the best question I can present. Maybe the alternative to this would be to give a very neutral response, neither promising support nor holding support from him. So that it could appear that we have promised nothing, but at the same time left the door open for possible support. With him we have to be so careful because of those powerful allies of his. And, as you stated, it is because of them that he remains aloof and where he is. Let's remember he is not stupid, couldn't be really, to have been able to hold on to his position for as long as he has, and while we all have our own powerful friends and allies, we cannot defeat him openly, so our letter to him, if this is what we decide to do, must be well written and subtle, and in all ways we must cover our behinds." Jaie could see the agreement from the others at the table as what had been both read to them, and what they had discussed so far. It was going to be a very difficult road to walk, full of obstacles, traps, blind turns, and unexpected outcomes, and it would all begin with this letter for all of them. They all knew that however this went that in the very end it would be affecting not only their careers, but their very lives.

* * *

Sabohl left his home early. It was to be a busy day since there were tests for his students, and the anticipation of a response from, well he'd guess that he'd give them a grudging nod as being near the top in their area of teaching, but in his heart he knew that they just did not match up to both his intellect, and his ties that he held that allowed him to remain as the only one on top. *Let the rest fight, scratch, and crawl for those few positions that are below.* No one could touch him, and with his spy network, and the power that he welded he made sure that it would remain that way. It had galled him that he had to stoop down to those underlings. But even with the size of his network, there was only so much he could do, and he suspected that this time he would need their help, and their networks to be successful and keep things status quo.

He lived on the grounds of the higher learning center but had other shelters in many of the villages, and while the breezes this morning were somewhat chilly, they held a promise of a warm day ahead of him. At times he wondered how it was that one could come to that conclusion, yet time and time it had been proven to be accurate. There must be some inborn sense that could predict this, but he had never figured it out, and in reality never truly cared anyway. History was his passion, and the weather could do what it wanted. After all, nobody had figured out how to control the weather, but with his iron grip he controlled the view and understanding of their history. Part of his persona he had developed was one of tolerance and acceptance to new ideas in his field, but behind this façade it was far from the reality of who he was. Walking through the doors into the learning center he smiled at the underworker who took care of the many small tasks that kept the center operating. Today Nacy, a female sat at the desk working whatever it was that she did. He really didn't know, and he really didn't care. He smiled and said as he bowed, "Ah good morn to you, Nacy. I would guess that it will be a warm day today, and is all well with you?"

Smiling back, although there was no feeling in it, as she understood where she and any of the other workers stood with this one she responded, "Yes, you're probably right, and it is a busy time for all of us. I see that you've arrived early today. I've just finished the sorting of the incoming letters for the staff here, and there's one for you that just arrived from that other learning center that you told me to be on the lookout for." She got up turned around to a sorting cabinet, and grabbed a handful of sealed letters and papers, turned around and handed them to him. "I do hope that whatever it was you were looking for is there." At this point after he had taken the pile she had handed him, she sat back down and returned to her work ignoring any further contact, which was fine with him.

Trying to keep an air of unconcern and normality he headed for his small office, just off the space where he did his teaching, entering the office, he closed and locked the door. He didn't need anyone walking in on him at this moment. Putting the stack aside he took the one letter that held the seal that this group used and opened it, reading it quickly, and when finished, felt anger rising, but with his iron control quickly squashed it. He then sat down and reread the letter once again.

"Sabohl, it has been so long since you've even acknowledged that we exist. It really must have been difficult for you in your high station to reach down to us commoners, the ones that you've always held in contempt. And how time after time, you've let us know exactly what our place is in your world. Yet now you are reaching to us for help. We must admit that this has come as a complete surprise, and we will take into consideration what you are asking, but at this moment that is all we will do. You have provided this group with very little facts, and since this can be taken in any direction, again since we only have your word for it, we will await further proof from other than you. Yet, if what you have stated in your letter to us is proven to be fact, we indeed will be able to possibly assist. But, as you must be well aware since you seem to know all, we have many projects operating at this moment and have no one we can spare.

"Still if what you are intimating is true, there is still plenty of time to end whatever imagined threat that you are seeing here. After all our history wasn't written in a day, nor have the discoveries and the writing of our history, as we now know it, written in a day. So with this in mind we feel that there is time on our side, and we can continue with those stated projects. It is something, from your letter and the tone it implies, that may at some time require our attention, but that time is not now. If you have more information that you would like to pass on, we eagerly await your response. And please, if you do respond, please provide more than just your word. Since it is easy to twist words to say only what you want someone to hear and see, hiding the true meaning and truth from all. As always, your fellow learned, we are eager to hear back with

such proof. Signed Jaie, temporary overseer of the historical learned."

Sabohl sat silently for a while staring out at nothing. He was furious, how dare they ignore his summons to action? He was sure that they would jump at the chance to assist in this endeavor; one that he was sure would keep them exactly where they were – the leaders of their field. But obviously he had been mistaken. Rereading the letter once again, it again set off his anger, and looking for something to take it out on, he found a hapless drinking glass sitting empty on his desk, which he then grabbed and flung it against one of the walls, shattering it in small pieces from the energy of the throw. *So they'll wait until I can provide more proof will they. They had their chance, now it will be me, and only me who will do this and take the credit in the end, putting out another of the many fires that have threatened our positions over the cycle of seasons. We'll see who will win this in the end.*

He suddenly realized that he could hear movement outside of his office, and some time must have passed since he had entered. And from the sounds and voices it appeared that the students were arriving for classes. So getting his anger under control, and putting on the air of a concerned learned, he exited his office, went down the hallway to the staff that kept the center clean and stated that he had accidently broken a glass, could they please clean it up for him while he was teaching. Getting the response that he expected he left to meet his students.

* * *

"Look you're better with the throwing knives than you are with the staff, but that still doesn't make you very good yet." Jura walked across the dirt area where the targets had been set up, grabbed the throwing knives and brought them back. "These that we are using are for training only. No reason to destroy a good knife when one is learning." She suddenly smiled and snuffed a laugh that was about to surface.

Looking at her with a questioning look he asked, "What?"

"Oh, I don't know where it came from, but with all the reading, writing, and studying of that history of your family, well let's just say that it brought up an image in my mind of a female back in that time doing what I'm doing for you, and how it would have been for both of us."

He thought a moment, and began to get an image in his mind of what she had just suggested, shook his head before speaking, "Yeah, I can kind of see it, and we both probably would have been disowned by the clan or tribe or whatever that's for sure. I can see it now, a female knowing how to use weapons and a male that doesn't. So what is this? Is what I'm seeing correct that we have a female that wants to be a warrior, and a male who can't seem to be one. Next thing we're going to see here is she'll want her own name. Her own name, imagine that." Standing there like he thought an unbelieving warrior of that time would stand, he continued. "Next thing we'd see is this female wanting to be the clan leader. Clan leader, imagine that. A female with a name and one that is a better warrior than this male, and what's to happen next, she refusing to carry?" This brought laughter to both of them.

With tears running down her face from the laughter she finally said once she could, "Not bad, and unfortunately probably much too accurate. Okay warrior want-to-be, let's do this again, and then before we go back inside to clean up, we'll work with the staff again. You're getting better, I think that you could defend yourself successfully against a child right now, but would be defeated by anybody with any experience."

Smiling he said, "Thanks for the confidence. Come on I'm not that bad, am I? I really thought I was getting it down."

Again she laughed, "And getting up off the ground too many times to count. Anyway this isn't getting any of this done, and we've so much to do before that trip."

Yeah you're right, and I've talked to the one who passed on that family document to me, and he said that he would take it and all of the notes and writings we've done, and keep it safe at his shelter while we were gone. I'm glad he agreed to do that, if no, I don't know who'd I'd fallen back on, maybe the bakery itself. I just didn't feel comfortable leaving it in an empty shelter, and the thought of taking it with us where it could become more damaged, didn't appeal to me either. Okay let's go through it again. Dusk is approaching and it won't be long until we can't see out here anyway. And again I know that you want to work with me with the staff in the twilight so I can begin to sense with my ears as well as my eyes what's happening."

Later as they were sitting around the table Kal said, "Come on Jura, I have to be improving. I mean I actually got you on the ground once."

"You mean when I stepped on that rock that rolled under my foot? I guess you can count that, but yes, in very small steps you are improving. It's just that you need to get past thinking about what you're going to do and just do it. I know, it takes time, and it takes practice, and I've had a lifetime of both. Still we both know the importance of this."

"Yeah we do. It's just that here in this village I never needed to learn this stuff, so I have to start from scratch, from nothing. Plus working mostly in the bakery, and not on the road with my father, who had his workers who were versed in defense it was something I had no need of knowing. But if we are to do what I want to do, then it must be learned. I know that once you get into the wilds, the outback, that life changes, and the ones who can defend themselves are the ones who survive. Look I've a full day at the bakery tomorrow and it will be dusk before I get here. I know that you have an earlier day, so if you would, can you drop off all of this work that we've been doing on this thing to my uncle, that way it will be one more thing out of the way. If you agree with my progress, I think that in another 9-day we can begin on setting the date for this first camp attempt."

"I don't see why not. We've everything we need, and I think, as far as the camp skills go, you've come far enough along that you won't burn down the camp area."

What could he say? It was true that he really hadn't done anything like this in his life. Even the few trips with his father, all the camp setup and work were handled by the workers, so he really hadn't learned from them. The rest of his time had been in the village and working at the bakery – so no experience at all. "Come on, I'm not that bad, am I? While it has been very obvious to me that this is your area of expertise, and I'm just a poor kid from the villages, I think I've picked up most of what you've been showing me."

"Yes, yes you have. But part of what I have planned for us when we are there camping is a day of nothing but hiking. There's some nice trails that climb through the foothills, and with some of the maps that I have, you can get some real experience comparing the area to those maps, and learn to read them better. While the copies that we've made of those primitive maps aren't equal to any we make today, we still have to try and follow them to the areas depicted in them."

The next 9-day truly moved by them was some speed. With work during the day, practice sessions at dusk, and the lessons on map reading, and skills for the outback, there was little time for more than a quick meal, a bath together, and falling into the bed exhausted. But the day finally arrived, and with the borrowing of one of the pack beasts, and this was something that he was better at than she, they headed out. He had to admit that he was somewhat excited about this. He was going to see first hand, if he could actually do any of this and enjoy this different world. Growing up, other than the brief times of play that all children find time to do, it had been learning the business of the family and assisting and learning responsibility related to his age at the time. So to take a few days off was a new experience, and to be able to do this with his mate made it even better. The two of them and only them was a rare thing even now, and there were no children in the picture as of yet. They both knew that when that time came that even those few precious moments of intimacy would be much harder to come by. And by knowing this that sometime in the future there would be a good chance that they would look back on this nostalgically, with smiles on their faces, as they recalled this small respite from their daily lives.

It took three quarters of a travel day to reach the camp area. It was relatively close, by travel standards, and actually sat between a number of small villages. They had stopped at one of these and had their zenith meal, and probably would stop here again when they returned. The food was actually quite good, and what surprised him was the fact that the products from their bakery were available here. This raised the respect he had for his father, knowing that not only he contracted for the supplies they needed to keep the operation going, but sold the products to many of the outlying villages and townships. Yes he knew that others had been responsible for the beginnings of the business, and because of the quality, it had grown, but when his father had mated with his mother and she joined the family it was then that business began to grow. Between his hard work and mother's business sense they had grown to be the largest in the surrounding area. In fact, if he had heard it right, his parents were planning on possibly purchasing other smaller bakeries, and begin selling directly in the villages and townships, making the product fresher, and thusly better. So to even get this time off was a privilege.

When they finally arrived Jura eyed the areas that were available with a critical eye before selecting one site that was close to a small hillside. "Here, I think this one will do. It will have some shade during the day, and by being here against this small hillside we will be safe from any major winds, and we're far enough back that we are somewhat isolated, but not really."

At first he couldn't see why this site, but as she explained it, it became obvious as to why. Another lesson learned, picking a site where to set up your camp is critical. "After you pointed out your reasons, I could see it, but I have to admit that I thought that maybe another area would have been better." Smiling he said, "Wrong again. Even with everything that we covered back at the shelter I still didn't see it. I can see why you wanted to take this trip. And as you've said time and time again, nothing like experience."

"Good, because now comes the fun. If one has never really set up one of these portable shelters then it can take much time to figure out. Even if you've done it a number of times, and then a great period of time has passed, you find it hard to do." She stopped a moment and swept her arms around to include their chosen campsite, "Then when you think you've got it right, one of the stakes that the ropes are tied to pulls out and the darn thing, if it's the right stake, falls down on you. Look once we get this set up we'll pick a place for the camp-fire, clear it down to just the soil, and while you wondered why I wanted to bring our own wood, if you look you'll see the area had been picked clean. And that's because the ones who come here either don't bring their own, or didn't bring enough. So anything that could be used has been."

Again she had been right. In what he thought would be a simple operation took many trial and errors before they had the portable shelter up and to her satisfaction. They finished the unloading of the pack beast, and she said, "I've been here before so I know a little about this place. If you take the beast around the hill just over there, there's a small area they've provided that has fodder and water for them. Plus it's protect-ed from any of the wild beasts that might be interested in having our pack beast for a meal. And that's one of the reason it costs us to stay here. Oh and before we put down the sleep sacks, and I know we've brought a little padding, make sure that all of those rocks and small pebbles are removed, it makes it so uncomfortable trying to sleep on them."

* * *

"I don't know 'bout you but now that we're back a bath would be a great thing." They had returned the pack beast to the pens after dropping off the packs in their supply shelter.

The suns were setting and dusk was upon them. Both were tired and he had to admit that he had learned quite a bit. And presently he had to admit it would have been stupid of him to go off tramping through the outback with as little experience as he had. In fact from what he'd been learning he knew that if he had survived at all, he'd probably would have been back, giving up on those wild ideas of his. Jura was leading as they headed for the door.

She stopped puzzled, turned and said, "Something's not right here. I don't know what it is at this moment but let's be careful. I can't put my finger on it, but even before we enter our shelter I feel that something's different." She'd taken the key out of her pocket to unlock the door, and when she had placed the key into the slot it didn't feel right. When she turned it, it just spun as if there were no guts in the lock. "This lock's broken. I think that someone may have broken into our place while we were gone." That stopped both of them as they looked at each other.

"I wonder why someone would do that? I mean, it's not like we have anything of value, really." Kal looked at Jura and shrugged, "Now what? Do we just go in, or do we wait?"

Breathing out deeply he said, "No, I guess with it getting dark we really aren't going to see anything, so I guess we go in being careful to not disturb anything and see if we can find anything missing." He replaced his mate and taking over the lead, quietly opened the door, just in case anyone was still there, and even though the door creaked a little, it wouldn't have been enough to alert anybody that could still be inside. But the shelter was empty. Lighting the lantern that hung inside the doorway, and then the candle that sat on the table to the right where they prepared their food, they did a quiet, slow, careful search and found the shelter empty. Whoever it had been was no longer here.

"Well, that's a relief." Jura turned and once again faced Kal and shrugged, "I don't get it. We didn't broadcast it to the world that we would be gone these past three days, and certainly there would be other shelters with much more valuable stuff to steal than our place, so why ours?"

Shaking his head in response Kal said, "I really don't know. It doesn't make sense to me at all. And when we looked around, again if that lock hadn't been broken showing us that someone broke in here, then it wouldn't have been obvious." This caused him a brief pause as a thought crossed his mind. "But if it was just some thieves that broke in here, why leave it like they weren't here?"

"I don't know, maybe to give them more time before we reported the crime, or maybe if it was something they wanted that we wouldn't miss for a while and maybe in the end think that we misplaced it. Who knows? But, that's a very valid question. In some homes of friends that had been broken into their stuff was scattered everywhere as the thieves went through the shelter as fast as they could, grabbing anything they could find of value, and getting out as quick as they could." She waved her arms around and said, "This, this appears to have been a careful, slow search, and an attempt to make it appear like they weren't here at all, and first off, if that lock hadn't been broken, the subtle items that were out of place might not have alerted us at all. No this was a careful well planned operation. Whoever this was took their time, tried to hide everything that they did, and tried very hard to leave everything as we left it."

"I don't know about you, but we're not going to solve it right this moment, and I'm itching from being so dirty. I did not realize that one got this dirty just camping out. Then once we're finished with a bath, and have eaten a little, we can write down what is out of place, and where it was. Maybe that will give us some hint as to what it was they were after. At this point I can't find anything missing, so we truly can't even report a break-in. And because both of us are really just starting out on our own, other than what we got as gifts at the mating ceremony, we have very little to interest any thief, and nothing that would be valuable enough to risk being caught."

She laughed lightly saying, "Yeah, you're quite right. I'll go draw us a bath. You get the water going so that it will be a hot one. Right now I think that would be much nicer than cold water. Besides hot water helps relax those sore spots one always gets when one does something different."

"You're not going to get me to argue. I do have to admit that I do have a few sore muscles. I never realized that sleeping on the ground or doing things around a camp could create so many sore muscles and spots. And a hot bath would ease all of that. I have to admit that I'm glad you suggested it, and then we were able to go and do it – camping that is. Okay I'll get a fire going in the stove and get the water heating. Maybe one day we'll be well off enough to have some of that new stuff that coming out, that only the rich can afford right now – indoor plumbing."

"Yes! How wonderful something like that would be. Then we'd no longer have to go outside to the privy, or to have our bath in that small attached room. Although I guess we're lucky with the bath. Most are still in their own small shelter a little away from the main one. And who knows, someday there might even be something to wash one's clothes other than by hand. I know right now that when we take the time at the end of the 9-day to do that chore, it's an all day job and that's when we're both working at it."

With a faraway look in his eyes he smiled, "Right, like that's going to ever happen. But I guess we can dream. And I have to admit something like that to help with those chores that never seem to end would be really nice. Yet, I guess, if we were to compare how we do it now, verses how it used to be done, then our ancestors would probably be jealous of us."

She laughed as, in her mind, she could see the females of the past standing, staring at her with help, first from a male, that alone would be a shock, and then to be able to bath in hot water instead of the cold river if at all. Then to take care of those daily chores and needs as they now did. Yes, they'd stand there with the hands on their hips just shaking their heads in disbelief. "I see what you mean. I guess each generation has its conveniences that the previous one would love to have had. But that still doesn't mean that I'll avoid dreaming about such things."

"I can understand that, hey better get that water moving, I'll help you haul it inside. I can see the water that's on the stove is beginning to steam, and I'll need to dump it into the ol' wooden tub and get more heating. Shouldn't be too long and we can jump in and soak off this grime."

* * *

Sabohl sat in his office dealing with student papers, one of the things he both hated and loved. Hated because it was something that involved so much of his time and effort, and so many were really bad. But, every once in a while, like his past student Kal, there would be papers that showed promise, and some were brilliant. In this Kal's case though, it was obvious that his direction would be the family business, and he felt that it was such a waste of talent. But one did what one must to survive. He shrugged as these thoughts ran through his mind. There came a soft knock on the door, and he looked up. He couldn't remember any appointments that he had with any of the students, and unless this was one of the staff, who knew better than to bother him as he worked the papers, there shouldn't have been anybody. "Enter", he said gruffly, and waited until the door opened, "What are you doing here?" He asked rather sharply. "We were never to meet, especially here."

The person at the door, dressed as a student bowed slightly with a smile on his face, came inside and closed the door. "That is true, but I felt that this chance could be taken, especially if I appeared to be just another student of yours. With so many running around this place, who would look at another such one anyway?"

Sabohl had to admit that he was probably right, but this irritated him to no end. There could be no known connection between himself and this individual or the others he was part of. "Okay, you've made your point, and again you're probably quite right. Still there is too great of a chance that someone could recognize who you are and my association with you must remain unknown. Why take this chance? This is something that can hurt both of our reputations."

"Let's just say I felt the risk was something that I could take, and as you can see, you have no choice, so accept that in what you are requiring of me and my own that there will be some risk to you. After all, it is unavoidable. Besides I will only be here briefly and be away. Then we can continue to communicate through notes and such at the designated drop points, and have no physical contact at all – protecting both of our reputations."

Sabohl leaned back in his chair put his arms behind his head, stretched, then leaned forward. "Okay, your point is well taken," he said rather gruffly, "so what is so important that it was worth this encounter?"

Smiling, although there was no humor in that smile the guest said, "I'm just reporting on that excursion that we agreed upon. I felt that it was important since you would not be at the exchange for a few days, and again I felt that you should be brought up to speed in person." Here he paused, leaned forward placing his hands on the small desk and said, "First off, as requested we searched, but found nothing out of the ordinary. It was just a shelter, and there really wasn't any-thing in it worth stealing. The couple is just above poor. I think, from what I've learned that the shelter that they are liv-ing in belongs to the family and bakery. From what I've learned and what is common knowledge, this family business provides shelters for their workers, and that includes family. And since this one is family, one would assume that the shel-ter that was provided would have been a cut above the ones they hire to work for them. But it is not so. We found nothing at all as to what your request stated should be there. So while it's not my place to say anything on this subject, I think you may be wrong."

"You came by to tell me this? This information could have waited until I picked up the letter. And you're right, it is not your place to tell me what I can and cannot do or assume."

Still leaning forward, and now with a look of hardness in his eyes, the guest continued, "Do not push that attitude towards me. I'm not one of your students that you can intimidate, and it will never work with me, so stop before you get yourself into something that you have no way out of. Yes, this information could have been left, but that is not the main reason for this visit. If you remember the specific orders given, stated that once we left there could be no evidence that we or anybody was there. Unfortunately they have their evidence."

"What? What do you mean by that? Evidence – what evidence would that be? I was very specific on that account. I cannot have this one suspicious that someone is trying to find something."

"It couldn't be helped, and it was unexpected. The one who was picking the lock to get inside cursed, and I asked, now what? He said that the lock was old and with his manipulation it simply broke. So when they returned they would know that someone jimmied the lock. And like I said, it couldn't be helped, and once it broke we couldn't replace it since we had no idea of what their key looked like, and besides any work would have been obvious."

Anger began to rise in Sabohl, but with effort he gained control as he stated, "As if the broken lock wasn't. You told me he was the best at this kind of thing, and now this?"

With no apology in his voice the guest said, "He is, and that's as much as I will say. Now that we are up to date I'll say good day to you." At which point not even waiting a dismissal he turned and left, closing the door behind him, disappearing among the many students walking up and down the halls. Sabohl sat at his desk looking at nothing still attempting to get his anger under control, taking a few deep breaths he thought. *This operation was supposed to leave no evidence that anybody had broken in. But that's not what happened, and now they know. But what do they know? After all it could appear that when the thieves broke the lock that they just panicked and left.* Sighing deeply and giving himself a shake he finally got back into control. *I've still a couple of classes to teach.* He got up went around the desk, opened the door, and headed down the hallway to his classroom.

* * *

"Jaie, Temporary Leader of the Historical Learned:

"Good day sir, it has been wise that I've been planted here at the higher learning center. As I have been instructed I have been monitoring the learned of interest. He had a visitor today, and while dressed as one of the students, one could see immediately that he was not. While I was not in position to overhear what was discussed, what I did hear suggested that whatever had been planned did not produce the expected results, and that there had been evidence left behind to give them away. As to what this endeavor could have been, I, unfortunately, have no hint. But suspect that it probably relates to the subject that had been broached in the correspondence to your people. I took the liberty of having this visitor followed, albeit discreetly. After all it would do us harm if either the subject we are watching, and the ones who made contact with him become aware of our interest. As new information becomes available it will be passed on. I know that this is beyond the normal reporting times, but felt that it was something that needed to be brought to the learned of the board immediately. May our endeavors be successful."

CHAPTER THREE

SUSPICIONS

It had been 3 9-days since they had returned and discovered the break-in. Yet with a careful search and discussion between the two of them, they found nothing amiss or missing. So whoever the thief or thieves had been they obviously were looking for something specific. They had reported the incident to both family and the local law, but with nothing to report other than the broken lock, there wasn't anything anybody could do, other than increase their individual alertness. But neither of them, Kal or Jura, could watch the shelter all of the time, so it was vulnerable to additional break-ins. Plus its location didn't help at all – since it was partially hidden making it easy for the incident to be repeated. After discussing things for a while, Kal realized that the only thing that wasn't in their home at the time was that family history. So as to keep it safe, they decided that it should remain with the uncle who had passed it on to him in the first place. At least there in that shelter someone was always present, making it almost impossible to repeat what had happened at their shelter. Besides, with the work that he had to do, he was quite busy. It was close to celebration time once again, and all of them were working especially hard to get the extra product out that would sell well. And when he would go home at night, and it was night, since they used all the daylight hours to work, he would be exhausted, and found that sleep was almost more important than anything else. As he sat at the table with his mate at the end of another difficult day he said as he breathed out deeply, "Jura, I smell of bread and sweetbreads, and am covered in flour. Need a quick bath, a quick meal, and much sleep. But I have to admit that this break-in still weighs heavily on me."

"Well, you're not the only one. It's something that's never happened to me before, and I suspect not you either. Here for the longest time you feel safe, and then this happens, shattering all those illusions that one has about being safe in one's shelter. I mean when we are on the trails or roads we could expect that there would be a slight chance of being attacked, but usually it's something that doesn't happen very often. Like you, this has bothered me a great deal. I'm just thankful that we weren't here." Jura shuddered at that thought and briefly closed her eyes.

"Yeah, I have to agree, but it also makes me wonder. While we didn't try and keep it a secret that we would be away for those few days, it seems that someone had been listening closely. And I hate to admit it, but maybe I wasn't as smart as I thought I was when I asked those questions of that learned."

She looked at him questioningly, "Are you accusing your old mentor of arranging this?"

Shaking his head he said, "No, not really. But you have to admit that this is a possibility. When you look at the way this was done, I mean that if there hadn't been that broken lock we probably wouldn't have looked that closely when we came back, and they would have gotten away with this. And the reason my mind keeps going back to him is this; he's considered top in his field, and with what we've learned from that family historical record would refute much of his ideas. So if that document should disappear, what proof would we ever have to present? We'd have nothing, nothing at all. So he could look at us, smile a sad smile, and ask us to show the world the proof, knowing that we couldn't do it. Thusly leaving he and his theories as the dominant ones."

Looking down at the table and thinking Jura said, "I see what you mean. And those questions you've been asking might have tipped him off. So, to protect himself and his position, he'd want to know what you really had, and if it was a threat to him or his theories, and if so, eliminate it. When you begin to think about it that way I can see why you'd come to those conclusions. But is it accurate?"

Shaking his head once again he answered, "I don't know, I really don't. And it is a worrisome thing. Because I've always trusted him, and his knowledge, plus he always seemed to be willing to take the time to listen and answer the questions I had. Of course putting it in this new light I can see it would be a great way to stay ahead of anybody who might be able to usurp him or his position – to appear to be friendly, knowledgeable, and willing to be there for his students. Again I might just be blowing smoke into the air, but if I was a thief breaking into a shelter, because of the risk, I'd steal whatever I felt was valuable and not traceable back to me, and that's not what happened here."

"Yeah, that makes perfect sense, so I guess I'm happy that we decided not to leave that family history here or it would have been gone, and we'd have no way of proving it ever existed. Hey it's getting late, go take your bath, and I'll have a bite for us when you get out, then we can head off to the sleeping space, tomorrow comes much too quick as it is." What they had been discussing made a lot of sense, but there was no hard proof. She turned and headed in to fix a quick meal. She heard him sigh, get up and leave to take that bath.

* * *

It was another 9-day since the celebration, and he had to admit that all the work had been worth it. With other family members and workers they had staffed their booth, and by the time the three day celebration was over they had sold everything, plus some as they had rushed to add to their supplies. That didn't mean that he and Jura didn't end up with some time of their own to enjoy the crowds, the music, and the festivities, to go to the dances, to enjoy the reenactments that were always performed. But now all of that was behind them and everything was returning to normal. His father was out on another supply run since the increase in uses for the celebration had depleted much of their on-hand stock. It was just after the midday break when his mother called him into her office and suggested that he sit down, which he did.

Once he was seated she leaned forward placing her arms on the desk in front of her. As usual the desk had its piles of work, but even though to the untrained eye it appeared to be a complete mess, he knew that this was far from the truth. She could find anything at any time she needed it. "Kal, as you know, your father and I have been looking to expand what we are doing. He recently came up with a very good suggestion and we've been pursuing it. And from the responsibility that you've shown, and the efforts that you've been willing to put forth, we felt that you should have the chance to help make this work." At this point she paused looking at him to see how he was reacting. What she saw was a questioning, and while it was subtle, a mother could always see what was happening with her children.

Now what? "What is it that the two of you have been discussing? I know that like the rest here that I work for the business, and family has no privileges. And we must earn our positions, and it is something that makes sense. Other than that and the fact that I've been required to learn the business from all aspects how does this discussion apply to me?" Then he had a thought but at first dismissed it, yet it persisted as he remembered when the business had been turned over to his parents a very long time ago. Was it time for that to happen for him?

She could see the thoughts, questions, and conclusions flit across his face as he remained open. Of course, in her mind, she doubted that others could read him like she could, well maybe Jura, but other that she, no one else. She smiled, "What we've been looking at is this; expanding this business."

"But we've already used up all the land and space available to this bakery. How'd it be something that could be done? Did you and father purchase the lands next to the bakery?"

"No, and I can see how that would make sense. No that would require too much of an investment, and the cost of building and converting is still beyond our money."

"So if that isn't something you can do, have the two of you decided to buy a mercantile instead, expanding beyond the bakery?"

Again she smiled, "That, by the way, is probably a pretty good suggestion – something that the two of us hadn't thought about, but no. Still it's surely something to think about in the future. No, what we've come up with is something that allows us to expand but at the same time to keep the investments within our means. Plus we've both seen how passionate both you and Jura are on following up on our family's history. Especially since that record dropped in your hands. In fact we, your father and I, suggested that he pass it on to you. We could see that history was something that held a serious interest with you. So who better? Now we felt that there needed to be a way that would allow you to pursue that, and at the same time help the family and the business that we operate, and to allow us to continue to grow, and what we've come up with allows all of that to happen."

How could all of what she had just related to him happen? He was definitely puzzled. "Okay, I may be a little dense here, but I can't see how all of that can be fulfilled."

"Simple really . . . In many ways I'm really surprised that nobody has done this. But from what we know, nobody has. And once I present it to you, you'll see it also. Instead of buying the land around here, doing all the required work and cost of adding what would be necessary, why not buy another bakery in a different village or township, and expand into a new place. Still using all the techniques and innovations that we've come up with and kept secret, and that's just what we did. We want you to go and be in charge of this new bakery that we purchased over close to where your mate is from. That will get her closer to her own family, and with the supply runs and such you'll still be in contact with us. And once it's up and operational, and all the workers have been trained, and you've found someone who can be an underboss, then this will allow you the freedom to search the family history and try and locate the places spoken in the writings. So how does that sound?"

At first he was stunned, and for the longest time silent. "Let me get this straight, you're saying that instead of just expanding here that you two went out and bought another bakery, and you want me to run it? Not that I don't appreciate it, but do I really qualify? There has to be at least one or two who have worked with you for turns that are better than I am."

"That could be, but we've been working hard on grooming you for taking over the business sometime in the future. But at the same time with what we've been doing the business has been growing and we needed some way of taking advantage of it. And yes there are a couple that have been with us for a very long time. In fact for a short period of time you'll have one of them with you to help get the new bakery operating to our quality. And believe me you will not be left on your own. Both of us will visit periodically to see how it's going. We know that for the first few cycles of seasons that we probably will be lucky to break even at the new operation, but that is expected. I suggest you talk with Jura and be ready in the very near future to make the move. At first you will be living in the back of the bakery, but eventually as the operation begins to show a profit we will purchase dwellings for the ones who work for us. Now get back to work, discuss this with your mate, and then be prepared to make this move. It has many benefits for all of us." With that she waved him out of the office and back to work.

The rest of that day as he worked his mind continued to go over the conversation, well more listening than talking, but it meant that he would be leaving the village that he had always known as home. Unlike his mate who had left her home to join his, he had never faced such a thing. At first it excited him, and then he became nervous. After all, all of his contacts, all of his friends, and most of his relatives lived either in this village or very close by. And before he knew it he was heading home, and still being deep in thought over the implications of this revelation found himself opening the door and not remembering the walk from the bakery to their shelter. Jura had arrived earlier. She worked part time helping out some of the older members of the community. She could see that faraway look in his eyes and wondered what was going on. "Kal, is there something wrong?" She asked cautiously.

"What? Ah, no, nothing's wrong."

"Okay, I know something's going on, so are we going to play twenty questions, or are you going to fill me in?" At this point she pushed him towards the table and then sat across from him waiting expectantly for an answer. As she sat down she crossed her arms, placed them on the table and leaned forward.

Not quite sure how to start he gathered his thoughts, and inwardly laughed. He then asked himself, wasn't this what he had been doing since he had received the news from his mother? Looking down and then briefly up, he cleared his throat and began. "I've been informed that there are changes coming and those changes will involve me directly, and truthfully both of us." Again not sure how to continue he paused. After all this had come as a complete surprise to him leaving him to wonder as to how would this affect Jura? "I've just learned, today in fact, that the family business will be expanding."

She smiled, "Ah, and that's the news! Great news if it is true." Again she paused because that comment he'd made did not match the look on Kal's face. With a look of consternation on her own face she realized that there had to be much more to it than just that. "Okay. I can see that there's more to it than what you just told me . . . oh, this change will somehow affect us, do I have it right?"

Smiling back at her, even though it was a nervous one, "Yes, as always you've figured it out before I could say anything." He then went over the conversation that he had with his mother and how everything would change for both of them.

It was her turn to be silent as she absorbed everything he had just told her. "So when is this to take place? I mean it will be wonderful to be closer to my own family and my old stomping grounds, so to speak, but I have to admit that I've established strong roots and ties here. It will be hard to give them up. So how long do we have?"

"I really don't know. Mother didn't go into a time line, but I suspect that it will be soon. So I guess we should be planning on making the move in the not too distance future. I know that we've been in this place for a while, so I suspect that as all of us do, we've been accumulating stuff." He laughed before continuing, "Look, if I remember it right, when we became mates and first moved into this place we barely had enough of anything to fill one room, let alone the whole place. Now look at it, every room is full and comfortable for us."

She had to admit that the shelter had filled up over time, but how else could one make a shelter their own? Yes, it would be difficult to decide what went with them, what they got rid of, and what they stored. From his description the space they were initially to live in would be much smaller than this. "Knowing your parents as I do now, I'm sure that they've planned this for a long time, worked towards it, and are just about ready to make it work. So I'm sure that in that planning they had you in mind all of the time, which means that they'll give us the necessary time to prepare and make the move. I suspect that we'll be using the pack and cart beasts that they use for the caravans that your father operates." Again she paused as another thought came to mind. "Oh my, that means that I'll have to leave what I'm doing and try and find something in that other place."

"Yes, that's probably true, but I suspect that there'll be plenty to do at this new, well new to us, bakery so that there will be no lack of work for either of us. And I suspect that we'll be using some of the earnings to support ourselves. She, ah mother, said that they didn't expect the operation to be profitable immediately, and while she didn't say so, I suspect that is because that part of what this place earns will have to support us."

* * *

It was now 1513TOG, and they had been at this new bakery for two cycles of the seasons. And all that they had speculated back in their old shelter now had answers. Both had worked hard and full time in the bakery. And as the bakery was named, back where the original one was, this one was also called, Bakery of Kaygor. With the skills that he had obtained from all of the time working in the family business, much of what he did not realize that he had learned, this new location began to grow almost immediately. And the time that was necessary for it to earn a profit turned out to be shorter than his parents had projected. But the work had been hard and both of them found no problem falling asleep at the end of another busy day. In truth that first turn of seasons found them working from dawn to dusk with no break, and all the 9-days were also worked with no time off. So now with the operation showing a profit, and workers trained, the two of them felt that finally they would take one 9-day off and be able to spend some time away from the bakery, and quality time with each other.

But before the opportunity to actually take that time off, fate once again intervened, and they received word that his uncle had passed away. His uncle had lost his mate a few turns earlier to some disease that slowly wasted her away until there was very little left. He hadn't fared well after her passing, and had withdrawn. The family had been quite worried, but there was very little they could do. So instead of joy and time with Jura they returned to the village where he had been raised, and where most of his family lived. In those two turns, two cycles of the seasons, he had all but forgotten about the family historical record, and his thoughts of finding the locations mentioned within. But now after the funeral, with the family gathered, all remembering the good of the dead, and of other family members, who had passed on, brought back what he had received from that uncle, and the fact that he had returned the family history to him to protect it. Now it would be back in his hands, and again it brought it back to the forefront, all that he had planned on doing with the knowledge that was contained therein. He remembered that conversation that he had with his mother about making this move working in this new bakery, and making it thrive. And that eventually once all was functioning as it should that he would be free to pursue the answers to the riddles this document provided.

While it had been a sad time for him since this uncle had always been a favorite, but with the work that the two of them had been involved with, there had been no time to stay abreast of family. The only contact that they had had with either of the families, hers and his, was by letter and by contact when his father would come by with the supplies. And even here, he did not visit every time. So he wasn't even aware of what had been transpiring with his uncle until he learned of his death. And now with the will having been read and the personal belongings passed to who they were bequeathed, the families returned to their own homes, sad in the fact that another member of the older generation was gone, and with the knowledge that slowly they were moving towards being that older generation. "I remember as I was growing up," Kal related, "he'd show me some things, and was always funny. Coming up with these little jokes and stunts to pull on others – I really wish I had known." But he hadn't, and no one had figured out how to go back in the past and correct mistakes. They'd been so busy that at times it seemed hard to breathe let alone get away.

Looking down at the letter that his uncle had addressed to him and only him, he stared at it unopened, not really wanting to open it and read the last words from him. After all if he put it off then he would still be with him with some wisdom or insight to pass on. It made him realize that his parents were not getting any younger. And while this uncle had been the oldest of the siblings he had died somewhat young. What made this sadder still lie in the fact that there had been no offspring from him and his mate. Kal suspected that was one of the reasons that they got along so well. He had become like a son to him. "Well," Jura asked, "aren't you even going to open it and read what he wanted to say to you?" They had finally returned to their shelter, which fortunately was no longer the back of the bakery, but a real separate shelter. They both sat at the table where they ate, discussed things, and worked the books.

Shaking his head and looking down he said, "I'm not sure. I know that once I do that he will be truly gone – not that he isn't. But this is the last of anything that is personal from him, and once I've read it then whatever I had of him will be gone. I mean, well I'm not sure what I mean." Sighing and taking a deep breath, "I'm saying this really bad, but as a child I looked up to him, and from there we begin to develop our views of someone else. I guess, even though there was no real reason to do so, I kind of looked at him as my hero. No, he never did anything hero like, but was there when my parents were tied up with some problem with the business. It seemed that he was always available if I needed someone to talk to or confide in. I'm sure that being brothers, my father and him, that if he felt it was important that he would pass on whatever it was we talked about. As a kid you don't think about such things. He'd take me on small outings and such. We'd have these great adventures, at least in my eyes, and we were close. So by not reading this I'm kind of trying to hold on to some of that, some of the mystery. This is the last of that and once I've read it then there will be nothing more ever."

Taking a deep breath herself before replying Jura said. "For someone who couldn't explain it very well, I think you did a great job. So I'll not push you to read this until you're ready, even though as a female I'm very curious as to what your uncle wanted to pass on to you. Okay different subject, but we have that family history again, what are your feelings on that? I know back when we were working on it all the time that you wanted to pursue what we had discovered. To find out if any of what is written there, and what we've been taught in the learning centers is accurate.

"I don't know at this moment, haven't even thought about it, let alone consider it. I guess for now until we've gotten everything where it needs to be it will just have to wait. I guess if time allows we can start working on it again to make sure it is preserved for others down the trails of time. I suspect that once we start that we'll become passionate once again."

"True, and while on the subject of family, mine contacted me recently and suggested that all of us get together for a couple of days, and I thought it was a great idea. And with us originally planning on taking some time off, for which we still have a couple of those days available, I agreed. Besides, this will be fun, and help you get over that loss that you just suffered. So we'll be heading over there the day after tomorrow." She smiled pausing a moment, "Besides I've been bragging about how much you've improved with the staff."

This brought his head up since he had been looking down at the table. "What? You've told them about me practicing with you? I admit that I've improved, but you can still beat me most of the time."

"Oh come on. You've come very far. Now I actually have to work at defeating you. Besides you've only had one person to work against. I want you to go against my siblings and if you feel up to it, mom and dad." Here she laughed when she saw the panicked look in his eyes. "Oh come on, it won't be that bad. In fact I think you'll have a great time, and if it isn't more than listening as all of us recall our good times."

"Right and me having trouble sitting because your family beat the crap out of me with the staff, what fun would there be in that?"

Laughing again from his comment Jura said, "Ah is my little male worried that he could be bested by my sisters, let alone my brothers or parents?"

From the tone of her voice he could tell that she was teasing and all he could do was smile and shake his head, "No, not really. I know they will beat me. While, as you've pointed out I'm so much better now I'm not good enough to beat champions, or in this case former champions. And working with you I've dealt with too many bruises and tender spots. So I can imagine how I would fare against the rest of your family." Sighing he continued, "Still, I have to admit that seeing your family would be nice and would take my mind off of my uncle's death. So what do we do with this family history, now that we have it back? I don't want to take a chance that it will disappear like it almost did."

"Good point." She stopped and thought a moment, "I don't know, how about the bakery? There's usually someone there all of the time."

"True, but there's that back entrance, the one we get supplies, and that area where we lived is just off of the hallway. It would be so easy for someone to sneak in there during the busy parts of the day. Heck you wouldn't have to sneak. It's so noisy that a crying babe couldn't be heard. It is a problem. When he was alive it was a great place for it to stay, but now . . ." Both were silent. Nothing had ever come of the original investigation from the past break-in, since all they had to go on was the broken lock. So whoever had been responsible was still free. And even though it had been two cycles of the seasons they had tried to keep vigilant, but had seen nothing to even raise their suspicions. He still believed that Sabohl was responsible, and because of this had never gone back to ask any more questions. Plus it was soon after that that they had made the move and had been heavily involved with making this new bakery work. And since that initial attempt there had been no others.

Breathing out and leaning back in her chair she said, "Well I really have no answers. And right now the fewer who know about this the better. But we do need to come up with something. I don't want to leave it here when we aren't. We still only have partially copied it, and if it disappeared we'd have nothing."

"Agreed, so I think that we'll take it with us when we visit your family, at least we'll have it with us, and maybe we can come up with some type of answer or solution."

* * *

He'd been right, while indeed he had improved, through practice; it had only been against the same individual. So as he went against other members of her family they found weaknesses in both his attack and defense, and had taken advantage. And for the first time he became involved in one of those free-for-alls Jura had talked about. While it had been desperate, since he was the least experienced, it forced him to react instead of think, and he found that he could make some of the moves quicker than he ever had. And while it would be time before the bruises disappeared he had to admit that it had been a lot of fun – rough fun, tough and brutal, especially since all of them were now adults, with no quarter taken or given. Even her parents would join and show the youngsters how it was done. And they still could whip any member of the family, and make it appear easy.

Breathing quite hard after the last free-for-all, he asked, "All of you did this kind of thing all of the time?"

Laughing, Fara the youngest sister of Jura's family stated, "Why of course. But we'd only be allowed to do such a thing after all the chores and such were done. And here there are always a lot of chores. I guess, in a way, this stuff was important too, but we looked at it as a game, as something fun to do. And as all kids have a tendency to do now and then, it could get out of control, and then mom and dad would come out and put all of us in our place." This brought a laugh from the rest of the family.

He could imagine, in his mind's eye, what that must have been like. The parents had been much younger then, and even now they could still whip any of them. Their skill was unbelievable. And he could understand why her parents had wanted them to become proficient with the staff. It gave them piece of mind knowing that any of their children could defend themselves if the situation warranted. Yet, when he had first witnessed one of their free-for-all's, before getting brave enough to join one of them, he couldn't believe the frenzied attacks and movements as they pushed to win the match. And while there were bruises that resulted there almost seemed to be a dance within the chaos he was witnessing, and as each one was eliminated until there would only be one winner, the dance would become almost beautiful. Then they would all laugh and do it again. Finally they convinced him to join, and the one thing that turned out to be consistent was he became the first to be eliminated. All of them were just too good, and that included Fara who was younger by many cycles of the seasons than he.

Finally, as in all things, it was time to return to the bakery and work. It was always there, and there was always work. They said their goodbyes and added promises of returning when they could. With the pack beast they headed away from the farm out to the main trail, and then to the major road that would bring them back to High Trail, the village where they were working and living at this time. Many of the villages were named far into the past as this one had been. The main road that they now traveled had originally be a trail out of the foothills and had picked up the name High Trail. Since this particular village had served the many travelers it had become known as High Trail, just as the one he had grown up in had been known as Cross Trails because it was where two major trails, which were now roads, had crossed. It had been a location that was perfect for a village. While Cross Trails was much larger than High Trail, neither had grown large enough to become townships. Both had farmlands that supported the communities. Cross Trails sat within the great grasslands, while High Trail nestled in the foothills on the edge of the great grasslands.

It was the beginning of the Season of Falling and when they had left it was early in the morning. They could see their breath in the cold crisp air, and coming out of a warm shelter had sent both of them to shivering as they adjusted to the cold air. With the feel in the air they didn't need to look at anything written to know the season. This got Kal to wondering, since they had just gotten back the family history, and had brought it along for protection, if that clan home could be somewhere close to where they were. After all they were in the foothills away from the Sacred Mountains, and if he re-membered right, this clan home wasn't that close to those mountains, and as far as the village of High Trail, and the family farm they were not very close either. But as soon as that had entered his mind he shrugged it off, since there were many areas that existed in the many foothills that were around, and much of them were a very long way away from the Sacred Mountains. What this began to do for him is to raise his curiosity and desire to delve back into that history and try and solve what was presented in those many words from the past.

Eventually as the suns climbed in the sky it warmed, and between their exercise and the warming of the air the chill left, and it became a comfortable day to be out and about. Breathing in and out deeply Kal said, "This is becoming a really beautiful day, and a good one to be doing exactly what we are. But it also brought to my mind my ancestors. They'd lived in an area something like this. I wonder what they were thinking when this weather hit. They had to be more knowl-edgeable than I, after all their very lives depended on knowing the seasons. They'd know that it would only be a short time until they would be locked up inside because of the winds, snows, and such. And at that point they would need to have enough of everything to get through that time, and if not, death would come knocking – not that death wasn't a constant companion. Between the fighting, diseases, poor health, and who knows what it's surprising that any of them survived. And the line I come from was a clan, and when you compare the clans to the tribes, well the clans, because of their settle-ments, were so much better off."

As they continued down the road, Jura listening to the clopping sound of the pack beast's steps, and the gentle creaking of the leather bindings used to tie the packs to the frames that the beasts carried, was quiet. She was enjoying the walk very much, and like him thought the day was a great one. Not only that, but the feel of the air, the smells of the land, the odors of the grasses as they had cured giving off a sweet smell, made her appreciate and remind her of the home where she had grown. The mornings were a little cold when they started, but from the feel of it now, the rest of the day, up until they reached the village at about dusk, should remain very nice. "As, I said in the past, I'm glad I'm living now and not then. And yes, at times one could easily wonder how anybody survived that time in our past. But it is obvious somebody did since we are here." Smiling and with a faraway look in her eyes she said, "I wonder how future generations will look back on ours. I mean that while we find what we have, and what we can do is good, and proper, and we live comfortably, even though we work hard to achieve it, but it really isn't an issue or a problem for us. Still they may look back at us and wonder how anybody would survive in this time just like we're doing when we're looking back."

Laughing Kal said, "You know I've never looked at it that way, and you're probably quite right. So I guess when we are directly in our time that it seems okay. I mean there are good times and bad times, and with the day-to-day stuff happening we rarely have a chance to look at the big picture, just trying to keep everything going. So I guess that it probably was the same for them. Still I suspect that with that lifestyle they really never looked back at earlier generations except as spirits. So I guess we should be happy with where we are and know that most likely our future generations are going to see us as primitive in comparison to where they are at that time."

She laughed and shook her head. "Now that's funny, I mean really funny. We don't consider ourselves anything close to that way. We see new things coming along all the time to make things better and easier, and while we can't necessarily afford this stuff right now, there's a great possibility that sometime in the future that we can. And when we have it we'll appreciate it so much more because we've done without all this time. Then to think that someone in the future will look back and feel pity for us because we didn't have something that they do. And they would wonder how those, you know ones like you and me, primitives could ever survive?" Again she laughed as the images flashed once again through her mind. "I guess it's all perspective. When one is in the midst of life it is what it is, and when one looks at another's life whether it is in the near past, or distant past we compare where we are to them, and probably while it's something that would be natural to do, is really unfair."

"You know taking these trips with you is really a wonderful experience. You bring up thoughts and ideas that I have myself, and it helps me make sense of what I'm trying to understand. I guess in many ways it is always great to have someone to discuss things. And I have to agree with everything you've just said. It makes perfect sense, but sometimes things that appear to make sense at the moment fall apart later when other facts are presented. But somehow I don't feel that's going to happen this time. Being a village kid I've never had the opportunity to experience this life style much. And I'm finding that I really love it. I guess with what we're planning on doing very shortly I'd better. Since I know that we will be out here much of the time, and again I know how we are, and I'm not just referring to the two of us here, never satisfied. If we are cooped up in the village we long to get away, once we are away, we cannot wait until we are back home, and when we are working we cannot wait until the day is finished so we can relax, and so on."

Jura cocked her head to the side, and smiled, "Very true. I can see much of that when I visit with my female friends. Some have children and some, like me don't. Now I'm not pushing for a child at this time in our life, especially with all that we're about to do, but I see that very thing in our conversations. Some of them are saying how wonderful it must be to have a child, and they have that romantic faraway look as they imagine how it will be. Then the ones with children comment something to the effect, *be careful what you wish for*, and so on. And I can see much of what you've just said in how I view things. And here I thought I was the only one."

"I guess it's more common than I thought. But it only makes sense when you think about it. If we were really satisfied with where we are, then there would be nothing happening to change anything, and there's a good possibility that we'd still be like our primitive ancestors and still have that dreaded lifestyle that led to short hard lives. This brings me back to this; what are we going to do with that history? I know that I've been given custody of it, and must somehow protect it. I know that we've continued to work on making legible copies of this thing, and we've almost completed that part of it. But we, I need someplace that is safe to store that thing. Since that attempt, at what we figured, to steal this document, I've been racking my brain trying to come up with a safe haven for it, and really haven't. I feel that someone wants this desperately, and we both know who that someone is. I know that we just got it back, but when I looked it over, I never realized that we were that close to finishing it.

"I thought about my side of the family, and all of them are quite busy with their lives, and while yes, this is about my side of the family, can I put them at risk? And at the same time, your side lives in the outback on a farm, making them an easy target if someone wanted to steal something from them." He paused a moment and actually laughed, "Now that would be funny really."

With a questioning look she asked, "What would be funny?"

"I was just imagining what a surprise a bunch of thieves would get if they tried to steal or break into your family's farm. Here these thieves would feel that they'd have it all under control and to meet your family with the matriarch and patriarch of the family staff champions and all of the children trained by them. I think the bad guys in this case would be in for a real surprise, let alone a good beating. I could see the surprise on their faces when they realized that they didn't have the upper hand, and that they had better leave or get beat up."

She was silent for the longest time, which made him wonder if he'd said something wrong. She stopped and faced him, "Well, it's not as funny as you make it sound. You see, that very thing did happen. Remember we are somewhat isolated, and as you can see, at this leisurely pace that we are taking, it will be dusk before we enter High Trail." She did smile as she recalled the incident in her mind, "And I think that you probably had it about right. We did beat them up pretty badly, in fact after that we were never bothered again. I guess the word got around that we weren't worth the trouble."

"Really? I was only thinking about something like that happening. And it actually did, wow, why'd you never mention it? After all it had to be a pretty traumatic time."

Again she paused before answering, "Actually the being scared part didn't happen until it was over and the thieves ran away. When they approached appearing to be innocent, we knew something was wrong, and when one of them reached out to grab both my mother, and one of us girls to get their way, we knew what was happening, and once we did it was just sort of reaction. It was touch and go there for a little while since they were spread out trying to cover all of us. And that probably was their undoing also. They expected just a normal farm family not us. They figured they could intimidate us into submission, and instead it was they who were put down. It was very intense and there seemed to be nothing but chaos for a few moments, but suddenly it was over, and the bad guys were running for their lives. It was then once we were all back together and found that other than scrapes and bruises, which we got when we practiced with the staffs anyway, we were okay. At that point we realized what could have happened and that's when we all felt it emotionally."

He realized that both of them had been standing there along the roadway with the pack beast patiently standing there waiting for them to continue, swishing its tail at some irritating bug. They both began walking again. "I never realized that something like that happened. And you say you or the family was never bothered again? How long ago was this?"

Shaking her head she said, "I really don't know, quite a while ago. I was still a kid. After all I'm one of the middle children, and I think Fara the youngest was just walking, so a very long time ago."

"And you and your family have never been bothered since. That must have been quite an impression you left on those thieves." Taking a deep breath Kal looked around, "I have to admit that I'm quite happy that it went the way that it did. I know that many times in those situations that the ones who try this have their way with the families and in the end just kill them to keep any from identifying them, allowing them to go do it again to some other unsuspecting isolated family. And if it had been that way, you and I would have never met, and fall in love and become a couple." This brought a smile to his face, "So I'm very glad for the way things turned out, and if you don't want it mentioned, I'll let it lie and just keep it between us."

Looking at Kal, Jura replied, "Oh we never tried to keep it a secret, but we also felt it wasn't important to announce it to the world. Doing such a thing might be considered bragging, and if someone thought it was such they might decide that we were a challenge and they would come by and try and see if they could succeed where that other gang of thugs failed. So we never made anything of it. Yes we passed it on to the other farms so that they would be alert to the fact that we had some bad ones working our area, but other than that we kept it low and quiet."

"Just had a thought, and then I'll just drop it. When these thieves first attacked, none of you had your staffs, right?" She shook her head, "Okay that means all of you were unarmed at that moment, so how'd that work out? I mean obviously well since you are here and your family is all okay."

She smiled as once again she remembered back to that moment in time. "If you think about it, one has to learn moves that allow one to defend themselves if they've become disassociated with their staff. So there are unarmed methods of attacks that allow one to recover their staff and resume the match. We've not practiced any of them, and back there at the family farm we all held on to the staffs during those few free-for-all sessions that you were invited to join. Obviously, well maybe not to you, but to the rest of us, we kept it toned down a bit for the rookie that joined us. And it was a couple of those unarmed moves we used that allowed a couple of us to get free, get the staffs, and toss them to the others. After that it was a rout pure and simple."

He smiled at her, "You're right, I couldn't tell that all of you went easy on me. From my point of view I was barely holding may own, and it was fast and frenzied. And I suspect that with this revelation that since all of you went easy on me, that the few times that I thought I had the upper hand, so to speak, truly wasn't the way of it at all."

"Before I answer that, let's just say that you've improved tremendously from where you started back a couple of cycles of the seasons ago. But honestly you're not in the same class as even my youngest sister, so yeah we went easy on you. But you have to admit that you learned some new things."

"Well that means I took a hit to that old male ego thing. Especially if the youngest female took pity on this male, but you're right I did learn a few things going against the rest of you."

"If it's any consolation to your male ego, as you know, we were trained by the best, and I think honestly that right now there'd be few out there that you couldn't defend yourself against if it came down to it. But I wouldn't go out and start challenging anybody as of yet. As time and practice continues and we have a few more visits to my home it will change. And to give you another hit to that male ego of yours, remember that I'm with you and if need be I can defend you."

"Gee thanks." And this brought laughter from both of them. "Hey where'd the time go? Look we're almost back and the suns are beginning to set. Oh well, back to reality on the morrow."

CHAPTER FOUR

THE ADVENTURE BEGINS

It had taken longer than he had expected to finish the re-writing of the family history. Once complete, they used only the copies, spreading the original among the family members, so that if any single part was either stolen or lost, it overall would be just a small portion, and with copies available they would be able to fill in the missing parts to present a complete history. With the help of her siblings there was now available more than one copy which, once again, was spread among her family. With the suspected attempt to steal it in the past it was the only way they could come up with to protect this precious history.

Sabohl continued to have them watched, albeit discreetly. He still felt that they, Kal and Jura, were a threat. And even though he had no proof that a document existed, he felt strongly that it did. Still two cycles of the seasons had come and gone and presently there had been nothing to show for all of this work. Yet he could not relax until this was confirmed one way or the other. He had thought that a second attempt to break into their shelter would be a good idea, but the only opportunity had been when a family member had passed away.

It really hadn't been that long since they had moved from the premises of the bakery to the shelter they were living in presently. And while they lived at the bakery there was absolutely no chance to sneak into their quarters and do a thorough search. There was always one or the other going in and out of their place any time throughout the day, and with no specific schedule, there was no opportunity. When they had finally moved into the shelter, she had remained there and put it together like she wanted it to look. Again with no schedule to allow a quick and thorough search it had to wait.

It wasn't long after that that they had left to attend the funeral, but while they were gone the workers watched the shelter continuously not allowing any stranger access. It, in his mind, was the proof that he needed that said they were protecting something. After all why go to all the trouble if there wasn't anything of real value? So with impatience he watched from a distance waiting for the opportunity to present itself.

"To the members of the Historical Learned, and Historical Society: I pass on my humble offerings as a fellow learned. As you are well aware, we of like thought have continued our monitoring of Sabohl. If nothing else, his resolve has strengthened, as has his contacts with his people, and you know of whom I speak, continue. He is more determined to find this mythological document, since at this moment he has no proof that such exists. But it is obvious to any who know him that he is consumed with this. In truth we are in no way positive that such exists. Yet if it does, it would be an important find and possibly shed light on our past. All of us who study the past know that we are making conclusions from very incomplete records and discoveries. And since no one is

around from that time we have no way of confirming any of what we've either found or conjectured. As you are aware, Sabohl has reached his high position through intimidation, politics, and pure guile. While much of what he presents could be a true history of our past, it isn't the only theory that is out there.

"So far we haven't been able to catch him doing something illegal. Although we know that he uses members of the thieves' guild, which by the way, doesn't exist, to accomplish much. After all if there is no hard evidence then he can continue to be the authority. And one of the easiest ways for there not to be hard evidence it to have it conveniently disappear. Again because of the way he operates, he is nearly untouchable. It was only because of that one visitor that we knew to tie him to this guild. And we've had to be very careful when we've followed him to his drops, for which there are many. But we've never been able to reach what it is that he leaves at these drops. Our best have seen that these are in such places that they are watched all the time. So if any of ours approached and attempted to gather this information they would know immediately that it had been compromised. This is as much as we can tell you at this point and we must continue our predator-prey game, and hope that he slips up at some point.

"As requested, we have continued to monitor the ones who may have that very important document, but if indeed they have it, they have also been very careful to both hide it from view, and give the appearance that it doesn't exist. We may know much more soon, as it appears that there is about to be a change. It appears that very soon the operation at the bakery will be turned over to the underboss, and the two of them,

Kal, and Jura, will be heading out – as to where, and as to why we haven't a clue. Yet if it has something to do with this document it should become obvious. We can see that we are not the only ones who are aware of this change, and there has been an increase of his agents here in High Trail. Will keep all of you informed as we can. With the increase in the presence of these it has become more difficult to remain hidden ourselves. So do not become worried if more time passes than expected – as always, your fellow learned."

* * *

"Sara, we really have no idea how long we will be gone. You've proved your worth and because of this have been handed the operation while we are gone. I'm sure that both Idala and Pehel will check in on you periodically which only make sense. After all they own the business, and want to see it grow. Jura and I have to go north for a family matter and the questions and problems left for us to solve will take an unknown amount of time." Looking down and trying to think if he had forgotten anything he felt Jura poke him in the ribs. He turned and faced her and asked, "What?"

Smiling she said, "I know that you are worrying over every little thing, heck I do it too. But she is more than capable to doing this. So let her do her job, okay? We've still a couple of things that need to be packed, and the daylight is waning fast enough."

"You're right." He turned back to Sara shaking his head, "Okay then, it's yours. I guess we'll see you when we do, and good luck with this."

Sara had remained silent throughout the final conversation that she was having with her boss. She remembered back when her mate had suggested that she apply at the bakery.

While the income he was bringing in was adequate, barely would probably be more accurate, additional income would be nice. And as things happened there never was enough to cover those extras. But never in her wildest imagination and dreams did she ever see herself in this position. But at the same time, knew that she had earned it. And with the rise to this position there had been an increase in earnings which had allowed them to live better than they ever had. Plus a shelter had been provided so that they no longer had the cost of paying someone else to have a place to live. "Yes, sir, and ma'am, I will not fail either of you. Now get out of here and do what you must, and know that this business is in the hands that both of you trained, and one that you've told a number of times that she was very good at this. Plus, as you have stated, I will not be on my own. Good luck with this venture, whatever it is."

And with nothing left to say Jura and Kal turned and headed back to their shelter. Kal saying, "Sara, such an unusual name, it's one that is rarely heard or used. In fact the only place I've ever seen it is in those papers. If I remember right it was the name of that female that came from those mythological lairs that our ancestors were destroying."

"Yeah, that's right. I knew that recently I had come across the name, but couldn't remember where. I thought when she was hired that it was a very unusual name. And she said that it had been one used in her family every couple of generations, and that they were proud of it, but really never knew when it had shown up in the family. When we go back to that time in the history we didn't have, weren't allowed names, so maybe because of this female who had one, one of the females picked her as a hero or something. After all she stood up against the males of that time and gave the appearance of being their equal. That would be a very good reason for someone to choose that for her name when we were finally allowed to have them.

"Of course when I start thinking about that time it always makes me angry. To think that we were thought so little of. I guess if I had lived then, and saw a female standing against the status quo I probably would have considered her someone to look up to. Although I'm looking at this from this time back to their time, and I suspect that I have it all wrong."

With a questioning look Kal asked, "Wrong, how wrong?"

"Well, my guess would be that when one lives in a society and the world at a particular time, one is what the society is. After all, from birth to death we are immersed in that life. So our world, our beliefs, and way of seeing the world around us is colored by that society that we live in. So if this Sara came into it from a different culture, then it would have been very difficult to adjust to this new situation, and the females that lived in our culture at the time would not have liked the new stock, so to speak, to come in and upset the hierarchy, that they enjoyed. With new females in the herds, these new females would have demanded the attention of the warriors, because they were new, taking away from they who were a part of the clan or tribe, making life for the new ones hell from both sides. Having to submit to the warriors, and then being put in place by the females, who has always been a part of the tribe or clan. Because we live in a different time, and different circumstance, we have a tendency to project our views and ideals to our past. This, many times, removes the truth and hardship that all of them lived at the time, and cleans it up, and makes it appear black and white. I guess because

I'm female, and I wouldn't change that for the world, I'm a little more sensitive to our past than you would be."

"I must admit that everything you've just stated makes absolute sense. I know that we've discussed this in the past, and I can see why you would have such strong feelings on this, especially since we are planning to search for this location in the northern foothills – the place where this supposedly took place. Not that we will be able to experience that time of our history if we do find it. But by finding it and comparing what we have with what was written it should make it more real, and by finding it we will be able to, and I know it's not going to be that simple, find those other mythological places that were talked about. From what I can gather from the records this clan home was occupied past the time of the revival of the gods, and then when or soon after the wars between the clans and tribes ended this place was abandoned. So it will have changed much over the time that it existed. This, of course, will make it difficult to pin down the right time period. But I suspect that there would have to be trails and such leading to and from this place giving us further help and following up on the rest. Well, I guess we can keep talking the rest of the day if we wanted, but this is not getting those final preparations completed."

The morning came quick, and as planned they had a small meal, headed out and packed the two beasts that they would be using, and before the suns crested the distant grasses and foothills, and with the gray of dawn, headed north on the high trail road towards where he had grown up at Cross Trails. Their plan was simple, throughout this day to travel, and then spend the night in one of the many points along the way for travelers. Then somewhere close to the end of the second day to be back at Cross Trails. High Trail was located far south, although there was much of the continent that continued in the southerly direction. To travel from High Trail to the Sacred Mountains would take two 9-days to accomplish, and to travel the full length of the grasslands, even though most was now broken up with the many farms, and beasts husbandries, would take so much longer.

No longer being the wild open area that it had in the past, it could take a full season or fifteen 9-days. This of course was north to south. Past the Sacred Mountains the area soon became another place of desolation, but unlike the great desolation that ran down the coast of the continent; this was one of ice and snow. The few hardy adventurers who had traveled there found no evidence that any people had ever lived and thrived there. But as harsh as it was, it was impossible to stay long, and to do a really good and thorough job of searching the area out. There was a long range of mountains – although not very high when comparing them to the Sacred Mountain range – that ran the length of the continent. From what they had learned, it was this range that helped create the area of desolation by blocking the moisture that came off of the one large ocean. As the ones who studied the lands and weather stated, "These mountains push up the clouds and rob them of their moisture, and when they get to the other side there is nothing left to nourish the desolation – simple and easy." Although it had been harder to explain how the rains and yes the snows reached the grasslands. And finally when an explanation did arrive it had been too technical for most.

If they had a way to view their world from above it probably would have made it much easier to explain the weather patterns since all of the land mass and the clouds would be observed. But there was no way to do that presently. Although the far thinkers believed that one day they would be able to do just that. Most just laughed it off as something that couldn't – wouldn't happen. It really hadn't been that long ago when they had finally began to travel to many of the islands, and now many had growing populations on them. Others, of course, were still unexplored. On the east side of the grasslands laid a couple of changes, one being the badlands. Rough harsh lands of canyons, and little growth of vegetation, with loose soils and falling rocks, seemingly hot all of the time, and the second, a series of steppes that had become known as the foothills. Her parents and family farm existed in one of these, as had the clan home in a different set. While not as rough as the badlands, there were similarities to both areas. Whereas the hills or mountains on the west were soft and rolling, covered heavily in trees and plants, these were covered in tough vegetation, the soils rocky with large boulders everywhere. Trees did exist here, but were more spread out. There were many places to hide from an enemy, and many places a large clan could live protected by what the land provided. If one traveled coast to coast, east to west it would take half the time, when compared to the north – south, even with the tougher terrain that one had to travel.

The desolation itself actually was broken up in a series of deserts with small oases between most of them. Very few of these deserts had any vegetation at all, and the ones that did, this vegetation barely hung on. Because of the mud hills and mud flats that existed in many of them, even though they had ceased being mud a very long time in the past, demonstrated that these areas weren't always dry. So with these facts in their minds, and knowing with such a large world around them, to find even one of these mythologies would be close to impossible. Many in the present and their past had attempted it, but so far none had been successful, and thusly the belief that all of this had to be mythology. But they felt that their chances were much greater on finding and solving this unknown past. They had something nobody else had. They had the direct record, the actual words written, had rough maps, had approximate distances. And even though those distances were more marked by days of travel than actual distance, it was more than the rest ever had. So as they began this adventure, they felt good about their chances. But doesn't everyone when they begin a new quest?

"Chill in the air this morn," Kal commented, "guess we should expect that. We are heading towards the end of the Season of Heat, and there's a taste of the Season of Falling in the morning air."

She shivered briefly; they had just left the warmth of their shelter into this cold morning air. She looked back as they had finished packing and had started down the road, knowing that it would be a very long time before she saw their home again. Sighing she said, "True. But shortly we'll appreciate it. Once the suns rise and start warming things we'll wish for just this coolness." Nodding her head as if in agreement with what she had said and looking at him, she stopped briefly and once again looked back.

"What are you doing?" He asked.

Smiling she said, "Look it's going to be a very long time before I see our place again. So I'm taking one last look, and putting this image in my memory."

He stopped at turned and did the very same thing, "Good idea. I probably would have kicked myself later when I thought about it. Guess we can do the same thing with the village as we leave. After all we've spent a lot of time here, and you of course, much more than I. We've got to know most of the people here, and it is hard to leave such a friendly place." They walked through a silent village that was on the verge of waking up to face a new day and the routines that made it normal and comfortable for those who lived and worked here.

In the shadows, for which there were many this time of the morning, two watched patiently as they watched the pack beasts and the ones leading them, head through a very silent village. They hung back so as to not raise any suspicion. Turning to one the other stated, "Go get word to our boss that they're on the move, and with this pace they'll be easy to follow. My guess would be that as they head north they will be going towards Cross Trails where he is from. It is time to alert all of the ones along this road from here to there. Catch up with me at the first marker outside of the village. I'll wait for you there, and we can continue to follow them and keep a safe distance until we hand it off."

The one he was talking to just nodded and silently disappeared. This other continued to wait with a smile. From what he could see this baker and his mate were unaware that anybody was behind them and held serious interest in them. *Well, let them continue to think like that. It'll make my job easier.* He continued to lean against one of the shelters in the shadows between two of the shelters until they were out of sight. He slowly entered the main way through the village and casually headed in their direction giving the appearance that it was just a random direction that he was heading. And unknown to these thieves, they were also under the watchful eye of others, others who were there to help protect whatever it was that Kal and Jura possessed.

Trehe turned to the others that were with him and quietly gave orders for these two to be watched, followed, and to find out whom they made contact with so that they could continue to find all the hidden ties, links, and directions that Sabohl had himself tied to. Soon they hoped to be able to topple his stranglehold within the learned community. But, as in history, time would tell, and nothing had been written as of yet to make what was transpiring history. After this one minor incident entered the history books it could be that nothing would have changed, or all would have. Would they look back and smile at their success, and the gains that they learned, or would Sabohl be the one smiling with another success at maintaining his position, running the present board into hiding and shame? A lot was on the line, and the two main players in this game hadn't a clue.

"Funny how it seems to chill," Jura said as she shivered from the morning breeze that had just reached her, "actually feels colder just before the suns crest and shine their daylight on us. It's like the night says I won't give up right up until the light wins out."

"True, and," as he smiled at her and she could see that from that smile he was going to make some smart remark, " You're not going superstitious on me are you – bringing back those many gods of our ancestors who controlled every aspect of their lives, by making a comment that gives the night life, and making the night alive."

She turned and faced him and gave him a loving shove and said, "No silly, and you know better than that, and besides I can tell when you're serious and when you're joking and you gave yourself away on this one."

Looking down and with that smile, the one that had attracted her to him in the first place he said, "I guess after all rest time that we've been together it's just hard to pull something over on you, but I have to agree with you it always seems to chill just before those suns approach the horizon. I guess I can see how it could appear to someone that this had to be a fight between two gods – one that ruled the night and one that ruled the day. With both dawn and dusk being a battleground as one fought to gain control. You know it's kind of strange when one actually reads the words in such a document as we have. While we may laugh, at times, because of how they viewed something, at the same time when one gets the mindset that they must have had, then it becomes easy to see it from their point of view. Well, maybe not easy, because, as you've said, we don't live in their world, but, it becomes easier to see it from their side." Since both of them had stopped briefly he turned around and looked back. Shaking his head he commented, "I guess we can say its official – can't see High Trail at all, now. For us it won't exist for a long time."

She turned around and looked, took a deep breath, "Yeah, and I already miss it. After all it's been part of my life for most of it." They both headed back down the road, soon, in the overall scheme of things, they would arrive at Cross Trails, spend a couple of days, and then continue north to what they would guess would be three days from the Sacred Mountains. In a way it was a surprise that these ancient mountains had never been renamed after the fall of the gods. This, of course was an unimportant point. Still, if they could find his ancestors' home, it would be from there that all of the rest of the locations that were considered part of mythology should be located.

* * *

"Look we've tried this from a number of directions, and so far none of it has worked. So let's think about this for a moment." Jura was frustrated with the results so far. Both of them felt that it would have been relatively easy to find this place, but as the 9-days had passed and no success she was just about ready to give up.

Taking a deep breath as he looked around, both of them were sitting in their camp that they had located just about three days from the Sacred Mountains. It was from here that they had been scouring the surrounding areas for some sign of that ancient site. "I know that both of us felt that this would be easier than it has turned out to be, but I guess if it'd have been easy someone else probably would have found it by now. We're having trouble and we have a rough, although I have to admit it now, a very rough idea of its location. I think I know why the exact location was never mentioned in the text. Well, at least I think I do. What comes to my mind is this; first off it would have been unwise during that time to reveal your location, and secondly they knew where it was so why state something that was obvious?"

Staring into the fire that they had built and then looking out towards the grasslands, their camp was located in area that hid them from the surrounding open country. They had located the camp at the base of the foothills knowing that somewhere in those foothills that clan home existed. Sighing she said, "Yeah, I guess that would make sense. But I have forgotten how tough 'roughing it' can be. As a kid I loved doing this, but now find it's not quite the same. I feel dirty, I itch all the time, and I have to admit it, to have a privy would be nice. Funny how important something becomes when you don't have it. I just figured that by going to the base of the Sacred Mountains and backtracking those three days, give or take, since I would guess that their three days of travel would cover a greater distance than ours . . . But I forgot how large an area we are talking about here. These mountains cover great distances to the east and to the west, and the foothills themselves while not as big seem to cover vast distances also. And from the descriptions of the area where they were located it could be a thousand different places. So much of the area looks the same when it is described in general terms as this is. I guess I was a little, well maybe a lot, optimistic about finding this place. I guess for both of us you could throw in naïve, which would make sense, since neither you nor I have ever done anything like this before. It makes one appreciate the ones who do this all the time. I guess we only see the results and not the work that went into the finding of these ancient sites."

"Hmm, sounds like the pot's boiling, would you like me to dish you up some of this stew?"

Nodding and smiling she replied, "I guess so. But I have to admit that I'm getting tired of this too. I guess the excitement has just left and for some reason I'm wanting some of the comfort that we had in our shelter."

"Okay, point taken. I know that you've done this because of me, and my passion to find out the truth. Yeah, and I know that the truth can be interpreted in so many ways and still be the truth, but you really didn't have to join me on this adventure. Oh don't get me wrong, I love having you with me, and sometime in the future we probably will look back and think that these were the best of times. You know times where we were free to do as we please, and not be tied down with whatever responsibilities that we will have then. We'll forget the bad and just remember the good – but point taken. Tell you what, tomorrow let's head into that village, you know the one that probably has been here at the time of these ancestors of mine. It's on the road that leads into the Sacred Mountains. We can take a couple of days, rent a room, and act like we are visitors on vacation. It will give us time to recharge, and buy what we need to continue this, how does that sound?" He had to admit that looking at her here at the camp, that she was still a beautiful female in his mind. Even with her brown hair somewhat disheveled and clothes that were loose fitting but couldn't hide her body, but he knew that right now a break would be welcome to both of them.

"Mother raised no fools, of course. I suspect that if it was possible that I'd soak all day in a bath and maybe even then not feel like I got all the grime off of me. I've never gone this long without a bath even as a kid when they were something to avoid."

"Okay then, we'll pack up in the morning and do it. Besides maybe we'll get lucky and something there might help us, I doubt it but one never knows." He stood up and headed around the fire and asked her to stand, he then gave her a loving hug for which she returned. They clung together for the longest of time, and then she began to laugh. "I think we better take that stew off the fire, I believe it's beginning to burn."

"He started laughing also and stated, "Are you sure it isn't us? After all that hug and the way we were close surely got me interested."

"Oh you males always are thinking that way." Then in a teasing voice she said, "I bet even as dirty and smelly as I am, you'd still think that way and if I offered you'd take me up on it immediately."

Smiling he threw his arms out with the palms up inviting her back into his arms. "Why of course. I find you attractive no matter what you look like, or how dirty or odorous you become. Besides if we do become involved tonight, we can always repeat it once we've cleaned up back in that village and having a room for a few days in the inn."

Coming back into his arms and putting her head on his shoulders she whispered, "Then, how can I refuse such an offer. After all you're not so clean or fresh yourself. And if you can stand me, I guess I can stand you. Just understand this though, we may be trying to find where your, and I guess if I really think about it, our ancestors and where they lived, but I'm not going to do what those females at that time did."

With a questioning look he asked, "Did?" Then as he thought about it he simply said, "Oh." Nodding his head before continuing, "Of course not. After all we are a very long way away from that time and place, and much has changed for the better since then, and you don't have to prove anything to me. Besides", he decided to tease her a little, "I'm the only male in this relationship and I don't require that kind of proof that you did your duty to the clan."

Then laughing and teasing back she asked, "Are you sure? After all with the way it was back then I would be dealing with many of you males." She saw the look of surprise in his eyes and just laughed harder. "Now come on, you are the only male in my life, other than, let's see, hmm, there are my brothers, and my father and then there's . . ."

Interrupting her he said, "Okay, okay I get the point. But I had to admit there for a moment you had me going." Then pointing to their portable shelter he asked, "Shall we?"

* * *

"Sabohl, this is an update to let you know what is transpiring with the two that you have an interest. They traveled to the Sacred Mountains in the north, and have backtracked just about three days from them and have been scouring the foothills. Whatever it is that they are looking for must be somewhere there. Although considering the very size of this minor range one could be searching their whole life and never find anything. They recently pulled camp and headed for one of the local villages. At this time we feel that we've remained hidden from their sight, and neither is aware of our presence. Because they have been somewhat stationary, we've added others to make it easier to watch. If there is a change we will pass it on immediately."

After reading the note he had to admit that whoever wrote this one was better educated than most of these he dealt with. *So they are searching for something in the northern foothills are they?* This confirmed in his mind that they had to have a source, something ancient that had sent them to this location, but so far nobody had seen it, and even with people eavesdropping on their conversations, nothing was discovered. Yet there had to be a reason for them to be there, and not only there, but searching all over those foothills. He'd need to get a note right back to those who watched. But even if he sent it out today to one of the many drops it would probably take at least one 9-day for it to reach them. Well that was something that couldn't be helped. There was no way presently to move something like this any faster. He couldn't use the signaling system that moved important messages, so he had to depend on the hand carried method, and dealing with these people who were less than trustworthy could actually add time to its arrival.

Still, he had to be careful to leave names and such out of these notes so that if they fell into the wrong hands that they could not come back and incriminate him. He could answer saying that whoever was accusing him of something couldn't prove anything. After all it was just a note and nothing more, and could mean any number of things. He was still angry with that one visit that happened a few cycles of the seasons in the past. It came close to exposing him and his many less than honest contacts that he used. But at this point in time it appeared that no one noticed, which meant that he was still in charge, and still safe. Leaning back in his chair with his hands behind his head he stretched, shaking his head, and sighing slightly he thought. *Still got more papers to read through and grade before I can get that response out to one of the drops so that it can be on its way.*

* * *

"Now that was a wonderful break, and to be clean for the last 9-days is wonderful." Jura stared into the fire at their new basecamp and actually felt relaxed and refreshed. It had been a nice diversion, which sounded funny to her. Since normally their diversions had to do with leaving the village and maybe go camping. Now it was just the opposite. They had found a place where a small stream ran. Upstream and just a short distance from their location there was a waterfall and at the base the water pooled in a small pond before continuing on its way. Surrounding this pond was a number of large boulders making access somewhat difficult, but accessible. Plus it provided privacy and while the water wasn't heated it still allowed both of them to bathe and not feel so dirty. The way the stream twisted and turned their campsite was completely hidden, making them feel a little safer than they did in their last campsite.

It had been an accidental discovery since small and large streams were a common sight here in the north. The plan had been to head back to their original site, but had detoured briefly because of a wild beast, and came across this stream. Pushing through some of the vegetation that grew because of all this water they found this place, a little oasis of clear ground surrounded by boulders and small hills with the only entrance and exit being through that vegetation. Smiling Kal said, "Yes, that was rather nice wasn't it? And you're right this is quite the opposite of what we're used to. And to find this place, for what we are doing I cannot ask for better. We have privacy, we have our own pond, to both bathe and fish, and plenty of boulders to take care of our nature calls, and all of this is invisible from the outside. Heck, even where that small falls comes in here you can't see in. It's like this is our own little world. Of course when we build a fire, the smell of smoke would draw someone to us. But there doesn't seem to be anybody out here but us, although there probably is."

"Yes there probably are others around; still I'm happy with this. Now if we had a permanent shelter built here it would be almost perfect, but since we can't this is just about as good as it gets."

"Yes, and this allows us to search a different portion of these foothills, and we double checked when we came back and we are still just about three days from the Sacred Mountains, so this could be the area."

For the next 9-days they searched the areas close to their new campsite and came up empty. Sitting by the fire that last night, with frustration showing in both of them, it just hadn't occurred to them that it would be this difficult. At least they were learning, and finding that slowly a map of the area was developing in their minds. And in those mental maps there were still a number of blank areas but slowly the large area was beginning to make sense, and as each blank area was filled in, the map shrunk in size. Warming his hands over their small fire, and then leaning back against a convenient boulder Kal said, "So far, from any of the descriptions and the rough map that we have none of this looks right. What is it that we're missing? I know that when maps were made during this era that there was never a specific orientation like all of them do now. It was more based on a key landmark, something that was familiar or commonly known at the time."

"Yeah, and that's the problem, we don't know what that common thing is. It would have been nice if it was orientated like all of today's maps with South on top, but I guess if that was the case then all of these ancient sites would have been located by now, and maybe the way we view our history would be different, but who knows that may not be true either. I wonder why it was decided to make south as the top of all the modern maps?"

"Could be because most of us live in the south, and because the weather gets a little nasty up here, that there are less of us here, it would make sense to base it on where most of us live. Of course this is just a guess, mapmaking wasn't something I studied."

"Well, being that I'm from the outback so to speak, we've used maps and been comparing them to the lands for as long as I can remember, and so far there's nothing at all that is similar to this map. Of course I know that if one approaches an area, one that they are familiar with, but from a different direction that that known area looks strange and unfamiliar until we change our position and then it just clicks. I suspect that this is what we are facing here. With no way to orientate the map, and not knowing what they used as their landmark, and who knows how much has changed since this place was abandoned, we've missed it. And let's face it; the land does change, even if it seems unchangeable. So something major on this crude map may no longer exist as it did in the days when this was created."

"True, so very true. I guess all we can hope for since this was made towards the end of their time at this place that the changes aren't great." Kal sighed, "I really did believe that this would be so much easier than it turning out." Looking around and then up at the night sky he continued, "That's really beautiful. Until we started doing this kind of stuff, you know camping and spending time away from the villages, I never appreciated the night skies or so many other things truly. Being one from the villages I was used to having noise and people around me all the time. So getting used to the quiet and the night sounds, feeling the soft breezes, feeling the changes that this world tells you have been a learning experience. I guess by being from where I am, and now doing this I can appreciate your life so much more and I'm finding that I prefer it over the life in the villages."

Smiling Jura said, "I told you it would be this way. But words can never, and I mean never adequately explain the differences. You really have to experience them for yourself. And in that I mean not just two or three days, but like now where you live it for a long time. It is only then when you shed your village ways and you begin to listen to what this natural world is trying to say to you, that you begin to understand the differences. Of course," she stopped and smiled with a faraway look before continuing, "there's many who try and before too many 9-days are over, are running, screaming and heading back to the protection of the village." She shrugged, "It's just something I'll never understand, but I guess some can only live that way. I know that while I've been living with you and we've been living in the villages it still isn't an easy thing for me to do. It's like there is a constant invisible pressure which places a restlessness on me, making me yearn for the outback. But don't take me wrong here, you're my mate and I'll be with you wherever we end up. Although I have to admit it, other than some of the necessities that a village can provide a female, I'm loving every day that we are out here." She looked up at the stars, looked down and was deep in thought and in her own world for a short time. He waited knowing that she still had something to say. "I don't know how to put into words, but being here in the natural world where we came from seems almost healing. Yes I know that it can be a dangerous unforgiving place, but at the same time when this soaks into you, you almost feel healed, whole, and feel like you've returned home. You feel more alive, oh I don't know, but it's the way I feel."

For a while both of them were silent allowing the night to surround them, the slight breezes to whisper to them, the small beasts scurrying along their way, the sounds of a night flyer passing overhead, and just the silence that almost seemed deafening. After what seemed a long time both looked at the fire and saw that it had burned down to just coals. Still neither felt like moving both lost in their own thoughts and the night. Finally Kal said, "I guess we could stay out here all night, and probably it wouldn't matter, but I think it's time to retire, snuggle a little bit, enjoy our closeness, and get some rest."

It was late morning with Kal sitting close to their fire. He looked around their private oasis, although this probably wasn't quite the right word for it. As far as he could remember it had to do with an area in the wastelands where there was water. Well, at least they were surrounded with water. Jura had commented that she needed a bath and had headed for the pond that was just out of sight of the camp. He heard something from that direction and figured it was her returning and got up and began to head in that direction only to be faced by Jura who was wearing only the moisture from her dip. Immediately he could feel the desire rise, and was sure that she could see it also. Shaking his head he stated, "Seeing you like this makes me want you right now."

Yeah, I'm sure, but I forgot to bring a drying cloth and a change of clothing. I had decided to wash the ones I was wearing as they were almost as dirty as I was. And on that other subject," there was a look of what he couldn't quite figure out in her eyes, "oh yes me female, you male. I must as a female submit to you since you are the male. No wait, that's not quite true. It is this way me female, you warrior, only then must I submit." She stopped and laughed before continuing. He wasn't sure where this was going, "No you are not warrior and as such I am not required to submit to your needs, but I am a better warrior than you, so you must submit to me!" She then walked over to him, they hugged, and he complained saying, "Hey, now you've got me wet."

She laughed again and said, "Well then, we better get you out of those wet clothes, don't cha' think?" After a rather passionate session, both retired back to the pond, this time with the proper changes and drying cloths and helped each other with their baths.

Later as both sat around their small fire both feeling comfortable they began to go over the rough map and notes that they had brought. "Look something we did consider is that the land does change. I bet even these small streams like this one moves its channels as things happen over time. Even though there are few trees in the grasslands, many of these streams have quite a few, so if, oh say because of a storm some of them would fall into the stream, then these fallen trees could force the stream to change direction. And who knows, while most of the time it would be a slight change, other times it could dam it in such a way that the flow has completely changed – never going past the blockage where it used to go but now in a new direction." Kal paused as he thought this through. "I know we are looking at around a thousand cycles of the seasons, and usually things don't change that rapidly, other than what we do to it. So, maybe one of the ravines that led from the grasslands to the somewhat hidden trail, which led towards that clan home, is no more, or so many other things. Who knows they could have deliberately misrepresented something on their map so that if it fell into the wrong hands that the ones who acquired this couldn't find their way there to be able to attack it."

Leaning back against a rock she contemplated what he had suggested. "Yes, any of those could be fact. Yet we have no way to prove any of it. So far we've been unable to orientate this thing with any of the land that we've searched. It's a very frustrating thing, it really is. Look we've kind of shot this day by getting such a late start. Let's just go out to some of the high points and look over the areas. Then as the suns begin to set we can watch the shadows to get a better idea for how the land really is. Maybe from that we can get some ideas of where to search next."

"Sounds good to me, I'm so glad that you showed me that. Being from the villages it is something you just don't think about. After all you have the streets through the villages and shelters of different kinds that are your landmarks so something like that wouldn't cross my mind. Besides not only is it educational as far as learning how the land lays, but it is also beautiful. You can feel the beginning of the evening cooling, and sense the increase in moisture and the shadows are beautiful as they stretch across the landscape." Kal paused in thought, "I think we should pack something to snack on, so how about we leave after the midday meal. That way we won't have to take too much and have half a day to explore."

"Works for me, let's do it." Jura got up went inside their portable shelter grabbed their carrying packs a brought them outside, tossing his to him. "I guess we should put these in order then."

* * *

There had been a rather stiff breeze off the grasslands upslope to where they stood on top of one of the higher foothills. Looking south they could see the foothills running up to the edge of the great grasslands, and in the vast distance to the west a slight haze that probably marked the edge of the desolation where it was not uncommon for dust to being stirred constantly by the winds. To the north stood the great ranges of what they had known as the Sacred Mountains, making the foothills a minor inconvenience in comparison, and to the east the vast foothills and somewhere lost within these was that hidden home of his past. It wouldn't be long before the shadows would show how rugged an area this truly was. Both had found a large flat rock to sit as they waited just a little longer. Soon they would have to head back, since they had no desire to work their way back to their camp in the dark.

Between them they studied a copy of the crude map that had been made towards the end of the occupation of the clan home. As the shadows lengthened revealing more of the hidden canyons smaller peaks, and ravines they turned and twisted the document in many different directions trying to establish some type of orientation that would line up what they saw on the map with the real world that they were observing. "I don't get it. There doesn't seem to be anything on this that compares to what we are looking at." He couldn't keep the frustration out of his voice as he looked once again on the scene before him and looking at the map.

"I know what you mean. I really thought that it would be a very simple thing. After all we had a map." She laughed, "I guess we set our expectations too high – very naïve of us if I do say myself." Taking a deep breath she continued, "Oh well I guess we can try this again in the morning. We really need to head back."

Sighing he said, "Yeah, I guess you're right. If we don't find something shortly that shows up on this map I guess we'll be moving our camp again – although it's going to be hard to give up this one. Okay, let's head back." They rolled the map back up and placed in her carrying pack got up and headed back for camp.

From a different hill and unknown to Kal and Jura, two watched them as they got up and headed back to camp. One turning to the other said, "From what I could see it looks like they were trying to compare something they had to this area. I wonder if they have a map or something. Look we need to follow them, because the last time they relocated their camp we never did figure out where it was. Who knows, maybe if we can locate the camp we can sneak in after they're asleep and steal it – but, on second thought maybe not. We'd be giving ourselves away and could come away with nothing. Besides we're being paid to do this and this is much easier than some of the other things we've had to do." The other one remained quiet and nodded in agreement saying only, "We'll watch."

And another team looked at each other with both smiling, since they were close enough to catch the conversation of the observers as they waited, until the two who had been observing Kal and Jura moved on down towards their hidden camp. "Seems for such an empty land it's getting kind of crowded out here. This brought a chuckle from his partner.

"Yes, isn't it? At least we won't have to reveal ourselves to protect them. Had these two decided to raid their camp we may have had to show ourselves. Guess we'd better be heading to our camp."

CHAPTER FIVE

OTHERS

Another 9-day had passed with nothing to show for their hard work other than covering more of the foothills. They had moved their camp, not wanting to leave such a perfect campsite, but nothing in the area had produced any results. So they moved two days hike to the east and while it wasn't as nice or as hidden as their previous site it would have to work. "I don't know how long we've still available to us. I've never been this far north and I don't know if the seasons are shorter, longer, harsher, or anything really." It was early morning and he and Jura were heading out to try and orientate the map once again, wanting to use the morning shadows created by the rising suns. There was hope that finally after all the time that they had been traipsing through these hills that something would finally go their way.

Jura shivered a little, "Yeah agreed. These mornings are becoming quite chilly. Definitely reminds me of the Season of Falling. So there's a good chance if we don't find something soon that we'll have to call it for this time and head back."

Breathing out heavily and watching his breath create clouds and then dissipate in the cool air Kal said, "It will be very frustrating to have spent all this time out here and have to return with nothing but our tans to show for it. At least we don't have to worry about those predators, you know the Skaiths. I think the last one was seen a very long time ago. I think that they were from a very early time in this world. And from what I've heard about them we would never know they were around until it was too late. With their speed of attack and strength, there'd be a blur and it would be the only warning we'd get. I know they sent fear through any who might have caught a glimpse of these solitary hunters. It was another reason to stay out of the Sacred Mountains, since they seemed to be mostly there. Although there had been reports that they hunted the herd beasts in the grasslands and foothills close to those mountains. And, of course, that's where we are. While, it's been frustrating enough to have this rough map and come up empty, still this is so much better than becoming a meal for one of those beasts."

"Agreed. I understand that just their cry was enough to send chills and fear in any who happened to be close. Should have worn something warmer, it's really cold this morning." As they had reached another of the many small peaks the morning winds touched them with a chill that penetrated to the bone. "Brrr, let's see if we can find a place out of this breeze. If I'm this cold I might be concentrating on being cold instead of looking over the countryside." They walked a little to the west and partially down and found a warm pocket of air, and by experimenting found that just a little way in any direction they were immediately back into the cold air. "I don't understand this, and probably never will, yet I ran into this very often back on the farm. There seems to be places that were either colder or warmer than the surrounding air and no reason that I could see for it to be that way, and here it is again right at this spot."

They got close together for each other's warmth and waited for the shadows to form. It appeared to take forever for the suns to rise high enough so that the morning shadows could form. At this moment the suns held no warmth as their breaths still came out in great clouds, and when the slight breezes touched them it sent chills through their bodies. Unfortunately, where they had retreated, their views in the direction that they wanted to observe were hidden, while the areas towards the grasslands were plain to see. Shrugging Kal said, "I guess if we want to see what we came here today to see, we can't stay here. Although right now being warm and being this close to you is a reason to stay here . . . but can't, so let's go see what we can see."

All she did was smile, stood up and together they braved the cold morning air and headed back to the top of the hill. Once they arrived both of them immediately forgot their chilled condition because what they were seeing, in the distance, in those morning shadows, matched the crude map that they had been using. Pointing Jura stated, "Look! I've stared at this map so often that I have it memorized, and truly thought that we wouldn't ever see something on the ground that would match it but look." She stopped briefly and turned to Kal and asked, "You see it don't you?"

He had been in awe when he had seen what she had. It had driven him to silence. He had reached a point that he had almost given up. It wouldn't have been much longer and they would have had to head back and wait through another Season of Cold before they could try again. But here before them, after all that time spent in useless searching, finally – finally it was before them. "Yes, I see it. But, how do we get to the path that goes there? From here I can't see it, and I think once we get back down into those small canyons and ravines that it will be easy to miss. From what I remember when reading my history, the pathway wasn't easy to find when it was traveled, and now it's been a very long time since anybody has traveled that way, and there's a very good chance that the entrance could easily be overgrown and hidden."

As he spoke these things she thought and had to admit that he was right. Up here it was plain to see, but once one dropped down and didn't have this view then everything changed. And because there had been no travel they could easily miss the entrance to the trail or path that led to the abandoned clan site. Plus he was again correct by saying that the entrance could be easily overgrown. So with the sudden elation from finding the landmarks noted on the map and thinking that finally they had found it, she realized that it might take days to find their way to what they had been searching. Trying to point out the positive, she said, "Well, at least we know we're in the right area. Look, I think we need to move our camp a little closer to what we've just discovered so that we can search this out. With all the failures that we've had up to this point, to be finally in the right place is a relief. It, in a way, simplifies things. Instead of all these foothills three days out of the Sacred Mountains, and even I was surprised as to how big an area it is, to finally have narrowed it down to this . . . well, I don't know, this area? I know to be this close, but at the same time still not there, and we've only got three or four 9-days left before we will be facing the Season of Cold." Taking a deep breath she said, "Okay, I know what we have ahead of us is still daunting, but standing here and reveling in the fact that we finally found it isn't going to get us there."

"You're right, so shall we go break the camp and move it then?" She nodded and both of them headed back down towards their camp to begin the preparation of breaking it down, packing the two pack beasts, but before all of this they would eat.

* * *

The two who were monitoring them had risen late that morning and were sullenly sitting close to their campfire. Every morning it was becoming colder, and this was getting old. At first it seemed like a nice break from what they normally were involved with. Besides, they had been almost caught the last time they had broken into a shelter to steal something, so this was a welcome diversion, and a cooling off time, a time to disappear. But now, both were missing their booze, and the companionship of a female, now and then. "Look, I'm just about done with this. They can't be out here much longer anyway. We can't be too far from the Season of Cold, and I don't want to be anywhere out here exposed during those storms."

The one he was talking to sat across the fire from him only nodded his head in agreement. At first he had been happy to be away, but now he would be very happy to be away *from this*. "Guess we better see what our two little fliers are up to." The other only grunted. So leaving their fire burning they got up climbed the hill that their camp was located behind and carefully peered into Kal and Jura's camp. "Crap! They're breaking camp, and we're not even ready to follow them." They turned rapidly around and headed back to their own camp and began hastily to break it down, not bothering to extinguish their small fire, as there was no time. All they did was to kick some dirt over it. Grabbing their dirty pots the one that had spoken earlier yelped, "That's hot!", and immediately threw it back on the ground where the liquid that was inside sloshed out and spilled out onto the ground. There was no portable shelter to pack as they were too lazy to put up such a convenience, threw whatever gear they had into their carrying packs, and rapidly climbed the hill where they had hidden behind to watch the two, and follow remaining out of sight.

"I wonder what prompted this move?" The other thief asked quietly. The only response he got from the other, who had made himself the unofficial leader, was a shrug of the shoulders. Well, he hadn't expected an answer anyway, and he was quite content to let him lead – meant less for him to do and be responsible for. Besides, if this went wrong he could blame it on him because of the other's choice and be free from any retaliation. Soon they were out of sight of their old camp and were concentrating completely their prey.

After they were out of sight three walked into their abandoned camp with the leader looking around and shaking his head. It was apparent to the three that the ones who had camped here were lazy, slovenly, and careless. Turning to the other two he said, "Better put out that fire we don't need it to escape. I've seen what fires do to the grasslands, and it isn't pretty." He watched as the other two carefully extinguished the campfire. While they did this he did a careful search of the camp finding nothing of importance. Turning back to the two who had completed their assignment he said, "Guess we better see what these two are up to, and soon one of us will have to return and update our contacts." The three left the camp, and with care, began tracking the two thieves, although a child from a village could have followed it.

* * *

As they hauled the pack beasts along Kal stopped a moment followed by Jura who had a questioning look on her face. He seeing this answered, "Look, I just realized from reading all of that in the document that there is a main path or entrance to the route from the grasslands. I know that it doesn't show it on this map, but I suspect that was to prevent someone using it, if, for some reason it fell into enemy's hands, at the time. Even close to the end of the time that they lived there, there was fighting, battles, and such all the time, even though things were beginning to change. It would only make sense to keep something like that out of this thing."

"I hadn't thought about it, but you're right. So what do you want to do? We're not too far from the grasslands, do you want to head back to them and see if we can find the entrance?"

"Jura, I just don't know. I suspect that the beginning of the trail was well hidden so that it couldn't be seen, allowing any enemy just to follow and attack. But at the same time, I don't know if we can come across the trail here in these foothills. It is a problem, what do you think?"

"You're asking me? That's a tough one. If the beginning of the trail was hidden in their day, it could be completely gone now, with no travel for all this time and no use, and there could be no possibility of finding it by cutting across the hills like we are doing now. Hmmm, okay look you have a good point saying that the entrance is from the grasslands so let's stop a moment and think about it."

"Yeah, let's see if we can put ourselves in the place of our ancestors, and before you say it I'm not meaning the place where you females were at that time, I know better."

Smiling at him although there was no humor in it she replied, "Better not, you know it's a sore subject to me." Taking a deep breath before continuing, "Okay, let's see . . . it would have to be easily recognizable, but at the same time defensible."

"Not only that, but there would have to be something close by that would place them higher, so that they could observe, in the distance, to prevent another tribe or scouting party to stay hidden and far enough away preventing someone approaching the trail to see them, but close enough to so they could mark the location."

She just shook her head as she thought about it, "Yes, all of the above. The problem is this, there's probably hundreds if not thousands of such places that all of this would fit when approaching the foothills from the grasslands."

The two herd beasts, unconcerned with what their masters were discussing, grazed contentedly; they knew that once this respite was over that they would be required to move again. "Okay," Kal said, "what if we work the edge of the foothills stopping periodically, climbing one of the hills and align the landmarks with the map. We should be able to make it line up and maybe the combination of that would lead us to it."

Nodding she said, "Yes, that might just work, although I wonder if there's something on this map that might give us a hint. After all the map wasn't made for those who lived at the clan home, it had been put together for the ones in the growing alliance. So there should be something there on the map, a meeting place that would have been in the grasslands. Something close, but not so close, as to give its location away. I'd suspect that they would have blindfolded the ones that they would bring into the clan home at least part of the way so that it wouldn't be revealed. Although from the description it would have been a difficult place to attack."

"That's probably true of leaders who were not members of that alliance. From what I remember reading, runners approached all the time, so its location had to be known. Still the less that knew meant less chance of attack."

By midmorning they had set up their next campsite and then, more by luck than design, they thought that there was a good chance they had found what they were looking for. It was an ancient trail, more sensed than seen, and it led in direction that would provide defenders the ability to aggressively attack an approaching hostile clan or tribe thinning their numbers as they approached. "If this is the right place," Kal stated, "then maybe we should have brought the supplies with us. I've the feeling that we're going to need to break camp once again."

"Yeah, you're probably right, but what if we hadn't found this trail, then what? I don't like trying to set up a camp at the end of a day. What's this?" She asked. It appeared that at this point the trail split going in opposite directions and not a hint as to where either direction would lead them. Before them was a cliff rising above them, again giving defenders a point to attack enemies. As they stood there looking in both directions undecided Jura talking as she thought about what was before them said more to herself than to him. "Hmmm, I wonder . . ."

With a questioning look Kal asked, "Wonder? Wonder what?"

Pointing in both directions of the trail where it had split she said. "Look, this is only a guess, but I suspect that both trails will meet and become one again on top. I know it's hard to tell right now because both sides run along the base of this cliff and then turn away from us and we cannot see where they go after that. Look I'll take the left branch and you take the right. We'll follow the splits as they go for a little while, and if either side seems to lead away, then we can backtrack to here and choose one that seems more promising. How does that sound to you?"

"Jura, you've had way more experience than I have on this, and really what do we have to lose other than time? And if I am honest here we've lost a lot of that with our fruitless searching, so what's a little more? Okay so how long?"

"Oh I don't know, we need to give it long enough that we can be sure what's happening. Okay let's use our shadows. When they have doubled in length from what they are now and we haven't met then we'll come back and meet here and discuss what we've discovered."

"Okay, works for me." He bowed and swept his arms out and asked, "Shall we?"

She laughed and curtsied and responded, "Why thank you sir!" Then on a more serious note said, "Okay if we don't meet higher up see you back here soon." She headed off on the left branch and he stood for a brief period of time until she turned the corner and was out of sight. He then turned and headed down the right branch and once he made the turn, in his case to the left, the trail immediately began to climb. It was a steep climb and it had a couple of switch-backs, fol-lowed by heading away from the area where they had split winding among large boulders, again a great place for defense, before turning around as he approached the top of the rise and headed back in the original direction.

* * *

"Hey, look they've split. It would be easy to kill them now and then we could get out here and just blame it on some predator that is out here. I'm tired of all of this and I long for a village and some wine and a little female companionship."

The other, the one who had unofficially taken charge looked hard at his partner, "What are you suggesting? We weren't sent here to kill these two, but to find out what they were looking for. So get any of those thoughts out of your mind. Who knows, maybe they'll return to this spot, and anyway, we can't take a chance of being seen, so we're going to wait right here." Both of them settled into as comfortable position as they could and still watch the trail, or trails since it appeared to have split. They would be paid for this work, and it was easy, so why sweat it?

* * *

Jura after making the right turn found that the trail continued up a canyon for a short distance and then started climbing out. Here the rise was gentle and the trail straight. The trail was sort of heading in the original direction that they had been going when they had reached that split, but as she neared the top coming out of the canyon it turned back towards the top of the cliff where the trail had split at the base. It dove back down into a large ravine again giving any defenders the upper hand in a fight. It remained this way for a distance and because of the depth of the ravine there were more shadow than sunlight, hiding any and all landmarks. Eventually it climbed out where there were a huge amount of boulders. She stopped and caught her breath. She was literally at the point on that cliff that they had looked up at. The view from here was over-powering in its beauty. And while hiking the ravine there was little air movement, once out the cool breeze chilled her as it dried her damp sweat soaked clothes. As she looked out over the trail that they had hiked earlier that day she heard a noise off to her left and turned to see Kal approaching with a smile on his face. He said, "Guess you were quite right. Although with you here ahead of me I'd guess your way is shorter." He paused and looked in the direction that she had saying, "Wow, what a view." He was about to turn and face her when a movement caught his eye. At that moment she had been look-ing at him so had not seen it, still he asked. "Did you see that?"

She turned in the direction that he had been looking puz-zled by his question. "No, see what?"

"I don't know for sure, but I saw movement out of the cor-ner of my eye, but by the time I tried to locate it, whatever it was quit moving." He studied the back trail as she joined him and from her silent question he pointed where he thought he had caught that flash of movement. Shaking his head he commented, "I don't know but I'd have sworn that I saw a person on that trail, or at least that's what my mind is telling me. But I don't see anything at all now, so maybe it was my imagination."

Quietly as she studied the area from their high point she shook her head. "No, I suspect that what your mind told you is accurate. You've got to remember that we are wired to catch movement. As my parents told me time and time again, it is a survival thing. And it would have held true for protection against those wild predators and when we became tribes and clans and were warring with each other it would have become even more critical." She paused thinking, and more to herself than him, said, "I wonder why there'd be someone on a trail that is no longer traveled unless we are the reason. Yes, that's the only thing that makes sense."

Listening to her conversation with herself he realized that what she said had to be correct. They were being followed, and it was only because of this accidental high point that that allowed them to look back over the trail they had just hiked. He suspected that his ancestors had used this point for just this purpose. "Okay, that makes sense, so now what? And why would anybody be interested in following us? I mean we have no treasure, our camp gear is anything but new, and pack beasts are cheap and available to the poorest of our villages. So that only leaves us, and it makes me wonder if we've been watched all the time we've been out here."

"A possibility," Jura said, "but we have no proof, and really at this moment we can't be sure that's what you saw, still I suspect it was, so like you, what can we do about it? We can't even know how many may be out there or what their agenda is." Both were leaning on their staffs, which meant that if it came down to close combat both were armed, trained and ready. "I think we better get back from being so exposed. If they wanted to attack us from a distance we have left ourselves pretty visible here." Both of them, at this point, looked at each other and carefully backed away from the cliff edge to the boulders that would provide protection yet allow them to monitor the trail.

"I wonder how long we've been watched?" Kal looked down at the bare ground and back to the trail, took a deep breath, "I bet that this could be from Sabohl, after all, it's the only thing that makes sense. We really, as I said, have nothing of value to attract thieves and such, and we aren't searching for some hidden treasure, and for most, what we are looking for isn't even worth their time to read it in a local paper. And we've surmised that he was behind that break-in a few cycles of the seasons ago. So it would only make sense that he hasn't given up. And what have we just done? We've led him right to what we think is the clan home. I know we haven't found it yet, but both of us are almost positive that we aren't very far away from it now."

"If what you're saying is right, then this is very frustrating. We're doing all the hard work and he has his cronies following to make it easy for him, and we've kind of just gave it to him. Like you, I thought that he had given up, but if what you saw, again, is accurate the obvious answer is, no he hasn't."

Sitting there and staring out at nothing Kal continued to be silent. How could they lose whoever was following them? And it was very important to locate the clan home since all the other locations that he wanted to find and rediscover would be based from there. "Of course I might not have seen anything and it was just my imagination, but I know I did, so wishing it away isn't going to change anything. So what do you want to do? The obvious problem is that we are on the trail and I suspect we will be close to the clan site soon. And whether we delay or not will change nothing."

Shrugging she said, "I guess we just go on. As you so aptly pointed out everything that we are trying to locate is based on this location." Both of them got up from where they had been sitting and with a sense of foreboding continued up the ancient untraveled trail and away from the cliff top.

* * *

"I thought we had waited long enough before starting to follow them again. Then as we moved they showed up on top of the cliff and looked right at us."

"Yeah, and both of us froze in position. I have to admit I was beginning to cramp from being in such an awkward position, and then they stayed there for a very long time talking about something before disappearing out of our sight."

The one who had taken the leadership role cursed, and kicked a loose rock that lay in the trail. "All we can hope is that they didn't see us. I guess let that be a lesson to both of us. We kind of got impatient there and almost blew the whole thing and gave ourselves away – although I have no way of knowing whether they saw us or not. Let's get off the trail and wait for a while longer. It's obvious to me they are going to stay on whatever this is. Let's go find some shade; it's hot out under the suns." Both of them left the trail and found a straggly tree that at least got them out of the direct suns' heat. "We'll give it a little longer and then we'll head up the trail and try and see ahead. But that's the problem. It seems that this faint trail is climbing so they will stay above us."

* * *

"Let's stop here." Kal had a thought cross his mind, "We need to look at that map again. From what we've found so far this trail has a number of overlooks and places where they could safely attack an enemy."

"True, so what's your point? Oh . . . hmmm, I don't know if these places would be marked on this crude map because had this had fallen into a rival's hands then they would know where to look or how to work around the ambush points. Also from looking at the position of the suns and our location I think that we'll be having a dry camp tonight. If everything pans out as it appears at this moment we can move our camp to the abandoned site on the morrow."

"I didn't think about that, but you're right. I suspect if we headed back now we would make our camp by nightfall. So what do you want to do, continue or return? It doesn't matter now since we've located the trail. One day or another isn't going to change anything. I know that if we dry camp it all of our gear in our regular camp will be okay. It's well hidden, at least I think so. And we've had to do this a couple of times." Kal stood up and paced for a moment as he continued to think this through.

"Going back isn't a bad idea, but if we are being followed then we probably would run into whoever it is, and we don't even know how many of them there are. And who knows, maybe it's just a coincidence and it was someone hiking through the area. Although, the chances of that happening, considering how remote an area this is, and with no isolated farms and such out here, I'd guess it's near impossible." Jura stood up also and walked back down the trail. Although from this point she couldn't see their back trail at all. "Hard decision, hard decision that's for sure. So what do you want to do?"

He laughed and said, "I asked you first. I must admit after all the failures we've had I kind of want to see what's at the end of this trail, but also know that if we are being watched that we're not going to be the only ones who know this. So if we go back to the camp and return tomorrow, will whoever is following us continue on and then claim they discovered this, and we have no right to be there? Or are they just some hired thugs who were sent to watch us and then report back to whoever it was that sent them here? Without more information I just don't know. Maybe we should go ahead a little further and see if we can find one of those ambush points and wait. Then if a small group shows up we can confront them and see if we can find out."

"Are you sure that you want to do that? If there are a lot of them we won't be able to defend ourselves at all and will be at their mercy. And if they are riffraff, I, as a female, do not want to be in their control. Since we are quite isolated, who's to say what happened to us if we never return."

Looking down at the ground with his hands behind his back as he thought about it, "I have to admit I didn't consider that. And you are quite right. We are by ourselves and it would be easy for us to disappear, victims of the outback, the wilderness. And as vast an area as we've come to know it, it would be easy to hide our bodies and we would never be found, leaving only the mystery of what happened. So now we've gone full circle here once again, I guess we better just continue on with the knowledge that someone is behind us and watch for them."

"Yeah, I think that's probably best." She came back from where she had been studying the trail behind them and asked, "Shall we?" They both had taken off their travel packs and now picked them up and put them on and headed back up the unknown trail with the knowledge that they were being followed, leaving them with an unknown future as well.

The trail wound and twisted through the foothills giving the defenders many opportunities to harass an attacking enemy. In fact they could see a number of places where there had been work performed to strengthen defenses along the way. There were a couple of areas where the trail wound through narrow canyons giving the high ground to the defenders. From the direction they had come there had been no way to climb to these defense points. It was only after leaving these narrow confines that the way to the top presented itself. Even here access wasn't easy. As the suns were beginning to set they turned the corner around a huge rock wall and before them was a plateau that sloped uphill gently. Ahead of them was a large grove of trees that blocked their view of anything beyond. Stopping and taking in the beauty and catching their breath, since the last portion of the trail had been a steep uphill climb, they studied the area.

Pointing Jura said, "Look, doesn't that look like stumps of some of the trees?"

"Yeah, it really does, but now the question is, is it because they simply fell and this is what's left, or is it because they were cut down."

She smiled and said, "We're not going to know just standing here so let's go look." They headed over to the stumps and inspected them, looking closely at the remains.

"I'd guess that either one of those small beasts that uses its teeth to cut down trees that they then use to dam streams, or crude axes. It doesn't look like the winds were responsible — besides there's not trunk on the ground." Looking around carefully Kal couldn't even see any branches that may have been part of the tree. "No, I'd guess that this was done by a person, you agree?"

"Yup. Let's head on in and see what's beyond these trees, shall we?"

He bowed and swept his arms outwards stating, "After you oh mighty one, I bow to your demands, and your expertise."

She laughed at his antics and took on the air of the rich and walked casually in the direction they both were going, which got both of them laughing. He caught up with her and they pushed their way through the stand of trees, dead branches, and debris, and stopped. Before them a rock wall rose and disappeared behind trees to the north and south. This rock wall faced west and at this time of day reflected the setting suns light. Towards the north end there was a split in this wall and they could see that at one time there had been work to reinforce this split. Both headed towards this point. As they did they noticed that south of this area there appeared to have been worked fields although long abandoned. And off of this south wall a small waterfall and a stream ran down through these fields and disappeared into the trees.

As they approached this split they found some of the tree trunks that had been placed here and a broken gateway. Again, as they entered the path that led through the split it continued uphill, again giving defenders the better position. This ran for a short distance, this narrow gap in the wall, and then it opened up into the compound which sat on a higher plateau and was relatively flat. *They found it!* And as the suns began to set in the west behind them, they were shocked at the size of this upper plateau. There had been nothing to suggest that the area they were presently in was anything but a small rise. Instead a village could have nested here comfortably. They could see where there had been shelters but with the passing of time most were just piles of rubble marking the locations of where the shelters had once set. Although the paths that had developed over the time from the many genera-tion who had lived here, as they had moved from place to place within this clan home, were very apparent.

For a moment in the elation of discovery, after so many failures, they had forgotten about the ones who had been following. And the two had lagged far behind, once that incident on the back trail had almost compromised them. But since then, the two that they were following had remained ahead and out of sight. But their trail was obvious on this little used trail. Shortly they climbed the last portion and entered the stand of trees that Jura and Kal had been in just a short time earlier. The one in charge looked at the other and said quietly, "Who'd have guessed that these would be here. Look we're out of daylight, so I guess we better set up a cold camp here tonight. It's quite obvious that they'll not be returning to their new camp tonight and had probably planned on staying over."

"Yeah, it does look like doesn't it? I'll get us some wood, there's no lack of dead branches here, and we can at least have a small fire to heat something up, and from the feel of the air it's going to get cold up here tonight, so the fire will help keep us warm."

"I don't know if that's such a good idea. After all if they're close by they probably could see it."

"Hey, we don't know if they saw us back there or not, and I'm not going to give up the comfort of a small fire. Look, we can head back down the trail and find a place that's hidden if you like, but I don't like being cold."

Shrugging, he had to admit they didn't know if they had been discovered or not, but he didn't like being cold either, and with the lengthening shadows he didn't think they could head far enough back down the trail to find a place the stay. "Okay, you've convinced me. We'll just stay on this side of these trees and away from this trail and that should keep us hidden from them." Both of them worked to the north of the trail, found a small pile of boulders that had flat ground inside and decided that this would work. There was barely room for the two of them plus their small fire, but at least with the rocks they could build a fire next to one and get heat reflected back at them and hopefully with this makeshift shelter keep most of the evening breezes from chilling them too much.

Kal and Jura carefully walked the huge area in the failing light both silent as they walked the grounds of his ancestors. "I guess," Kal said quietly, "we better find a place to set up camp before it gets too dark. I don't think we'll lack for fuel for our fire." He stopped and looked around and just to the south of the entrance the land fell away into a natural bowl. Looking inside this bowl they could see that at one time it had held a rather large shelter. Pointing he said, "That might a good place, out of the cold night winds, but the cold air might settle in there, what do you think?"

"Don't know really, but there's a good chance for the air to settle there. Hmmm," she mumbled as she looked around in the dimming light. "I don't see anything that would be better so why not?" Both of them headed back to this natural bowl and when they descended they found that at this moment the air in the bowl was still and a bit warmer than the surrounding air. Smiling, she said, "I think I like it already – hadn't realized that it had cooled that much already." Looking around at the openness of this plateau she commented, "Bet the winds just whip across this place. There's absolutely nothing to stop them. It has to be a miserable place in the Season of Cold."

They worked quickly with practiced ease as they set up their dry camp at the bottom of the bowl close to the ruins of what had to be a large shelter. Once set up both headed out and working through the compound where a number of trees had grown since the place had been abandoned they found plenty of wood to feed their fire. As both of them got back together with their armloads of wood Kal asked, "Thought I smelled smoke from a campfire when I got close to the entrance to this place. But it was only so brief that I wasn't sure. Did you by any chance smell such a thing?"

"Now that you mention it I think so, but it was so subtle that I almost immediately dismissed it. Well, if both of us smelled it then it has to be real. I guess the only question is; where is it coming from?" Thinking for a moment and climbing up the slight rise out of the bowl she sensed the direction of the breeze, stood there for a few moments to be sure and said, "With the time of day, we have an up canyon wind, which means that it would be flowing naturally from that tree stand and lower plateau up through that split that leads into here. So that fire has to be where we came from, probably the ones who are following us, I would suspect."

"I guess that this would confirm it then", Kal paused, "but we probably should sneak down the slash and see if the smell gets stronger. If it does then we know that they are behind us, and then maybe if we are careful we can try and locate their camp and find out how many are following us."

"I concur with the first part of your idea, but if there are many of them, they'll probably have guards out and neither of us is good enough to sneak up on a camp. So let's just head down and see if the strength of the smell gets stronger, if so, then we can be pretty sure that it's them. Besides, we need to stay on this side of those trees, because there's a lot of debris, dead branches fallen leaves and such, and in the dark we won't be able to see any of it." Careful, because it would be much later when one of the minor moons rose, and even with their eyes having adjusted to the darkness, it was still very difficult to see anything, they worked their way back to the split in the wall that gave them access to the lower plateau.

With a rock rolling out from under his foot Kal went down on his backside. He fought down a curse and tried to slow his slide as he slid down the steep slope that they had just tackled. After finally being able to stop and stand back up he whispered to Jura, "really hope that wasn't too noisy, and that hurt." He could feel a burning on his hands and arms making him realize that he had lost some skin as he had slid down the path.

"Yeah, I bet it did, but I don't think we have to go any further, the smell of the smoke is definitely stronger here and I suspect that there's a camp close by – probably on the other side of those trees."

"Yeah you're right, it's really strong here, and I think if you look over there to the north end there seems to be a small amount of haze hugging the ground – could be the smoke laying in there in a pocket of slow moving air." She nodded in agreement, at this point both turned around and headed back to their camp inside the ancient compound.

* * *

"Do you think that the two we are following continued up the trail that they found?"

The one who had taken charge just shook his head and said, "Nah, don't think so. They know nothing about what's ahead of them any more than we do. So I suspect that they are camping just as we are. After all they did have their carrying packs on so that means that they were prepared to camp overnight somewhere if they needed to, and again who knows how long this trail goes, I don't. And once it started to get dark they would have to stop, and before you ask, no I don't think there's another way around and they have headed back to their other camp. I believe that they would have to go past us and we would know."

Both were staring into their small hidden fire, making them night blind. Once they had picked the area they were going to build their fire they walked away to see if the camp was hidden from any who would walk the trail and as far as they could see it was. The only factor they didn't take into consideration was the three that were following them. These three were on a lower level looking up and as it darkened they could discern two glows that marked the two campsites.

"I guess this Jura and Kal are safe for now. There seems to be a little distance between the two sites so they haven't been bothered yet. Although, I don't know what we'll do, if these two who are following them, decides to attack them. I guess that we will have to stay out of it because we cannot be found out." They were staying in their own camp, a dry camp with no fire and cold travel rations.

One of the underlings with him smiled, "I really don't think that will be an issue. If you remember, Jura is an expert with the staff, and I suspect that she's been training Kal. So if those two decide to attack them, up close and personal, I believe it is they that will be in for a surprise. They'll go in thinking because there's a female that it will be easy pickings. In a sense I'd like to be there, you know a Loki in the grass, as those two low life's get what's coming to them if they are stupid enough to think that they can bully the two of them." This brought a chuckle out of the three as they pictured the surprise on the two who would have thought they had the upper hand only to find that they didn't.

* * *

With morning Kal and Jura were up and exploring the discovered site. He stood in awe and felt more like whispering than saying anything out loud – in a way this was a sacred site for his family. This was the place where the alliance had begun, and it was from here that all of the rest that was written in the journals could be located. He realized that even with the size of this small plateau, in the Season of Cold where you would be isolated to your shelter, that it must have closed in on everybody. While this would have been a place that would be easy to defend in time of attacks, the area was exposed enough to allow the winds to whip through the area sparing no one. It truly had to have been brutal. Clearing his throat Kal said, "It's hard for me to believe that we've actually found it. If I remember right in the reading of the journals that area where we camped last night is the location of the female shelter, and if that's so, to the north of this would have been the leader's shelter. Then further to the east we should find where the compound was divided between the warriors and the priests. Plus on this side of the compound there would have been shelters for the rest, the ones who kept this place going – you know, like the slaves and young males in training, and the ones who just did all the other mundane things that it takes to make it work. I think that we should probably spend all day here sketching everything we can figure out, and mark its location on one of the better maps that we've brought with us. Maybe spend another night before heading back and getting our gear and setting up a camp right here. How does that sound to you?"

"Okay I guess, but I don't know if we have enough food and such for another night. It might be better if we just went back and got our stuff and moved it here. After all, this place isn't going anywhere."

"True, but I worry about what the agenda of those who are following us may be. If we leave will they move in and claim that they found it and that we had better leave?"

"Darn! I forgot about them," Jura exclaimed, "I was wrapped up in looking this over and in the excitement they slipped my mind. Maybe with full daylight we should go see what we are facing, and if it's only a couple maybe suggest that they leave?"

"Yeah, but would they? This is a problem, I don't want us to be separated but maybe it's a way of doing it. Look you're better at sneaking than I am just because of where you grew up, and I'd feel better if I knew that you were away and safe. And, before you point out that you're much better with the staff and defending than I am, I think that if we do it this way they are less likely to come after me as a male than you as a female. They might think that you'd be an easy mark and make it difficult. As it is, if you were to leave now you wouldn't be back here until dusk."

He could see the attempt in her eyes and her face of trying to counter what he had just said, and was remaining silent for a moment. Finally she took a deep breath and shook her head and said, "I can't argue against that logic, you're right even with my skill, by myself, I'd be a target even if there's only a couple. Out here a female alone, against who knows who, could make for a very bad outcome. But I'd be alone heading back to our camp, packing it, and then coming back, so I don't know which is worse, do you? Tell you what, let's go down there and see what we are facing. The drift of the smoke from their fire put them on the north end of that lower plateau, probably on the other side of the stand of trees that is there. If we sneak around from the south we can do two things. First we can locate their camp, and second if we get lucky we can see how many are following us. Hmmm, I just had a thought . . ."

Trying to lighten the mood a little he asked, "You had a thought, really?" He then he smiled showing that he wasn't serious. She went ahead and hit him on his shoulder anyway which did hurt, "Ouch! What was that for? You know I was only kidding."

"Yeah, but so am I. If I'd been serious you'd be picking yourself off the ground just about now. Anyway there may be a way that both of us can chance it and go. I really don't like the idea of separating. We become much easier targets then even if there's not many of them. We know that both of us, I'm speaking of those unknowns behind us and you and me here. All of us had to stop because of darkness and camp for the night."

"I'm with you so far, please continue."

"Well, who's to say that we found anything at all? I mean that these unknowns have probably been following us since we've been up here and we've hit nothing but dead ends and returned to our camp to start over, so what if we head back down the trail talking like we were very disappointed but this promising lead turned out to be nothing but another dead end and we need to get back to camp, pack it up once again and then head further east and see if we can find something else."

"Yeah, that would be consistent with what's happened so far, but would they go and look where we spent the night . . . Because, if they did that they would know the truth."

"Yeah, that is a problem. Hmmm, what if we do it this way then – we both leave and we show our disappointment that this trail was a dead end, possibly a hunter's camp at one time and we discuss this just as I suggested, and we both are mad because we just wasted all this time on another dead end. We both slowly head down the trail, and then pick one of the points where we can watch our back trail, soon after we leave and go past where we suspect that they are camping, to see if they follow us. If they do that immediately then we'll know our discovery will be safe, and if they don't, we can turn around and come back. The only problem with coming back is that we'll be giving ourselves away and they would know that something's up."

Kal was silent for a moment, thinking. *What a dilemma, should we go or should we stay? Either way there could be problems.* "I don't know, because really, if they don't see us, then they'll assume we've just continued along the trail, not knowing that it ends here, and when they came along to continue following us they would walk right into our discovery. So I guess we'll have to chance it and make an appearance and do as you suggest. That way we can see if we can make them follow us back and head back to our camp and break it down and maybe figure another way to get to the trail head."

"Then we'd better do it," Jura stated with some urgency in her voice. "We really don't have anything to pack other than rolling up our sleeping sacks. I think that shortly the suns will be cresting that rock face that sits on the east end of this place. We can still make a quick sketch of the area, with two of us working the sketch, so that we can say that we really were here, and maybe help protect our rights to discovery."

With the decision made and while it hadn't been spoken they had decided to leave together, once the quick sketch had been created, and to announce to the world that this was another dead end and they needed to head back to their camp."

* * *

The two that were following had had a bad night and when the dawn came both were deep in sleep unworried that their quarry would escape them. Even though there had been a close call the day before, it appeared that they had gotten lucky and had not been viewed or discovered, and that was very good news. This meant that they could continue to do little to nothing, other than follow them, and with a little care, remain an unknown. As it got closer to the time of the suns showing above the foothills both of them still in the twilight of just waking up heard voices which immediately brought them fully awake. They looked at each other and then at their dead fire and then froze in position as the voices became stronger. Listening, all they could hear was disappointment in the voices, as they lamented another failure and another dead end. Peering around the rocks where they were hidden they saw the two talking about the fact that all they found was a dead end and an old hunter's camp, and what at first held promise led to another wasted day, and there were so few of the days left before the Season of Cold would be upon them and they would have to give up until the next cycle of seasons. The voices faded as the two headed down the trail and out of sight.

Grabbing their gear, and not taking the time to make sure that their fire was truly dead they hurriedly threw their gear together and took off after them, not bothering to check the camp where Kal and Jura had spent the night. As in so many other attempts, it was obvious that this wasn't what they had been searching for either, so why bother searching the area where they had spent the night? The two who were following, hung back just far enough so that they would remain unseen, and shook off the dregs of waking from a deep sleep and felt once again that luck was with them. Now they had to be careful, and trail a little further behind and make sure that the ones they were following didn't take off on some side trail, thusly losing them.

The three who were following the two who were following Jura and Kal had remained further down the trail with one scouting ahead, when the one who had been doing the scouting ran back to them. He stopped to catch his breath before being able to say anything. "All of them are heading back down the trail towards us, and we only have a very short time to disappear." Looking around, there wasn't any place to go so they headed rapidly back down the trail to where there was a ravine that cut into the side of the trail and curved around out of sight. Unfortunately it wasn't very deep but with the concentration of the four coming back down the trail they hoped that they wouldn't be looking too hard. The only advantage they had was twofold, first this wouldn't be some place that one would normally conceal oneself, and secondly they were not visible from a higher point on the descending trail. They had to lie flat, barely hidden, with only the grasses providing anything to block one's view.

They heard, more than saw, the first two pass their location and continue on, none the wiser that they were here. Their positions were uncomfortable but they had to wait what seemed like forever before the heard the second pair approach their position, quietly talking as they slowly continued down the trail. The three waited until they were sure that enough time had passed to safely come out of hiding. The one who had been scouting simply said, "That was too close."

* * *

Jura, as they headed back down the trail at a rapid pace to force the ones following no time to check out their camp commented, "Look I have a feeling that whoever the ones are they aren't very good in the outback. I guess in some ways yes they are since we didn't even know that we had someone following us from the beginning. But look," as she pointed to the trail, "their tracks are as plain as daylight. If any of my family had been doing this we'd eliminated our tracks so that they couldn't accidently be found later like this."

"At least by them doing it this way," Kal replied, "we can see that we're probably only looking at a few of them, which means if we did have to face them it would be a little more equal." He stopped, and it took a second before she stopped, as it had been unexpected. Shaking his head, she could see that there was a little bit of anger in his stance. Breathing out a deep cleansing breath Kal said, "This just sucks. And to think I trusted that learned, that Sabohl, and now he has been watching us ever since. I know I don't have any real proof, but who else could it be? It makes me want to confront these few that are following us and get the truth out of them. Although I suspect that they aren't tied directly to Sabohl but someone else. Look we have another issue, and I know we briefly talked about it before heading out this morning, but I've been thinking about it as we led them away. And it's not only the fact that when we return that we'll give ourselves away. We can only stay there so long and we have to head back. We'll be the only ones who know that we were the first, and there's no quick way for us to get back. Plus, I wouldn't know who to report our find to anyway.

"Originally I just figured it would be you and me and the families who would know about what we've found. Then when we would have had the chance to search out the different locations and have an understanding of what we've found find the right people to report it to and go from there. By us being followed like we have been, none of this is going to happen. At least we now know that what the journals say is accurate, and that they weren't some forgeries that had been planted in the family in the past. What they say is true and real, which means that the other places talked about are real also. Meaning that the way we are viewing our past is not right. These places are not myths or creations of our ancestors, they are very real.

"I guess, like so many things that we do, we go into it with an unreal expectation of how it will go. And if we both think about it, finding or trying to find this site is a good example. Both of us figured that with the crude map that it would be easy to just use the map and walk right up to the clan home. Well, we both know how well that worked. Here it is almost the Season of Cold and after working through the end of the Season of Heat and most of the Season of Falling we've finally located it only to find that we have been under observation the whole time and none the wiser for it. And teaching the ones who are behind us a lesson will not change anything. They'll still know and we can't change that. And I can't just kill them, although I suspect they probably deserve it. So I guess after this long winded talk it comes down to, now what?"

Jura listened quietly with her hands on her hips as he spoke. After finishing, she remained quiet, cocked her head to the side, and said, "Here's a thought, and like leaving this morning it has risk, not that everything we've been doing doesn't. Instead of heading back to our discovery we could just pack up, look dejected and defeated and call it a season of failure, even though we know better. We might be able to give them enough of a misdirection that this will remain safe until we can find someone who could help us. And it's becoming obvious that we're going to need help. Although who to ask, I really don't know either."

"It's something to think about, and I know that we have some time before we reach our camp. In fact it will probably be between the zenith and dusk before we get there. So we'll be spending at least one more night in our more permanent camp. Maybe we can come up with something, and I think your suggestion is a good one. But anything we do is a problem at this point. Well this isn't getting us back to camp, shall we continue?"

CHAPTER SIX

INTRIGUE

It had been a hard decision since they had actually been, even if so brief of a time, in the clan's ancient home, the home of his and hers by becoming the mate of Kal, ancestors. But now they were back in High Trail checking on the bakery and all the paperwork that seems to always multiply. One would swear that it could reproduce itself. While they had been away the business had grown under the care of Sara and she had suggested that they pick up a second site as they were now outgrowing the one that they were in. So for the Season of Cold they would work through all that they had to do, touch bases with his parents, and bring the family up to date with what they had discovered. For now it would have to remain within the confines of the family. And they hoped that it would be enough, and the ones who had followed them through their season of searching hadn't returned to that last place where they had made their discovery.

Then the word got out that in the near future that Sabohl would be making a major announcement about a discovery in the far northeastern foothills and one of importance. And at this point they knew that he had stolen their discovery, but even if they tried to counter this *up and coming* announcement that Sabohl would be sure to silence them. If they hadn't been sure of Sabohl's position, they now had personal proof of the way he worked. Again, while there had never been proof that the break-in had been requested by Sabohl, this reinforced this thought that he had a strong role in it. Too many coincidences, too short of time between knowledge that Sabohl had gained to the actions, and here was another. Breathing out deeply and feeling somewhat defeated, Kal said. "We were so hoping that when we left like we did that whoever this was that was following us would just ignore what we found and we could safely go back in the Season of Greening. But I guess we were wrong. Probably should have moved our camp and at least tried to check out a couple of additional areas to, as you call it, lay a false trail. Something made them curious enough to go back and find what we had found, and now it's lost to us. Who knows what mess he'll make of the place, and how he'll bend it to fit his own interpretations. This is so wrong!"

Feeling helpless Jura could only be silent as she listened. She felt betrayed also, but who were they but just a couple of bakers? How could they go against one of the most important people in their world? She knew that he wasn't really expecting any answers from her, but it seemed so unfair. *Yes but life is unfair.* She heard her parents telling her that in her mind. Sometimes you saw someone who never deserved what they had, continue to receive undeserved rewards, acknowledgements, and the ones who actually should have remain unknown. It was that way of the world now, and as far as she knew, it had always been that way, and probably always would be. "I know you don't expect me to answer those questions since I have no answers and you know it, but there's got to be some way, or someone out there that can help us. There's just got to be." Again she was silent. Then in a much softer voice, one that held no confidence she said, "Although I have no idea who that would be or where to even look."

She leaned forward on the table that both of them were sitting around. It was the end of another busy day with not enough time to accomplish all that had been set before them, and she had to admit that she was tired. Yet the next few 9-days were going to be no different, and once everything had been brought up to date with the bakery, they needed to start their planning for the next season of searching. Yet, before any of that could be accomplished they had to find someone who could help, pure and simple. If they continued like they were doing, then as they made their discoveries, Sabohl, who seemed to have them watched all the time, would just claim it as his own, as he had on their first major discovery. It almost made one want to forget the whole thing. But now that they had located the first she was finding that she had a desire to continue, she felt that she was catching fire like Kal, and wanted to go find those mythological places and prove that they were real. Shaking her head she said, "I just don't know, there has to be someone out there who knows about how this Sabohl works, and is trying to end his reign. I'm sure that we aren't the first that he's stolen from, and if he continues in his place of power, we won't be the last."

"True, but I don't have any ideas as to where to even begin to look. And I'm sure if we had a way to see in the dark we'd find that there are people out there watching us. I mean it took us almost all the time we were out there searching to discover that we were watched. It was a shock to say the least. Now if . . ." His thought and statement uncompleted, as out of nowhere there was a single knock on their door, this being a complete surprise since it was dark, and rarely would any come by this time of night. They looked at each other and then the door, "Now who could that be?" Carefully he got up and peered out the window that allowed them to see the entrance, but there was nobody there. Now curious he went to the door and opened it and confirmed that there was no one there. Puzzled he stepped out and almost tripped over a small bag that was all but invisible. It was something that hadn't been there earlier. So instead of bending down to pick it up he kicked it inside, closed the door, walked to the window and looked once again trying to see if anyone was there, anyone at all. But the roads were empty, and all that was visible were the lights from the other shelters in the area.

He was now more in the dark than he was before opening the door. Once outside he had searched carefully, with his eyes, every place he could see, which truthfully, wasn't much. It was one of those rare nights that none of the moons would be visible, so it was as close to pitch black as one could have. So after seeing nothing with his eyes after giving them time to adjust to the night, he listened very hard for any sounds that would have been unusual, but again it was silent, other than the normal night sounds. Once back inside he looked at Jura shrugged and shook his head when he saw her questioning look. "I don't know, there was nothing, no sounds and it was too dark to really see anything. And whoever tossed this," he pushed the small bag with his booted foot, "made sure that they couldn't be seen or heard." He breathed heavily undecided, but eventually bent over and picked up the small leather bag which was tied shut with a leather string. From the feel he could tell that there was a rock to give it weight and what felt like paper inside. He brought over to the table and sat back down across from Jura tossing the small bag on the table, where both stared at it.

After what seemed much too long of a time Jura finally broke the silence and said, "Well, I guess we better see what's inside, don't you think?"

"I guess so, and we really aren't going to learn about what's here just looking at that sealed bag." He reached for it and with some work was finally able to untie the knots. He examined the bag as he did this and found that it could have been any of the thousands that were made and sold so there was no clue as to the owner from the bag itself. The string was threaded through the top of the bag and took some work to get the bag fully opened. The rock that had been placed inside was large enough that it took some real work to remove it, and in the bottom was a tightly folded paper. After removing the paper he examined it and saw that once again that the paper was just that – ordinary cheap paper. Looking up he could see that Jura was burning with impatience and curiosity, so he handed the folded paper to her and signaled her to go ahead unfold it and read it, which she did. He waited patiently and really couldn't read what she was reading but shortly she passed it to him and he then read:

"You've now learned the extent that Sabohl will go. Just know that there are others who are just as aware. We cannot reveal ourselves to you at this time, but know that we truly know who discovered the site that Sabohl is claiming as his own discovery. There will come a time when all of this will come back and haunt Sabohl, but as you have so learned, he has much power and control. Remember you are not alone in this."

It was short and sweet, but left neither closer to an answer of the owner or owners of this unorthodox delivery. And while the note promised an accounting sometime in the future, and that there were others aware, it didn't improve their present situation at all, and truly left a bigger mystery. Like how could they know that the two of them had discovered that site? "I don't know how to take this? I mean this could just as easily be coming from Sabohl as well as someone else. So we could be fooled into thinking that there's help out there, well maybe help out there since there are no promises, and in the end it being Sabohl manipulating us to do his bidding. But if it is someone else, that means that there had to be a lot of people out there following us around while we searched. And if that's so, how many, and how does that reflect on us? I mean we weren't looking for people out there watching us, and as a result we didn't know until it was too late. Would we have been able to see them earlier than we did, or were we just too wrapped up in what we were trying to find to notice?"

"Yeah", Jura responded, "everything you've asked are valid questions, and this is getting much more complicated than I ever imagined. And when we started this I just figured that we would be out in the outback, the wilderness, by ourselves, trying to find that ancient site. Instead we seemed to have led an army around those northern foothills and never saw them at all. Like you, I figured that once we moved to High Trail and had worked all that time before starting this that we were free of Sabohl and his minions, but I was obviously very wrong. And now, if we are to believe what is in this, this unusually delivered note, then there are others who are just as aware and are working against Sabohl."

"Yeah, but can we believe it? I know that the delivery was dramatic, if one wants to think about it, but if, well not if, since we know that we're being watched, that means that this other shadowy group is also staying out of sight, staying in the background and trying not only to remain hidden from us, but from Sabohl and his organization also. Hey, I'm just a lowly baker, who like everybody has a family history, and I know that I'm not the only one who can claim to have come from the clan that K'jor was the leader of, and part of our historical past. After all there were lots of leaders over the time that clan existed. Yes we can trace the beginnings of change from him and his time, but we also know that there are other influences and it was a very long time past his time that the changes truly began – so why the interest? What is really happening in the shadows, in the depth of the night, and how'd we get mixed up in all of this?"

"I don't know, and I don't like it. After all while you, and I guess me now, we are bakers, but in the beginning I was just a female from the farm. One who only visited the villages now and then, and dreamed of someday doing something other than farming. But this – this is nothing I want to get involved with. No I don't mean chasing your family history, but this *intrigue* that involves ones in power. Like you I thought it would be nice to actually find those places that are talked about in those documents, those journals from your family, and whole heartedly wanted to search for this as much as you did. I guess in some ways it was being romantic. In those cheap stories that one can buy, while the hero and the heroine go through tough times they always triumph in the end. And even there they leave out much of the hard boring stuff. So when one tackles something like this it is easy to forget that there's lots of hard boring stuff. And I have to admit that there was or is." She paused for a moment and smiled, "But I suspect that after much time has passed both of us by that we'll personally forget the hard boring stuff and create a romantic story of our own."

He laughed which turned contagious and she joined him. Once they could catch his breath once again he said, "You know I never thought about it that way, but I suspect you're right. I know that when I was still young, very young really, we'd go see family and there'd always be stories going around. And I have to admit that many of them left me in awe to what they were talking about. In my mind I would create adventures from those stories. But like you just stated, all the boring stuff probably had been left out, and the stuff where they got hurt or failed, and only passed on the good stuff. Do you really think we'll be like that when we get old?"

She shrugged, "That's hard to say, but I suspect that it will be the way of it. I've seen the same thing in my family gatherings and there are oldsters who are living around this village always willing to pass on some gem of wisdom, or tell a tale from their past. So maybe as we get older and begin to lose much of the vigor of youth, the strength, and mind begins to fade that one only has their past to live for." She stopped a moment took a deep breath and let it out slowly. "I guess when you look at it that way it's tragic. We work and try and accomplish things in our lives, some work, some fail, but suddenly what you are no longer matters and the young ones have taken over and you are now the one looking in and wondering what happened. It really has to be hard."

With the swift change he hesitated as he thought about what Jura had just stated. "That's very true and really has to be hard. It seems that time robs us of our strength, our ability to think and act, and it happens so subtly that one never notices it until one day it hits you in the face and you're old and, well maybe not useless, but one probably feels that way. I know that with my sires that I'm beginning to see much grey in their hair, and while they still seem strong and virile, it's obvious that in a few cycles of the seasons that they will be moving over as their parents did before them. And it seems to happen so fast." He got up and paced for a few moments with his hands behind his back. The direction that their conversation had taken was off the mark to where it had started, but that seemed to happen often. It was as if the mind was unruly and needed to be disciplined to keep it on track. "Look we kind of gotten off the subject where this all started, and like we said, we're nothing more than simple bakers, and this stuff that's happening behind our backs, unknown to us, is so far beyond that I would never have guessed such a thing exists. So now we're in the middle, and if the rumors that we've read are correct, then our hard work, or discovery, will become someone else's, and that sucks. I suspect that this is common, but until it happens to you, you just don't realize that it's this way."

"Yeah, I surely didn't. But what can we do about it? I know that we wanted to go back and map the area better than the quick sketches that we did before we left . . . ." She paused deep in thought for a moment.

Curious as to what she was thinking he waited before asking, "What?"

She shushed him and continued to think. "Look we need to find out who these people are who contacted us tonight."

"Why? We don't even have a hint to as who they are, let alone know a way to contact them."

"Yeah that's true, but look we need to find out because if they are part of the search for our history, maybe, just maybe we can beat Sabohl at his game and get credit for the discovery."

"How? Really?"

"Yes, really. Look we've worked hard on finding the clan home, and I would just hate to have Sabohl grab all the glory from it, so if we can contact this other group, if indeed there is another group, then with the rough drawings we did, and the marking of the location on our maps we could get this out ahead of him and claim it as our own, which it is."

"Okay, I agree with you, but now we have two mysteries to solve. First who is this group and where are they? And secondly, how many does Sabohl have watching us, and if it is a lot can we make contact with this other group and not give them away, and will they be willing to help? I know that they, in their note said that they are here, but that's a long way from coming out in the open."

Jura then added, "But there's a third also, and that is this; do we have enough time to prove it was our discovery before Sabohl and his release the details, undermining our facts, and truths? Hmm, let's look at that note again, maybe there's something there that we missed. I'm sure that there wouldn't be much on it in case it fell into Sabohl's hands, but it probably wouldn't matter, because even this much would be enough for Sabohl to probably figure out who this was. So they were taking a very big chance getting this into our hands." They spread the crumpled, folded note out and studied it closer, but could find nothing, until they turned it over, and there on the back was a small mark. But neither had ever seen such a mark, and really if they were truthful, it could have just as easily been just part of another correspondence, and this scrap of paper could be just that – scrap.

* * *

Sabohl felt satisfaction with the results that had come out of his feelings that that upstart had been hiding something from him. To have kept the surveillance up for as long as had been required had cost him much in both time and finances. Now, because of them, he sat upon one of the largest discoveries in his field in two lifetimes. He laughed quietly and asked himself just what could they do about it? Answering himself he said quite smugly, "Why nothing, nothing at all." There was no one who could challenge him or his position and it was going to remain that way. He was very good on putting up the front of being the helpful friendly learned, but if any knew him as he really was they would've realized that this was only to gain possible information that he could use later, and he had a great memory. Soon, with this discovery, he would be able to cement his position and leadership to the point that absolutely no one would be able to challenge him, and that damned board would just vanish as all did in time.

He lived alone and preferred it that way. And if he had need of a female, and what male didn't, he'd have some of his female students who looked up to him until he grew tired of them, or maybe a female or two from the society that he frequented, and if all else failed there were always those of the lower caste, or the shelters of females for that purpose. So he had no need of a companion, and friendships were a way of learning something he needed and nothing more. Besides he was enough company, and by being this way there could be no accidental slip up because he let his guard down at home.

After it had become obvious that the two, Kal and Jura, headed back at what seemed to be an unsuccessful search in the northeastern foothills, he had become frustrated. He knew in his heart that they weren't there just to be away from the business. And by the way they were up and down those hills it was further proof that they were looking for something. So as the sparse reports came back he encouraged his contacts to keep following them. And in the end these two were never the wiser that they had been followed, being watched. And when that last report had come back saying that the two were done for this cycle of the seasons he thought it a little strange. Yes it would only be a short time before the Season of Cold would be upon them, but there was still a few 9-days left before it would strike – much too early in his mind to be quitting. So he sent word back to have the ones that were close to that final area to contact the two that had been following and with the four of them to retrace that last place that Jura and Kal had been before they quit. Soon word got back to him that indeed the two had located an unknown ancient site, and what did he want them to do?

With the flush of both excitement and confirmation that he had been right, he moved quickly to secure the location and to claim another discovery. But before he could officially make that claim he personally would have to make the journey to give credence to the fact that he actually found this site. And he had to make sure that the higher learned center was aware that he was out searching, and the reason was some old document that he had discovered, which of course, led him straight to this unknown location and unknown ancient site. He would be gone three 9-days to give the illusion that he was out attempting to nail down the exact location, but really had just spent it in the closest village under an assumed name remaining comfortable. Yes he had taken a single trip out to the location so that he could officially say that he had actually been there. And once the time had passed he returned and announced his discovery with maps and rough drawings. Now let any try and take it away from him. *Yes, I need to continue to watch these two. I really suspect that this isn't the only place that they will discover in the end, and it all will be my discoveries when it's all said and done.* Again he laughed as he drank his liquor. All was going well and all was going to be a part of his long ranged plans.

* * *

Jaie, standing as he faced the historical society said, "I really didn't expect him to move that fast. But I guess it makes sense. He didn't get where he is by sitting on his rear end. What we need to do now is find out if we want to make ourselves known, more than that note that was left at their door. Are we ready to come out in the open, and with what Sabohl has done to them, would they be willing to accept our help? I think that with the results of their hard work and the subsequent loss to Sabohl of that same hard work, they just might. Although we will be walking a very fine line if we do. There's a good chance that Sabohl will figure out that we are more openly opposing him, and with the speed that seems to surprise us, do something unexpected that could be a major problem for us." He sat down and for a while it was silent.

Tesam stood and voiced their dilemma, "True, absolutely everything that you just stated is fact. Yet, if we do nothing he'll continue to build his power, and nobody, and I mean nobody will be able to challenge him until like that old male in the herds who is the one servicing the females, some young one comes along who is stronger and takes his place. He could easily destroy us, and with his claim that he located this site, unless we can inject some doubt on that claim, it may be enough that he will be that old male, that old bull who is wily, and even though the young males are stronger and probably faster, it is his experience that allows him to continue to rule over the females. We cannot allow this to continue, but honestly I have no answers on how to prevent it. So maybe it will be in our best interest to actually contact these two, the ones who actually made the discovery and see what they may have that can counter Sabohl's claim of being the first." He sat down.

Shahe then stood and was quiet for a moment as he thought through what had been presented, "Okay, I think we're all coming to the conclusion that we will need to make contact with Kal and Jura and find out what they have to counter Sabohl's claim to this site, and we must do it quickly or he can claim that they only copied what he put out there, and that what they are saying is false, trying to take his discovery from him, and after all, everyone knows that he, Sabohl is the greatest in his field, and there are always upstarts trying to take it away from him, so why not now? So I guess the question is this; how do we contact them, and still keep it a secret from Sabohl's minions?" At this time he sat down and the hall where they were meeting was silent.

* * *

It was an unbelievably busy day at the secondary bakery. With the innovations that his parents added, and the varieties of breads and such, it seemed that soon, even considering the small size of High Trail that they would have to expand again. They were getting well known in the area and were drawing people in from well outside of the small village. And there had been a rather large order from a private learning center slash religious shelter. Yes they still existed, but no longer did any worship the old gods. Instead they now considered that there was only one God who ruled not only the creation of this world but of all that they could see. And because this order had not been given to them in advance it had put them far behind and their normal on-hand amounts dwindled rapidly. Turning to Jura Kal said, "Look I'm going to make a quick trip across the village to our main bakery and see if I can get some stuff from them. We've run out of the sweetbreads that are in such high demand. When we got that order from the learning center it included almost all of our fresh supply. I just hope that they're good for it." At this point he took off his apron and turned the selling counter over to her; he smiled and said, "Be back as quick as I can."

Stepping outside he shivered involuntarily as the cooler air struck him. But it was only momentary. As always it was warm in the bakery, and even though the smells of fresh breads were pleasant, he found the fresh air sweet smelling and invigorating. Taking a deep breath and throwing the large empty sack over his shoulder he headed out at a rapid pace. About half way to his destination someone tripped in front of him and stumbled into him. The stranger apologized profusely for being so clumsy. All he could do was shake his head and smile. If he wanted to be honest he had to admit that he could be that way himself. The interruption only delayed him a moment and finally he reached his destination, and found that the main bakery was doing a lively business also. Taking out the large key that opened the back door and with the rattle of the small chain that the keys were attached, he entered the maelstrom of organized chaos. He heard orders for the different breads being yelled out and the staff was in a frenzy trying to keep up with the demand. One would have thought that they were close to one of the holidays. Catching Sara as she flashed by him he yelled to be heard over the noise and asked if she could see him for a few moments after she finished helping the customer that she was filling an order for. She nodded and pointed to the small office for which he returned the nod and watched her as she headed out to the front and was gone from his sight.

He headed inside and closed the thin door and was rewarded with a reduction of the din that had assailed his ears. Taking a deep breath he let out a sigh of relief. Who'd have thought that a bakery could be so noisy? He reached in his pocket to pull out the list and found something else in his pocket along with the list. *How'd that get there?* He thought. *I distinctly remember putting the list there, but the pocket was empty.* At that moment Sara entered the office completely out of breath, and taking a deep cleansing breath herself said, "It's crazy out there! I know on the first of the 9-days we are busy but nothing like this. I mean I'll take it over being bored with nothing to do, but this was a real surprise. Okay boss, what can I do for you?"

Looking at her he smiled as there was flour in her hair and a smug or two on her face, "Well if it's anything to you we're running crazy over there also. So much so that we've run out of some of the breads. I'm hoping that you can give us some of what we need, and to keep the books straight I have the money to cover the stuff." He handed her the list and waited as she looked it over with a look of concentration on her face. "Hmm, I think we can fill most of this. Look I'll be right back. Better give me that sack also then I won't have to make two trips." And with that she was back out the door.

Shaking his head the thought, *who'd have thought that it would be this way? After all most make their own, and while a bakery would provide some stuff, it was never a lot. Now we can't keep up with the demand, and when a special order, like what we got over there, comes in, it can push us beyond what we have on hand. Hmmm, I wonder if we should make it a requirement that special orders be given to us in advance, that way we can be prepared – something to think about.* He leaned against the small desk that was piled high with unfinished paperwork and unfiled reports. If things continued like this for both locations they would need that third location very soon.

In what seemed to be a very fast time she came back into the office like a whirlwind with not only the filled list but the detailed billing. She was breathing hard from the effort that she'd put forth. "Look, I grabbed a couple of the workers and we were able to get this together much quicker, and we did have enough to cover what you need over there, plus while they were getting the product I ran a cost on it." At this point she handed the totals over to him and set the heavy sack on the floor.

He glanced at the figures and agreed, pulled out the money, paid her, thanked her for the speed, and she smiled back and was back out the door to continue the supervision and work. All he could do, once she had left, was to shake his head. Such efficiency, they all could learn from her. He took the receipt and lifted the now heavy sack and left, heading out the side door, the unknown note completely forgotten. He needed to get back since what he had in the sack was needed now, not later.

It wasn't until that night and the chaos of the day had vanished, with the quiet of home both sighed and let out a slow breath, finally this day was over. Both of them smelled of the bakery, the breads, the yeast, and their clothes covered in flour dust. It was time to change out of these work clothes and get into something more comfortable, something that they could relax in. As he went through his pockets to clean them out that he found that folded note once again. Unfolding it he found that it was too dark in the room that he was presently to be able to read what it said. So he headed out to the table where they had a lamp sitting that cast a brighter light. Jura was already sitting there snacking on some crackers from the bakery while she studied the books, looking over the lists of supplies and what they were short and what would be in need of replacing. Looking up as he sat down she commented, "We're going through this stuff faster than we projected. I'm going to need to get an order out to your father's caravan so that we can get the shortages in, and Sara stopped by briefly at the second bakery to pass on her needs list. She's in just about as bad as shape. Who'd have thought that we'd become so popular here and in the surrounding areas. Not me." Spying the folded paper in his hand she asked jokingly, "What's that, something from a secret admirer?"

He smiled, "Ha ha, very funny. Actually I don't know whose it's from. Somewhere along the way from the second bakery to the primary this ended up in my pocket. I know for a fact that I didn't have it when I headed over there, and when

I reached in for the list that we had put together it was there. The roads were pretty crowded, especially for a small village like this. You'd have thought that we were heading into a holiday or something important, but it was just another day. So it could have been anybody, anybody at all." He paused as he thought about his trip and remembered that someone had stumbled into him and had fallen. He had assisted the individual back up before continuing. "Hmm, that must have been it. Someone fell and I helped them back up. It would have been the perfect opportunity to slip something into one of my pockets." He looked down at the small folded piece of paper and noticed that it was similar to that other note that had been left on their doorstep.

Curious now, Jura asked, "Well, are you just going to stare at it, or are you going to open it up and read what it has to say?"

Again smiling he said, "I thought I would just stare at it." He could see that she was just about ready to hit him, and it was obvious she was burning up with curiosity. "Okay, okay, I was just thinking that this paper looks much like that other scrap we got the other night. So there's a good possibility that this is from whoever passed on that other one." He carefully unfolded the note and was silent was he read it. After reading he was quiet and she asked, "What?" He passed it over to her and here she read the words on the note.

"It is important that we begin to work together. We know that with what has transpired with Sabohl that trust is not an easy thing, and we could easily be working for him. We will be contacting you further, but must remain in the background so that Sabohl doesn't get wind of our involvement. We are aware of your discovery, and can help you beat Sabohl at his

own game, but we must do this before he has a chance to pub-
lish and thusly establish your find as his. We will be in contact
with you in the next few days so be prepared with whatever
notes and such that you have. Our options and time are very
limited."

Like he she was silent. Looking up and then at Kal she asked, "What do we do? We were both discussing the fact that we needed help, and suddenly it's being offered. But can we trust this offer, or is it like it so stated that they could be working for Sabohl, I don't know, I just don't know. But I will say this, if there's a way to beat him I'm all for it. We did all the hard work, did all the searching, and to have him claim that he was the one and that no one other than he is responsible for this find just burns me up."

At this point trying to keep it light although he felt much the same as she, he touched her and said, "Ouch!"

Questioning that comment she asked, "Ouch, what do you mean ouch?"

Laughing now he said, "Look I know it's a very serious situation, but your comment about burning up made me do it. I know you are a hot female and I just wanted to see if your body agreed with your statement." Again he could see that she did see the humor but didn't feel it was the right time. "Look, I know, and what we have to decide is whether to trust whoever this is, or continue on our own, and the one thing both of us have already concluded is we cannot continue on our own. So now the question becomes, what can we reveal to this mystery group and what do we want to keep away from everybody? This is a very fine line that we are walking here. But at the same time I don't want us to get so wrapped up in this *intrigue* that we aren't we. That could be a bigger disaster for the two of us."

As she thought about it, what he just said made sense. With so much more going on and with everything becoming very complicated, with no clear answers, it would be so easy to slowly let their relationship slip away, and not be the wiser that it was happening. And if that did happen, and both were at that point in time, would they be looking back, questioning what had happened to bring them to the breakup? "You know I would say that what you just stated would be something that a female would figure out before you males. So I'll give it to you this time, you're right. As we've been discussing, this has gotten far beyond what we thought it would be when we, with your family's blessings, started our research and searching." She sighed, "I guess in the end it's never as simple as any of us think it will be. And I never figured that there would be outside influences and all of this happening just because you wanted to discover your, and I guess because I joined your family, and my past. Why has it gotten so complicated?"

In a soft voice Kal said, "I don't know, I just don't have any idea." At this time both were quiet with their own thoughts, Kal thinking – *We just don't have much to make a decision here, so what's the answer? If I really admit it, I haven't a clue, not one. When I had asked those questions, innocently of course, who'd have guessed that that old learned would be one who stole from his students –not I.*

Jura, leaning on the table and staring at the lantern that sat in the middle of the table, was completely at loss as to which way to go, or even to know how to come up with a decision on this one. As the note stated this could be a ruse to bring them further out into the open and then steal the rest of the valuable information that they had in their possession. And if this other group was legitimate, who could say that they wouldn't do the same thing as Sabohl? They – she and Kal – knew nothing of them either, and it could mean that they would be stepping deeper in the quagmire with a heavy fog rolling in obscuring everything – leaving them no direction, and no way out at the end of all of this.

"Look," Kal said, "We're going to have to trust someone, and right now if this note is from someone inside of Sabohl's organization, then there's little we can do about it. Still if it is someone else, then they may be our only way to keep this. I feel that we've no choice here, and if you think about it, which I know that both of us have been doing, then we've got to do something. So I think we'll need to trust this group, at least initially, and say yes. But at the same time reveal nothing about what we have as far as the family history that revealed this location to us, and if at a later time they've proven them-selves then maybe at that point we can let them in on more of what we truly have."

"I guess that makes sense." Jura leaned back in her chair put her arms behind her head and stretched. "All I can say is that for me, as I've been thinking about it, I've only gone in circles with no answers at all. I know that we need help; I know we need to trust somebody, but whom? And because we know that we've been backstabbed by Sabohl, someone you trusted, then who's to say that it will be any different with these guys? We don't know them at all. For all we know they may be laughing at us right now knowing that we have no real choice in this, and in the end they'll get what they want, and we will be the ones who do the work and get nothing." She shrugged, and threw her arms out in surrender, "I just don't know. We know so little, just so little. After all, like you said, we're just bakers, business people trying to earn a living, and learn about your family's past. Is that so much to ask? Is it so much to ask people to just leave us alone and let us learn the truth?"

Again, in a quiet voice Kal said, "I guess it is, I guess it really is."

* * *

It was the middle of the present 9-day and the bakeries remained extremely busy, again as to why they had no answers, but appreciated it. Still it meant that there was too much to do and too little time to accomplish all that needed to be done. So the notes were temporarily forgotten until in a transaction another note was exchanged. When he realized that was what had happened he could only see the back of the individual who had passed the note to him as he left the bakery. With the crowds of people still waiting to be served, he couldn't stop and follow, and there was nothing out of the ordinary for Kal to be able to identify this individual. Shaking his head, he put the note away and promptly helped the next customer in line. It wasn't until he broke for the midday meal that he remembered the note. And as he and Jura sat in the office he looked up at her and said, "We had another note passed to us."

"Really?" She was sitting on the opposite side of the small desk with a sandwich in her hand and water sitting on the table. She placed the sandwich down and asked, "Did you see who it was?"

All he could do was shake his head. "By the time I realized what had happened, whoever it was was almost out the door and all I saw was his back. His clothes were nondescript, average build, nothing to identify, and no, before you ask, it's been way too busy to even find time to read it. So we can read it together." Taking a bite of his sandwich he could hear the din from the floor of the bakery. Even though many took the time to eat at the midday, it was still chaos out on that floor. He unfolded the small note, noticing that once again it was written on the same paper as the others. He read aloud these words:

"Time is very short. Sabohl is putting together his report. If we do not have something before the end of this present 9-day then he will have won this round. We will stop by every-day around the time you received this note. If you are with us then it must be now. Place your response inside the sack. The contact will be wearing a dark shirt with a torn pocket, and will comment that he had just caught this pocket on a nail, and it was his best shirt too. He will then purchase one loaf of your heavy grains bread, and be flustered as he can't find his coin purse. At which point he will look down and comment, "Ah there it is". According to the response that we receive will determine how we will proceed."

"Pressure's on that's for sure, so what do you think?"

"Too little time, too little knowledge, and still we have to make a decision – this sucks."

He laughed a little and commented, "I don't think we can put that in the return note."

"And why not? After all that's exactly the truth.

"You know you're right, but I think we need a little more than, 'it sucks', don't you think?"

CHAPTER SEVEN

THE ANCIENT CLAN SITE

It was cold, and it was snowing intermittently. Again he asked himself, why the heck was he, and especially Jura, here? While they had beaten Sabohl on both the announcement and the location, it did not matter because at this moment his minions controlled the site. Although there wasn't anybody here that could be tied directly back to him – he wasn't stupid. Kal, Jura, and the field members of the Historical Society or board, and again these members couldn't be traced back either, were looking at the entrance to the ancient clan home. They could see the smoke rising from a couple of fires, but other than that there was no movement. Not that the movement could be seen from their location. It had always been one of the advantages of this location that any attacking force would have to attack uphill and the only entrance was through a choke point giving all the advantage to the defenders. When he had finally viewed the location for the first time he really wondered how his ancestors had conquered this place. Whoever had occupied this location before his ancient ancestors would have become extremely careless to have lost it.

Well, it didn't matter now, since this place had been abandoned for a very long time, and now a descendant from that clan had come back to claim it. Not really, but in a sense this was exactly what was happening – although what was here belonged to all, not just he and his family. So here they stood in the snow and winds, remaining within the small forest out of sight.

Trehe, facing him asked, "What do you want to do? It would be nice if we could have a fire since it's so very cold right now, but I know that's not an option. We have no idea how many, or if they've just hunkered down or they have guards up and watching. There's just no way to look into that place at all to get that information."

"Yeah, and it's no wonder my clan kept this until they abandoned it. Besides I'm just a baker. I never knew anything about making attacks or searching out some place to see how many might be defending a place. So this is something you're much better at than I am."

Trehe shrugged, "Not really. I've been assigned, well the group that I'm a part of, is assigned on keeping track of everything that Sabohl is involved with. And believe me, that's a full time job all by itself. He's smart, and he keeps his ties hidden as much as possible. And, as you've learned, much of his ties are to less than reputable members of our society. After all, as we explained to you, it was this group who were responsible for the break-in of your shelter when you were gone. Look I'm freezing out here. We need to come up with some way to get inside there and expel the ones who are there, some ruse or something. I really don't think there are that many, but I could be wrong. Oh, by the way can you use that staff?"

"I'm okay with it, but I'll never be as good as Jura."

"Jura? Your mate? A female who is good with a staff, really . . . Now this I've got to see."

Kal smiled, "I wouldn't challenge her, it might damage your male ego."

Trehe laughed, "Then this I've really got to see. You must be just fair if a female could beat you."

Shaking his head, Kal said, "Don't say I didn't warn you." He turned around and signaled Jura to join him and once she did he said, "Jura, Trehe wants to challenge you to a round with the staff. I warned him but he can't believe that such a small female, or any female, could defeat such a big male as he. So let's head to the other side of these trees — besides the exercise will warm us up." They headed out the backside of the trees close to the area where the original two that had followed them had camped. The others followed not knowing what was transpiring. Turning to the rest Kal said, "Your leader has challenged Jura to a round with the staff. He said that he would go easy, after all there's no female out there that can defeat a male. Not my words but his." He looked over at Jura who had an evil smile, and he knew that from being with her as long as he had that Trehe was just about to learn an important lesson."

As they entered the area where the boulders were Trehe stated, "Look I'll go easy on you. After all you are a female and aren't very big."

"She smiled back saying, "Two falls is standard for a round. Is that okay with you?"

"No, I said I'd go easy so one is fine, unless you want it the other way."

"I think two is better. That way if you fall both times it can't be the result of you tripping or something, leading you to believe that this was just a fluke."

"Okay, shall we?"

A line was drawn in the dirt, although because of the cold and the light snow it was more a scratch than a line. Both toed the line to signal they were ready and she at first appeared to handle the staff a bit clumsy. Trehe seeing an advantage immediately attacked but to his surprise she easily blocked his attack followed by a quick counter that swept his feet out from under him and he landed heavily on the ground at which time she placed the end on his chest marking a fall. She turned demurely and casually toed the line allowing him to see her very feminine posterior, turned around and leaned back on her staff. She smiled and simply waited until he stood up and carefully approached the toe line. "That had to be an accident young one, but you won't be able to do that again."

Again she smiled and didn't say a thing. She stepped back casually again inviting him to attack which this time he refused. He was noticing that there appeared too much efficiency and fluidity to her movements. So with heavier concentration and care he came at her with his staff at the ready position. No, he wasn't going to allow some slip of a female beat him at this. Attacking with a feint, followed by a sweep at the knees meant to bring a person down she easily dodged the move and then blocked the follow-through. Again she smiled at him and at all times didn't appear to handle the staff well at all. Yet, everything he had tried, to this point had failed. It was time to just finish this and put her down. So he attacked with the idea of coming down on her head followed by a strike with the lower portion of the staff aimed at her hips followed by an upper cut directed at her chest and neck. To his surprise she easily blocked every one of those moves. *Who is this female anyway?* She teased him with what looked like an unskilled move, but with what he had experienced he didn't take the offer.

Again she looked at him and smiled. The ones who were witnessing this were silent. Their boss had bested every one of them a number of times, both in practice, and in some of the rounds they had worked to keep in shape. Here was a female who had already put him on the ground, and so far he hadn't been able to get past her defenses – unheard of. Both came to the ready signaling that they were ready to continue. Using what he considered his size, weight and strength he feinted with an attack low using his left hand to bring the lower end of the staff at speed to her legs followed by an immediate swing through to bring the upper end of the staff to the top of her head. While this move looked awkward, he had practiced it much and it had been one of the moves that he used to successfully defeat the ones who worked with him. Inwardly he was smiling because it seemed that the move was going to work as it always had in the past. With speed and precision he made his follow through expecting to make contact, only to find that she had immediately blocked the move and had followed through with one of her own using the left end of her staff to hit him in the stomach.

The move was completely unexpected and had pushed him back and off balance, and instead of following through, and putting him on the ground a second time, she deliberately placed the left end of the staff on the ground and held it at the ready giving him a chance to recover. *Again, who is this female?* Now cautious, he approached studying his opponent.

Yet there seemed to be nothing special about her or the way she held her staff. He was at loss as to how she had been able to block his attacks and feints, let alone turn the tables on him. He decided that he would use a flurry of combinations to overwhelm her, starting with an attack at the legs with the bottom of the staff, bringing it around at her head with the upper end followed by a thrust and then an attack to her mid-section, but she blocked every one. She smiled at him and said quietly, "If you want to stop now and save your male ego we can, and I'll even allow you to call it a draw and that you just had a bad day."

Here was a way out. He suspected that with the ease that she'd defeated all of his favorite moves that most likely she could have put him on the ground a second time and won the round. "Okay, I'll accept that, but I don't want you to go around bragging that a mere slip of a female defeated me."

Again she smiled, "I said that we could call it a draw. I'm not looking to brag about anything like that. After all it would mean that there would be many out there that would want to challenge me just to prove I was lying. Besides, whether you want to accept it or not, I'm better than you, and it has nothing to do with your abilities, which I have to admit, are pretty good. But you see my sires are regional champions with the staff, and I, with my siblings, have been trained since we learned to walk on how to use the staff. Then we used to have free-for-alls involving all of us children and then every once in a while my sires would join the fray. We'd all end up with our share of hurts and bruises, but it was fun. So instead of proving that I can beat you, which I think you now know that I can do, I thought it would be just as wise to test your skill and just give you a taste of mine. Kal did warn you not to do this. He's had a taste of our wide open staff sessions where all of us attacked each other."

Shaking his head and smiling looking briefly over in the direction of Kal and then back at her he said, "At least you could have warned me, then I wouldn't have made a fool of myself."

Again she smiled, "Would you have believed me if I suggested that I was better than you?"

Shrugging he said, "Probably not. I've never met a female who was interested in the use of the staff, let alone be good at it. I guess the joke's on me." Turning and facing Kal he asked, "So I guess you did warn me. And you being her mate how have you fared against her?"

Kal laughed, "I have more bruises, bumps, and hurts to count and that's not including the many to my ego as she easily bested me and still does. But you see because of where I come from and do I never really needed to learn to use the staff. So I was clumsy and awkward, slow, and she was patient to bring me along to where I am. But I don't come close to her competence, or ability. Then I visited her family on the farm and witnessed one of their free-for-alls, and then got involved with them. To be honest I got beat up pretty good. And even her youngest sister bested me without even raising a sweat. Look they told me a story and after watching them in action I know that they didn't exaggerate anything at all. Let's just say that the ones who attacked them got a surprise and quickly left."

Laughing now Trehe said, "At least you could've reinforced that warning to me."

"Well, if you think about it," Kal replied, "I did warn you, but for some reason you didn't believe me."

"I guess that I have to admit that's a true statement. I figured that she was just putting me on and that I needed to put her in her place." He then laughed harder, "Guess it was me who got put in his place." He stood quietly for a moment deep in thought. "This gives me an idea, since I now know that I won't have to worry about you, Jura, and it's this . . ." He went on to explain and the two of them could see the logic in it. It would be a way to get inside the site and with the two of them, Kal and Jura drawing attention to themselves the others could sneak in and then drive out whoever was occupying the site.

Even though it was difficult to tell through the lightly blowing snow that was falling, dusk was on its way, and the dropping temperatures were reflecting that change. "Hey Kal," Jura said, "There's a chance that we can get out of this up above." It was hoped that the ones who were occupying the site presently didn't know that it was the two of them that had located this place back in the Season of Falling.

"Are you sure? I mean we've somehow got ourselves all turned around and we need to find a place for the night." He was trailing a little behind giving the appearance of reluctance for passing up the shelter that the trees may have offered.

She stopped and turned around. "Look I know that the trees could have provided some protection. But both of us know that when we were standing in there trying to decide whether to continue or stay that the winds just cut, so there's a chance that just a little ahead there might be someplace better. Besides if we don't then we can always return to those trees." Not waiting for a response she headed up through the gap in the rock face and he followed.

Both of them had spoken loudly making it appear that they were trying to be heard over the growing winds, but were actually putting on a show for the ones that were just a little ahead of them. They were hoping by being so obvious that any attention would be drawn their way, and as they passed through that gap, the others hid behind that rock face so that they could listen for the expected challenge. "Hey Kal, I smell smoke. I think someone has the same idea." Jura stopped and waited for Kal to join her, and both took a deep breath as they were nervous at this point, since shortly they would be challenged, and they would know how many were here. They didn't have to wait long as from the direction where the leader's shelter had originally stood they were approached by four individuals. "Whew, are we glad to see you," Kal said. "We made a wrong turn somewhere down below and it wasn't until we got up here that we realized it and then the winds picked up and it got colder and the snows started blowing and we knew that we needed to find some place to wait out the night. I wanted to stay down in the trees, but my mate here," he pointed at Jura, "wanted to look a little further before it got dark. And I guess she was right. Since it appears that the four of you have already established a camp which means that it has to be a better place than where I wanted to camp. You know down in those trees."

The one who appeared to be the leader looked at the other three knowingly and then at Jura and Kal. He smiled and said, "That's true. This is a better place for a camp. What are you doing out here in this remote place? There's nothing around for a very long way from here."

Jura looked disgusted and pointed her finger at him saying, "He thought he knew a quicker way through this area. We were heading for that small village that sits close to the Sacred Mountains. We are to meet some of his distant family members who wanted to meet me, but I guess they'll just have to wait. Hey maybe you guys know the right trail." She smiled and then with the encouragement of the leader the two began to retreat towards the hidden fire. Jura then asked, "By the way, what are the four of you doing out here? Did you get lost too?"

This brought laughter from the four. Since they were from the underworld, thieves and such, they felt that luck had just turned in their direction. After all they had been complaining about being stuck here in the cold, with no female companionship or any ale to drink and what shows up at their proverbial doorstep but a female, and accompanied by a single male. And with the remoteness of this location, if the two disappeared and were never heard from again then it would be chalked up as the outback taking two more. Yes it would be an enjoyable night, at least for the four of them. The other two, well that was their problem wasn't it? So concentrating on the two of them, the four surrounded them and casually led them back to the fire with all sorts of imaginings in their minds of what would be happening this night. But when they headed around the small obstruction that hid their fire both from sight and the winds to their surprise six unknown males were standing there warming themselves.

Looking over at them Trehe said, "Nice fire you've going here and such a nice location. Oh I suspect all those plans you had wanting to take advantage of the two poor lost travelers isn't going to happen. Instead the four of you are simply going to pack up what you have and leave. Now before you say anything you have two choices in this, you can go without putting up a fight or you can, but in the end the results will be the same. Besides knowing the type I'm looking at here I suspect that what you had planned wouldn't have happened anyway. You see that female that looks like such an easy target would have whipped all of you and probably not even raised a sweat doing it." He could see the disbelief in their eyes and he smiled. "You know I'm almost tempted to let you try. But that would be a waste of effort and energy and you'll need that energy to get back down before this storm moves in with full force. So be good little ones, grab your gear and just leave, and let your bosses know that this site is no longer yours."

* * *

Sabohl was furious. He wasn't used to the idea that someone would do to him what he had been doing to others for many cycles of the seasons. He figured that even though the two, Kal and Jura, had gotten the information and announcement that specifically identified the site that they had discovered, in the public view ahead of him, that in the end he would still win. He had control of the site after all, and later he could claim that they were the usurpers claiming something that he had discovered with his team and they had ridden his coattails so to speak. Then came the word that not only had they beaten him to the specific announcement, but now had ejected his people from the site and they now were sitting on it. *Well, one thing for sure, this cannot stand. I've got to get them out of there and immediately begin to undermine this whole thing. Just because they did the legwork means nothing, the site is mine. They have no right to it. I'm on top because I know better how to treat the site, how to let others know what is there, and most of all, how to interpret what is found.*

The blowing storm outside rattled his door and with the air that escaped into the room where he was sitting caused the lights to flicker dangerously, coming close to being blown out. None of this helped his mood. He stood and paced a bit and went over to his rather large roaring fire and warmed his hands. At least he had this one consolation; he was here where it was warm, while they were on that site of his in this storm. This brought a chuckle to his lips and an evil smile. *They weren't going to be there long.* He'd be sure of that – although at this moment he really had no plans of how he was going to remove them. The only satisfaction he had, even though the news had been bleak, was the cowering reaction from the ones who had reported the failure to him. He remembered yelling at them and literally throwing them out of his shelter. He really needed to learn to control his temper. *Let them freeze, in the end I'll still have the site, and I'll still be in charge.* He paused a second in his thoughts as another crossed his mind. *Who's behind this? It can't be just those two. Even with family help they wouldn't have the understanding or wherewithal to pull this off. But from what I've gathered nobody recognized the ones who were with the two of them. Is there someone else working in the shadows?*

He looked around his shelter in that particular room. It all appeared to be too ordinary, too normal, *why is this happening, why is this particular operation falling apart*? Hadn't he planned well, and hadn't he kept on top of all of the developments, hadn't he kept the two under constant surveillance, yes, so why were things going so wrong? Well, this had to change and change now. With a decision he sat back down, wrote a quick note, shrugged into his heavy coat and exited the shelter. It was night, and nobody was here to notice that he had left, and nobody would think it strange if he went out at night. It was another one of the many ruses that he had developed over time. This going out at odd times so that it would appear to be something that he normally did. He stuffed the completed and folded note into his pocket and headed out the door only to be hit was a very strong and cold wind that snatched the door out of his hands and slammed against the side of the shelter, blowing loose papers off the tables inside, scattering them everywhere. He cursed, grabbed the door, and slammed it shut. *Damn, now I've another mess to straighten out, and damn my temper.*

Unknown to Sabohl, like he, and his many minions who kept watch on the ones that he deemed important, he too was under observation. And as long as they remained unknown to him, they would be able to track and document his night time travels, which in the end could, and probably would become critical in finally destroying the power that he held . . . Finally eliminating his narrow minded views, and the refusal to accept any others however compelling – other than his own. "I wonder where the great Sabohl could be heading out on such a night as this?" One of the unknown watchers asked.

"Don't know, but I suspect that when he got that news earlier today that it didn't bode well for the ones who had reported it to him." This brought a quiet laugh from the three of them who had the duty tonight. "I guess", the first one said, "that we had better see what he's up to." He stood up in the shadows and asked, "Shall we?" Knowing most of the routes that Sabohl took, the three of them spread out and covered them while remaining hidden and in the shadows. They suspected that he was heading for one of his many drops, and because it was as nasty as the weather was, maybe for the first time they might get a chance to see what was actually written there, but they really doubted it. Besides it wasn't worth the chance of discovery. It had taken too many cycles of the seasons to establish their network and to have him discover them now, well that could end their chance of toppling him and getting someone in there who was more conducive to the ideas and facts that were being presented and uncovered.

* * *

The storm had rolled in with its full fury – winds, blowing snow, and so much of the white stuff falling that it was almost impossible to see. Jura wondered how their ancestors survived in this stuff. And while the location was such that it was an easy place to defend, it surely didn't protect one from the elements. The eight of them had moved their camp back against one of the rock faces that was located on the east end of the site. She suspected, from the reading of the journals, that this was where the priest compound had been located. And when she saw the layout of this area it made complete sense. The priests were the warriors of their ancient gods and not warriors against other tribes and clans. So to have the whole clan of warriors between the entrance and the location of the where the priests lived meant that if an attacking force reached the priests' compound, then all was lost anyway. Still that didn't help keep one warm when facing one of these storms this far to the north.

If anybody had any sense at all, and that includes me, none of us would be out in this. I'm an outback female and used to nasty weather, but this is so much worse than anything we face down from where we are from. I thought those storms were bad, but now I've been proven to be quite wrong. And it would now make sense that the ones they were supposedly chasing, that remnant from one of those lairs, the ones who died in the Sacred Mountains would have to face even harsher storms than this. With them having to fight for every step and not prepared for any of this, plus to have been with child and from the words this female was late in her carrying, it's no surprise that they died. Although that doesn't explain the death of that patrol, who knows maybe they had some bad food or something. Anyway with only three surviving to that point it would have been easy for them to sneak around that encampment and disappear into the Sacred Mountains only to succumb to the weather. Now that sucks, it really does. To have been so close to safety, and away from the attackers, only to die in one of the storms. I wonder who these people were and whether we needed to bring destruction down on them like we did.

Well, maybe, since we did find this site, this could mean that the rest that are mentioned in the journals are real. Even though they are dead and gone now, and not just from de-struction and death, but almost from memory, and who would have thought it would be that way? Actually so close to being forgotten completely, and then their whole lives were being turned into myth instead of being real. Yet being here right now and being cold was very real. She wondered how her an-cestors could live like this. At least the clans had permanent shelters, but the tribes moved all the time with those tempo-rary shelters, and they had to be so much worse than the clan homes. But all of this was unknown, conjecture on her part. Shrugging, she didn't have any answers, and she snuggled deeper down under the coverings to keep warm. While the rock faces kept most of the winds away, every once in a while a gust would find its way in and chill them more than they already were. Finally she moved closer to Kal and snuggled up close to share their body heat. The fire that the group had burning was more for cheer. The storm seemed to steal the heat right from it, although if one got up very close they could feel some heat. Smiling and trying to keep it light Kal whispered, "Careful there Jura, I might think that you're interested in getting physical as close as you're getting."

She forced a smile and shook her head. "Yeah I can see that, but I'm not the type that will perform in front of an audience, and you have to admit we have one. Plus, even though I know you're joking, you'd not get me to undress in this kind of weather. So we'll just have to share each other's body heat and try and keep warm that way."

He put his arms around her and pulled her closer saying, "That's fine with me, at least we're together. And I don't think we'll have to worry about anyone moving in this weather – although I doubt that Sabohl will take this well. I suspect that we're going to have to face something after this storm clears. After facing this one, and knowing that there are probably others on their way, storms that is, I think I'm quite happy not to have lived here back in the distant past. This would have been just pure misery. No wonder there were so many deaths recorded during the Season of Cold. Our shelters we have now are so much better built than they were in the days of the journals; at least I think so from the descriptions. Although I have to admit that having you this close is so tempting – something about being male with a female this close to me, especially you – oh well, so be it."

She smiled back at him even though it was a weak one. *Yes getting physical would have been nice.* It would have taken her mind off of being so cold, even if it was for a very brief period of time. And the physical activity, while not vigorous, would warm one, followed by the afterglow and the closeness, sharing everything they had. *Yes, such a nice thought.* This brought her full circle as she thought about the life style of their ancient ancestors. The idea that a female, when requested from the herd for breeding would be required to be ready, which meant that she'd be without her clothes – in weather like this, right. There had to be something that wasn't written in those journals that covered weather like this. Well, she'd have to search them out and see. One thing for sure being a female and having to live that life style was beyond her comprehension. So what did the females do? There was some distance between the shelters where the female herd lived and where the warriors' shelters were located. And a warrior would have to first go to the herd's location, make his request, and return to the warrior's shelter where the female would make an appearance. *Guess our ancestors were much hardier than we are today. Because there's nothing mentioned it probably was considered unimportant. Wow, unimportant? For one to have to move through this stuff, not fully clothed, and consider it nothing – almost impossible to believe. I guess that would make one appreciate the warm body on the other end though, but afterwards to immediately return – still beyond me, that's for sure.* Still, she had to admit that right now that warm body next to her was very nice and comforting.

Kal had to admit that having Jura this close to him made it almost impossible to think of anything else other than mating. It was the nature of the male, at least from what he had gathered in his short life, to be physical with a female whenever she'd allow it. And even though many males felt that they controlled such encounters, it really wasn't true. Of course if the encounter was forced, that would be different. But in a normal relationship, since the female received the male, it was her decision if and when it would happen. And, of course, there had to be included in this, the fact their fertile cycle led to the bleeding at which time mating was not allowed. Although here and now, while they were under the large cover they would be out of sight of any here, but it would be obvious to any who looked their way what was happening. Then they faced the problem of how to handle cleaning up afterwards. So he knew from a practical point of view he would have to leave it at the thinking part, and leave the physical part out. Even though he had fun teasing her, and at the same time he had to admit that she returned it in like. Taking a deep breath and letting it out slowly he said. "Yeah I know that we'd enjoy it, but it's just something that we'd probably regret later. I mean I know that we'd both enjoy the closeness and the heat, but there's no place to take care of what we'd need to afterwards, and there's always that particular odor that tells anybody who's close by what one was doing." Shaking his head he continued, "Although . . . Although with you this close . . ." He hugged her tighter which she returned and the clung to each other for a while listening to the howling winds, the whipping of the small portable shelter flap where the supplies were kept, and the crackling of the blazing fire. Soon they would retire to their own cold portable shelter.

* * *

It was two days later when the storm finally blew itself out. When they all emerged from the portable shelters it was to a transformed white world. Yes there had been a little snow around before this, but just enough to say that it had snowed. Now it appeared to be closer to the middle of the Season of

Cold, although it truly was only beginning. Trehe turned to all of them as they stood there and stated, "If this amount fell from this first major storm, then this place will get buried pretty deep in this stuff." Turning to his group he continued as he pointed to four of them saying, "As you know there's a village close, a couple of days away from here. I need you to go and pick up additional supplies. Plus we'll need to get something that will allow us to build some better lean-tos. I can see that these portable shelters are just not going to work by themselves. So go and there's an account set up there so place these items on that account. The ones that we work for will be sure that what we get is paid for. Now go and be back as quick as you can. Yes I know that knocks us down to just four of us here, but I think if we do this now that we will beat any retaliation that Sabohl will be sending. And we all know that somewhere and somehow he will not take this lying down."

As the four left he turned to Kal and Jura and asked, "What were your plans for this place once you discovered it?"

Looking at each other and then back at him Kal said. "I, we really never thought that far ahead. I mean while I have enjoyed history and excelled in it really, that was in the learned centers – I really have no practical experience in this at all."

Laughing, even though there was no humor in the laugh Trehe said, "You really didn't consider what this would mean to our people? That finding this place would start the change of how we view our past and could change what had been conjectured about that time?"

"Well, yes, actually that part did come to mind. But once we found this place," he paused trying to find the words, "hmmm, what I mean is that we really never knew if we could find it. Yes we had this rough map, but it had never been made with the idea or the way maps are made today with south being on top and north being on the bottom. So as large, as we learned, an area as these northern foothills are we could have spent a lifetime looking and never find the proper orientation, let alone the proper place, in these foothills to match the map. We were lucky that it only took a season, but even still we had some hints that helped. But we hadn't really thought much beyond just finding it."

"I guess that makes sense. Well, now that you have found it, now comes the problem of keeping it. Because soon we will be receiving guests, guests from Sabohl – he won't give up this easily. Especially since this is a very, very important abandoned site, critical really. And I can guarantee that if he fails in his next move that this won't end it either. The Season of Cold is long and we are in a very remote area. Even with the advances that have been made, since this place was active, people are lost to be never found out here. So if for some reason you were to disappear and your bodies never located it would be just be a case of someone else falling victim to the outback. While I cannot begin to know what is happening back where Sabohl lives and who he has contacted, I know that he has something in the works and that will bode bad for us. It will mean that there will be little or no chance, other than maybe mapping this place, to work or research it. Instead, once we have the tools, we'll have to do as your ancestors did and make this into a fortress once again. So we have much work ahead of us."

Shaking his head Kal said, "I really didn't expect any of this to happen. I mean when I got this information," thinking as he was passing on this he thought. *So how much do I dare tell them? I know that they are risking their lives to be here and to help. But what is their agenda, why have they gotten involved? And I really haven't even begun to know who they represent. This still could be an elaborate ruse by Sabohl and we are the ones that it's being played against.* "There was a great possibility that what I had wouldn't be worth the paper it was written on. It could have been something that was added to my family long after this place had been abandoned, and since my family claims to be from this clan, the clan of K'jor, then there was always a possibility that someone in my line decided to create a map to give credence to the family history. So, in the end, it easily could have been a chase after those twirling dust spirals that we all like to chase when we are young. It was another reason why neither of us had thought beyond just finding this place."

Throughout this conversation Jura remained quiet, but what Kal was saying wasn't quite the truth. Later she would confront him as to why the deception, but for now, because she didn't understand, she remained silent. *Just what is he doing? Doesn't he trust these people? Well, I guess I can understand that. This adventure has turned out to be so much more complicated than either of us thought it would be. With the blessings of his family of course, we went out looking for his, well ours, since I'm now part of his family also, past. And while, yes, he's supposedly from an important clan, and again supposedly a direct descendant of K'jor, the first leader to unite the tribes and clans, it was still kind of a private thing.* Sighing quietly as she continued to watch and listen to the exchange her thoughts continued. *But here we are just after one of the storms in the north inside the abandoned clan home and who'd have thought that, not me. At first I had held out little hope of finding this place, and then when we did that that would be it. Great! We did it! But instead here we are in the middle of something that's so much bigger than the two of us and this truly beyond our understanding.*

She found that she had been staring out at nothing and had actually quit listening and was caught off guard when she heard her name. "Yes?" She turned towards the one who had mentioned her name and it was Kal who signaled her to come away with him to a different part of the site. She followed as he headed back towards the rock face that they were using as a windbreak and sheltered area during the storm. She waited until they had reached the area where they were staying and asked, "So why the misdirection? The ones who are here are helping us, and as far as I know, they don't have to."

"Now I can't say for sure if that's true or not. I just don't know enough about them to really know who they are and what organization they're a part of. They've been pretty secretive on that aspect. So I don't know anything really, and because of this I still don't trust them. They could be laughing behind our backs with the secret knowledge that they actually work for Sabohl, and all of this is to get us into their confidence and when we fully trust them we then become their victims. This has gotten so much more complicated than I ever expected. Yeah, I knew that this site could be important, but I didn't expect all the trouble finding this place has caused and from what I can see, will continue to cause. In a sense, even though we are the discoverers here, we are the ones on the outside. And as we continue, it just seems that things are becoming as clear as mud and we know less and less. I'm almost sorry that we started all of this and sometimes wish we could just go back to before this started, before we made a decision to pursue this, change our minds and let someone in one of the future generations do the discovering. But we can't change any of this and so here we are. And because of this I'm not going to reveal any more than I have too."

She paused thinking about what he had just said and could see the logic in it. Truthfully what did they really know, and like he said, the two of them were the ones on the outside. From her observations of this team that was helping them, and especially Trehe, it appeared to be an old game – one that they had played too many times. Who'd have thought that all of this was going on all of the time and ones like the two of them being completely unaware? And if it was like this for the learned, how was it for others vying for power? She had to admit that this was a very scary thought. That there was always someone in the background trying to get on top and stay there and others just as determined to topple them. Taking a deep cleansing breath she let it out slowly, "Yeah, I guess now that my eyes are being opened it would be nice to just go back to when I was ignorant of all of this. But, as you've said, we can't undo any of this and we are very stuck – and unfortunately, as you just pointed out, at the mercy of Trehe and his group. In a way I wish I hadn't tipped my hand back there and shown them my skill with the staff. If they are working for Sabohl then we would have a chance to get away because of their ignorance."

"True, in a way this is like one of those really bad books or bad dreams where you know what's coming but can do nothing to stop it. And what has been aptly pointed out is our isolation, and we are really isolated here." Kal began to pace just a little, realized that was what he was doing, and stopped. Shaking his head he said, "Don't want to it to appear that we may be doubting them." He was silent, shrugged, saying, "I'm out of ideas of how to get us out of this mess, and I have to apologize to you for putting you in the middle of this."

Quietly Jura replied, "Not your fault. I walked into this with my eyes open. I just hope that Trehe and his are here to really help. And yes, we stupidly walked into this and have completely isolated ourselves – not a good thing, that's for sure."

DEFENSE

It took a 9-day for the ones who had gone for the supplies to return. In that time another storm had blown through and for now it was clear and very cold. So other than when they went down to the tree line to gather firewood and look to building up the fortifications, they all stayed close to the fires. Nothing throughout this time had led either Kal or Jura to completely trust the group that they were staying with at this time. While they were not prisoners by any means, with the weather as it was, they were going nowhere. So other than trips to take care of nature they remained together. But at the same time were attempting to make it appear that they had no suspicions or fears. It was a difficult road to walk. For all they knew, they had enemies within, and enemies without. Still both had to admit that at this point, other than the suspicions that they harbored, Trehe and his seemed only to want to help protect this important site and the two of them.

Now with the full crew back, and with the tools that the ones brought with them, they began to build a gate across the open path into the ancient clan home. To put up a similar defense that the ones who had lived here so long ago had done, successfully defending it until it had finally been abandoned. While weapons had improved over time, as is usually the case, this location still had the advantage that to enter and attack required the attackers to go through a bottle neck with the defenders being on higher ground, leaving the advantage to the defenders. Still with such a small group and their constant need for firewood, they had to leave the protection and work the trees and haul the dead wood up to where it would be available. At this time it was the weak point in their defense. So once they had finished their rough gate all of them proceeded to drag as much of the wood and scrap up to their camp within the compound.

"You know," Trehe said, "that moving this wood warms you twice."

"Twice?" How can that be?" Jura asked.

Smiling he replied, "It's quite simple really. As we work to move this stuff up to our camp, the exercise warms us, so that's the first time. Then we burn it and feel the heat and it keeps us warm, and that's the second time. So it warms us twice."

"Okay smarty, I guess that's true. I must admit that I hadn't thought about it that way, but you're right." She stopped and rested a moment as the piece of dead wood she was dragging up was heavier than she thought and she needed a break to get her strength back. Looking around she could see most of the ones there was doing the very same thing – moving the large limbs, stopping, catching their breath, which was coming out in clouds of steam, and then continuing the trek up the hill. Eventually she was ready once again and began dragging her piece up into the area where they were stockpiling the wood. She stopped suddenly as an idea crossed her mind.

Grabbing Trehe she said, "Look I just realized that we may be making a mistake."

"Mistake? How so? Do you mean moving wood up by the camp?"

"No, no, we need to do that. But we are putting all the wood in one pile. I think we need to put it into a number of piles because it is the one thing we have no way of replacing. If those others that you suspect are coming find a way to set it on fire, then we would have to abandon our defense because it would be too cold for us to be able to hold it."

"You know you're absolutely right, and I didn't even consider it. Hey, I'm the one with the experience here, and I missed that one completely. Okay we'll do that immediately."

That night they rested since it had been a full day of hauling the wood up to their camp, and both Jura and Kal were finding muscles that they didn't know that they had. The skies were unbelievably clear and the stars were so bright that it seemed one could reach up and touch them. As they stared up at the night sky it suddenly lit up with a bright fire as a fireball streaked across the sky briefly lighting the area. It had begun it's streaking above the sacred mountains in the north and appeared to be traveling completely across the visible sky until it disappeared in the distance slowly growing dim as it traveled away from them. "Wow! That was spectacular!" Jura exclaimed. "I know that I've seen a few of these things back on the farm but nothing quite as bright or as large as that one. I always wondered what those things were, but I probably will really never know."

"Know what you mean. Although from the village and the light that comes from it you never see many of them. It's only after you've gotten away from those lights that one can see more of them. And I always liked the lightshow anyway, didn't think anything about them. I guess I can see how our distant ancestors would have considered them something from the gods." Both of them moved closer together because of the bitter cold. With the clear skies it appeared that any of the heat, not that there had been much, had been sucked away from the earth leaving only the cold. This made the warming fire so much more inviting as well as each other.

* * *

For the next several days it remained clear and cold. While it was necessary to continue to work on their defense, one couldn't remain too long from the heat of the fires. Kal thought, *what a miserable place to have to spend the Season of Cold.* The area was exposed to the winds coming from above off the higher peaks in the northern foothills. He began to understand why his ancestors had finally abandoned this place. With the exposure they had on this small plateau, once the need for defense was ending, there were many other locations that would provide a better place to live. Yet, he had to agree that it was a place that would have been hard to conquer. Making him again wonder how it had first been done. Looking at his hands he could see blisters forming. While no stranger to hard work, the life as a baker created other calluses and these did not come into play with the cutting and moving of timber as they worked to create a new stronger wall and gate to block the single way into and out of this area.

Inside the site they were careful to only walk and travel along one path so as to not disturb what history might still be locked here. And even though most of what had been here was constructed of wood and had long disappeared over the interval of time that had passed, there would be other such things that would remain. But these thoughts at this time were the furthest thing from his mind. Sabohl would be doing something to take back this site so that he could claim it as his own. It had become obvious to Kal that this one was very smart to have been able to maintain his position of the learned and leader in his field and at the same time be ruthless in the background to maintain his leadership. So he really had no idea what would transpire and had to depend on Trehe who appeared to be experienced in dealing with Sabohl. His thoughts were interrupted when he heard one of Trehe's team yell out that someone was approaching. Looking up from the log that he was dressing, removing the limbs and smoothing so that it would fit into the hole that had been dug, as it was to be the support for the gate, the one that the rest attached, he paused.

Leaning back and stretching his back and twisting his neck to relieve the pain from bending over so much, he looked towards the trail where any that came here would have to approach, and watched as Trehe and the rest headed down to the tree line and disappeared. He turned at the sound of approaching footsteps and saw that Jura was approaching with a questioning look. Shaking his head he said, "I don't know."

She came up and stood beside him shaking from the cold a little. "Getting away from the fires makes one appreciate them," she said. For now she had taken over the cooking duties, not that she couldn't have assisted with the building of the gate, but someone needed to do this chore, and right now to build this thing required brute strength and she hadn't been blessed with that. So together the two of them stood looking over the tree line waiting to see what would happen. Turning once again and facing Kal she said, "I barely heard the yell, couldn't make out the words really. But the others took off quick. You didn't go with them?"

With his arms folded and continuing to look out over the lower area he said, "No, Trehe signaled me to stay here, so that's what I'm doing. They didn't look worried so I don't know if there was only a couple of whoever it was or maybe something else. I guess we'll just have to wait and see." Looking at her he could see that she was shaking so he put his arm around her. At this moment from the work he had been doing he wasn't cold, but suspected that if they stood around too long that he would join her. "Why not head back to the fires. You can at least look over at me and I can either yell to you or signal to you what's going on. Truthfully it's no fun being cold and I have to say this makes me appreciate my ancestors much more if they faced this every Season of the Cold. Suspect that they probably spent most of it inside their shelters anyway. I know that I would."

"Okay, I have to admit that I'm very cold just standing here. But, well, if you keep me informed I guess I'll head back." She gently pulled away from his embrace and reluctantly headed back to the fires. She had to admit that this place was so much colder than where she had grown up.

As he waited he found that he was beginning to cool down and soon he would have to join her by the fires if there was no sign of what was transpiring soon. Turning so that she could see him he smiled, although from this distance he didn't know if she could see that or not, then signaled that nothing had changed. He turned back around to see Trehe emerging from the trees and with him there were now at least nine others that he had never seen before. Alarmed now, he turned and signaled Jura that he wanted to meet her and hurried in her direction as she did his. "I don't know what's happening but we have at least twice the number that we did just a short time ago. I truly hope that they are really here to help, because if we've been fooled there will be no way out for either of us." This raised the tension level on both of them, but there was nothing that they could do to change it now. "It would be so easy for us to disappear and never be heard from again, and with all of this open land our bodies would never be found, and we'd just become what so many others have. Darn! I know I've said it before, but I almost wish we were back just working the bakery and ignorant of this, being warm and safe, maybe looking to the day when we became a family. Yet, here we are." Shrugging and shaking his head he was silent. *Why us? Why has things just gone this way? Am I so naïve that I couldn't see this coming? Well stupid, obviously the answer is yes.*

Jura remained silent she was at loss as to what to do. While Trehe had appeared to be just who he said he was, there really had never been any proof one way or the other, leaving both of them unsure. Sure everything seemed to be in order all the way back to when they began to contact them through the notes and bakery, but all of this had been beyond her and so subtle that it was well beyond her grasp. Were they now to be at their mercy, and especially she since she was the only female here, to be played with as these wanted? It was a scary thought, and one she wanted nothing to do with. But she was learning that one could easily walk into something completely ignorant and then pay the price for that ignorance. She looked at Kal and asked, "What do you want to do? It's not like we can just get up and walk out of here. In fact with the ones who

are here we were never really alone. There was always someone with one or the other of us. And now there are more."
Closing her eyes and grimacing, she quietly said, "I can only
hope that what we've been told is true. Otherwise I believe
that we are in a very big mess and there's no way out." *I
thought that at the beginning of all of this we would be having
fun, well in a sense fun. We'd be having an adventure that in
our old time we could look back, tell stories about that time,
and smile as we made the adventure seem so much more than
it truly was. But now is there even going to be an old time for
us? Are we going to leave a next generation to learn, to grow,
and to discover things that we've never dreamed of? Or, is
this where it will end for us? Well, I guess we'll know shortly.*
"Let's go back to the fire, I'm getting cold."

Together with arms around each other's shoulders they
strolled back to the fires and sat down on one of the logs that
had been dragged here for just that purpose and waited. After
all, what else could they do? In moments they would have
their questions answered, one way or the other, and in the end
it probably didn't matter since they had no control on either
the answers or the outcome. They didn't have long to wait as
the much larger group approached the campsite and both of
them could hear the pleasant conversation and some laughter
that was being spread among the group. Jura's ears perked up
as she thought she heard some higher voices. *Did that mean
that they brought children with them? Now Jura that doesn't
make any sense,* she admonished herself. *Well, if not young
ones maybe a couple of more females?* She wondered why she
had come to the conclusion that there was more than one.
Since she only had heard the voices. *The voices that's it.
There is more than one. Hmmm, this could change that fore-*

boding feeling I'm having. If they have brought other females then maybe it's just as Trehe has said. She laughed inwardly at this conclusion. *Now that really is stupid. Not all females have mates, or are nice. They could as easily be here just to service these males and make something for themselves out of this.*

Jura and Kal didn't have to wait very much longer as the combined group reached the fire. Along with the group came a couple of pack beasts fully loaded with supplies, and now counting all the new faces there were a total of eleven, making the group that was part of Trehe seventeen. They definitely were outnumbered, very easily could end up being prisoners, but as he looked over the group saw that there were three females with them. Okay what were they doing here?

Trehe looking at the two of them could see a little fear and a very questioning look. He smiled and said, "I know that this is unexpected, and I wasn't sure that we'd be able to get them to come. That's why I didn't say anything to the two of you. But now that they are here and obviously made it I can bring you up to date. When the four left to get those additional supplies, part of what they needed to do was to send out a call for help, but again as I just stated I didn't know if we would get any help and would be left on our own. Again we'll go over the introductions later, but let's just say that the ones who joined us will help in the protection of this place, and begin the real research here. We need to do both if we are to establish this as an official ancient site." He could see that Kal was about to say something and he held up his hand and shook his head. "Kal just let me finish please. I know it appears that we are trying to take over your discovery, but you did discover it, and all the records will reflect that. And we know, unofficially, that this is an important site. But until we can prove it by doing digs here, it is only conjecture. And to keep Sabohl from claiming that we took this away from him we need the proof as soon as we can get it. So this is why it was important to get these people in here."

He looked at Jura, and continued. "Look I knew that once this group arrived that it would look very bad to you. After all you're the only female here, so along with the request for this help I stated that you were here and because of this any who wanted could bring their mates along. I felt that it was important for you not to feel either so isolated or threatened by there only being males here, and having other like-minded females would help put your mind at ease. We really are who we said we are. I know that with some of what's been happening, it's hard to remember that. I hope that this helps put your mind, both of your minds at ease, and what we've said all along is the truth." Trehe waited with patience knowing personally that having this go the way that it had that he would feel much the same way, have the same doubts, and of course, fears. While he wasn't a female so couldn't know exactly her feelings, still it had to have been real fear and worry. Had they been bad ones then she would be paying a horrible price for making the mistake of being here. In truth, no matter how careful one was, it was still too easy to step into something unexpected, and find one in serious trouble.

Jura and Kal looked at each other, and then Kal took a deep breath, again paused before speaking. "I know you keep reassuring us that you and the ones who are here are on the up and up, but it surely is difficult to believe. Every time we turn around you're surprising us with something else, some new revelation. Of course we're on edge. What did you expect?"

Jura thought, *I really am worried. What other surprises are they going on spring on us?* "I really don't understand this. Is the threat that Sabohl presents that great? After all he is only a male, and yes one of the learned, but only one person."

Pausing before replying Trehe said, "One male, one person yes. But he fought his way to the position that he's in. He is smart, and has no allegiance except to himself. He uses whoever he can, and when he has what he wants then he dumps whoever it was that helped him get that piece of whatever it was. And, not that you don't already know this, he can and does put on a front of a learned that is willing to help any who want to learn, to find out things, to research to help unlock our past. Then he pounces, takes whatever work and effort that these did and claims it as he own. And he's always looking for ways to cement his power and to remain the one who is the only information that will be accepted for the way our past is. A very narrow view of the world, don't you think? But that is unimportant to Sabohl. Just as long as he has the power to shape things in the way he sees it that's all that matters to him.

"Have you ever wondered why he has no mate, or companion?" Trehe looked directly at Jura when he asked the question. He knew that it was something that she had noticed, and had actually pointed out at one time. "Because, first off, no female could stand his selfish ways, his air of superiority, and secondly if he needs to take care of his physical desires he takes it from some adoring female in one of his classes, or delves into the underside of the villages and townships and gets a female that sells her services. From his point of view, that's what a female is for, and that's all she's worth. He could have easily survived back at the time in our history where we only had the clans and tribes. In some ways he's a throwback, someone out of time. And he fights to win, no rules but his own. Yet none of this can be seen from the outside, by his students, by our society. He appears to be friendly, always willing to lend a hand to help, one who only wants the truth about our past to be learned so we can truly understand where we came from and where we can go. Always willing to listen to a student, answer their questions, and direct them where they might find the answers.

"Yet, in the end, one only has to look up those he stepped on, and continues to step on to learn the truth. But even here he's very careful to make sure that any of these victims are placed in such a way that they become ineffective and thusly not a threat to him, or if he sees that they can and will be a threat, well then through some accident or other situation they die or disappear, very conveniently and in such a way that it can never come back to him. We've followed his ties to the underworld, but he is so very careful. While we and our network are quite aware of his movements, his contacts, and his life, he has yet to slip up allowing us to catch him. And since he has isolated himself as he has it makes it easier for him to keep those slipups from happening. And while I know that this has been a long winded explanation, it's necessary so that you can understand why it is necessary to bring these others in here.

"If anything, Sabohl is consistent – predictable really. You see this isn't the first site that has been found by someone else. But are they around, are they still alive – probably not. Once he has confirmed this or that discovery, and he has his ways of keeping track of what's happening in the field as we call it, he has his underworld contacts come into the site, take it over, hold it, and then moves his own teams in, announcing to the world of this new discovery that he's made. And you've had personal experience, so you know that what I'm saying here is the truth. You were watched the whole time you were searching for this site – the whole time. How do I know this – simple really, we have teams whose job it is to keep tabs on his contacts from the underworld. They follow them wherever they might go. And there were two constantly dogging your searches, and it was only through accident that you discovered this when you found the trail to this place. Again, how do we know this, because one of our teams was there when it happened. So in some ways it was you two out searching being spied on by Sabohl's people, while we followed them." At this point Trehe laughed, "Look, in a way while this area usually has none of us around here since it's so isolated, for a while there it was actually crowded, and unfortunately before this is over it's going to get even more so. In fact it may look much like it did when this site was occupied with an attacking force trying to get inside to claim it as theirs. And remember we are very isolated here. So whatever happens and the results from the actions that happen here will never get out. And the only information that the world will hear will be what this site is and what it represents, nothing more."

Looking again at the two of them Trehe looked as if he was about to go and join the newly arrived members, but instead stopped and began to speak again. "Look what we play here – although play is probably not the best of words – is a very old game, one that has been played out here from the very beginning of time. And what I mean is this, there was a time, and not one of us knows when that was, we became conscious thinking creatures. I suspect that at the beginning we only survived because we could think and outsmart the other predators that were looking for a meal. But eventually we started to get together to form what eventually became our clans and such. And at this point we had become the top predator out there and began to fight with each other. Probably the competition was one of the reasons we continued to grow, to improve in our abilities to think, to act. I guess the pressures of the times kind of forced this growth on us.

"I know this is getting a little long winded again, but I think once you hear me out that you will see that while the times have changed, we really haven't. Maybe it just dressed up and a little more sophisticated than it was in the past. But if you strip away everything that it hides behind, then it's really no different than what we were when this site or any of our other people during that time were here. The only difference now is that it happens more with words than with the long knives and bows. This is not to say that those are no longer used. All of us know better than that. And I suspect sometime in our future because we've descended from warlike people that this is still in our blood and as such we may find ourselves in wars of unimaginable size compared to what it was, again when this site was occupied, or even what we can imagine today. And because we can see that we've advanced one can only assume that our weapons will do the very same thing – which means that our ability to cause misery and death will increase.

"I suspect that the ones who will live during those stressful times in our future will wonder why we do this and why it is so, and this is why the past is so important. So important that one person shouldn't control what is put out there, to make sure it is only his ideas that control. Because it is our past that leads us to our future, and to interpret it correctly requires many disciplines and much thought and study at the very ancient sites such as this one. Then this information, as it is gathered, must be passed out to as many of the learned as we possibly can get it to. Because we never know who will find that one key that will unlock a mystery that no one else had been able to solve. So in a sense we are fighting just as our ancient ancestors did. Only here the battle is for knowledge, and who knows, it still may be survival, but again knowledge. Since having the knowledge and the understanding that sites like this can provide, allows us to understand who we are, where we came from, and possibly where, in the end, we will go. But when one like Sabohl is controlling all of it then none of this is happening and as long as he can control this, we, as a people, as a society, will be the losers.

"Sorry about this, but I cannot help but be passionate about this. No one person should control this. It's just too important, and it's the reason that I'm in this fight right up to my ears. I've watched as Sabohl has changed and twisted the facts to fit his ideas and theories, and he is so closed minded that he refuses to allow any competing idea or theory, and crushes any unmercifully. You see I was one of those he crushed. And no, before you ask, it is not the reason that I am doing this. I'm not looking for revenge." He smiled before continuing. "Although I suspect that at the beginning of this it was that. And if we look at our past I'm sure many of the battles that we fought had revenge as the motive. Now it's more to do with the restriction of knowledge and what this knowledge could do for us if we could get it out there. I know with life as it is, not many have time to do other than what is necessary to survive, and so much of this may seem unimportant. Yet, if we are to better ourselves, we really must know who we are, who we were, and what has changed, why we've gone the way we have, and so many other things. Without this knowledge and it must be as accurate as we can make it, we will find ourselves repeating things that at best should be left alone and never repeated.

"Okay, again, sorry about this. It's just when I have an audience, and in your case a captive one at that, I kind of preach. Anyway, I'd better head over and join the others, and you can join shortly and we'll make the introductions and then begin to decide how we'll tackle this project as well as the protection of this site from not only Sabohl and his minions, but once word goes out, there will be looters and others who just want to see our past. We have to try to work this in a way that anything that we recover can be authenticated and not messed up because we have someone here who just wants to dig everywhere because they think that there might be some treasure here. In truth the only treasure that truly is here is the knowledge about our past, but we of the learned would only see it that way." At this point Trehe turned and left heading over to join the others leaving Jura and Kal alone.

Both were quiet and then they looked at each other. "Wow," Jura exclaimed, "passionate about this isn't he? I guess if we both think about it we won't have to worry about them being secretly part of Sabohl's team. At least I don't think so."

"I think I have to agree. And unless he's that good of an actor you could really see, as you said, his passion for this work, and his dislike for Sabohl and what he is doing." Kal took a deep breath, and looked over at the other group who were in a separate camp. "I guess we'll see some others set up in their own portable shelters since, if I heard right, there are other mated couples in that group. At least I'm happy that there will be other females here now, but the only downside is that we don't know them. Still if I've learned anything since we've been together, it won't take too long before all of you will be chatting like old friends." Again he looked up and across to the other gathering and saw that Trehe was signaling the two to come and join them. He breathed out heavily before continuing. "I guess we'd better go and join them then."

Arm in arm they headed over to the others with no expectations of how this would go. After all the rest knew each other, and even though this site was their discovery, they were still the outsiders. As they approached they could hear the voices of the many as they talked among themselves, but as they got close it became silent with an air of anticipation. Smiling first at them and then turning to the rest Trehe said, "And here are our discoverers. As you know this place has, in many ways, been our special and probably one of the most important sites that had never been located. It is here that the leader was able to create the first alliance that eventually led to what we are now. But with so much time that had passed since his time as leader, this place, and its location has passed into the realm of myth. And in many ways the history that we study reflects that. Well, now with the location known maybe we'll be able to find if other parts of our history that is marked as this was, myth, may in fact be real. Not that you don't know but these two are Kal, and Jura. Kal's family history says that he's a direct descendent of K'jor, and this clan. Again, with the way things were done back then, and he agrees by the way, it would seem to be impossible to know who one's sire was. Still if that cannot be determined, at least it can be said that he is from this clan." Trehe then introduced all the new members that had just joined them here at the site, and they all seemed to be friendly, and just about as passionate about the past as he had assumed Sabohl had been.

Later when both of them were back inside their portable shelter Jura said, "Well that was a spirit-spiral introduction and evening. With all these new names it's going to take me a while just to put the faces with the names, but I suspect that we'll not be having a lot of contact with them anyway. I'll, most likely have more contact with the other females since with me there are only four of us, but there are now thirteen males including you. And from what I could gather from the conversations, most of them will be setting up areas to begin to learn about this place with all of us taking our turns at guarding this place from Sabohl and his cronies. But this is only the first night, so who knows, things might and probably will change." Smiling she looked deep into his eyes and said. "Not to change the subject, but to change the subject, I would really love to have you very close tonight,"

What could he say about that? He had to admit that he just loved to get as close as he could. He smiled back and said, "For me that's never a problem. I love getting as close as we can, and enjoy each other's bodies."

* * *

The following few 9-days just flew by as they continued the reconstruction of the gates, bringing in the additional wood for their fires and began the tedious work of working this site. And, of course, the weather refused to cooperate with storm after storm hitting them with a fury that none of them were comfortable with. And as another storm raged pushing all of them back into their shelters Kal looked out stating, "If I had a choice, and from what I've learned so far, this would not have been a place that I would have chosen to live. Yeah, because of the lay of the land it is one of the most defensible areas that we've seen. But that is just about the only good you can say about it. This is surely a miserable place to live during the Season of Cold. And if our history says anything, nobody moved in that season. So why not find different Season of Cold headquarters and avoid all of this."

"I'm sure that it crossed their minds a few times." Jura replied, "But I suspect that if they abandoned this place for a warmer location that when they returned they would have found someone else occupying it. And from what I can see it would have been nearly impossible to take it back. So they would have just stayed and suffered." Jura could understand, since she had to admit that it wasn't a very nice place to live this time in the cycle of seasons. As of yet she or Kal for that matter, had no opportunity to experience it in any of the other seasons. It had been close to the Season of Cold when they had discovered it, and had returned back to their home in High Trail almost immediately.

Both of them heard the crunching of the snow as someone approached their shelter. While they were still living in the portable shelter that they had brought with them, it had been reinforced with other materials to keep it from being torn and destroyed by the winds. Trehe then called out, "Are both of you decent?"

They looked at each other and then at the portable shelter flap and Jura replied saying, "Yes, just trying to keep warm and out of those wicked winds, and why wouldn't we be?"

Trehe laughed as he replied, "Oh I don't know, let me see . . . very cold, by yourselves, mates, trying to keep warm – you know, things like that. Conditions like this have led to new lives."

She laughed and said, "I guess that's very true, and it does seem like when you get close together to keep warm that it does go further than that. Yeah, we're decent, so come in, come in."

They could hear the stomping of feet and then the flap was pulled back and Trehe crouched down to get through the opening, entered, and sat down next to the entrance. With him came a blast of cold air that immediately sent a chill through the two of them. Seeing their reaction Trehe said, "Sorry about that, but there's just no way to keep that cold air out when you enter a place. In a way wish we could build some more permanent shelters, but until we know more about the layout of this place we can't afford to mess something up."

Looking at the two of them Trehe leaned forward placing his hands over the small fire. He noticed that the fire was close to smokeless and what smoke was produced curled up towards the roof and out through a small opening that was there for that very purpose. The materials that the portable shelter was constructed from made it somewhat stiff, but with these winds it still flexed and snapped giving the illusion that it could fall at any time. "Look, first off now that we have close to a full team here, you truthfully don't have to stay here. Once the Season of Green arrives it would be a great time to be here, but now it is just miserable. As you know we've been more involved with making this place defensible once more than actually doing any research. And the way these storms are rolling in here I suspect that we won't be doing much research until this season is over. Now I'm not telling you to leave, but I want you to know that it is as option

– not that traveling in this kind of weather would be easy. And if you decide to go nobody will feel that you just cut and ran. In fact some of the others suggested it. In a way we'd love to just leave a very small crew here, someone to just occupy this place to keep it under our care. But with what may show up here at any time we really don't have much of a choice, but you do." He could see that they were about to protest so he held up his hands to cut them off and continued. "Look, we don't need an answer right now. Discuss it between the two of you, come to us and ask questions, anything. Just be sure if you decide to ask any of the other mated couples here that you announce your arrival. That way nobody gets embarrassed when one walks in on a compromising situation." Here he laughed again and said, "After all like we both agreed it is quite cold and such situations does lead to other things."

He paused a moment cleared his throat and said, "Not to change the subject, but enough on that. I understand that the two of you have a general map of the layout to this place, is that right?" He waited as again Jura and Kal looked at each other before looking back at him. "Look, we know at least this much, and while we never discussed it directly, you had in-formation that led you to this site. It was obvious from our field operations, as the two of you searched all the areas that you did. There was nothing random about it at all. So if you do have something that would help us when we are finally able to actually work this site it would be much appreciated."

Kal looked at Jura who just shrugged. "Look, I know that you know that I'm supposed to have been from this clan. A little had been passed down through the generations, and I guess either because I have an interest in history, or maybe because this is the first time in history that it would be safe, well not truly safe, but maybe the first chance to actually go out and search I was sort of elected. So, yes, I had something to go on. But what surprised me, and I know Jura, is just how large an area this is. So I, we feel very lucky to have located this in our first season of searching. And yes I do have a very rough drawing of what this place was supposed to look like when there were people living here. I know that we've tried to be very careful, all of us that are here right now, of avoiding any obvious areas of past occupation, and from what I can see we have. I know that *note taking* is a very big part of such an operation. Besides all the digging and sifting, and so many more tedious things, so if you could give us some paper I could probably transfer the rough drawing I have, which I want to keep since it is part of my family, and then you would have exactly what I have. Look, it still worries both of us, even with the assurances, that we could lose this site. So we are trying to be so very careful."

"That's a very understandable position," Trehe shrugged, "and even now there's no way that there can be real trust between us. Too much has happened. And in that I mean this has all transpired rather quickly, and the two of you have had to react more than having the time to really think it through." Again he paused and took a deep breath. "Look, I don't know why but life just seems to be that way. So much that happens is unplanned, unforeseen, and all we can do is adjust as it happens and hope that what we decide is the right decision. Yet, as you well know, many times those decisions are made with too little information and, usually, too little time to make those decisions. It's no wonder that so many times what we decided, once we have the time and a chance to look back makes us think that if we only had better information, or more time, then what we decided would have been so much differ-ent.

"In the games that we play when we are young we find that we can always start over and do it again, but life doesn't give us that opportunity. So we muddle along from one decision to the next, never knowing what our future or the outcome of those decisions will be. And many times we sit there and curse ourselves for being so stupid or reacting in a certain way, wishing that we could go back and change it. But I guess the real question would be, would we? Even if we knew all the facts, and knew what the possible outcomes would be, would we truly make a different decision or go in a different direction? But since we cannot go back and try, all this is no more than an exercise in futility. So all we can do is go on with our lives, and hope that we've learned something from our past, and this is the whole past – you as an individual, the two of you as a couple, the places that you live, our society, and even all of us – if we don't, then its shame on us, and rightfully so. And I guess that's one of the reasons why I do this, and go against Sabohl. What he does is to maintain his position of power and appear to the rest as the one in the know. But what he really is doing is quite wrong, since his version of the past isn't necessarily the correct one. And as you have seen he is ruthless in his pursuit of maintaining that position. It leaves the rest of us searching for ways to defeat him. And it's sad, in some ways, because if he would be will-ing to accept what there is out there, work with the ideas and such that have been presented, then we'd know so much more, maybe understand much more. But alas, it's not to be. So here we are fighting our own little war. And like in any war there are casualties, but most of these casualties are the destruction of knowledge instead of individuals, but the tragedy is no less.

"By narrowing and restricting what we know of our past and why we are where we are is truly a dangerous stance to take. It means that somewhere in the future, because of what we think is the way we were in the past, the decisions could be completely wrong and lead us to our own destruction. If you think about it, not that you haven't, what we did in our past put us here where we are today. Sometimes the changes took a very long time to happen, other times very quickly. I guess a good example of this would be how some tribes over time established more permanent homes and became the clans. Yes we still had the nomadic people, and in some ways we still do. But this change continued until we now have our villages and such – a very slow change for sure. Then we have the forming of the alliance, no not the small ones, but this really major one that was brought about by your ancestor. This was a rather rapid change, and from what little we can understand about it, it was outside influences that brought about. Yet at this very moment, we have no idea what those outside influences are. This was followed almost as quickly with the disillusion of the same alliance by the mythological meeting of the gods in the mythological valley. Still when one looks at the brief time it existed this was the real beginnings of change. But we know so little and with Sabohl using his power to keep the history as he sees it, there's a great chance it will remain that way.

"Look again I didn't mean to spout off to you like this, but whatever your decision, to stay or to leave, it's up to you. Again I know that there's no way if what we, the group I represent, are being honest with you or not. I know I can stand here, well it's really not that easy to stand in these shelters, but you know what I mean, and tell you that we are here to learn, to help you establish this site, and still be lying. In fact everything I've just said could be a lie. So again with too little information, and too little time, both of you are left with making a life changing decision." He shook his head and smiled, "But as both of you know too well, that's life." He turned to leave stopped a moment before exiting and said, "I don't need an answer now, so think about it and when the two of you are sure come to us and let us know. Either way, stay or go, we'll back you." Taking a deep breath he steeled himself for the cold harsh weather outside of the shelter and exited leaving a fresh blast of frigid air behind as the flaps opened and closed.

Again both looked at each other and remained silent. Trehe had been quite passionate in what he had relayed to them, and what he said was very true of life. "Wow!" Was all that Kal could say.

CHAPTER NINE

SABOHL RETALIATES

Sabohl sat inside his study. It was warm and comfortable, but he didn't feel the comfort. Whoever this was that was attacking him they had beaten him at every move. He was not used to losing, and soon with his spies in place he would learn who was behind this, and when he did they would pay. He'd been too long on top not to know how to play the game, to find out who was behind this. Obviously it couldn't be those two naïve ones who, unknown to themselves, had located this most important site for him. All had gone just as everything in the past had up to a point in time. It appeared that once again he had won, and soon the accolades would be coming forth praising him and his efforts to advance their knowledge of the past. He had to admit that it had felt great to be back in the game, of taking advantage of those minor players. It had been a long time since such as this site had been found. And he had heard rumors that he was starting to lose his place, his position because he hadn't found anything new, hadn't advanced any new ideas, and appeared to be set in his ways, like that old bull herd beast who was beyond his prime still fighting off the younger to keep the right of breeding with the females that he ruled.

So when Kal had approached him with those questions he knew that here was a chance to prove his detractors wrong. Once again one of his students would provide a new site, new research, and conclusions – his conclusions of course. He knew, because of his experience that his conclusions were the only ones that mattered. No matter how logical, or how much the facts might have supported others out there, he ruthlessly suppressed both their theories and the ones presenting them. He had immediately put this Kal and his mate Jura under observation. Knowing that eventually they would slip up and reveal what he wanted to know. And if not then he would use his underworld connections to steal it. It didn't matter, as long, and in the end that he had the information and received due credit for the hard work, even if this hard work wasn't his own.

It was night and the soft glow from the candles created a room that was both cast in shadows where the light didn't reach, and yet at the same time comfortably lit, giving the feeling of warmth. He could hear the fire snapping and popping, and every once in a while the sound of water sizzling as a drop found its way down the chimney. There was a rain storm raging out in the night, but as well as his shelter was built he barely noticed. Again his anger seethed. *I'd better get myself under control. I know about my temper and if I release it, which has happened much too often lately, I could get careless, and that's something I cannot and will not do. Someone out there is beating me at what I do best. Well, so be it. But once I find out who this is, then we will see who wins in the end. This is only a skirmish in a small battle, and it's a battle I intend to win. So whoever you are, enjoy it for now. Because in the end I will have my victory, you can count on it.* He started to sip the wine that he had in the glass that was in his hand but noticed that the glass was empty. Sighing he got up went over to his supply and refilled the glass returned to his chair and sat heavily staring out at nothing, not even hearing the winds that were buffeting his shelter.

Tomorrow would be another day, and it was a day full of classes, so he wouldn't be able to devote any time to the problem before him. Besides, he had to maintain this front of the learned, the one who wanted to teach, to assist. It had worked well for most of his life, and he saw no reason to change now. It had given him all that he needed. He was the leader in his field, he could have female companionship whenever he needed it, but not the attachments that lesser males seemed to need. With his place of power it had brought him wealth, and with his contacts he controlled so much more than any realized. *Yes, so why change now?* Yet he felt restless, unsure, as for the first time in for as long as he could remember, it hadn't gone his way. Was he losing his touch, his ability to move, to out-think his opponents? He snorted at such a thought. Again this was only a minor setback, and soon he would counterattack and be on top once again.

After refilling his glass a second time he sat back down and again stared into the fire. He could feel his anger once again trying to control him, and he fought desperately to bring it under his iron control. If he didn't come up with something shortly, maybe this very night, then that thin veneer that marked him as one of the betters might just be destroyed – but, what to do? Yes, there had to be something that he could do to retaliate even if it was against his former student. He knew from his network that they were presently on that site that they had discovered, proving that they indeed were the discoverers and not he. Again from that same network he knew that there were others with them, so making a direct attack and blaming it on the many criminals that lived on the edges of society would prove to be impossible. And, from the ones who were monitoring the site, there were too many there, and the original place where there had been protection through that gap had been replaced making the site virtually untouchable. Even the archives spoke of this location being impregnable, and continually occupied, until abandoned when such places were no longer required. But there were other ways to defeat any enemy. This thought brought a smile to his face. Yes, definitely, there were other ways.

At this very moment a heavy blast of wind struck the shelter shaking it to its very foundation, snapping him briefly out of his thoughts, but at the same time a glimmer of an idea was forming. *Yes, yes, there are so many other ways of attacking while leaving no evidence behind that I am responsible.* He laughed, even though it was dark and the laughter had no humor in it. *This storm is perfect.* It would cover what he would do, and so very few would be out in such nasty weather, and with the rain falling as hard as it was, it would wash away any tracks that might be left making this appear to be an accident. Then once he had accomplished this he would head for the down side of the village pay for a female, and afterwards head back here, show up at the higher learned center and feign surprise that such a tragedy happened. After all, with all this wind and rain how could such a thing happen? With his mind made up and the anger still boiling just below the surface, again threatening to erupt, he got up from his chair, dressed in dark clothing appropriate for both the night, and the weather, gathered the materials he needed, and prepared to leave. This time he would do this himself, something that he hadn't done in a very long time – actually since he had attained his position as the leader in his area of study.

* * *

The two who were watching the shelter shivered when the last gust of cold wind struck. There just wasn't any place they could go to get completely out of this miserable storm. It would have been easy to abandon their post, since Sabohl rarely went out in such weather. Yet, from time to time he did, and because of this they stubbornly remained watching and waiting. Soon, others would relieve them and they could, at the time, get out of their wet clothing into something dry, and get warm before finding something a little strong to drink and head off to get some sleep. But until that time here they were. The one in charge turned to the other and said, "This is bad, and it just sucks. It would be so easy just to go and just say that we were here, but I know better. The moment we would do something like that would be the time he would decide to leave."

The other smiled, although it was a smile of misery, and just nodded in agreement. *Who'd be stupid enough to be out on a night like this?* He asked himself. Then he laughed quietly when he realized that he and the other was out on a night like this. "Yeah, it would be so much nicer if we could be out of this looking out instead of being in it." He shrugged before continuing, "But what can we do? He has beaten us time and time again over the cycle of the seasons. And as time has passed he's gotten only stronger and more cunning, holding on to his position with the tenacity of one of the old clan leaders. I guess what they say is true . . ."

"True?"

"Yeah", he laughed, even though it was a bitter one, "theories and ideas change within academia and science, one death at a time."

The leader thought about the statement and had to admit that it was very true. It seemed that even when something was presented with all the proper research and data to back it up, that if it went counter to the thinking of the time, this person would be belittled, black listed, and ostracized, and could even be destroyed. And, if later, much later usually, what he had originally presented had proven to be accurate, vindicating the person who had presented it originally, it was much too late. "I can't disagree with you. Not at all, I've seen it happen . . . hey, he's leaving, and dressed in really dark clothing. With the night like this, he's really going to be hard to follow. I wonder where the ole anarchism is heading now." With the cold and dampness that had become a part of them, all of this was forgotten as they set to follow Sabohl, and remain hidden.

Sabohl didn't head for the main thoroughfare through the village but immediately headed for the back trails to remain hidden from sight. That he was up to something was quite obvious, but what, was the question. With the lateness of the hour and the miserable storm there was little chance that any would be out and about, so why go this round-about way? All they could do was speculate, and follow. That he had a destination it was obvious, but from other times of following, this was not a common direction for him. Sabohl was keeping up a very fast pace making it more difficult for the ones who were following to remain hidden. Thank the gods for the storm and darkness. Without such they would have been discovered. Eventually Sabohl turned a corner around one of the many shelters and headed out into an open area. It became obvious that he was heading to the storage shelters.

With the winds blowing as hard as they were, driving the rain before it, so when it struck the raindrops felt like spikes, it hurt. Both of them stopped and watched as he disappeared into the storage shelters before moving across the open area between the shelters where business was carried on, and the shelters that were used for storage. The one looked over at the leader and asked, "What do we do? We can't follow him too far into this area, there's really no place that we can be out of sight."

Shaking his head the leader replied, "I don't know, I really don't know. Somehow we've got to figure what he's up to, and why he decided to come here." The leader looked around, even though there was little to see with it being as dark as it was. "Look let's slip in a little closer and get out of this wind. At least between a couple of the shelters we'll be out of most of it and maybe something will come to either of us as to how we can cover this." The other with him affirmed the thought and they carefully moved deeper into the storage shelters, trying to peer around them and locate Sabohl.

Even though he had been told the location by his spies, Sabohl, with the deep black of this stormy night, had problems in locating the one he wanted. And with the frustration of the failures of the near past his anger threated to break free once again and become a furious rage, uncontrollable until it burned itself out – taking its revenge on anything or anyone who happened to be near. He fought hard to maintain control, and stood there motionless as he fought this inner battle. Finally after who knew how much time, he had the anger under control once again, although he could tell that it would be easy to give in to it. Looking around the many shelters he finally located the one he was searching for, and with his strength and tools he brought with him, broke the hasp that kept other than the owners out. Once inside and out of the weather it was as if a weight had been lifted. By being out of the storm it was almost deafly silent. Well, it wouldn't matter as he was only going to be here for a short time and be gone.

From under his clothing he pulled a small candle and using the striker lit it. Then surveying the surrounding floors he began to spread lamp oil on many of the items within. Near a stack of flammable items he placed a small saucer filled with the lamp oil. And on this he floated another small, short candle. Then into this saucer he placed paper that would absorb most of the oil and trailed this paper over the sides. So with what he spread throughout the shelter and this timer, it would give him time to be away, but not too far because he wanted to see his handiwork. He repeated this in a couple of other locations, lighted the short candles, and exited, heading now in a different direction and not back to his personal shelter. When this succeeded he would celebrate. He smiled. *So you think you can beat me do you? Well, we will see about that.*

The two remained hidden behind one of the supply shelters watching for Sabohl when suddenly he reappeared and headed off in a different direction. There was a small open field that he was heading across, completely open, and even in this darkness the two would have to wait until he finished crossing or take a chance on being discovered. *Just what was he doing here?* They moved towards the last row so that they could continue to observe when the heard what sounded like a "whoomp". Turning towards the source of the sound they saw a fire's glow in one of the shelters. "Of the gods", exclaimed the leader. "The fool has set one of the shelters on fire. You continue to follow; I've got to get some help. If this fire gets out of hand, and with these winds we could easily lose all of these shelters. The only good thing out of this is that they aren't very close to the village. The bad is much of what the merchants own is here – now go!"

The other took off to continue to follow while the leader ran back to the center of the village and sounded the fire alarm, a bar of metal hanging from a chain with a striker. By the time, since it was the middle of the night, people began showing up the fire was quite visible and raging among the storage shelters. Quickly a fire team was organized and they began to attack the fire. But it had gotten a strong foothold and was now beginning to ignite the other shelters around the one that was burning. The winds were roaring and rain coming down in sheets, but the rain had little or no influence on the intensity of the raging fire. As the villagers fought desperately to put out the fire they found that either they were soaked by the pouring rain, or scorched by the heat from the fire. "We've got to knock some of the shelters down!" Someone yelled. "We've got to create a break or we're going to lose them all." There must have been close to a hundred shelters here, for which at least one third were presently either burning or about to burn. And as each new shelter exploded into flame, the heat and intensity of the fire increased to the point that no one could approach the flames. No one needed any light to see as the fire with its great yellow flames leaping high in the air lit the surrounding area in its yellow light turning the black of this stormy night into day. Soon shelters that were rows away from the head of the fire began to smoke and then burn. Even destroying rows of the shelters wouldn't work now as the sparks and coals being thrown into the air by the massive fire storm began to rain down on other shelters, and since all were constructed of wood, began to smolder and burn. It soon became obvious to the desperate villagers that there would be nothing they could do but watch as the roaring ever increasing beast of flames spread beyond anything they could do.

How'd it start? What and maybe who was responsible? In the chaos from the first alarm to the present no one knew who had rung the alarm, but it hadn't been soon enough. And standing there in awe as they were watching the power of the flames continued to destroy. It was no surprise to them that their ancient ancestors had assigned a god to this force of nature. From the intensity of the fire and the heat being generated they were forced back away from the destruction, and with trepidation watched as, for some, their life work was disappearing before their eyes. Many would be wiped out by this, others would recover, but it would be many cycles of the seasons before the village could be as strong as it had been before this devastating fire. With shoulders slumped and depression setting in they watched helplessly as shelter upon shelter collapsed into flaming ashes.

* * *

Once away from his handiwork Sabohl turned and watched for a short time before heading deeper into poorer side of the village. He needed a female to finish out this evening; one he felt was going to be quite successful in his revenge against Kal and Jura, and the unknown ones that seemed to be behind them. He heard the fire alarm and was surprised that it was discovered this quickly. *Oh well, probably some passersby.* So he turned once again and looked towards the storage shelters and even though he couldn't directly see them, he could see the yellow glow reflecting off the low cloud cover. He laughed quietly. *Success! Let them try and stop me. Let them try and topple me from my position!* He then continued his interrupted journey and headed down towards one of the smaller rivers that flowed on the edge of the village. Here was where the females who sold their bodies to any male were located. And for either a short time or for the night a male could have a female companion. It came down to what one was willing to pay. Yet when he reached the entrance he was barred from entering. "What's this?" He demanded.

"Sorry about this sir, but you have been banned from this establishment, and are not to be allowed inside or to be with any of the females who work here."

Sabohl could feel the anger rising again. With the fire he had just set some of it had abated, but now with this new aggravation it threatened to engulf him once again. "What do you mean barred?" He bellowed.

Without batting an eye the guard, bouncer really, stated, "It seems that you were overly rough with one of the females last time you were here, and she was unable to work for almost a full season. And while your coinage is good your behavior is not. None of these females who work here will have anything to do with you or your ways. So I suggest that you leave and not return."

"And if I decide that I don't want to leave, what can you do about it?" Sabohl asked angrily.

"Then we will make you find reasons to leave. There are more here than just me, and if necessary all of us will be sure that you leave, and, I might add, we will not be gentle. Consider it a reminder that roughing up can work both ways. Plus it would be easy to get word out about your activities down here. And while this is something that is known about, this place here, it really is never mentioned in polite conversation, nor is the males who use our services ever identified, *unless there are problems* – if you get my drift. So please just move along and nothing need to be said, or acted upon."

Taking a deep breath and barely able to keep his rage under control Sabohl smiled, although it was quite forced. "Okay, you're point is taken. I'll quietly take my leave." He turned and with the blind rage filling him, headed in a direction that he had never been, deeper into the poorer and bad side that all villages seemed to have.

From the shadows the second watched and listened to all that had transpired, and all he could do was shake his head and continue to follow. But where Sabohl was heading wasn't safe for anyone. Especially one of his rank. But he couldn't do anything about it other than follow, keep his notes, and eventually tie in with the leader of his team, who at this moment, was quite involved with that conflagration that Sabohl had caused. And if Sabohl got into trouble what could he do about it? Nothing, nothing at all. Heck, he would be putting his own life in danger by following him into this area. So with all the stealth he could manage he continued to follow and remain hidden from all. And shortly what he feared began to develop as he lengthened his distance. He could see a small group begin to gather and follow Sabohl, who appeared to be completely unaware of the danger he was in or even that he had gone in the wrong direction.

* * *

With this refusal to be allowed inside Sabohl's anger began to get the best of him. Yet, through this fog he realized that he needed to leave before he really did something stupid and forever get banned from this place. So he stomped off not looking at all as to where he was going or the danger he was putting himself into. Because he had strong contacts with the underworld, and as far as he was concerned, was safe anywhere he wanted to go, he headed out. Although in saner moments he knew better. If he wanted to be honest the group he dealt with was only one of the many who lived in the shadows of society. But with his anger in control he really was being careless. He didn't notice when he had turned in the wrong direction and now was heading into a part of the village that even the group he contacted would stay away. He just needed to push through and let his anger burn out and get back in control. At least he had been successful in extracting revenge earlier this evening. Suddenly he realized that his surroundings were strange to him, and he looked around and could see shadowy figures converging on him as if he was prey and they were the carnivores.

His mind flashed danger, danger, danger, but it was too late. With the fires he had set all the village would be there, and here where he presently was, would be no help. He was completely on his own. Could he talk his way out of it, or would he have to fight? In a sense the latter part of this question brought a grim smile to his face. With his mood tonight fighting might be the very thing. Again, reason pushed its way into his mind as he knew that there was no way that he by himself would be able to overcome the size of this gang. He stopped and searched his surroundings for a place that he could better defend himself and allow these to only approach from the front making it more difficult for them to attack. Yet, at the same time, he needed a direction available that would allow him to escape if the opportunity presented itself. He realized that he was still close to the river, and there was an old dock, rotting, unused, and falling apart making it an ideal place to protect himself. If it became too hard to defend then he had the river to jump into, and with the darkness of the area he would be unseen once he was in the water. Yes with this storm raging it would be dangerously cold, a raging torrent, but the danger just about to approach him was greater. Quickly he picked up his pace and feinted away from his planned point and then picked up his pace even more and cut to the old dock, and headed out towards the end being careful to keep his balance as it swayed under his feet making him realize that the dock was in worse shape than he first thought. Looking around in the dim reflected light he could see that there was debris and trash scattered all over the place. There seemed to be a few stacked empty shipping containers which further narrowed the approach. He hoped that because of the instability of this old dock, the stacks of trash, debris, and old containers that it would further his advantage making this gang have to approach much more carefully than they had planned.

* * *

The one who was following looked at the movements that Sabohl was making and at first it didn't make any sense to him. It was obvious that he was now aware that there was a gang of thugs closing in on him, but it had been too late to avoid a confrontation. As he watched he saw Sabohl appear to head in one direction to suddenly dodge and head out on the old dock. *Why'd he do that?* It didn't make sense, but it must to Sabohl. He saw the old dock sway a little, and knew that it was in very bad shape – but what to do, what to do? He, by himself couldn't help, there were just too many of them. And besides his orders were clear – Sabohl could never learn that he was under constant observation, and was followed everywhere he went, and if he revealed himself, then as smart as Sabohl was it wouldn't take him long to figure it out. So, with a helplessness of events beyond his control, he remained hidden and watched as everything slowly unfolded before his eyes.

* * *

As the villagers watched, the final shelters that were on the edge were consumed by the roaring conflagration. And slowly with nothing left to burn the flames began to slow in their rage, and now the storm with the winds and rain became, once again, the dominant force, slowly overcoming the flames. Now instead of the roar of the fire, there was a replacing sound of hissing as the rains finished what the fires had begun. With most of the village turned out to attempt to suppress the fire they stood there numb and in silence at the destruction that lay before them. Too much in shock to even think, or contemplate how such a thing had started, or the results of that fire, or what the true loss had been, at this moment. Then, slowly, since there was nothing left to do, they broke up and headed back to their personal shelters, defeated by what they had just witnessed. Tomorrow they would return and see if anything, anything at all could be recovered. Although from what they had witnessed, and how they were feeling at this very moment, it was very doubtful.

At least they could be thankful that these particular shelters were not very close to where they actually lived. Had it been, then there could have been many deaths, as the fire tore through their places of work and personal shelters, leaving nothing but the ashes of the village. If that had happened would they rebuild on top of the ashes of their previous shelters, or would they have moved? That was an unknown. It would have been something that would have been a hard choice for any of them to make – something that none of them had ever contemplated. It probably would have come down to how many would have died and who had survived. By the fire starting when it did, it easily could have caught the whole village sleeping, and with no warning or no time, the deaths could have been very high. So with these thoughts they quietly returned, smelling of smoke, and covered in soot. Eventually leaving only one or two who continued to stare unbelieving at what they had witnessed.

One of these slowly withdrew and was out of sight. He had been the one who had sounded the alarm, and now needed to find the one who had continued to follow Sabohl. But with the storm still raging, and only a general idea as to direction, he really had no idea. At least he could head to one of the planned rendezvous points that had been set up for this side of the village. There were a number of these marked for the teams throughout the village and surrounding area, and since he had seen them head in the direction he was presently going, he decided to head to the closest one. It was a cold depressing night. With what had transpired, and what he had witnessed, it made it so much more so – but what to do? It was obvious that they knew who had started the fire. Well, sort of. Since they never really witnessed him setting the fire, it could have been coincidence after all. But he suspected that there was a connection between Sabohl and what had happened here. Yet, one didn't just go and accuse one of the most important learned of such crimes. Shaking his head, he realized that there was no proof, and if they came forward, they could be accused of starting the fire also. And how could they explain it away? It angered him that Sabohl was going to get away with another one.

He finally reached one of the meeting places and began to pace. The other hadn't arrived yet. He wondered what was transpiring, but there was no way to know. If truth be told he could be waiting at the wrong place, since it was likely that Sabohl had just circled around and headed back to his personal shelter. And with that thought he wondered if maybe he should head back there, but decided against it and wait a little longer. If he didn't show up soon he'd head out over that way and see if that had happened. And with that decision the time continued to drag by slowly without any change. So he decided to head over to Sabohl's shelter and see if indeed the other was there. Unfortunately it was completely on the other side of the village and would take him some time to reach there. So before leaving in the dim light he left a brief, very wet note that stated for him to wait here if he came to this meeting point. Taking a deep breath and shaking off a shiver he headed out rapidly to see if they had returned. Yet, when he arrived back at the place where they would observe Sabohl's shelter no one was there and the shelter was dark. *So they hadn't returned. Where'd they go? And where are they?* He laughed a bitter laugh, if he knew that he wouldn't be running around like this on this stormy, cold, very wet night.

He waited what he considered was a reasonable amount of time and when no one showed, he headed back to the other rendezvous point, taking his time to check on other locations as he headed back across the village. Soon he and his assistant would be relieved and the dawn couldn't be far away. But with this storm he suspected that it would require the suns rising to lighten the area well enough to know that it was dawn. At each point he checked he came up empty and eventually returned to his starting point after leaving the devastation left by the fire. Again back, he was alone. With no idea of what to do or where to go, he was becoming alarmed. Normally they were to stay together, but tonight there were extraordinary circumstances that had required them to split up. Now he was here with not a clue as to what had transpired after they became separated. Shrugging inwardly, at this moment there was very little he could do but wait.

The only advantage to this location lay in the fact that it was out of the way, and there was very little chance that one of the villagers would come by and start asking questions. So he waited, hoping that his partner would show, and in what seemed much too long he could finally see someone approaching his location, and once he was close enough in the uncertain light, he recognized his partner by his walk and waited as he slowly, cautiously approached this meeting place. He wanted to shout out, "What has happened?" But held this in check, and when the one who had followed Sabohl had joined him, he found that this one had an odd look about him. So he waited, and found that he didn't have to wait long as his assistant took a very deep breath, shuddered a little, leaned back against one of the stacks of unused lumber and shook his head.

"I think Sabohl is dead." He whispered.

Shocked at what he had just said, the leader asked, "What? Are you sure? What happened?"

"Look, when I left you and followed Sabohl he headed for that shelter down by the river where females sell their favors. It seems that once he had accomplished what he had set out to do he was going to celebrate by taking a female. But he was denied access. From what I could gather, in a previous visit he had roughed up one of the females, and now is barred. This set him off and it was obvious that he was furious, because he took off in the wrong direction. I think if he had been in control of himself at this point he would have just headed back to his shelter and leave it at what he had already done.

"I've heard word that the whole storage complex was destroyed, is that right?"

In a subdued voice the leader answered, saying, "Yes, the whole thing. Once that first shelter's roof collapsed the winds drove the fire into the rest of them. By the time anybody could get there, even though we tried, there really wasn't much that we could do but watch as it burned."

"Then this has become a very bad night." He paused, as he absorbed this information, and sighed a bit. "This is going to destroy many of the businesses here. I guess we can be considered lucky that it didn't get into the living shelters."

Nodding in agreement, the leader said, "Very lucky indeed. Anyway continue on if you would."

"Oh, yeah, I guess that would be a good idea." He looked out over the leader's shoulder and paused as he stared out into the distance. While this wasn't the meeting point where they would change shifts it was the secondary location. "I think that our replacements are arriving."

Turning around and looking in the direction that the other had been looking he saw two figures materializing out of the darkness – dawn must be close. They waited until the two arrived and the leader of the night shift then signaled him to continue.

"Okay. Anyway, like I said, he must have been angry because instead of heading back in a safe direction he went deeper into part of the village where it is very dangerous. There are a number of gangs, much theft and murder, and who knows what else, since good people just stay away – especially if they want to come out alive. And you know, the deeper you go the worse it gets, and he continued to go deeper. I became worried not only for him, but for myself. Then, I really had hoped because of the time of the night, but it was a lost hope, one of those roaming gangs found him . . ."

"And they killed him right there before your eyes?" The leader asked.

"If it only had been that simple, no, and that's why I can only say I think he's dead."

The two that had just joined them had very questioning looks on their faces and the leader of this team asked, "Killed, who was killed?"

The one who had been following Sabohl said, "The one we have been assigned to follow and report on, you know Sabohl."

"He's dead?"

"I, think so, but let me finish, and I think you'll understand. When the gang showed up I didn't know what to do. Should I go in and help, should I stay and watch – that kind of thing. I realized that even with two of us there'd be no chance, and our orders are very clear. There must never be any contact between us and Sabohl. So I watched from a hidden place, deep in the shadows. I could see that Sabohl was still furious, but he seemed to realize his situation and began to look for a place that he could defend himself against a group this size. Personally I wouldn't have picked where he did, but when there is no time to really look one takes what seems to be convenient, and for him it was an old rotting dock. In a way it was a good choice forcing the attackers to come at him with the maximum of two at a time giving him some advantage in the fight.

"The leader of this gang yelled at him saying, 'Just give us your valuables and we might let you live.' At this point the rest of the gang laughed, immediately letting anyone who happened to be around that living past the next few moments was quite unlikely. Sabohl bellowed something back at them, and while I couldn't hear the words it incited the leader and the gang to go after him immediately. But with the restrictions only a couple could attack at a time and for a while Sabohl held his own. The problem was the dock. With all the bodies that was on it, and its poor condition it began to sway, throwing the ones fighting off balance. And during one of the shifts of the dock I saw Sabohl lose his balance and one of the attackers was able to stab him once. But at this point all this action was too much for the dock and it collapsed into the river taking half the gang with it and, of course, Sabohl.

"At this point the rest of the gang left quickly and began to head downstream to see if anybody had survived. But with this storm raging the river was a maelstrom of boiling water, tearing downstream at a terrific rate. In fact from what little I could see it wouldn't be long before the river would go beyond its banks and begin to flood the lower areas." He shuddered for a moment before continuing. "I just don't know how anybody could survive that even if they were strong swimmers and were in great shape. While Sabohl is big and strong, he had been stabbed just before the dock went into the water. No, I don't know how bad, and because of the bad light, I don't know if he was able to grab some of the flotsam or other debris that was both from the disintegrating dock and what was already in the river or whether he was able to get back ashore. So I can only assume, at this point that he drowned. But, I have no proof, none at all. And with the speed of that water his body wouldn't even wash up on the banks until a very long way away from here, if ever."

The other three were silent for a while, and the leader of the relief asked, "What should we do now? I mean there's no one to know what happened, or where Sabohl is, or even if he's alive."

The leader of the night team thought a moment, taking a deep tired breath since this last night had been very stressful and very eventful. "Look, if he survived then somehow he'll return to his shelter, so I guess the best thing would be for the two of you to stake out his place and see if he does return. After we get some sleep we'll put together a report and get it off to the history board or society leaders and after that it's in their hands as to what happens." Again pausing because he could feel the weariness pressing in on him now, and it was becoming harder to concentrate let alone think, "Look, I think that this is out of our hands and all we can do is watch his old haunts and see what happens. I don't know what else we can do."

CHAPTER TEN

FROM SITE TO HOME

Storm after storm rolled in on the site and it was another 9-day before they finally broke, and with the morning light it was clear, calm, and very cold. Jura and Kal were thankful to finally be able to leave their portable shelter into the cold crisp air. With their breathing producing great clouds of steam, it had become obvious to all that this was a horrible place to spend the Season of Cold, and probably one of the main reasons for its abandonment once the skirmishes and fighting among the tribes and clans became a thing of the past. There were so many other places to live that could provide more comfort. Still as they stood outside in the frigid air it wasn't long before they were shivering and retreated briefly back inside where the fire kept it warm. "I must admit", Jura said, "that I was looking forward to getting out of this shelter and into some fresh air. But after doing just that, well, here we are back inside." She laughed and just shook her head. I don't know which is worse, the raging storms that we've just experienced, or seeing the suns shining and finding that it's so cold that we can't even stay out and enjoy it."

"Yeah, I have to agree. Maybe as the day moves a little it will get a little warmer, and if we stay out of that icy wind and find a sheltered area maybe we can soak up a little of that sunlight, and I'm all for soaking up lots of that right now." They heard the crunching of the snow which meant that someone was heading their way. So both of them opened the flap and headed back out to see who it was and found Trehe approaching. "Good day to the two of you. It's so nice to see that there are still two suns in the sky. After this last series of storms I began to wonder."

The two smiled and Jura said, "Yeah, you and me both. But once the suns did come out I didn't think it would be this cold." She was stomping her feet as the cold from the frozen ground began to penetrate her footwear. Then that icy breeze reached out of them and they involuntarily shivered. "Boy that wind is cold!"

"So what brings you our way this day?" Kal asked.

"First off to make sure you were okay. With those storms raging as they were nobody was out and about to check on each other, and secondly to let you know that we will be expecting someone to show up today and bring us up to date on what has been happening away from this isolated site. I think when these last storms arrived that whatever resistance that may have been camping outside this place probably gave up and headed for warmer grounds. I know I would have if I could. This place is just miserable this time in the cycle of seasons. All I have to say is that our ancestors, and of course yours, since they were the ones who occupied this site, had to be hardy people. Between the fighting, and health issues that would have existed because of improper things like hygiene and such, creating disease, and then with these storms brewing as often and as hard as they seem, it would force them to remain inside giving a chance for clans to be wiped out with some disease, and if I remember right that almost happened here. And now I can more appreciate and understand why they left once they could. Great place to defend, almost impossible to attack, but a really really bad place to live for almost everything else. Look, both of you are shivering, not that I'm not very far from it myself. We have a bonfire going and some hot drinks let's get over there and enjoy the heat of both the fire, some nice conversation, and grab one of the cups so that it will warm our hands as well as our insides."

Jura smiled, and said, "You don't have to ask twice, lead on please as that just sounds wonderful." Together the three of them went across the site heading towards another part of the rock face that was the back defense for the site when people had lived here, and as they approached, Jura and Kal could see all the rest standing around the fire taking advantage of the heat. It also became obvious that the location of this fire was out of the winds which helped. They could see the welcoming smiles as they joined the rest of the team that was here. One of the members, she didn't remember what his name was said, "Ah to actually see sunlight, and enjoy the warmth, even if it is this fire, and to be able to actually get out, what a relief."

She couldn't disagree with that statement. She had to admit that with all the time that they had spent inside their portable shelter with the storms raging one after another and with little or no break between them she, and she knew that Kal also, had been going crazy. She had heard it called shelter sickness, but until now had never experienced it personally. Well, now she had and wanted no part of it. She smiled as she faced the roaring fire putting out her hands and feeling the heat as the clothing she was wearing began to warm and transfer heat to her body. The only problem with these fires was that one could only warm one side at a time, leaving the other side cold and miserable. So, one played the game of continually rotating different sides to the fire, hoping that eventually one would get comfortable and warm. "So how did all of you fare? I mean we are all living in small places and those storms just wouldn't end. I was going stir crazy and time seemed to drag. And the continual winds, the howling it set up as it came roaring out of the lower places was deafening. Then it seemed to always be gray and at times hard to see the difference between night and day it was so dark out. Being from a farm I felt that none of this would be an issue, but I was wrong."

This brought a bit of laughter from the others gathered around the fire. And she could see a lot of nodding showing agreement in her assessment of situation. One of the other females who were here with her mate said, "You surely have that right. I've been on a few of these sites with my mate and figured that this one would be no different, but . . . but most of the time we've only worked the sites during the Season of Green, or Season of Heat, wrapping up during the Season of Falling and not being around when the storms really begin to roll in. I have to admit I was ready to run outside in those storms screaming bloody murder. That shelter where we're staying seemed to be closing in on me and kept getting smaller and smaller." Again this comment brought a chuckle from the rest as similar sentiments seemed to be the way.

Trehe then commented, "If things go well we should have supplies arriving later today. And on a side note, I wonder how our watchers have fared? Guess we'll know later once our supplies arrive. I was beginning to worry that we'd run out with the way these storms had continued unabated. I have to admit that it will be nice to get both the supplies, since we are running out of just about everything, and updates." Here he paused for a moment let out a deep breath and said, "With the size of this group we go through a lot of food, and, of course, the second and probably more important part, to find out what has been happening in the rest of the world. That's always the problem when we work these sites, we have no idea what's happening at all, and when we do get updated it's already old news – of course not as old as what we are working on at the time." This elicited additional laughter since most of the ones here had worked together a number of times in the past on other ancient sites.

* * *

It was working towards evening and the needed supplies had yet to arrive. But then again because of the severe weather that had just passed it was no surprise. They had briefly checked the camp of their watchers and had found it abandoned. So, for now, they were alone. They figured that the storms had driven them out. And here again there was no surprise since the watchers were in the open with little to protect them from the storms. So a couple of the team stood watch where they could see down into the valley that led into the grasslands. Eventually, as dusk approached they signaled that the supplies would be arriving at dark as they could see them approaching, but with the distance still to go it could easily be very dark. At least tonight the major moon would be casting light making it easier to see. The ones watching then built a large fire to signal the approaching supply train that they had been sighted and expected.

As the night approached the rest of the team joined the two and all began to watch the progress as the supply train was climbing the last portion and then arrive at the flat area. At this point Trehe approached the leader and they embraced. "It is well that you have made it." Trehe stated.

"I cannot agree more. The storms were delaying us much too long, and I, we were worried that things would have been bad here. I know that there's always an emergency cache of food, but that can only last so long, and we are already a 9-day behind because of the weather. So with what we normally bring we've added additional to resupply that emergency cache. Hey, it's cold out here, so shall we continue on in to your camp, or are we going to just stay here all night?"

Laughing Trehe said, "Oh I thought we could just stay here. Of course, of course, let's get into the camp. The ones who have the cooking chores have been busy, although what we have will be pretty bland, since we have run out of any variety and were getting pretty deep into those emergency supplies. And as you know what is there is stuff that is hardy and keeps one going, but has never been the best tasting stuff around." He swept his arms in a welcoming way, and asked, "Shall we go then?"

* * *

The two of them had packed hurriedly since the news that had been brought by the suppliers had relayed the incidents in High·Trail. Their supply shelter would have been one of those that had been destroyed, and with no word directly to them they really had no idea what kind of loss they faced. At least the bakery was part of a larger operation, so recovering would be easier for them. But with the total loss of everything that had been in those shelters others had not been so lucky, and this would have an effect on their business for some time to come. And once down and away from the dig site and back on the main trails it would take them at least another couple of 9-days to return to their home in High Trail. The Season of Cold was still raging but the Season of Green would be arriving soon, even though from the ferocity of the storms it would be hard to believe.

At least, as they dropped down in altitude and headed south, the snow and icy winds were changing to rain making the main trail and road a muddy mess, but still better than the icy cold. Yes, where the road was more traveled it had been graveled, but not much more than that. So it was subject to the soils that lay underneath. And much of that was a red sticky clay that the gravel sank into and it then stuck to one's footwear causing one to have to stop periodically and scrap it off. Two days earlier they had split with the supply team as it headed north towards that same village that the two had stayed in when they were searching for the old clan home. Now night was approaching and they were not close to any of the villages that existed along the road. So looking for a place to spend the night they left the road and headed east towards a small grove of trees that at least promised some protection from the winds that were chilling them.

The clouds hung low and a heavy cold mist was falling obscuring the distance, covering them with a wet gloomy depressing landscape. Both were wet and miserable and quite happy to call it a day, but again had wished they could have made it to a village and find a place to stay for the night that was out of the weather. But the gods hadn't favored them that way so here they were searching for a campsite as dusk approached. Kal turning to Jura said, "I had hoped, but I guess because we are still so far out that the villages are more than a day apart. If the farms and such aren't around there'd be very little to support a village, since travelers in either direction are light, and certainly not enough to keep a small village going." Taking a deep breath and looking around he could see that the trees were further away than they had expected, but at this moment they were finally approaching them.

Jura, shivering a little when the winds struck her, just nodded her head. She was more than ready to call it a day. When they had started, the skies had promised this mist, and after they had started, it had begun and refused to let up, and from the look of the clouds would be continuing through at least this night. As they got closer to the trees she saw that they had grown close to a small hill and off of that hill ran a very small stream. Still by not really knowing the area she had no idea if it ran all the time or was dry during the Season of Heat. Yet the way the area was put together it appeared to form a small bowl with the exit for both them and the stream facing towards the road. "I'm ready for a fire, some real heat, and some hot food. Originally I was thinking that we could forgo the temporary shelter, but now I want to get out of this, dry my wet clothes and get into something that is dry. I'm tired of being drenched to the skin."

He nodded in agreement as they arrived at the trees. And once there could see that others in the past had used the area for the same purpose, as there were a couple of fire rings and ashes from long dead fires. The trees provided plenty of dead wood, so fuels to maintain their fire wouldn't be a problem. Looking over the area they decided to build the fire in one of the pits that hid the fire's reflection from the trail. While they were armed with their long knives and staffs, and felt safe, it was better not to advertise their location. They were still isolated enough that they could depend on help from no one, and after spending so much time with the size of the team they had left; they had become comfortable with all those additional bodies around. They quickly set up camp and staked out their pack beast so that he could get both graze and reach water, with the two of them between the entrance and where the pack beast was located. After the portable shelter had been erected she unpacked the cooking gear, and began to put their sleeping sacks together while he went out and gathered wood for the fire. After the fourth trip he felt he had enough for their needs and to maintain a small fire all night to help keep away any of the wild beasts who might be curious.

He then built a fire, even though it was a bit difficult with nothing but wet wood to work with. Fortunately, from all the time that they had spent in the outback, they always carried dry tinder and small materials to get a small fire going. Still even with this help the dampness of the wood made it a very slow process with much smoke, hissing, popping, and spitting, as the small fire fought to overcome the moisture trapped in the wood. Looking out from inside of the portable shelter Jura said, "Lots of smoke and steam, no heat, and barely a fire."

"Yeah, ain't it true, and I've got to stay on top of it or this wet wood could put it out. This heavy mist isn't helping either. I guess once I get it going we'll stack the wood I brought over here close by so that the heat can dry it out and make this easier." As he continued to work on the fire a large gust of wind entered the bowl, swirling around and spreading the burning tinder for a few moments, and briefly extinguished the fire. And while they were just outside the trees great drops of very cold water still fell on him, making him shiver. "I guess the wind and storm doesn't like the idea of us building a fire here," he commented as he went back to the chore once again. Fortunately there was a very small bed of coals forming from his fire starting materials and soon had a weak fire going once again. In what seemed like forever he finally had a roaring fire going and for both of them steam was now coming off their wet clothes, slowly overcoming the additional moisture that the mist provided. "Oh, does that ever feel good," Kal commented.

She smiled although it was forced. "Yeah it really does. The way this day has gone I felt that I would never be warm or dry again, and the way that fire refused to burn I was beginning to think that we'd have a cold wet camp tonight."

"Well, I guess we could have gotten real close and let our body heat warm us," he said half in jest. Seeing no humor in her eyes he shrugged. "I guess we better get to cooking a meal so that we can get something to eat other than cold trail rations."

"Again, you're not going to get me to argue. Right now anything hot, this fire, the food, and even you dear one is welcome." She smiled at him even though it was a tired one. She would be happy when they finally were back in their own bed, and shelter.

It was almost full dark and they huddled close to their fire trying to keep warm in the heavy mist. The heat at least kept them semi dry, but if the storm decided to change its mind and go to full rain then cold or not they would have to retreat inside of their portable shelter. As they stared into the fire, which for any who lived in the wilds knew was wrong, since it destroyed your night vision, they were half asleep. But, at this point, both were weary from the cold nights on the site and the time on the road. Unfortunately they were still quite a few days away home. It was then when both jumped when someone out in the darkness hailed them, "Yo' fire!" They looked at each other and then out in the darkness and Jura moved into the portable shelter and both withdrew their long knives not knowing who could be out there. Then in the way of their time Kal answered, "Come and set", then he added, "But come friendly."

This brought a chuckle from the unknown individual who within a few moments approached their fire, and to their surprise was riding a pack beast. Once in the light of the fire he climbed down. Again he chuckled when he saw their disbelief. "Get that a lot when others see me do this. I'm really surprised that others hadn't thought about it. After all we've trained our pack beasts to carry our supplies, why not us also? Anyway, you'll not have to worry about any others I always travel alone." He looked at their camp with a practiced eye and smiled. "Well set up, defensible, and not visible from the trail – good, good."

"If what you just said is true, how'd you find our camp?" Kal asked.

"Oh, I've spent a night or two here, and because of a delay I got here later than planned, and was actually surprised to find this place being used. Not many are around here this time of the seasons – too miserable." He squatted down put his hands to the fire and smiled once again. "I really wasn't looking forward to getting my camp set up in the dark, and with it as wet as it is, to get a fire going. But imagine my surprise when I found one already burning – can make one right curious." He leaned back and sat cross-legged and continued. "Yeah, yeah, I know it goes both ways."

They looked at him and guessed that he had to be twice their age, and was dressed in rough handmade clothing. He looked as if he belonged to the hills and grasslands, as if he was as much a part of them as they were of him. "Ah, I thought the two of you looked familiar."

"Familiar, have you seen us before?" Jura asked from just inside of the portable shelter. "I know that we've never seen you."

He then laughed a full deep laugh and said, "I'm never seen unless I want to be." He then leaned forward before continuing. "You're the two that has been traipsing out here in the wild lands, the outback. Lookin' for something say I, and unknown to you others who were watching what you were doing and where you were goin', with not a hint that you had that they were there. Well, I said to myself, this place is gettin' crowded so maybe it's time to head somewhere else. But I was curious. After all there hadn't been anybody in those foothills that I could remember, other than a traveler now and then. And you were lookin' for something – it was obvious. So I decided that since there wasn't much happening anyway I'd stay and watch, and see what this was all about. Had to admit with everybody that seemed to be there it was almost too much for me. You see I'm a loner and prefer it that way. Don't like people. Oh I can take them now and then, but eventually I have to get back and away, live off the land, and enjoy the solitude. Villages and such are just too noisy for me. So I'm happy with just my beast and this world around us here." At this point he took a deep breath and shut up.

Jura and Kal looked once again at each other and then at this stranger, with Kal stating. "You say you were watching us, and those others, and nobody saw you at all – that's hard to believe."

Again he laughed. "Did ya' see the ones who were following you all the time you were searching? And to think that not only were they watching you but another group were watching both you and this other. All I could do was shake my head, and you were none the wiser about any of this. And both of those groups were clumsy, thinking that they were good at what they were doing. By the gods I could have come into both of their camps and stole them blind and they'd been none the wiser. Thought about going in and shifting things around a bit, just to mess with their minds, but it was more fun to watch all of you stumble about thinking that you were alone and were good at living out here." He again leaned forward and said, "Look, I don't know about you, but my stomach thinks my throat has been cut and I have a few items I can add to the meal so let's continue our conversation after we eat something. Besides I need to take care of her, my beast. Mind of I stake her over by yours. That way they'll have a little companionship. After all they originally were from those wild herd beasts and are used to company, other than you and me."

Silent for a moment after this one relayed to them what they had been doing for the last cycle of the seasons, Kal had to admit that they had thought the two of them were alone, but it had proven otherwise, and here was someone who thought it was a joke watching all three groups move through the wilderness. "Sure," Kal said, "It's okay, and what you just said is true. I know our beasts originally were of the wild herds, but that was a very long time ago. And . . . yes I guess you can join us, since you've almost invited yourself anyway. Besides it is a very miserable night and some additional company can't hurt."

Again this stranger laughed, "Okay then, it's settled. I'll go take care of the ol' female and be back before you can get the pot on the coals." At this point he jumped up and was out of sight into the darkness almost instantly.

Jura turned to Kal and whispered, "He really moves fast and is very quiet. I've the feeling that if he had wanted to do us harm that it would have been very easy, and we'd be none the wiser."

What could he say, she stated it so well. "Yeah, but maybe this is a good thing. At least with another in camp it would be less likely that we'd be attacked by bandits or such."

With a large smile on his face the stranger reentered their camp saying, "Ah talking about me are we. Not that I can blame you. But you have nothing to worry about me. In fact before you move out in the morning I'll be gone and you'll wonder if I was ever here. Mark my words, I rarely reveal myself to anyone, but I have to admit you've left me curious, and I felt that this was a good chance to maybe get that curiosity answered."

"Why would you be curious? We were just out and about searching for some ancient site, that's all, and we aren't the only ones to have done that." Kal paused, looked over at Jura and then back at the stranger, "Nothing unusual about that."

"True, true, and if it had continued to be just the two of you I probably would have watched a while, and got bored and then moved on. But when these others were out there too and everybody following everybody it becomes more of a puzzle. Now I like puzzles and solving them. This wild world is full of them and they change all the time keeping me on my toes. Make a mistake out here and you're dead, just that simple."

"That's probably true. And I guarantee that we were quite unaware of the others until we saw them following us when we were higher than they were and we caught them in the open." Here Kal paused again wondering if he should say more, and decided while he was beginning to like this stranger he really didn't know anything about him and it was still important to keep it quiet. Even though there was a possibility that Sabohl was dead, knowing him, there was just as much of a chance that he was still alive and biding his time. And, who knew, this stranger could easily be an agent of Sabohl's who used different tactics to get information. "I really don't know why. I just know that after we discovered them that they became more of a problem, and then that other one showed up and offered to help, and that's really it."

Waving an index finger at them the stranger again smiled and said, "Say what you want, but just from what I observed I know better. But stick to your story if you want. Besides what was so important about that place anyway? I've been there a few times — found some old pottery and places where fires had been built. Felt that this had been a place where some of our oldsters had lived temporarily. Nothing important though. Found other places with much the same stuff. Although, different stuff in the desolation. Tough dangerous area — no water, no game, no nothing but heat, dust and a land that looks the same no matter which way you enter; easy to get lost, easy to die, and none the wiser."

Suddenly interested both Kal and Jura leaned forward with Kal asking, "You've been to the desolation? It's a place that is shunned even today."

"Yeah, it's one of those puzzles. Yah see I haven't always been the wonderer that I've become. I went to the learning centers; I know our history, and the myths surrounding the desolation. And it was a puzzle . . ."

"And you like puzzles!" Jura blurted out.

Laughing and slapping his leg with his hand the stranger said, "Yup, you're learning, you're learning. So I've been working the edges, been deep into the Sacred Mountains too — mighty strange stuff up there, mighty strange. Did you know that there are caves everywhere, and that there are a few where no beasts will enter? Not only that but they seem to have their own heat, and once you're inside they seem both to glow with a soft light, and remain warm. Strange. Now I would have considered it something that didn't need second thoughts if there had been only one of them. If we want to be honest we have no idea what this place can create and it could just have been a freak, some peculiar combination that created it, but I found many of them. Still there was nothing, no other sign, so maybe they are from some of our ancient ancestors." He shrugged, "Who knows, not me. After all it's another . . ."

Again Jura interrupted saying, "Yes we know, it's another puzzle and you like puzzles."

Taking the plate of food that she handed to him he laughed again. "Yeah, and this one is probably one of the many I'll never solve — too cold up there for me. So those caves were welcome. But they are located high, nowhere close to the bottom. Nobody goes there — no reason really — just rock and trees and water and such. Nothing to keep one alive other than the herd beasts, but even most of them keeps to the lower areas. Did you know that there are places where there's boilin' water, and at times this hot water is blown high into the air —

quite a sight, but dangerous so very dangerous." He leaned forward and pointed to a massive scar on his left arm. "Learned the hard way, I did. That's from that hot water. Hurt like the dickens it did. So now I stay away from any of those things I find. My mom didn't raise any fools, and I learn quick. Of course, if one doesn't out here they aren't around very long – become food for the beasts."

Kal and Jura looked at each other and both thought what a strange person he was, but he had been to many of the places that they wanted to travel, but it was obvious that while he liked to talk that there was very little chance of getting his help, but would it be wrong not to ask? Kal taking a deep breath as they ate; actually needed to finish eating before the food got cold as it did in such weather. "Look you really seem to know a lot about the outback and we could use help. We are trying to locate a number of places that our ancestors frequented, and we only have vague clues."

Shaking his head the stranger said, "No, no not interested at all. Can't abide by people very long before I go crazy and have to be out on my own. And on that note, did you know that the Valley of the Gods is real and not a myth like they taught us in the learning centers?"

This got both of their attention immediately. "It's real?" Jura asked.

"Quite, but don't ask me where it is because I don't know."

"But you just said that it's a real place and the only way you could know that would be if you had gone there." Kal looked at him questioningly. "So which is it? Myth or real?"

"Oh it's real, but I found it accidental like. I was following my supper, trailing it and had gotten a shot off with my bow – thought I had hit it, but off it went so I continued to follow."

Staring out in the distance as if remembering he continued, "A very remote place, close to the desolation, very hilly, very rough, and again like the mountains a lot of caves in the hillsides. I seen it duck into this crack and wasn't sure if I wanted to follow or not, but I don't leave no wounded beast so I followed it into that crack and to my surprise there was a trail that twisted and turned through a very narrow canyon with the mountains, or foothills probably is more accurate, holding tight. Looking up I could see no way one could get atop these things other than the fliers, so didn't worry about something coming after me. After a while I finally emerged in what could be called a hidden oasis. Meadows, herd beasts, even a small lake and a waterfall. Many trees and from that lake a stream ran all the way across the area. It was shallow and easy to cross. I was frozen in awe for a few as I drank in what was here.

"Then things began to click in my mind. I mean I'm pretty good a remembering my learning. First off even though it is a peaceful place, it felt haunted. I felt like I was watched and continued to look around, but really there was very few places one could face danger. So carefully I explored, and like outside this place there were caves everywhere in the faces of the cliffs. And then I found it." He stopped to grab more food from his plate.

"Found what?" Jura asked.

After taking a few more bites and wiping his mouth with his sleeve he smiled and gave the look of conspiracy, lowering his voice he said, "The altar to the gods that is described in the myth. It's right there exactly where it said it was, and at the moment I knew I had to leave. I know that we don't believe in those gods anymore, but it explained the strangeness I was feeling and I got out there as fast as I could, and no I never saw that beast that I had targeted. It was like it just disappeared once it got inside that valley. Anyway, later, much later really, I decided that maybe I should go back and make sure I was right. But was never able to find that entrance, and I tried a number of times. Suspect that the valley keeps its secrets and knows who is close and who isn't. So if it doesn't want anybody to find it, the valley confuses the mind, changes the trails, makes one go in circles. After a while and too many attempts I gave up and haven't gone back, and I don't plan on it. After all the valley allowed me to see that it wasn't myth, but decided not to allow me back, and as such I decided that it could be dangerous if I continued to search.

"Look, like I said, I'll be gone before you are moving in the morning, but if you plan on pursuing these places then I might drop in on yah now and then, maybe point you in a particular direction, and don't ask me my name, I feel that when I'm out here that I have none as the beasts that live here. So when I'm here I'm nameless and prefer it that way. But don't you worry if you are out here, somewhere along the line, I'll know it, and be watchin'." He stood up handed his empty plate to Kal, stretched, and said, "Haven't done so much jawin' in a very long time, and I'm jawed out. So I'll be sayin' good night to the two of you. I'll be with my beast. We kind of protect each other, and thanks for the eatin' it was good, but I'm already feelin' a little crowded. Thanks for everything." And with that he faded into the darkness and was gone – leaving only the dirty plate as a sign that he had even been in their camp.

In the short time that he had been here he had passed on more information than they had before, and sat in awe and silence as they absorbed it all. "What do you think?" Kal asked.

"I really don't know. Almost feel he's kind of crazy. But there surely is a ring of truth to what he said. So maybe it's a smart kind of crazy. Guess we better clean up our camp and head for the sack. With all the time we've been on the road and trails I'm exhausted and could use a good night's sleep before we head out again.' She paused a moment and stared out into the night in the direction that the stranger had disappeared. "I wonder . . . I wonder if we'll see him again."

"It's obvious that he goes where he wants and is good at this life he has chosen, so I suspect that if he wants us to see him we will. He did say that he'd show up at our fires now and then, and I believe he will."

As he had so stated, when they rose in the morning he was gone, and no sign that he had ever been there. Both wondered it maybe they had dreamed him up. The night before had been miserable, wet, cold, and they had been very tired. Maybe the fire had hypnotized them, or they had drifted off to that twilight place where you're neither awake nor asleep but somewhere in-between. But when they looked they found their fire had been built back up and was burning brightly and a fresh pile of wood was stacked nearby. "How'd he pull that off without us hearing him?" Kal asked. He felt, while not the best of being outback, that the time that they had been doing this, his skills had sharpened, and even Jura had mentioned that he was much better at living in the outback. But this stranger had entered their camp while they were sleeping, brought new firewood in and stoked their campfire with them being none the wiser.

"Well, I guess we aren't as good as we thought, or we were so tired last night that we just didn't hear anything." Jura paused as she thought a little, "And that isn't a good thing." She took a deep breath and said, "I guess we might as well get something to eat, break our camp, and get down the trail. We still are a very long way away from where we need to go."

* * *

They had been back at least one 9-day and were still catching up on the news of what had happened. They found that the business had been lucky, far luckier than others who had lost everything in that conflagration. They had gone out to where the storage and supply shelters were located, and while much cleanup had been done it was still quite obvious from the complete destruction how hot this fire had been. One would have thought with the rain falling as hard as it was that the fire wouldn't have been able to do this, but it had. And the information they had received stated that the area remained hot for at least two 9-days, and it had rained most of that time. It had turned out that their supply shelter had been almost empty. The load of new supplies was late in arriving because of the rains. Had the supplies arrived on time then the shelter would have been filled to the top. Since, under the guidance and hard work of their foreman, Sara, the bakery continued to grow, and thusly why the use of one of these isolated shelters instead of the one that they had used in the past. That one was still being used but only to keep what they needed daily on hand and close by.

They had asked, of the group who had been keeping tabs on Sabohl, "how'd he get up here", since he had been living and working in the learning center back in Cross Trails. It was then relayed to them that after a cycle of the seasons Sabohl took a leave of absence stating he needed some time to refresh and had moved up here to High Trail, and maybe teach as a guest learned in High Trail. Because he did have a shelter here it would be no issue. And after he had refreshed his mind and spirit he would return. One of them stated, "We knew that the real reason was to be closer to the action, to be able to watch the two of you, and to be able to get his underground moving much faster . . . since it would take quite a while for a message from here to reach him down in Cross Trails, with the returning message doubling the time; much too much time as far as he was concerned. And we figured that had to be the reason, since immediately upon arriving he made contact with his network."

They then learned of that tragic night when the shelters burned, and how this team had followed him and once the fire had started, had to divide up with one staying with the fire to alert the village, and the other following Sabohl, the rejection, the bad choice of direction, the subsequent fight, the collapse of that old dock, and the disappearance of all who had been on that dock at the time it entered the swollen river. "So we have no proof as to whether Sabohl survived that plunge or not. With the waters flowing as strongly as they were, his body would have been carried far downstream and maybe all the way out to the ocean, since this one empties into it. Plus the one who had watched it all transpire swore that Sabohl had been stabbed at least once. But in that uncertain light he couldn't be sure."

"And there's been no sign of him?" Kal asked.

The others just shook their heads with one saying, "No, none at all. A few of the bodies washed up on the banks much further down, but none were Sabohl. So what happened is truly a mystery."

* * *

They remained throughout the remainder of the Season of Cold, and helped the village wherever they could. Nobody knew how it had happened, and again the secret team that had been keeping track of Sabohl had no direct proof that he was responsible so couldn't say anything. Because that storm that had been pummeling them at the time of the start of the fire, it was the reason for the lack of on-hand supplies. The storm had come out of the north, and the same storm had been responsible for the supply caravan delaying and finding shelter to wait it out. So the bakery was almost completely out of the necessities when the fire began. Yes there had been a number of sacks of different flours and grains, but most of what was there had been unusable, giving the appearance to any who happened to be inside that there was more there than there truthfully was.

Contacting the rest of the family, who by now had a number of bakeries throughout the region, being operated by his siblings and overseen by their parents, much information was available. Available simply because the supply caravans, the contracts with the farmers, and the many bakeries provided a continual flow of what was happening. And because of this the forward thinking of his parents the whole family was becoming quite wealthy. Yet, it was hard work, diligence, and the many hours of planning that made this possible. Also because of their growing importance and having such a great source of information, the family became sellers of information. This wasn't known to the general population, and was never to be revealed to the same, for obvious reasons. So when word was put out to be watching for Sabohl, there was confidence that if he had survived his ordeal that this would be known. Yet, all inquiries came back negative. So with no body, and no proof, everything hung in limbo. Still the general feeling was that he had died and his body washed out to sea.

When the word went out of the fire and loss, the Kaygor family and their many workers descended upon the village and offered assistance wherever they could. They cleaned up the burned shelters, helped the many families that had lost everything to the fires, and had only their personal shelter and little else to live in. Kal remembered his mother and father saying, "There's enough evil in this world, and as we continue to grow and become more successful, when something like this happens it is important that we help, that we provide what has been lost – all within our ability, of course. You see, a little charity now, can benefit not only the ones in desperate need, but can provide a favorable image of us and our business. It is easy to be greedy and turn one's back on others who have not been so blessed, to let one's ego get in the way of helping where it is needed, all because one is above such things, such suffering. Yet, were these same ones not customers, the same ones who were buying our products? Yes, we do provide a good product, and with care we've done well, and built our business. But, if we are not willing to give back, then, no matter how good we are, the quality of what we sell, in the end it will leave a bitter taste in the people's mouths and they will look elsewhere, and then we will be no more. No more because of our indifference, of our failure to show compassion to those who through no fault of their own need help. Yes, some will never recover from such as this, but others will. And all of them will remember, and remember who helped and who turned their backs. And while they may say nothing, those feelings will be there deep inside. And while it may not show immediately, eventually these who observed will use their abilities to move away from those who turned their backs.

"And if they, the ones who ignored the plight of their fellow villagers then run into dire straits, it will be then that they learn, the hard way, the cost. Most are willing to help where they can. But most do not have the means in which to do too much. Most of the time it comes down to their physical selves, and of this they give freely, and when it is over, whatever the emergency or loss, they will return to their lives, and go about the day-to-day thing never looking for rewards or even recognition for what they did. It takes families like ours who have prospered to be able to help beyond just the physical, and as long as we are in charge of this family it will always be that way. And, in the end, we hope that once we have left this world that it is the same with all of you."

It was a good philosophy to live by, and once the work had been done they all returned to their interrupted duties and lives, not looking for any personal reward, and it was time, since the seasons had moved forward, as they always do, to prepare for the next search. Word reaching them from the ancient site that they had discovered was promising, as the different areas of habitation had been mapped out, a burial site discovered, which was strange – not that there was a burial site discovered, but the method and markings used were so different. When they had inquired how so, the response simply stated, was, "These burials were vastly different from any that have been uncovered in the past, and most appeared to have been female skeletons, although there were some males. And because of the type of landscape, and weather all that remained were the skeletons. So no further answers could be drawn."

Both Jura and Kal discussed this, but by not being on the site they personally hadn't seen these burial sites, and the drawings really held no clue. Was it the beginning of another change in how their ancestors viewed life, or was it something else? "I don't know about you, but when we both started this search because of your family archives that were given to you, I thought this would be easy. Well," Jura paused a moment, "well, easier than it turned out to be. And who'd have thought that we'd become part of some larger intrigue, so naïve that's what we were."

"Yeah, really. Here I thought that I could get help from Sabohl, not realizing that it was one of the methods he used to increase his reputation, and to steal discoveries from his students and others in the field. May the gods look well upon him." He smiled and said, "Yeah I know, we don't believe in those gods anymore, but the saying has been with us for who knows how long."

CHAPTER ELEVEN

THE SEARCH

They decided that this time since they had a starting point, the old clan home, that they would attempt to discover the location where the warriors hunted every Season of the Green to replenish their meat and skins after the tough Season of Cold. Because it was here that the story in that archive really began. For generations they had traveled to the same general area, and while, at times there had been rare confrontations with other clans and tribes, this was the norm. If that one wounded herd beast hadn't darted into the desolation at that very moment when K'jor was the clan leader, then their history and how they lived presently could be far different.

Buoyed by the success of finding the original clan home, well the one mentioned in the records, they felt that it would take no more than a season to locate the clan's hunting grounds. But they were wrong. They worked the areas to the south of the clan home covering every space from the clan site to a number of the smaller villages and farms that existed in the great grasslands. While the location of the clan home was mapped out, and had assisted them in finding its location, there was no such thing for the hunting grounds. Only brief descriptions, and because it was common knowledge among all of the clan – the hunting grounds – nothing was written, other than it was a few days travel to the south, by a small stream, with trees, and close to the desolation to the west. While the description of the actual camp was very specific, time would have changed even that. Trees die; streams change direction or dry up, even the land itself changes. And with the description, by being as vague as to the actual location, it could have been thousands of places that all had similar lay-outs. If one wanted to be honest, the desolation ran the full length of the continent from the north at the Sacred Mountains to the southern foothills before meeting the seas to the west.

And the final direction, south, didn't help at all other than point them in the right direction. The warriors could have just as easily headed directly west until they made contact with the edge of the desolation using it as a barrier against attack from rivals, and then proceeded south. And if this had been their route, their final location would have been vastly different than if they had gone directly south or had stayed in the foot-hills weaving their way through protected trails and valleys before emerging into the grasslands and heading for their camp. Sitting by their campfire during the middle of their sec-ond season in searching Kal said, "This is so very frustrating. Here we are in the middle of another season, and on the verge of the Season of Falling and we've found nothing, no hints, and are no further along than when we decided to look for their hunting camp. I know, I know, this camp was just a tem-porary place that was convenient, and there were no permanent shelters built, but one would think that with the generations that used the same place that there would be something. And to think that there had been a meeting with one of the tribes during the time of the alliance meant that others knew of its location also. So why can't we find it?"

She shook her head, "You know why, and while the location was known at that time and in that world, so much has passed by, so much has happened since that time that what was once known by all is now known by none." She sighed and took a deep breath, "I know that we've gone over the notes at least a hundred times, but we must be overlooking something. There's got to be some kind of hint that we've missed and are continuing to miss."

"Yeah, you're right, and I think part of the problem is our way of thinking has changed."

"Changed, I don't understand."

"Okay, look we are no longer a warlike people. Yes there's still fighting, and there's a lot of bad people out there, but it is so different from that time where anyone away from their clan or tribe was fair game. If the person was a male, they'd be killed, and if a female she'd be bred. The clans and tribes fought all the time, and until that first true alliance had been formed it remained the way of life and death. Yes disease and childbirth took many also, but if one was a male, the most likely form of death was battle against any of the rivals out there. So this camp had to be such that it would have been easily defended, and while known by others, it was such that they wouldn't attempt to attack it. So we probably need to look at factors that make a location good for defense as well as for the required hunting." He took a deep breath, paused, and shook his head, dropping his voice to almost a whisper. "The only problem with this is what would fill all those requirements? I mean it could have been a small ravine, or depression where the water ran close by, or it could have been wide open not allowing any to approach unseen."

She laughed, "Oh yes, that really narrows it down. I think you just described just about any place and area out here. I'm glad you thought it out. Now I'm sure we'll just go out and find it in the morning." This brought laughter from both of them. As they settled back down she said, "You're right you know. We have no need to be continually on watch for a rival clan or tribe looking to attack us, so in some ways we've grown less watchful, and aren't always looking for the best trail, the best direction that would give us the advantage during a fight. This will take some thinking. Maybe we should stay here for a couple and start trying to put ourselves in their situation. Maybe, by starting in the daylight, we can study where we camped, and see if we can find out how badly we did in choosing our camp, from their point of view."

"You know, that might be a great way of trying to get our minds going in the right direction. But, in the end, I'm sure that we'll only appear to be babes when comparing what we will come up with, compared to them who lived this life for as long as they remained alive."

"Very true, but at least we'll begin thinking like they did, and I'm sure that will eliminate many areas that we would have searched."

With the rising of the suns in the morning and after the first meal of the day, taking care of what nature did to everybody, they looked at their present camp with different eyes – finding both good and bad in their choice of a campsite. First, the good; water close by, camp located against a small hill that hooked around in such a way that it was partially hidden, and very defensible from at least one of the approaches. But both had to admit that the bad far outweighed the good. Their choice of camp allowed too many approaches, so that an enemy could be almost in their camp before being seen, the hill they were camped at the base of allowed easy access to an enemy approaching from the back, giving them the higher ground, and most of the approaches from that direction were protected. So all an enemy would have to do would be to keep their attention drawn forward and then make the attack from the top of the hill, and that would have been that. "You know, at first I thought we had done pretty good job of picking our campsite. We're close to water, partially hidden, plenty of dead wood for our fire since there are many trees close to that stream, and we are far enough back not to keep any of the beasts who might get their water from this point. But I can see how poor a job we did from the defense part of it, and as you said last night we are just babes at this." As Kal continued to look around he was seeing more that made their choice a bad one. Taking a deep breath he said, "If we had been here back then we wouldn't be here now, and I can see that quite clearly."

"Yeah, I see it also. Of course there would have been more than just the two of us. Nobody during those times went out alone, let alone with two. And if it was just two it was usually the warriors who used their skills to remain hidden and out of sight as they moved. And while we've improved since we've been out here for so long, I'm sure that we again are poor at doing just that. This means that even when they hunted they worried about being hunted, so all their concentration couldn't be just on the hunt. They must have always had other members of the hunt being lookouts for rival tribes and such." She paused a moment as another thought entered her mind. "So how did they determine the lay of the land? I mean we get up on top of a high point and look it over and plan how we are going to travel, but to do that would expose you to being seen, and seen from a very long way off. So they must have had other ways."

As she asked those questions he realized that they really knew so very little. What is common knowledge is rarely recorded or written down since everyone knows. So when such is lost there are no records to recover that lost common knowledge. And it would only be through similar circumstances that that knowledge would be rediscovered. "Yes, very good question. How would one go about figuring all that out and not reveal their position?"

". . . Nothing in those pages about that that I can remember . . ." Jura walked over to a log and sat down with Kal joining her, actually standing behind her and massaging her shoulders and neck. "You're so good at that," she whispered

He hadn't realized that he was doing that, but knew that he enjoyed it and that she did also. "It's one of those joys, and I'm glad that you like it. But like you, back on that original subject here, I don't remember anything on those pages about this either. So here we are so many cycle of seasons later, and we don't have a clue. Maybe if that character that came into our camp that rainy night showed up we could ask him. He seems to know how to disappear into the lands. I know it was dark when he showed up, and it rained most of the night, and once we were up that next day he was gone, yet he moved with a grace that made it seem like he and these wilds were one and the same. He probably does much of what our ancestors did with little or no effort, and probably doesn't even think about it. It's as much a part of who he is as is breath-ing."

"I almost forgot about him. But you're right. He seemed to just flow, to move in such a way that it appeared each and every move he took was planned, but at the same time you could tell it wasn't a conscious effort, and it was just a part of who he is. Yes, but I suspect that if we asked he probably couldn't tell us – probably doesn't even think about it or how he does it. He just does it and it's become part of his nature – who he is. Just like you're a male and I'm a female."

He laughed at that and said, "Amen!"

She looked at him questioningly and asked, "What?"

He smiled, "Oh what you just said. I'm quite happy that I'm a male and you're a female. It works out well for both of us." He then got this wicked grin on his face and said, "Shall we go and prove it?"

"Oh you males, always have that on your minds." She smiled and just shook her head.

"Can I help it if you bring the male out in me? After all I love all of you, and that definitely includes your body." He began to teasingly touch her in places that would get her in-terested, and she put up a token fight but he could see that she was beginning to respond to his touches. At first he was only going to tease her, but he could sense the passion rising in both of them, and they, hand in hand headed for their portable shelter.

Later, after both of them had bathed in the stream and were absorbing the warmth from the suns, he reached out lovingly and touched her hand, and she returned the touch. "I love times like this. I guess one of the advantages of being out here trying to find those places from the past, that we can explore each other and learn more about each other, and get even closer."

At this she laughed, and said, "Now I don't think we could have gotten any closer than what we were, but I know what you mean. And yes being out here like this allows us a little more freedom on our loving each other." She sighed, took a deep breath, grabbed her clothes, since both of them were lying on the grass naked, allowing the suns and the heat to dry them, got up and began to head back to camp. "I know we could spend all day doing what we did, and I'm sure that we'd enjoy every moment of it, but we've got to get our journal up to date, and then begin again."

When she got up and he could see her in her full naked glory he could feel the passion rising in him again, and reached up and pulled her down to him for which she giggled, and said, "Never satisfied are you."

He smiled lovingly up at her and asked, "Can I help it if you do that to me? After all you looked so inviting I just couldn't resist a second chance."

With a look of devilment in her eyes she said, "Okay, but after this we really have to get something done."

He laughed and said, "I thought that is what we are doing."

All she could say was, "You!" And she then laid a very passionate kiss on him which excited him even more, not that her naked body didn't.

Later as the suns were setting and they were back in camp both looking over the journal Kal asked, "So how do you want to word our discoveries?"

She looked up innocently and asked, "Discoveries, which ones – the ones where we decided to attack this problem by trying to think like our ancestors, or the one where we discovered our bodies?"

At first he didn't catch what she was saying since he was deep in thought, but then what she had asked penetrated and he began to laugh. "I would think, since somewhere in a future time that these journals will be read, by other than you or I, the former would be what is important. From what I've learned about you females – such a discussion between mates is fine, but it is not for public consumption."

"While you males like to talk about your conquests," She shot back.

"Now, now, now that's not always true. In fact, yes there are a number of males that brag all the time about such things. But I suspect that quite the opposite is true."

"Opposite, how so?"

"In my humble opinion, the ones that are bragging are probably not getting any. It seems to be an axiom that if one is physically involved that one doesn't hear much about it, but if they aren't, then the mouth runs over."

"Well, I wouldn't know. It's not that way with us females, I can say that for sure."

"It could be, since I really only know one female intimately . . ."

She looked up at him once again with that innocent look, and asked. "And who would that be?"

* * *

With frustration in his voice Kal said, "These maps are next to useless. Yeah they show many of the villages, but the lay of the land is only general at the best, and even this isn't very good. Heck it's almost impossible to even pinpoint exactly where we are on these things. I really thought that they would help. I'm no cartographer or artist so I can't add a darn thing to them." They were standing on the rise that was behind their camp as they watched the suns rise out of the east. Even the stream that they had camped close by wasn't accurately represented. In fact it was depicted as having ended further east than their present location. "I wonder how much of what is here is as inaccurate as what we are seeing now."

She couldn't disagree with him. She was becoming as frustrated with these things as he was. When they had brought them along forsaking something else, it was with the understanding that these things would help. Well, they hadn't. "I guess if someone isn't living in the area then it might as well say, 'here the land belongs to our mythological gods, and we will only mark it as such'. Yeah, I was really hoping that they would help. But probably the best use we could find for these things is kindling to start our fire. What a waste of finances to have even purchased them. Well, I guess if this is the only disappointment we have in life, then we can count ourselves lucky."

Breathing out heavily he replied, "Yeah, I guess so. Still it would have been nice . . ." Both of them jumped when another asked, "Nice, what would have been nice?" Both sort of recognized the voice, but couldn't immediately place it. Turning around rapidly they both saw that individual who had stopped by their camp that cold rainy night.

"Where'd you come from?" They asked in unison.

He gave them a funny look and said, "From right down there, isn't it obvious?" He looked at them and said, "Oh, it's you two . . . Been a while. So you out looking for those ancient places again?"

Answering back in the same way Kal said, "Yes, isn't it obvious?"

"Well, one never knows what one will find out here. So from where I was I seen your camp, not very well hidden. In the old days would have been a target, that's for sure. So again I was curious."

They smiled and Jura said, "Yes, and it was a puzzle as to who was out and about, and you like puzzles."

This brought laughter from him. "Remember she does, yup, remembered. True, true, and there was something familiar about the camp, but I couldn't figure it out, so decided I would come closer. Now I know why. It is your camp. While most camps are put together much the same, there is always differences." He tapped his forehead and said, "An' I remember differences." He saw the large paper in their hands and asked, "So what's that?"

Kal replied saying, "Something worthless. It's supposed to be a map of the area out here, but it's next to useless. Nothing on it is right." Pointing over at the stream that they could plainly see below them he said, "See even that is wrong. By this thing it ended quite a distance to the east of here, yet here it is."

He glanced at it and said, "Don't use those things, have no need, already know what's there and what's not. Waste of space, waste of time." Then looking at the two of them he asked, "So what puzzle you solving this time, what place are you looking to find?" Again he laughed a little. "I may have been there, might give you a hint, but not give it away. Let you solve the puzzle —it's so much more fun that way – makes one think, makes one grow."

The two of them again looked at each other and back at him. With what little they knew of this person he could have been to where they were searching, but how far could they trust him? Yet, they had been unsuccessful all of last season, and this one was getting late. So any help, any help at all would be appreciated. So with a silent agreement between them Kal said, "We are looking for the hunting camp that K'jor and his clan used. From what we could discern, they used the same camp every hunting season. And while locating the clan home was important, it is what happed after that that changed us, changed our history. So we want to find that place where it truly began."

He was silent for a while. It was obvious that he was thinking. "Hmmm, good puzzle, interesting, out in the open, but at the same time hidden. Not like you – easy to see, easy to find. I'll think about this, but you must remember that there were so many others who also had their camps, who also returned season after season. So to find only one . . . yes, a good puzzle . . ." It was obvious that he was deep in thought and actually appeared to have forgotten that the two of them were there. Looking up he seemed surprised to see them, and then he smiled. "Will let you know, but not today. But will say this, while the herds are no longer large and they originally ranged all the way to the Sacred Mountains, most of the tribes and clans hunted to the south of here. In places where it became green earlier in the season to give the beasts time to put on meat. Others waited until the migrations took the beasts north, but most did not." Then apparently tired of company, and of talking he just walked off the hill down to his beast and then disappeared behind a small hill and again like when he had left their previous camp it was like he had never been there.

"There's one quiet, sneaky person. We never heard him approach and we just watched him disappear in broad daylight. If I believed in sorcerers and magicians I'd swear he is one." Kal turned back to her and shrugged. "I guess we can guarantee one thing."

"And what would that be?"

"Oh, now that he's found us again that he'll be showing up now and again and asking more questions."

"Yeah, that's probably very true. At least he gave us a direction to look. By what he told us we are still too far north. I guess it's still early enough in this day that we can break camp and head further south, and set up again before dark."

"Guess so. It's obvious that he knows more than he's saying, but at least he pointed us in a new direction. I really didn't think that they could have gone any further south. We are a few days out of the clan home. But that is the way we reckon it. We really have no idea how much ground they could cover in a day, and from the records they were three days away from the clan."

"The land is quite open here," Jura said as she looked around again, "and we have had it proved that we definitely set our camp in a place where it was easily spotted, as he just showed us. Darn he makes me jumpy when he does that." She paused a moment before continuing, "Yeah, I didn't think that they could have gone too much further south, but he could be right. Still the only way we're going to know is to head that way, and standing here isn't getting us moving, so shall we?"

It was mid-morning by the time they were packed and heading south, leaning a little west. Using the suns to mark their direction, with the surrounding landscape being similar there was nothing to mark, as a distant point, to keep them on the line that they planned. In truth, since there was not true destination, in the end, it probably didn't matter. They were searching for signs of ancient occupation, and not a particular place. Water wouldn't necessarily be an issue as small streams crossed these grasslands creating islands of trees that hugged the banks or at times grew in the shallow waters redirecting the water around them, and eventually changing the course of the water's flow and direction. As the day progressed the winds picked up and it grew warm. They knew that as they continued their general and slow movement to the west that the grasses would become sparse and the heat would increase as the desolation became a stronger influence. Since this was something that never had been studied that they knew of, it was unknown as to whether the desolation was growing or remaining the same.

There were some theories as to why the desolation existed at all, since the storms that provided the moisture for the grasslands, came up from the south where the grasslands bordered the sea. It was just north of that point that the hills on the west began to influence and to funnel the storms away from the coast and up through those grasslands, denying rain and water to that strip. As the storms would move north, the lands slowly rose in altitude until they struck the Sacred Mountains, which pushed the storms higher into the air changing it from heavy rain to snow and ice. And now that there had been some exploration beyond those mountains here was a place of permanent ice and snow – very inhospitable to life in general. It had created another one of those historical mysteries that someday they hoped to solve, as they were attempting to unravel the surviving ancient writings they were using as a guide. That other mystery had to do with a clan only known as the travelers who consistently, over the generations talked about their home being north of the Sacred Mountains, but nothing had been found to indicate that such a clan had ever existed, further strengthening the myth theory.

They broke for a midday meal and watched as thunderheads began to develop over the eastern foothills. It was travel rations since they wanted to be moving as quickly as possible. "He said that many of those hunting camps were set up further south, but that doesn't mean that any of those can be tied to our clan. It'd put us at least five days out of where they lived, and the writings specifically state that this camp was only three days out." Kal just shook his head, it didn't make sense. But where they had been searching further north there was nothing.

"True", Jura said, "but we are looking at this from what we can cover. We still don't have a clue as to how far warriors could travel in a day. I suspect that physically all of them were in better shape than we are now. Even though I suspect that our health is better . . ." She paused and shuddered as she thought about this. "So dirty and unhealthy the way they lived . . . I'm really surprised that any survived long enough so that we can now look back on that time."

"Yeah, but it must have worked because we are here, and you're right we really have no idea. To cover this much distance in three days would have meant that they probably jogged the whole distance, and that would have included the females that went with them. Those were some tough people. If that idea is true I probably would have been beat up by any of those females and they wouldn't have raised a sweat, and the warriors would have probably just shrugged it off as they would a crawler."

She smiled and said, "I beat you, and not once but several times, and I suspect that I still can."

"Well, true. But you know what I mean. That had to be such a hard life no matter which sex you were. I think I prefer now to then."

"Yeah, me too. But I wonder . . ."

"Wonder? Wonder what?"

". . . What you would have been, oh mighty baker that you are. Would you have become a warrior, a priest, or just one of the workers who remained with the clan to handle the slaves and other such stuff?"

"I really don't know, but we know where you'd been stuck, and you've already given me your opinion on that." Standing up and stretching he said, "I guess we better continue on. We have half a day to travel yet, and still need to find a campsite for tonight."

* * *

It was dusk when they found their next camp, and this time they had studied it from their new found way of looking for a campsite. One that offered defense, provided water, and fuel for their fires, and still allowed them the ability to observe what was happening around them. Here, as they had approached this area, they began to see the first signs of ancient campsites and ancient fires. So that, well, they still didn't know what to call him, since he refused to give them a name, still insisting that when he was in the wilds that he as the beasts required none. Anyway the information that he had passed on to them seemed to be accurate. What else did he know and wasn't willing to pass on, or maybe didn't know he knew, and it was only when they met and they passed on what they were trying to do that it would remind him. He surely didn't appear to be hiding anything and had been forthwith the information that they received from him so far.

As night closed in around them it gave the appearance that they were the only two that existed in this whole world. There were the sounds of night, and the coolness that slowly increased as the time moved by them. "I wonder", Jura asked, "how it was before the clans and tribes, when there were only small groups of us around. How lonely it must have been. How scary knowing that the creatures out there could be your meal or you could be theirs. Now slowly we are taming this world, but there are still a lot of dangers. Yet, to do what we are doing without a large group around us would have been unheard of – not that people don't just disappear out here, because they do. Still, to be here back at the beginning of our people when it could have gone either way . . ."

"Yeah, that would have been an interesting time . . . time before any history that we know. And no, I wouldn't have been interested in living then either. Death had to be very high, and I'm sure that there were many groups that were wiped out, from who knows what. Disease, attacks by the beasts or rival groups, floods, landslides, and so many other traps that I can't think of right this moment. Not a time to relax at all, no time to think about what might be, just a struggle to make sure you lived to face another day, and with no guarantee that when you made it to that day that you would be around to finish it." He laughed, "Enough on that depressing subject. It's part of our distant past and as far as I'm concerned it can stay there. We have enough mystery with what we are trying to solve, thank you."

They both lay back and stared up into the night sky watching the stars, and then every once in a while something would

streak across the sky in a blaze of light and be gone. "I wonder what those things are?" Jura asked.

"Don't really know, but that reminds me of that really
large one we saw back at that ancient site. The one that came
out of the north appeared to be right over the Sacred Mountains – never seen something so big or bright like that at night,
other than our moons."

"Yeah, that was pretty spectacular, that's for sure. Well,
whatever they are, they can stay up there. Think I'll turn in,
lying here I'm finding that I'm falling to sleep anyway . . .
New areas to look at tomorrow . . . g'night." With that she
slowly got up and headed inside the portable shelter leaving
Kal alone. He felt tired himself, but at this moment couldn't
get up the energy to move from his comfortable position, and
continued to stare at the night sky, only waking later realizing
that he had fallen asleep. The fire had burned down to just
glowing coals, so he threw a large piece of wood on the coals
figuring that it would last until morning, and headed to his
sleep sack, morning couldn't be too far off.

* * *

Through the next couple of 9-days they searched and continued moving south until just before the zenith they came
upon an ancient isolated camp. Looking at their notes and at
the surrounding landscape this came close to matching. They
were approximately six days away from the clan home – six
days! Yet the words within the text spoke of the distances being only an easy three days away. Was it deliberately
misrepresented, or could their ancestors actually cover this
much distance in the time stated? Yet, everything that had
been confirmed within that text has proven to be accurate, so
why would they misrepresent the distance here? Still the texts

never mentioned the return times only what it took to reach this location.

Yes the site showed changes since the time that the clan used this as their hunting camp. The stream was no more and the trees that had provided shade during the heat were just snags. Sometime in the past the stream either dried up or changed course isolating this location, leaving the trees without a ready source of water. And if they were to stay here they too would have to find a new source of water. Still when looking over the descriptions given, the directions given to any who sought this camp and comparing this to the actual lay of the land there could be no doubt. Highly defensible, easy to see any enemies approaching, and close to where the vast herds once roamed, with the desolation not too far to the west of them – in sight really, but probably at least a half day away. And they began to really appreciate the location as it was virtually invisible until you almost walked into the camp. In fact that is exactly what had happened to them as they continued their searching. When looking from the outside of this location it could have been any of the thousands of ravines, or small depressions, never giving a hint to the large area that was here or how uninviting it appeared from the outside.

As they had noticed once inside, it was easy to defend. Any place an enemy would approach they would have to expose themselves to the sky, to highlight themselves, making them an easy target. While the ones inside of this location would be difficult to locate, and with water readily available, plus and since this was a hunting camp, food would be of no issue, so the idea of a siege became no option either. It would take an overwhelming force to rout and kill the ones within this camp, and since the main purpose was to hunt for all, there truly would be no reason to attack. Again, from the writings, it stated that attacks did happen, but of these, most were from opportunities presented or a particular tribe or clan had become troublesome to all. And this would be those rare times when a couple of the tribes or clans would ally and attack. Yet all of this during this time of the cycle of seasons happened very rarely – so much so that it happened less than once a generation.

In quiet reverence Kal walked the camp where his ancestors had used for generations of hunting. It was here that the whole story truly began. It was here that was the beginning of the change of direction for this whole world. Even though at the time that it had happened, no such thoughts were in any of their minds. The leader, K'jor, had been left with a puzzle, and it was one that he, for who knew why, needed to solve. Yes, this camp continued to be used long after K'jor was no more. Yet . . . yet it had been here that what they were as a people today could be traced back to this very location, this very spot of earth. While the finding of the clan home held importance, in his own mind it was this place, a camp that was used once a season that held a much greater importance, a greater value, to all of them. While it had been important to find the clan home, it had been necessary so that the rest of the story could be located and told.

Jura watched as he walked quietly around the site. She didn't say anything, knowing or at least guessing what must be going through his mind. Now, with the writings that they had, they had been able to locate two places that had been placed in the myth status by the historians. Those writings that his family had held on generation after generation were finally bearing fruit, and slowly uncovering their true past. What was still ahead of them, what was still to be discovered? She really didn't know, but the writings had been accurate, so all she could assume was that the rest of what was written there probably was accurate from their ancestors' point of view. She looked and could see that they'd been here for a while and the suns were beginning to head towards the hills that were located in the desolation and quite visible from here. "Kal, we need to setup camp, and while we have water enough for now, we'll have to find more."

Kal barely heard her as his mind was drifting to images of what must have transpired here, cycles of the seasons after cycle of the seasons. He could almost see the ghosts of the warriors and the females who would prepare the skins and meat for the trip back. See them bring in the large herd beasts that required at least three warriors to bring down, and twice that many to bring the carcass back to camp to be efficiently processed and packed. It was like he was being allowed to look through the veils of time and see those ghosts going about their lives, unknown to them that one of their future ancestors was watching. He could see the almost smokeless fires, the numbers of warriors and females here. There must have been a least fifty warriors, with a minimum of ten females if not twice that number. It was like a small village with all the activity going on. Yet there was a quiet the defied the size of the group. They moved with a grace and seemed more to flow than walk. As if they were part of the land, part of the wild places. He knew that there was no way he could ever be that graceful, obtain that way of moving. It was completely unconscious on their part, and he knew if he tried that he would have to think about it all the time, taking away that awareness of the surrounding areas that also seemed to be a part of them.

They were never still, their eyes were forever moving, never staying on one point at any one time. Yet, when they did remain still, it was as if they were the land, it was as if they became invisible, disappearing from sight only to reappear when they moved once again. In that movement, and those times of stillness nothing was wasted. It seemed that each move, each pause, had a purpose. In some ways he envied what he was seeing. Still, he realized because of their lifestyle, the continual fighting and hunting that this was a very necessary part of who they were. If they made a mistake or hadn't learned their lessons well when they were children they wouldn't be here now, but dead. As he remained on the edge of this ancient campsite he could also see the seriousness of what they were doing. The clan depended on them for their meat, and all the work that he was witnessing reflected that goal. He noticed that the portion of the camp where the females resided was the center where they were protected by the warriors who surrounded them. He became alarmed when one of them looked directly at him and he flinched, but then shook his head and smiled. There was no way that this warrior from the past could see him, or if he did, there was no way he could touch him, since the veils of time stood between the two. Then as it appeared the scene faded and he was alone with Jura and they were standing in this long abandoned camp of their ancestors. Quietly he said, "Yes, you're right . . . we do need to set up our camp." Yet, he continued to stare, trying to understand what he had been shown; but no answers came.

CHAPTER TWELVE

THE DESOLATION

"That was quite a vision you had a 9-day ago. I wonder what brought it on and why you were allowed to see the past that way?" They were standing on the edge of the desolation, knowing that shortly they would make their first foray into that inhospitable place. Jura looked carefully at what they were planning and since neither had ever been this close, they really didn't know if their plans covered everything, nor did she like what she was seeing.

Kal shrugged and said, "I really don't know if what I saw was real or not, or whether it was just my mind playing tricks on me. But there had to be something to it, because we found proof that the camp was laid out just about the way I saw it in that vision. Who really knows what exists in the natural world. Maybe there was a brief rift that allowed both the ones from the past and me to look across that veil, even for a moment and see, for them, that there would be a future, and for me, proof of our past and how they lived. I just don't know. I do know that after the vision was over I began to doubt it. Still as we worked the site and we found evidence that it was as I saw, it left me more puzzled, and I guess if I admit it, still doubting, even though the proof was being uncovered each day." He looked into the desolation and honestly didn't want to set foot in there. It had a reputation and that reputation was very bad.

"Now that we are here it makes me wonder what was going on here. I mean from the writings it speaks of many smokes coming out of the desolation at the time there was renewed belief in the gods. You know when the rumbling began again in the Sacred Mountains. It wasn't very long after that, that the smokes, up and down the length of the desolation, are recorded. But look, there just doesn't appear to be anything that can burn here. It's barren, there are no grasses, except here on the edge, and it's still early in the day and I can already feel the heat building, reflecting off that bare land." He stared into the desolation once more and could see that on the edges that the grasses attempted to invade but was largely unsuccessful.

"Look, if I remember right, those writings stated that the priests were brought out at a later time to get their take on what was found – you know right after they had destroyed the lair. Also from the descriptions made by the warriors, and by K'jor himself, it was almost impossible to find your way around in there. So my thoughts are this; they probably marked a trail into the area they wanted to go. So let's hike the edge, and see if we can find some type of marker that would lead us in. Remember they were hunting when they trailed that wounded beast into the desolation. That means that they were not a very long way away from camp – far enough to hunt, but not so far as to make it difficult to bring in their kills. So, I'd guess no further than a half day out, and then, only if it required that distance. If you think about it, traveling a half day, taking down a few of the beasts and then having to haul them all the way back to camp would be a waste of time and effort considering the amount of meat they would need."

"Makes sense to me, besides the longer we can remain on the edge, at least until we have a better idea about this place, the better I feel about it. And that idea about leaving a marked trail is probably true. I'm sure that for the first few times in they tracked. But looking at what we are seeing here, tracks wouldn't last long. There's already a dusty haze as the breeze is picking up. I think that tracks would be wiped out rather quick leaving no sign of one passing through. In fact, if I remember right, it said that in the writings."

Taking a deep breath and shaking her head Jura continued saying, "I guess we're just stalling a little here. So let's work the edge." They were just outside of the camp carrying enough supplies to last for a couple of days, if need be. But both of them suspected that where the ancestors had entered the desolation chasing that wounded beast couldn't be very far away. Still what they considered not far away and what their ancestors would have, had proved to be vastly different.

It was pushing the zenith when they came upon a rock cairn. And until they found it there had been no sign of any entering, leaving, or the placing of markers of any kind. Looking further to the south, still on the edge of the desolation, they could see nothing else that resembled this. So using this point they stopped and had their travel rations. They had brought their pack beast with them, not wanting to leave it alone. Also the beast was now carrying all their water and knowing what had been told about the desolation, they knew that there would be no water. It had been another reason for the present belief that the *priests and servants of the gods* couldn't have lived here, and as such was just a part of the larger myth surrounding this time in their history.

As they sat there staring into that foreboding place Jura asked, "What do you want to do? How do you want to tackle this? I can't see anything, at least from here that shows us any other markers. Yet, there has to be, especially if this is the right place. Distance was a little further than I thought it should be, be that's me not them. We already know that they could travel over greater distances in a day than we do, heck almost twice the distance. So it could be the same about their hunting range."

"I think what we should do is just work inside this area to see if we can find any other rock markers or cairns. Half of this day is already gone, and I'm not of the mind to be inside the desolation in the dark. Again from those writings, wherever it is that we need to go is probably at least a half day inside. So let's just do a cursory look, and then move our camp. There's a stream close by so we won't have to keep going out like we are at our present camp to get our water skins refilled."

"Okay, it works for me. I have to admit that the idea of getting stuck in there in the dark isn't something I want to do either."

The next morning as the suns touched the horizon they were ready to make their first trip into the desolation. The plan was simple really, just work in far enough to be able to see their camp and to see if this cairn that was positioned on the edge of the desolation, was the starting point they were looking for, or that it was just another dead end, left by a later or earlier group representing something long forgotten. Yet there was also a worry about those mud hills, well they weren't mud now, but there was nothing on them but the exposed earth flashing back colors of red and yellow, with large boulders exposed half buried in those hills and they appeared to be close to the edge. Meaning that it would be easy to lose one's way almost immediately. And if the writings said anything at all, it was a warning that even for an experienced warrior these lands looked the same no matter where one was, and tracks disappeared almost as soon as one made them, leaving only the suns as a marker as to the direction one traveled. It definitely was a land for the spirits, not the living.

And as the cycle of the seasons had passed with hundreds passing, the feeling hadn't changed. Many had tried to search the desolation, and many never returned. The ones that had sworn that they would never go back to that place, as it was only a place of confusion, dust, and heat. Cooking one's body and mind, confusing even the most experienced – yet it was here where K'jor and the clan had gone, discovering the servants of the gods, those mythological gods that they now knew never existed. So what was it that they had found, and what had caused all that smoke when it was quite obvious there was nothing here to burn? So with this knowledge and with some trepidation they began their journey into the unknown. Looking into the desolation they could see that there was already a haze as the morning breezes began to pick up, causing the light powdery soils to begin their daily ride in the currents, and to once again settle at night when it calmed, leaving the ground without a mark, without a track, leaving no trace that any had passed here.

Had anybody been standing there as they made this first exploration, it would have appeared that they were slowly turning transparent as the dusts swallowed them, making them disappear from sight as if they were no more. Kal coughed and sneezed before reaching into the pack he was carrying. Looking over at Jura he could see that she was doing the same thing. They stopped as they dug in their packs for something to cover their faces so that it would be easier to breath. The fine particles of dust were too easy to breathe in. Even though they had seen the dust clouds forming, they hadn't considered the consequences. At least the herd beasts had a natural defense against this, and wouldn't be having the issues they were. Both turned and looked back to where they had entered and found that it was already obscured to the point that they couldn't be sure of its location. "How'd they do it?" Kal asked, "I mean they supposedly followed a wounded beast in here to finish it off, and then found that male and female here. They then returned to the camp with not only the slain beast, but the clothing of the two, and from the writings made it sound like it was no big deal."

"Yeah, big difference between reading it and living it." Jura looked back once again. "Look, I think we're going to have to come up with a better method of doing this. We're really not that far into this area and already we've come close to losing sight of where we need to return. And looking at this, this dust and such, how would the ones who entered mark a path? From what little I can see, and I really mean what little I can see, there are no paths, nothing that one can latch onto to know where you are or how you can backtrack. And if the winds really start blowing hard I have a feeling that it will be almost impossible to see anything at all. Yeah, this is making me respect our ancestors even more. Like you said, from their writings it was just another day."

With an unspoken agreement they turned around and headed back to the cairn that they were using as a landmark. After reaching it they looked at each other and both of them were covered in a fine dust with the footwear full of silt, changing the color of their clothing to that of the desolation. "No wonder there's never been any bodies recovered from here. We've only been in there a short time and look at us. If someone died in there it wouldn't take long to bury the body or make it invisible just from this dirt. Besides I don't think many would have spent too long looking anyway. We're already learning, personally, what the dangers of this place are." Kal looked back over his shoulder into the desolation and could only shake his head.

Jura began to brush herself off raising clouds of dust as she did. "Well, one thing for sure, if there were people or clans that lived in there, they would be safe from anybody out here. And that's a very big 'if'. If it hadn't been for that accident they would not have been discovered and our history would probably be very different. You know it's kind of funny how just one small incident like this ended up bringing major change to us. Makes one wonder, what other inconsequential incident that happened in our past may have led to some other major change for us, and this world. I guess we'll really never know, since such things aren't considered important at the time, and it's only after much time has passed and one can look back to that point in time that it becomes apparent."

They hiked up and down the edge of the desolation to see if there might be an area where the powdery dust wasn't being stirred by the winds producing that haze that obscured everything. "We're going to have to rethink this. I felt that we could just hike in there keeping that cairn in sight and mark something so we'd have a direction to both go into that place and find our way back out. I really didn't think that the dust would be that big of deal. Boy was I wrong. How'd our ancestors do this anyway?" Kal stopped and stared knowing that while the desolation was so close, it was still beyond them at this moment.

"Yeah, I just figured it would be easy too, at least take a small excursion into the area – kind of learn a little about it and then come back out. We spent less than the morning time in there and learned nothing – exasperating to say the least." Jura stood there next to him with her hands on her hips coming up with no solutions. Both hiked back to the cairn and began searching around it to see if there was something that identified why it had been built here, but after a long period of time had passed and they came away with nothing, it just added to a very frustrating day. "There's got to be a time when that dust isn't so bad, and maybe back when our ancestors entered here it wasn't this bad. Things change and I'm sure it's the same for the desolation." With nothing found and no solutions, they returned to their camp somewhat depressed.

Once they arrived back at camp they unpacked the pack beast and staked him out on some of the grasses where it began eating, unconcerned about what its owners were thinking about. As long as he had food and water and was treated well he could care less. "Well, this has been a successful day." Kal said sarcastically. "I surely have a puzzle to solve, and speaking of puzzles didn't our friend say that he had been in the desolation?"

"Yeah, I think he did, but he didn't say how far or whether it was just along the edge like we ended up doing today. That's a very dangerous place, and a tough one to crack. No wonder people get lost and die in there. And I didn't see many rocks and such when we went in there either. That's not to say that there isn't any, but that means if we are to mark a trail by using stones then we'll need to bring our own, and from those clouds of dust today we'd have to plan on marking our trail at least twice as often as we would normally. That's a lot of stones."

All Kal could do was nod his head in agreement. They really didn't have any idea what the interior of that place held. There could be plenty of rocks for them to use, or like the edges have none. Stones added up to much weight, and that would mean that something else would have to be left behind. The beast could only carry so much, and even with their packs they were limited to what they could carry. "At least there are plenty of stones here by this stream but with that dust how large of stack would it take to remain visible, or not get buried?" It was a very good question, and another for which they had no answer.

Jura took a deep breath and let it out slowly, saying, "I guess we can finish out this day here, sleep on it and try again tomorrow. With the after-zenith still ahead of us we can begin to pack some of these river stones and at least try setting up a few inside the desolation to see how many we will need, and what the maximum distance will be to allow us to see them. I think for the next couple of days we should experiment and see what works and what doesn't."

"Good idea and I think we probably should do that away from where we plan to finally go in and explore. That way we won't get confused by some of our experiments if we tripped across them. Of course if we did, and we had set them up somewhere else, then we'd know that what we finally settled on didn't really work since we would have come out in a different area than where we went in."

* * *

For the next several days they tried a series of methods and found that on some days the dust wasn't as bad, but others it was worse. They finally settled a method that would use the smallest amount of stones, and yet point them in either the direction they headed going in, and the direction necessary to head back out, and finally after a 9-day, they were ready to attempt it once again. They were hoping that as they headed deeper into the desolation that they would come upon markers left by their ancestors, especially if this cairn represented the entrance that they had used. Their strange visitor never entered their camp during all of this time. But that didn't mean that he wasn't watching them. He had already shown them his ability to stay hidden. So there was no way to know if he was around or not. So with hopefully enough stones, and enough supplies and water packed, and with the rising suns, they began their trek back into the unknown.

Once again inside the desolation the cairn disappeared from sight and the mud hills became more visible and were closer than they thought. The clouds of dust made it appear that they were further away than they really were. Upon examination they were of a crumbly type soil that once wet probably made clay of some kind, but once dried out would break apart killing any plants that might try and grow. Here the land was very broken, with the hills and the small depressions all looking similar, making it easy to become lost. So far the supply of rocks that they had brought with them was holding out, and that was a good thing since they had yet to locate any within the areas that there were traversing. The dust was less of a problem the deeper they got in. It seemed that these mud hills provided a partial wind block, which was nice, but the downside came as the suns rose higher in the sky. With no vegetation, and little wind the ground began to heat up and shortly it was almost unbearable – it was downright hot.

Taking a break in what little shade they could find, they could see that their clothes were becoming soaked from their sweat, and this wetness was picking up the dust, creating a mud layer on their clothes making the situation even more uncomfortable. "Why would anybody want to live here?" Jura complained. She was uncomfortable, hot, and felt dirty from her head to her toes. And while working on a farm, such work could get one dirty – this was far worse. She itched, felt like she was in that oven that they used in the bakery. And there was no place to get relief. What made it worse still was the fact that they hadn't reached the time of day yet for the maximum heat. They were still short of the zenith when it would become the warmest, hold that way until late after-zenith, and then begin to cool. Now the worry was did they bring enough water? Oh they had plenty, but they were sweating it out almost as fast as they drank it. Looking around where they were they could see their last marker, which was a good thing because no matter what direction they looked, it all looked the same. All the hills were rounded, the depressions slight, and only the shadows gave a hint to direction. Once the zenith had been reached, even that would be taken from them.

"I'd say we need to find a place out of the direct suns, find shade and wait until it cools a little before continuing, but there's no place to do that. This just sucks. Why would anybody want to live here?" Kal swept him arms around to emphasize his question. After all there were so many other places to live than this. Still, at this time, they stopped to take a break.

"I don't know, and I don't know if we'll find proof one way or the other. But maybe, whoever they were, they had little or no choice. I know, there are always choices, but we really have no idea who these people were, if they were, so I don't know."

"I know, I was just spouting off. This place is unbelievable, miserable and whatever other words I can come up with to describe it. I know one thing for sure; I wouldn't want to live here. The grasslands during the Season of Heat gets warm enough for me. This, this is so much worse than I ever imagined it could be, and we're in the Season of the Falling."

"Point taken, and to add to that is the fact that we are only a few 9-days out of the Season of Cold, which means that it's not nearly as hot as it would be at the beginning of this season." Breathing out heavily and standing back up, she asked, "Shall we? Sitting here or hiking and being uncomfortable isn't going to make much of a difference, and we can't find anything sitting here."

They began moving off in a southwesterly direction, now being surrounded by these dry mud hills, small valleys, ravines, depressions, and nowhere water or vegetation of any kind. It was a very dead world. No wonder their ancestors had considered it the land of the spirits. Nothing living could survive here and this only deepened the mystery. How would anyone survive in this, let alone a clan or tribe? There was absolutely nothing to support life. Since entering these hills they had been forced into the direction they were taking as any of the other directions were blocked, and the trails, if that is what you could call them, were narrow and went through the small breaks in those hills. Eventually they came upon another cairn and from that picked up a trail marked in stones. Most of these markers were half buried in the fine powdery soil that they were hiking through. Each step they took created a small cloud of dust at their feet, and their clothes from their knees to their feet were heavily caked with it.

With the stones that they had brought with them, they added to these old markers to make them easier to find when they left. And because they couldn't be sure that this old trail would lead them back out, the made sure to heavily mark where their markers joined this one. They knew from the writings that the hunters had trailed the wounded beast deep into the desolation, although it was still on the edge when compared to the actual size of these lands. It had taken the hunters about half a day to do what they did here and to return with their tale that they had passed on to K'jor. Then once they had returned to the hunter camp the following hunting season, K'jor had explored some of this area trying to get answers to his nagging questions, finding , in the end, that hidden lair of "magicians and sorcerers", as they had called them. It meant that they were presently walking the same grounds that their distant ancestor walked. And all who had followed him, to destroy that hidden lair in the distant past.

And one of the lessons that they were still learning had to deal with distances traveled in a day by their ancestors' verses what they could travel in a day. Their ancestors could go double the distance as they flowed over the landscape, moving with stealth and grace, covering vast distances with little or no effort. So, taking that in consideration, they felt that it would take them at least a day to get to where their ancestors had found the beast they had wounded, and of course, those two strangers. At least for now, with the existing stone markers they were traveling much faster than they had when they blazed and marked their own trail – eventually, as the suns were setting only to enter another bowl like area, where they found another cairn. It was too late in the day to do any more exploring so they set up camp here, and once set up began to look this area over. There were a couple of small caves, and from the descriptions in the writings this had to be the place where this encounter had happened. Although how they determined it was an unknown, since once again, those writings spoke of confusion and the similarities of the landscape, which they could now personally attest.

They had packed fodder for the pack beast and water for all of them. Their plan was simple, be here for no more than two or three nights and leave on the third or fourth day to be back at their camp they had set by that cairn that marked the division between the two areas – the grasslands to the east, and the desolation to the west. Yet as the shadows began to grow and the suns set, there became a chill to the air that was unexpected. Still if they had thought about it they would have realized that with nothing to hold the heat of the day it would just evaporate as their sweat did. And once the suns did set it became a very cold and uncomfortable night. With their fire burning, again from the wood that they had packed with them, it was silent – a too silent world – making them feel that they were being watched by unseen eyes. But there was no one other than the two of them and their beast. But the feeling was overwhelming and they became jumpy. No wonder their ancestors felt that the spirits roamed here – it was a dead haunted land, and once they were done with their exploring they would be glad to leave, to be gone. And if they found nothing, there would be no reason to return, which was fine with both of them.

Eventually both them fell asleep, although they awoke often thinking that they heard something approaching their camp. They would listen hard but hear nothing, only to fall back into a troubled sleep, and with the first gray in the sky found both of them shivering and building a warming fire. Both were blurry eyed and exhausted as if they hadn't slept at all. No word was spoken as it would have taken effort and energy which both felt that at this moment there was none. Sighing Jura finally said, "Bad night, hate them."

He nodded in agreement, not having the energy at this moment to put it into words. In a way he thought it was funny that right now as both of them sat shaking from the morning chill trying to get this fire burning hot enough to get some heat out of it, and that he, and he was sure she, looked forward to the rising of the suns and the heat they would provide them, only to curse them later in the day.

Eventually as the suns touched the horizon they began to move a little. Anyway they looked at it; this would be a tough day. With as little sleep as they had, even thinking clearly would be hard if not impossible, and they would have, also, to be careful with their tempers. Both knew that they would be short today and it would be easy to find faults that could set either of them off. Again, with the lack of concentration, it would be easy for their minds to drift off the task, and here, especially, it was very dangerous. While they were still close to the edge of the desolation and the grasslands, they were far enough inside that if they got themselves turned around it could mean failure and their very lives.

So with these thoughts, they picked up the trail and followed the old stones with care. And as the previous day they added their own to be sure to keep this pathway visible to them. The trail wound through many of the mud hills, small depressions, shallow valleys and ravines giving one no idea where it was leading. Soon they were longing for the cold morning as the heat became oppressing, closing in on them, and with the small breezes giving only temporary relief as they dried their sweat soaked clothes, leaving them worse off as the heat sucked the life right out of them. In the distance through the heat waves there appeared to be another cairn which lifted their spirits a little. At least they knew that they were still on the marked trail even if there was no true trail there. When they reached the cairn they found themselves in an enclosed bowl which concentrated the heat even more, making it almost unbearable. It appeared to be a dead end. Had they come all this way only to find nothing? It surely appeared to have been a waste of time. Jura looked at Kal and asked in a tired frustrated voice, "Now what?" She was exhausted and quite done with this, and finding this apparent dead end caused her flagging energy and spirits to collapse.

He was at loss for words as he looked around this sun baked landscape. Why place a cairn here of all things? There seemed to be no reason, none at all. In the unbearable heat and the waves of heat, causing the lands around them to shimmer, he walked further into this bowl and began to walk the perimeter, and hidden in a fold that was invisible from where they had been standing, he found an opening. Turning around and facing Jura, who hadn't moved, and to his eyes, appeared to be on the verge of collapse, pointed and said, "Looks like it might continue here. This is kind of hidden unless you get in the right place." He signaled her to follow and found himself in a narrow ravine or small canyon, the floor covered in loose sand. It wound and twisted through a number of turns and then the hills that formed the sides began to drop away with the path he was following change and began to widen and open up. As he made the final turn he stopped and his jaw dropped. He was at a complete loss for words. It was as if the words in those writings had come alive and he was now standing as his ancestor had described the scene.

Jura was trailing a little behind and when she saw him stop, even though he was still partially hidden by the twists of this trail she wondered what happened. Only to stop as she came up beside him and see the very same thing he was staring at. Both were silent for a while and in silent reverence entered into this hidden area that his ancestor K'jor had first set eyes upon. The very thing that had set their world on the path it was presently on. Before them sat those same shelters that he had seen. Only time had not been kind. Still because of the dryness of the area these shelters were still somewhat intact. Although the roofs have collapsed a very long time in the past, and many of the walls had collapsed together forming piles. Yet enough remained so that they could be identified for what they had been – shelters. As they approached these long empty and abandoned shelters they could see that original strip of vegetation, now long dead that had blocked the view of that wall, and below and ahead of them the other shelters constructed as the tribes had, again showing the wear of time. "It's just as described in the writings," Jura whispered.

It was almost like they had entered sacred ground. For this had been one of the strongest myths, and one, that any in their world thought would always remain as such. Yes, in the past others had tried, and many had died in their attempts. Making most believe it wasn't worth the cost to prove it one way or the other. Yet here they stood as K'jor had. Only in their case they wouldn't be facing the same issues, the same problems or puzzles, since these had been solved so long in the past. The present puzzle was; why did someone live here in the first place? Now, from personal experience, it made no sense. It was a land of the dead not the living; unbelievably hot during the day, and very cold during the night – making this land un-inhabitable for all. They had yet to find any living thing be it plant or beast, in the torn ragged land. "I really don't believe what I'm seeing. It's got to be a mirage. But we can reach out and touch this so I know it isn't." Kal was almost as quiet in his response back to her as his eyes took in the sights. The heat forgotten, they quietly walked the area where the two places were located – the clan home and the tribe home. In a way it was a learning experience since there hadn't been any-thing like this in at least a thousand cycles of the seasons so no one really knew what these shelters truly looked like or how their ancestors arranged them.

After spending some time among these ruins of their past, they headed towards the wall that was visible beyond the dead vegetation that had originally blocked the view of any who had entered this small hidden valley, and began to follow in the footsteps of their ancient ancestors. For them it was just as it was for their ancestors. From this point on it was into the unknown. What was it that lay just beyond that wall? That wall that was still too high to climb, too high to see over, leaving everything that existed beyond to speculation. Yet the writings had described what had transpired back at that time, and the killing of the ones who had lived in this place. As they approached, their appreciation for the ones who had constructed it increased. Its sheer size dwarfed them, and while much of whatever had covered it had been blasted by the winds over time, there was still a slight hint of the color that it had originally been. Sort of an off white that rivaled the colors of the surrounding hills leaving just enough of a contrast to make the wall stand out from the barren land.

Again silence was upon them. How was something like this constructed? There had never been found in any of the discoveries anything like this. And, as far as they knew, they had no ability to do this today. Kal reached out and touched the wall and found that it had the feel of a rough rock surface, and of course was warm from the heat. As he ran his hand over the rough surface he could see small grains of something falling off. Both stood there in awe of this massive construction, so simple, and yet so beyond anything they could do themselves. "It's no wonder that our ancestors thought that whoever built this was magicians and sorcerers. It had to be shocking to find this kind of barrier and know that it isn't natural. By the gods, I almost feel that way. This is just unbelievable." Looking up he felt that it had to be at least twice his height and maybe more.

Jura remained silent as she stared at it. *Who could have done such a thing?* With what they had discovered so far, she was expecting something completely different than what was here. Even now, like Kal, it would have been easy to pass this off to the supernatural. Quietly and with reverence she said, "Shall we walk along it and see what we can find? But if this is what these people were capable of, I'm almost afraid of what might be on the other side of this wall. I mean look at this! Really look at this. It's so simple, but at the same time demands our attention. It reflects strength and power without being obvious. And why is it here and why did these people do this? From what we can tell there's nothing in the desolation that could require such a thing. Yet, here it is. And if I remember, in those writings, every lair that they attacked and destroyed had one of these surrounding it where there were openings in the land. So what we are seeing here isn't isolated, it was common."

"Yeah, but that brings up another question."

"Another one? I thought we were finding too many already. But what would that be?"

"Well, think about it Jura. I mean really think about it. It's obvious that we couldn't do this when this was discovered, and we still cannot today, so who are these people? I mean who were they that they could do all of this, and live here where no one could or should live, and from the size of this it was more than one or two families. Plus, in those writings that we are using, they said that this was one of the smallest that they discovered and destroyed. We already know that we can't live here, and that's why this place is largely unexplored. As experience has shown, most that go into the desolation don't come back out. And now that we've had firsthand experience, we know why. So again, who were these people and how'd they do it? And I guess that leads to another one. I know that we've been trying to find the hunter camp and then this place, but from what we've seen so far, and I know this is just the beginning, do we announce our discovery or do we say nothing about it? I mean, look at this, really look at this. What does this say about us, and then comparing what we are seeing here, and I know we aren't even inside of this yet, are we really ready for what this both reveals and says about our world?"

They began walking along this wall before he continued. "Look, this flies in the face of logic and in what we truly know about our past. There is no record anywhere that supports what this represents. This changes everything. It raises questions such as; were we more advanced than now at some time in our past? And if that's the way of it, what is it that caused this world to lose what it had and became the clans and tribes of our past? There's just so much that something like this makes me want to question, and of course, I have no answers."

Jura remained silent once again as she absorbed what he was saying. It was a dilemma that's for sure. They had been eager to search and find this place – the place where their history began to change and lead them to where they were presently. But this was so beyond expectations, so beyond anything she had imagined. She honestly had thought that the writings had exaggerated this wall, but found in fact, that it understated it. *I really don't understand any of this.* She thought. *And Kal has raised some very valid questions. I know that I'm overwhelmed with just this wall. What is it that we will find beyond this? I'm almost afraid to find out. In a way I guess that I feel that we are so far above our ancient ancestors with what we are able to do. But here, right here is this. And it's old, so very old, and so far beyond us. What does this truly say? What does it say about us?* They came upon the jog in the wall, the very one mentioned in the writings, and before them was that doorway into that unknown world that K'jor and the clan destroyed so very long ago in the past. What would they find when they passed through that door leaving this world behind and entering into the lairs, as they had been called at the time of their destruction. She paused not sure if she really wanted to, and at that moment shadows started to build. She, looking around, realized that the day was just about over and they would have to wait as night was approaching and they'd need to set up camp. Thinking about what they had brought with them, tomorrow would be their only chance as they would be running out of what they had packed. In a way she was glad for the respite, since she wasn't sure if she really was ready for what was through that doorway. This wall had been shock enough for one day.

As it seemed to be in the desolation, the suns rose early. There was no trees, no mountains, nothing to block their early rise. So with a quick morning meal out of the way they made their way back to that wall, following it down towards that single entrance. They had camped by the ruins of the shelters that were like the clan shelters of the past. Something familiar, and at the same time there was additional wood so they could avoid using their meager supply. Now with the shadows stretched deeply from what shelters remained standing and that wall both could feel that morning chill that penetrated deep making both of them cold. Both looked back towards their campsite which wasn't visible here. Since there had been a warming fire there, and as of yet the suns hadn't begun their job of warming the area, and what surprised them was their breath coming out in clouds of steam – that fire was beckoning. There was reluctance in both of them. The wall had been a shock and was enough to make them feel inferior to whoever had been the ones who had constructed this thing. The writings had said that this doorway had been sealed at the time of discovery and after stopping whatever monster was responsible for that deep vibration that was more felt than heard; the doorway opened and had remained so since that time.

And that became the next mystery. They had expected a swinging door, the same that was on every shelter that ever had been built, yet this was not that way. Instead it appeared to have withdrawn into the wall. How could that be, and how, if they were seeing it right, did it do that? Again, this was something that they couldn't duplicate even now. In a subdued voice Kal said, "I guess we'd better go inside. You know I just can't get over the feeling that we're being watched. But, other than us, I haven't seen a living thing, and all I can feel is this very cold morning breeze, and hear nothing but silence. It really does feel like a haunted land. But, again, I don't know about you but that breeze is cutting, and I'm thinking that on the other side of this wall we'd be out of it. So shall we?"

Jura just nodded her head. She really wasn't sure she was ready but had to agree that getting out of the cold wind would be nice. She hated being cold. She signaled him to lead. He shrugged and took a tentative step through that opening in the wall. He really couldn't see much as the light from the suns was directly in his eyes, but once inside it cut that wind and it immediately felt warmer. They stood side by side looking to either side of them seeing a large avenue that followed the base of the wall in both directions. And while broken and cracked it appeared to have been some type of hard surface now gray with time, but giving the appearance of having been originally a much darker color. Picking up a small fragment Jura asked, "What is this stuff?" Handing it over to Kal all he could do once he had it and had inspected it was shake his head in the negative.

Where the suns light were striking them they could see another avenue that moved directly towards the suns. Soon they would be high enough that what the bright sunlight was blocking would become visible. Kal pointed to their left and said, "Let's go that way for now. At least we'll be heading back in the direction that we came from." So quietly, as to not disturb any of the dead, they walked along the wall on the inside passing a number of shelters and avenues. All of the shelters that faced the wall were nothing but walls. There were no windows or doors at all. Yet when they passed the avenues between these shelters they could see small porches, doors, and windows. As they continued their circuit of this strange place they found that it was laid out in a circle with the avenues acting like lines heading to the center. Making it easy for anyone who had business towards the center to head back out to where they may have lived. These shelters appeared to be made of the same materials as the wall. Yet here they could see that many were damaged and that there had been fire in others. All that they were seeing, as far as the damage, had been reported in those writings. It was uncanny – the accuracy. It was like they arrived days later to find this place, and then describing what was found to a scribe so that it could be there for future generations. The clan of K'jor had done their job well.

Finally, with the suns to their backs, and both had to admit that it felt good; they were more clearly able to see the layout and the size. This place had to be as large as Cross Trails if not larger, and Cross Trails was one of the larger villages. So far they were only searching the outer areas of this dead silent world, and there was plenty to see. As they worked their way towards the center they found other avenues that ringed this place so that any could go to any portion within that they desired. They realized that they probably could easily spend a few 9-days and not see everything that was here. And they only had today in which to explore. They finally decided to choose the large shelter that was in the center of the, well what would they call it? So going back to the writings they learned that the ones who were called sorcerers had called them cities, whatever that was? So using that unfamiliar term they found themselves at the shelter in the very center of the city. It was larger than most that they had passed and this one had no windows, and the doorway was twice the size of the others that they had seen. Like the entrance into this place through that wall, the opening into this shelter was also open, and it appeared that the doors retracted in the same way. As they studied the doorway they could find no hinges that a door would have hung on, and there were grooves in the floor and wall showing where doors would have been.

As they entered it became darker and they had to wait until their eyes adjusted. Looking up they found that there had been openings created in the roof to let light in. Dust lay on everything, and there were no tracks of any kind here. So they would be the first to disturb the sleep of the dead, and the silence that permeated everything. As they crept across the floor they found that it wasn't just dirt, crushed stone or rough wood planking. There appeared to be something on it that formed patterns. Both of them crouched down and with their hands pushed away some of the dust to get a better view of what this was. It appeared to be large squares of some material that made the floor shine, and whatever these thing were, they formed an understated checkerboard pattern. "What is this stuff?" Jura asked.

Again this was something that was beyond them and Kal replied saying, "I don't know. And with this dust and dim light we're really not seeing it very well."

"Yeah, that's very true, but I sure would love to have something like this on my floor. It'd be so much easier to take care of and so much more pleasing than what we have."

As they crossed the room there seemed to be some type of equipment that lined one of the walls, but what this was and what it did was completely unknown. Afraid to touch any of it they stared in awe. There were chairs for people to sit, but again these were unlike any they had ever seen. Kal accidently bumped one as he was trying to get a closer look at what appeared to be a smoked glass panel and the chair moved away easily and actually the seat spun slightly. "Did you see that?" He asked

This place was making her nervous, almost frightened. There were things here she didn't understand and felt that she would never understand. It was another one of those moments that brought understanding to her as she realized that their ancestors probably had felt the same way. And for them it was a different situation. The writings stated that what was here seemed alive. But how could that be? What she was seeing didn't – couldn't have been alive, yet that is how they felt. This place almost made her believe in magicians. How else to explain this? "Yes, Kal, but I don't like the feel of this place at all. Can we go look somewhere else please?"

He could see that she was shaken so he nodded and they walked quietly to a railing that was on the far side and across from where they had entered. But once they reached the railing they were disappointed as there were no skylights to reveal what was below. The light barely penetrated and what could be seen were just the very edges of a floor further below and past those shadows nothing but darkness. Looking to the left both could see a set of stairs leading down in that darkness. Both were reluctant to use them and enter that dark area. They looked at each other and they could see that they were more than willing to leave things as they were. Kal walked over to the walkway and found what appeared to be a chain hung across the entrance and a small sign attached that simple stated "POWER UNIT # 1". These words meant nothing, and the script was foreign to their method of writing, so they couldn't even be sure that there was a meaning attached to what they were seeing.

They headed back outside and had to admit that it was great to be back out in the sunlight. Just what was it in that strange room inside that windowless shelter? "You know, like the bakery, this place could have been used for business or such, But, that's only a guess. I didn't recognize anything in there. Even the familiar things, like chairs, are very different." Kal looked around and the shelters he saw more or less reminded him of the village center. The place where business was handled, and when he thought about it the shelters they had first passed as they came here looked to be places where one would live. "I think we should look in some of these others that are close to this one, and then finish by looking in a couple that is further away from this center. What do you think?"

She didn't know what she thought other than she didn't want to go back into that one they had left. Still curiosity drove her on and she looked around seeing if any drew her attention. Looking across from where they were standing she spied one that seemed a little different. There appeared to be a curved area in front and a large round, well she wasn't sure what to call it, but in a way it looked a little like a bowl that they would serve soups and stews in. But this was huge. Pointing she said, "Let's go over there. I want to see what that thing is, and the whole front of that shelter appears to be made of glass or something like it. Look how it reflects everything. And I think if you look closely we can see us in it, and all the other shelters around."

Both headed over and inspected that large bowl like construction, and when they looked inside as they approached, there was nothing to indicate what it may have been used for. They found that the edges were large enough to sit and was of a height that invited one to do just that, so they sat down. At this point Kal looked at the sides that curved down and away from them and noticed some type of material sticking to the sides. He scraped a small piece off and studied it for a moment. "I think I know what was in this thing. I think it was water."

"Water? Really?" She leaned over and looked at what was sticking to the sides and realized that he was probably right. But this would mean there was a lot of water, and here, in the desolation? Where'd it come from? Looking at the center of this – what would she call it – an artificial pond, there appeared to be some type of sculpture, but again, what it represented or what it did was beyond them. Kal climbed in and carefully walked to the center where the sculpture was, walked around it and then joined her. "Well," she asked, "figure anything out?"

He shook his head and said, "No." At this point he climbed out. Shaking his head he thought, *another question to add to so many others. I really thought that this place was myth, and yet here it is. Then I thought that my ancestors had it wrong considering the people who lived and died here were sorcerers and magicians, and yet here we are this many cycle of the seasons later and I feel the same way. Can I blame them when I have the very same reaction?* This place was strange, foreign, beyond anything they could have imagined. That it was old was quite obvious. And yet, except for the dust of the ages that lay upon everything, one could imagine people living out their lives here today. But why in the desolation, and where did they get their water? They had to get it somewhere, and this thing that held all this water was proof. But again, where, and how? "Okay, another mystery. Shall we go inside this shelter then?"

She agreed and they once again entered through what appeared to be a double doorway with those mysterious doors that had retracted into the walls. Light streamed through those open doors and what appeared to be glass walls at least making the interior space brighter and more inviting. One of the first things they noticed was that it was cooler inside even with the open doorway. Although, as they moved back and forth, passing that entrance, they could feel the heat as it invaded this space. Just past the entrance was what appeared to be a large desk – one who was standing could comfortably approach and lean on. It seemed to be made of some polished wood, but where would that come from? Looking over again they saw those strange chairs and more of that equipment. Looking back behind to the wall they saw normal doorways, a couple behind the desk and more running down the back wall to either side of the desk. On the front of the desk was another sign of that strange script that stated, "ADMINISTRATION".

Leaving the desk area, they walked up to a number of the doors, and each had a sign on them. All these doors were closed and appeared to be more along the lines of doors they were familiar with. They also saw a couple of areas where there was seating, and some strange machines marked with that strange script once again – one stating "SNACKS", and the other "BEVERAGES". Again, like their decision to leave the other shelter, they decided to leave without further exploration. Their time was very limited and they really couldn't spend much time on any particular shelter. And, once again outside, the bright light momentarily blinded them. "I think that you're right, this is just like our village center. I think I'd like to see how these people lived, so let's go out a little further and check out their personal shelters." Jura turned around and looked again at shelter they had just vacated and wondered what it was like when the living had been here. And at the same time felt lucky to even have the chance to find and explore this place. The writings spoke of the other lairs found, and their ancestors had destroyed these others with fire. With this being the first, their ancestors had simply attacked and killed the residents.

It was somewhere between the fifth mark and sixth, and their stomachs were reminding them that it was getting past the zenith and they hadn't taken time to eat anything. So once they had left that last shelter they looked around for any shade that they could find, finally settling on a shelter that had a small overhang. Here they leaned back against its wall, taking off their packs and digging out travel rations and a container of water. Their day was divided into ten marks as was the night. They were running out of time for this trip. And on the morrow they would have to make a quick trip back to the base camp in the grasslands. They had entered the desolation heavy, but would be returning light, and since they wouldn't be trying to locate the way to go, the return trip should be faster. They were quiet as they ate, not really tasting what it was that they ate as their eyes roamed these strange silent shelters. What had it been like when there were the living here? Yet, as it had been since they entered the desolation, they still felt as if they were watched, that this dead land, this dead lair was filled with spirits that watched everything that they did. But all that moved in this silent world was the winds, a bit of dust, and debris that the winds picked up. It was like they were the last of the living.

Jura shuddered saying, "I don't know about you but I've not been comfortable since we've entered the desolation, and once we came in here it's been worse. I feel like I want to panic, to run away screaming, from, oh I don't know what, but whatever. This place depresses me greatly, and I can't even tell you why." She fell silent not knowing what to add to what she had just said, yet she felt as there was more that needed to be said. "It's like, again, I don't know if I can even find the words . . ." Here she trailed off and just shrugged.

Quietly Kal responded, "I know. This place feels like death. Yet, when you look at the shelters, what is here, none of it reflects that – none of it at all. Okay, let's go through a couple of the ones we think that people probably lived in, and really our day will be close to over and we can leave this haunted land. And once we're back in our camp in the grasslands we can decide what we want to reveal later. But we will at least need to bring our writings up to date as to what we found here, and update our personal maps – especially if we ever want to come back . . . Although, truthfully, if I want to admit it, I really can't figure out why I would want to do that. Like you, I feel that this place, these lands, seem almost alive in the sense that it doesn't want us here and is letting us know. Making us feel uncomfortable, making us feel like we are being followed, watched. Yet, everywhere we look, every place that we've been, everything that we've touched shows no sign of the living – just us."

What could she say? It was exactly like this, and it made no sense, no sense at all. They got up from their zenith meal and randomly picked one of the larger shelters that appeared to be a place where one would live. One of the signs that they took for this was the doors. These doors were similar to what they were familiar with – none of the type that disappeared into the walls. Most of these shelters had small overhangs to project shade, and many of these areas had chairs made out of an unknown substance, furthering the illusion that the owners were away, and would be soon back. As had been the case of the large central shelters, many of the doors were open and the one that they had chosen was one of these. Before entering, they looked through the dirty windows that were located on either side of the entrance, but couldn't really see anything. So quietly they entered not knowing what they would find. Again, like when they had left that previous shelter, their eyes had to adjust to dim interior. So they waited a moment before continuing. The first thing they noticed was an odor that spoke of age. This room appeared to be a place for whoever had lived here to gather. There appeared to be something soft on the floor, and it covered the whole room. It kind of reminded them of rugs, but there never had been any of this size, or texture. It begged them to take their shoes off and walk barefoot across it. But it was also covered in dirt and sand that had blown in through the open door.

Now that their eyes had adjusted they went from room to room looking at what was here finally reaching what had to be the sleeping areas. Many of the rooms in this shelter had doors, which were a surprise, and one of the biggest surprises was upon opening one they found what they thought had to be the room where one took care of nature calls. This was something that was rarely part of the main shelter, but usually a small shelter close by. Plus there was a place to bathe, and clean up. There was a small frosted window which didn't admit much light, so most of what they saw was in heavy shadows. Yet, they felt that their conclusions had to be right. Thinking about it they didn't remember seeing any of those out-shelters when they had come into this place. Neither spoke as they searched and explored this shelter. It seemed that silence was appropriate. So they moved on to the next closed door.

Upon opening it they both stood shocked at what they saw. This had to be the sleeping area and on, well it wasn't a sleeping mat since it was much taller than that, were two bodies, more skeletal, although there still was skin attached. And it was obvious from the dark stains that surrounded them that they had been killed here and their blood had stained what had covered them. From what they could determine the two remains appeared to be male and female. They closed that door, went to the other side of the one that they had inspected before opening this one and opened another closed door. Here they found another room like the sleeping room, and in it were smaller versions of what the two had slept on, including one that had to be an infant sleeping mat. And like that other room, there were bodies here – obviously children. Both of them entered the room just far enough to be able to see the whole grisly scene. Jura picked up what had to be a child's toy and idly turned in her hands as she looked at the bodies.

Kal turned facing Jura and saw tears forming in her eyes, and a couple beginning to run down her cheeks. He could understand her feelings. Taking her into his arms, he gently led her back out of the room and quietly closed the door. The urge to explore more of this shelter was now gone, and he led her back outside where they sat on the chairs under the overhang feeling the warm breeze. He didn't say anything but let her cry it out. It was so different to have read it in the writings. Now facing the reality of what their ancestors had done shocked him, and he knew her. When the writings said that they had killed all that lived within this evil lair, it never dawned on either of them that this meant literally everyone – males, females, and all the young ones. How could they not have realized that? Breathing out quietly he asked, "Should we look through any of the others, or should we just leave and call it enough?"

Jura had finally quit crying and looking at him through her red rimmed eyes and dirt streaked face from where the tears had run she said, "I'm done. Let's just leave and let this place return to the ones who died here so very long ago." So quietly both of them got out of the chairs and headed back out through the doorway in that wall, back to their camp by the clan like ruins and shelters, packed everything that they were not going to need for this night and watched as the suns set, ending their time here in the desolation, even though they wouldn't exit until the morrow.

CHAPTER THIRTEEN

VALLEY OR NO VALLEY

They had all of the Season of Cold in which to bring their notes and thoughts up to date. Both had begun to realize the hard work that went into these searches, and to be prepared for anything when they discovered what they were searching for. Who'd thought that once those ruins were located in the desolation, with the passage of this much time, that there would still be evidence of what had transpired there – not either of them, that was for sure. Both learned that experiencing it had a much greater impact on them personally then reading it in the old writings. It seemed so much more impersonal. So much so that it was easy to separate one from the idea that real people had died, and from what evidence they had gathered with their brief time in those ruins, it became obvious to them that these people had no weapons. Yes, they had argued, their ancestors may have taken whatever weapons that these people had, but there was nothing in the writings suggesting such a thing, nor was there any proof on the ground that such existed. This meant, their people had attacked, and wiped out, a clan that had no way of defending themselves, resulting in the slaughter that they had discovered at that site, after all this time.

They had yet to come to any conclusion as to what they were going to reveal about their time in the desolation. After all, their main objective had been to locate the hunter's camp to demonstrate the range that their ancestors roamed. The trip into and the attempt to locate that first, again what was it these people had called it, oh yes, city, was just that. So that portion of their research writings and field notes they kept separately. Instead they wrote detailed notes covering the camp, from its layout and the finding of broken spear points and other arti-facts. While all of this was true, it reflected more time than they actually spent, yet it gave the appearance that they had, thusly covering their time in the desolation. Those ruins felt haunted, felt as unseen, unknown eyes were watching them during their whole time there. And the ruins spoke of a differ-ence, and a knowledge that was well beyond them even now. So, they felt that it should remain unknown to the world as it had until it was rediscovered sometime in the future. Later they might change their minds, but for now that place would remain vacant with its ghosts and spirits and be left alone by any from this time and world.

Once all of this had been written, discussed, edited, and finished to their satisfaction, it was time to prepare for the next season. They had plans on locating the mythological place, the Valley of the Gods. Until that incident recorded in the writings of not only K'jor's clan, but of many of the tribes and clans that had become part of the alliance, this valley had simply been the place of meetings and gatherings of the alli-ance. The place where they planned and carried out their attacks on what they called the sorcerers and magicians and their hidden lairs in the desolation. From their talk with that, well they still didn't know who he was or what to call him, so they settled on the wild one, they knew that the area they needed to search was north of where they lived in High Trail, and south of that hunting camp. And again, it had been located on the west side of the grasslands and had bordered the desolation with at least two ways directly into the desolation from it, but only one entrance from the grasslands itself. The description given in the writings suggested that it was located in an area of much broken land, with many dead end trails and canyons, and among all of this was the valley, a hidden oasis with grass, trees, and water, while much of the area was drier than the grasslands themselves.

Again, with their conversation with the wild one, they had gotten a better idea of what they faced, since he had stated that at one time he had actually been in that valley, but had never been able to find his way back. Suggesting that the entrance was well hidden and even if found could easily be lost again. Also, from the writings they had studied, they learned that the entrances, or at least one of them on the desolation side, was open and was very easy to travel. Although if one was looking at the entrance from the desolation, this one held no promise of going anywhere at all, looking like so many of the other dead ends. So if one didn't know, then with little promise of going anywhere it would be passed up and ignored. But both of them admitted that they had enough of the desolation and decided to try and locate the entrance from the grasslands, leaving the desolation entrance, if it still existed, until later if need be. But, again, it stated that when the gods had made their appearance that the two exits into the desolation had been destroyed, so these probably were not options anyway. Still they wouldn't know until they were actually in that valley.

Both had spent a lot of time in each other's arms after their grisly discoveries, making them realize that there was much on the outside that could influence their lives, and nothing was promised or guaranteed. What they had discovered there had changed both of them forever. Again what had started out as wanting to discover their true past, but not really being too serious, had turned to just that, and with the discovery this further changed their personal views of their world, their lives, and just how fleeting all of it was. Not that they weren't close, because they were, but these discoveries brought them even closer together, trying to live and accept every moment, knowing that they could end up being like those dead. Through the Season of the Cold, they spent time with their families, worked the business, and talked long and many times deep into the night. Family now meant everything to both of them, and both knew that someday they would have children, and raise the next generation who would continue in the ways of their families. This was the way it had always been, at least after the times of the clans and tribes, and should continue long into the future.

* * *

The Season of Green had been well along when they began this cycle of the seasons search. There still had been no word on the fate of Sabohl. His body had never been found, so this was still an unknown. With him out of the picture the others had replaced him in the hierarchy and new ideas were being put forth. With the discovery of the ancient clan site and the discoveries made there, some of what had been considered myth had been shown to be fact, requiring a reexamining of their history. Most of these new discoveries, because of those ancient writings that had remained within Kal's family from the time of the ending of the clans and tribes, were the maps, in words and drawings that led them to these places lost in time. Some of the discoveries included tools, long knives, and to their surprise some ancient bow strings – although, the bows themselves, hadn't survived the passage of time. And that left them with another mystery – who had created these items?

While the condition of these discoveries were poor, it was obvious that even with the abilities that they had now to forge knives and braid bow strings that gave the strings strength and longevity, these were far superior to what they produced. It was suspected that these were trade items from the travelers, who had stated, as quoted from the writings, "They lived in a cold wet place requiring their people to come up with solutions to prevent their bow strings from stretching when wet, and for the knives to hold an edge and not rust." Whoever these travelers were, they had been lost in time. Their home never located, and whatever methods they had used to create these items had been lost with them. So the tribes and clans coveted the few that had remained when the travelers came no more. And as it was the first time they had disappeared it was the last. There was no tapering off but a sudden and instant end, with no explanation or reason as to why, and thusly why these travelers had ended up as myth in the present time.

Still with the travelers being mentioned quite prominently in the writings, to both Kal and Jura, they had to be real. But that was for another time. They were out to locate the Valley of the Gods, again another location placed as myth. Because of what was known it would have been impossible for the incident described by so many of the clans and tribes to actually have happened – it just did not make any sense. Especially now, since they were aware of many of the laws of nature – not all by any means, but discoveries were being made all the time. So what had been witnessed by them, in that time, was tied to something they may have eaten that caused mass hallucinations. Yet with the consistency of what was reported, none could explain it away – so another mystery. And there seemed to be so many more of those mysteries than hard facts. Why was this so? Both of them wondered, since their ancestors had lived during that time, had recorded what they had witnessed. Of course it was interpreted by the way they viewed the world in their time. Still, even looking at it that way, no one could solve this riddle. This led to the theory that what had been witnessed in that valley was something that had changed over time and had become the myth that they now knew – but no one really knew.

So they had two and half seasons this cycle to attempt to locate the hidden valley. Fortunately, that accidental contact with the loner who roamed the outback had given them hints as to where to look. They remembered coming out of the desolation hot and tired, seeing the heat waves move across the landscape and what seemed to be a very large male standing there. He appeared to be twice the height of the normal male and they could see that he was watching them. So they approached cautiously not sure what they were going to face. And to find, as they got closer, his size began to shrink, and once nearly out of the desolation, they could recognize who it was. They didn't know why, but for some reason he had attached himself to them, showing up now and then to see what they had learned or found. It must have been something to do with his curiosity, his liking of puzzles. It was the only explanation that they had. Still that brief time with him, before once again he tired of being around people and disappeared, they had learned the general area where the hidden valley was located. So it was here that they would concentrate their exploring. Who knew, maybe this time it wouldn't take a couple of cycles of the seasons to locate this place.

Yet the word from the ones who had been in that area spoke of a broken land, a smaller version of the Sacred Mountains, some said. That led them to believe that it was probably the same forces that had formed both of these areas – although it was only a guess on their part. He, after all, was just a baker, and she a farmer. They headed out early in the morning on the eighth 9-day of the Season of Green, and headed north and west since High Trail was located on the eastern edge of the grasslands up against a number of low lying foothills. It was in these foothills that Jura and her family had farmed for generations. This trip would probably require at least two 9-days to reach the beginnings of the area that they wanted to search. Then from the description they had been given, they knew that they probably could spend the next several seasons there and not locate all the canyons, valleys, and hidden areas. There didn't appear to be any one person who knew the whole area. So over the time that they had spent back in High Trail, they had gathered what information was available and had a rough, albeit, inaccurate map of the area. Even with this, there were many blank areas and lots of conflicting information. They truly had their work set out before them. Still, with high hopes and copies of those ancient writings, they headed out.

* * *

They had already spent a 9-day in the area more setting up camp and getting a feel for the surrounding terrain. On the edges of this vast area it was hilly, and as they worked their way deeper into what they were now calling badlands they found sharp rises, cliffs, canyons cutting through plateaus, some areas heavy with trees, others with grass, and then like the desolation a few of what they saw was bare of any vegetation at all. It was a tortured broken land that one could easily get lost in. And when they first saw it they understood why their ancient ancestors had chosen this area. If an enemy were to attempt to follow them into these broken lands it was so very easy to spread out and disappear leaving the followers too many directions to go and by doing so weaken their own forces. The area had a raw rugged beauty about it that drew one in wanting to see what the next rise and valley would present. And this was a danger in itself – it would be easy to become lost, with the washes turning and twisting in multiple directions, branching off, and turning in on themselves. Many of these narrow canyons showed signs of heavy flooding, and because of their narrowness they also were in shadow a good part of the day. So using the suns as a way to determine direction, many times was impossible.

The area spoke of a rawness that said don't attempt to tame us, we have always been here and will be long after you are no more. It was a land of many streams, a few rivers, and many waterfalls. Here caves abounded with some hillsides filled with them giving the appearance of villages in the hills. At no time did they find sign of any ever having been here, let alone living here. They found that they could hike all day running through a series of those small narrow canyons only to turn a corner and find themselves looking at a large meadow being fed by one of those many streams and see in the distance another waterfall. And the waterfalls were of infinite variety. Some fell from great heights while others were a series of falls, and still others broke and split and ran off the cliffs in different directions. Never were there two alike, but each unique to itself. In some areas they could find long dead cinder cones, proof of this area's volcanic origin. Then close to a series of these cinder cones they found hot springs, and a series of geysers. Since this was the first time they had personally experienced geysers, even though they had read about them in the learning center, the view took their breath away leaving them in awe of what this world was showing them. Out of those hot springs ran small rivulets that created small streams, and as the water flowed, it left colored deposits on the soil adding further beauty to this hidden world.

Because of the remoteness of the area from any village or farmland, they kept their pack beast with them fearing that there could easily be some predator that would attack and kill it leaving them without a way to move their supplies. As they worked their way through the land they added to their maps, and while the maps in their mind were very incomplete, as the ones they were creating on parchment, slowly they were beginning to see and understand this place. A number of times as they had worked their way west they would find places where a particular canyon or valley that they were exploring would open into the desolation. Showing why this area had been chosen to organize those attacks on the hidden lairs. Yet, the prize eluded them. Time and time again they felt that they had been close, and studying the ancient rough map that they had in their possession, it looked right, or felt right, only to find that it wasn't so.

As the Season of Green moved on into the Season of Heat they were beginning to have doubts that the entrance would ever be revealed to them. Both were sure that they had to have gone by it a number of times. Both remembered the words of that wild one who stated that he had been in the valley once, but when trying to find it again could never relocate it. And knowing what they did about this one, if he couldn't return to it, then the entrance was well hidden and only circumstance and time of day would reveal it. Finally narrowing their search down to a specific area deep inside these badlands, they had set up camp after moving it from the hills just outside of the badlands. They had decided that they needed their working camp to be in the area that they were searching, and they had discovered enough meadowlands within to keep the pack beast fed. With a new site established, both were sitting watching the suns set over the cliffs off to their west, seeing the shadows grow and the light soften towards dusk, it had been another frustrating unsuccessful day. "Look, I don't know about you," Kal stated, "but I feel like we are so very close."

She laughed and asked, "How do you mean that?" She reached out and put her arms around him and asked, "Do you mean like this?" At which point she kissed him, smiled and pulled back, and leaned forward before continuing in a little more serious tone. "Know what you really meant, but I just couldn't help it. You just seemed so serious and your statement could have meant so many different things. But, I don't have any answers. Just like when we were trying to find that old clan home, we've run into obstacles and part of those is the map that our ancestors provided. Again, like we discovered last time, there's nothing consistent in what's up or what's down, or what direction is what. And some of the things they've used for landmarks have disappeared over time. Orientation is also hard to figure. Both of us have decided that if a tribe or clan were newly added that they would be given a map like this to lead them to the meeting place. But at the same time they left something out so that if the map fell into the hands of an enemy they couldn't discover this meeting place and set up an ambush."

"Yeah, and the problem that both of us are facing is that we can't speak to any of them since they've been dead for such a very long time. So without that verbal key we're banging our proverbial head against a wall."

"True, true, at least we can say we've seen some very beautiful country, and seen sights that others haven't. So if nothing else is to come of this we have that."

He couldn't help but smile. She always had a way of bringing out the good side of what they did, even if he hadn't seen it at the time. "You are so right. This whole area is very beautiful, and because of its isolation very few come here. So it's almost like we're the first, even though we know better."

They spent the night in each other's arms. It had been one of those romantic nights with the major moon rising giving the lands a magical feel leading them to being physical a couple of times. Finally satiated from their love making they both fell to sleep with a soft warm breeze coming off the desolation which lay to the west of them. The night was slowly cooling and later before the morning chill made them cover up; they remained on top of their sleep sacks with only a light covering to keep them warm. And with the morning both of them took a quick invigorating dip in pond that they had camped close to. Shivering from the cold water both headed back to the roaring fire that they had built before heading for that morning dip. Wrapping a drying cloth around themselves they absorbed the heat the fire was throwing out.

Finally they grabbed their clothes that had been placed close to the fire, dressed, enjoying the warmth of the clothing on their cool skin. Finally warm and with only their hair now wet, Kal walked out and away from their camp while today Jura had the kitchen duty and was fixing the morning meal. It had been a magical end to the day and a wonderful night last night. Still, they were no closer to solving this puzzle. And when he thought about it that way, it brought a smile to his face, since that wild one liked puzzles and had dropped in on them a number of times since that first visit so long ago. Well they surely had one here. Kal knew that they were close. This area where they were camping matched well an area on that primitive map that marked a gathering place that was close to the hidden entrance into the valley. He stood and watched as the suns began their daily rise above the canyon walls promising the heat that would be arriving soon. Yet right at this time the heat the suns produced felt great. About this time he heard Jura say that the food was on, and if he wanted it hot he'd better get over here. Turning around and smiling, even though, because he was between her and the suns, so she couldn't actually see him well, he said, "Yup, that's how I like my food, and my female – hot." This brought a laugh out of both of them as he came back to the fire and joined her.

Later, after the camp had been cleaned up, and the suns were up high enough to cast some deep shadows, they began to study the canyon walls that surrounded them. Seeing how the lay of the land truly was. Both sat on a small rise arm in arm, enjoying the peace and slight breezes that surrounded them at this very moment. It seemed that all was right with the world, and with them, as they reveled in each other's company, not speaking, but enjoying the closeness, the quiet, and each other. What more could they ask for? Well, other than the shadows revealing the trail into the valley, but there was a warmth, a deep companionship here, and both realized that these forays into the wilds had made them ever so much closer, so much deeper in love with each other, leaving them with a deeper commitment and desire to be with the other. It was one of the important aspects of these searches that hadn't originally been considered. They spent the time this way until midmorning talking about nothing and just holding each other.

Finally Kal said, "I think I could spend all day just doing this, and by the gods, why not. After all a down day now and then is nice and necessary, so let's just take a leisurely stroll around this canyon and just idly look around, take it easy and not push anything today. This day, so far has been very nice. I feel the need just to be close to you today – can't explain it, but it's so."

She smiled, even though it was one of those rare shy smiles. She'd been thinking the same thing actually. The last day or so she found herself being drawn closer to him, and last night had been wonderful, and now today it just seemed right to let it just continue. She looked into his eyes and said, "You're not going to get me to argue. I feel very much the same way. So, I know what you said, but is there something specific?"

He smiled back at her and said, "No, not really. I know originally we were going to do some searches here, but it can wait. Just let the day become what it will. Although with last night being as good as it was, I think that if the day goes as well, I'd like to repeat it if we could."

She laughed. "I thought as much. But you're not going to get me to argue after all I agree with you, it was wonderful last night. Okay, we'll take the day as it comes and then we'll see."

* * *

After a very relaxing day the day before both felt recharged and ready to tackle their task at hand. They really couldn't remember the last time that they had taken a full day to just enjoy each other and block out the world. But time moves on, and it was now in the past. With the primitive map in hand they were comparing the landmarks on the map with the canyon they were presently in, and so far had been unsuccessful in making anything match once they got beyond the area that they had identified as the initial gathering area before heading into the valley. With no distances marked they could still easily be at least a day away or it could be here. But with all the growth of the trees and bushes nothing was easy. Yes there were a few trails through this stuff which allowed them to approach the canyon walls, but all of it was hard going. Where they had their camp was grasslands like where they came from, a rather large meadow, but as they approached the water flowing through this canyon, the trees became thick as did the bushes. And for whatever the reason, it seemed that these bushes were thickest at the canyon walls.

Another 9-day had passed without much success when, as the suns were setting they watched a shadow fall wrong across one of the faces of the cliff. It should have lain straight against the wall but instead dipped and disappeared showing that there had to be a crack or something else here that wasn't normally visible to the eye. So with the fading light they quickly headed towards this illusion before darkness claimed it. And if that happened they weren't sure that they could come back to this place and find it again. The wild one had stated that he had only found the entrance by following his intended target and after leaving had never been able to find his way back. So if one did not mark the entrance, the chances of finding it again were close to zero. Most surprising of all was the fact that the area they were heading to, was out in the open, not blocked by either trees or bushes. It was a spot that they had passed by, who knew how many times, giving it little thought. They had studied this face a number of times but have never seen anything to would lead them to believe that there was a way through. This wall appeared to be solid.

Even as they approached the wall they couldn't see the break in it and once they reached it, it still wasn't obvious. No wonder this trail had never been found and thusly had been placed in the myth category. If there was no way into such a place, then the place probably did not exist, and if it did not exist it had to be myth. And it was now almost too dark to see so one of them stood at the point where the shadow had appeared and the other went quickly to gather what stones they could find to place a small cairn here to mark it so that in the morning when they would have the whole day ahead of them they could come back to the exact location and do a much better search. It would be awhile before the minor moons rose tonight, so with care they stumbled back to their camp full of energy and anticipation for what they would discover on the morrow. In a sense it was frustrating to both of them, but there was little they could do about it. Of course what was there could turn out to be just another dead end. There were breaks and cracks all through the walls of this canyon and most were just that. So the odds were that this would be the same. But, this couldn't be answered at this time.

It was late before they could wind down enough to sleep, and with their expectations high they had a wonderful physical session that left both of them breathless. They lay in each other's arms for quite a while afterwards, and slowly their breathing eased and both fell asleep until later when the chill of the night finally penetrated and they climbed into their sleep sacks, and fell immediately back to sleep. Both surely hoped that, with all the time they had spent in this broken rugged land, with the Season of Heat winding down, and the time of harvest was fast approaching, this was what they had been searching for. They were once again running out of time. One did not remain out here in the Season of Cold. It was obvious to them as they had explored the many canyons and valleys. There were signs of flash floods and high water everywhere. So it was an area to stay away from if one wanted to remain among the living.

The morning broke bright and cold. One of the signs that signaled the Season of Falling was approaching. The morning chill had a bite to it that made them want to stay close to their fire. Their breath was coming out in clouds, being quite visible in the morning light, before evaporating and disappearing completely. Looking over at Jura, Kal thought. *She doesn't look so good this morning – hope she's not getting sick or something.* "Is something wrong? You're looking a little off this morning."

She smiled at him even though it was a weak one. "Don't think so, but my stomach seems a bit queasy this morning and these smells that usually seem to cheer me up almost make me sick just by smelling them."

He saw a surprised look on her face and she got up rapidly and headed back behind their portable shelter and he heard her throw up, not once but several times. Yeah she definitely had caught something. This surely would put a damper on the day and what they had hoped to discover, but her health was so much more important to him than finding that entrance. He watched her as she came back around, appearing to be a little shaky, and sit back down. "That was unpleasant", he said. No sooner had he said that that she was immediately back up and headed once more behind the portable shelter and he heard her heave again. *Wow, whatever it is its nasty.* "Are you all right?" He asked He heard a bit of mumbling but couldn't make out what she said. Finally after a while she finally came back around and sat down once again, looking a bit white under her dark tan. "I guess we'll just stay in camp today and see how this progresses with you. I'm not going to leave you by yourself when you're obviously sick." He could see that she was about to protest, but he put up his hand to silence her, shaking his head he said. "Look, this can wait, you are what is important. Not some old trail or valley that will still be there long after you and I are gone. So don't protest, we still have time . . . I just don't want you getting any worse."

This had come out of nowhere and was completely unexpected. She had felt great last night, and buoyed by their possible success yesterday it had even given her more energy, and she had to admit that last night they'd been as close as they ever had been, actually almost desperate for the need of each other. This had only happened a few times in their relationship and every time that it had happened in the past, they would look forward to those rare times when it would show once again. *So, why now?* What did she catch? Well, whatever it was she didn't want it to be around very long, they had too much to do, and the seasons were winding down once again towards the time when they would have to abandon what they were doing. She watched, as Kal puttered around the camp, watching her as she tried to put on a happy face trying to look better than she felt. Inwardly she had to smile, because the concern that he showed was very genuine, and she had to admit that she appreciated it very much. With their research of the past she had become very knowledgeable of how life had been for females and it wasn't pretty, nice, or anything that she could think that she'd want to live or do.

Yet, as the morning progressed her stomach began to settle down and she wasn't feeling like she'd need to go behind their portable shelter and lose whatever was still there. Truthfully, with all she had done this morning there really couldn't be much left. Sitting there she drank cold water and attempted a little of that bland travel bread that they had with them. She wasn't sure if she wanted to put any food into her system, but felt that she needed to try. The last thing she really wanted to do was repeat her earlier episode. Gingerly she nibbled the bread, and drank a lot of water and found that she could keep it down. Then, to her surprise, she felt fine. *So what is that all about anyway?* "Kal, I think the worst is over, so why don't we go over and at least look. It's really not that far, and if I begin to feel bad again it's a short distance back to here."

He looked her over carefully, and still could see some paleness underneath her tan, but at the same time she didn't appear to be as drawn out as earlier. He breathed out deeply still concerned saying. "I know, but are you sure?" He walked up behind her and gave her one of those shoulder rubs that she loved and heard her respond as she sighed with pleasure. "We can wait, we really can."

Looking over her shoulder and up at him she said, "That really does feel good, but I'm okay. It seems whatever that this was has faded and right now I'm good to go."

Still reluctant he shrugged. "Okay, I'll let you set the pace, and if you feel like you need to come back and lay down or something just say the word and we can come back."

She stood up, looked him in the eyes, smiled, saying, "Works for me." And headed off in the direction where they had discovered that crack in the wall. He paused as he watched her walk away, shook his head, shrugged, and then followed.

It took them the rest of the morning to reach the split in the wall – not that this was the only such place. They had checked out a number of these cracks or splits finding the rest nothing but what they appeared. As they approached, they looked at the ground and could see a subtle trail or path that appeared to be heading directly into that crack, and once they reached and studied what was there, were really surprised by the size of the opening. There was some low lying brush that had grown over the opening and this crack ran parallel to the cliff making it appear to be just a small crack unless one happened to be standing at the right place to see that it went deeper then it appeared. Once they entered into it, they got their second surprise. The actual entrance was narrow but immediately past that point it opened up wide enough that they could walk side-by-side. Still the cliff walls remained tight along this trail making it impossible to go anywhere but along this trail. And because of the steepness of the sides and the overall narrowness, the trail remained in deep shadow furthering its invisibility. Absolutely nothing to show that this trail had existed from the outside, making it easy to overlook.

She shivered briefly because of the change in temperature, leaving the sunny canyon that they had been in to this perpetually shadowed trail. With her shiver she could see once again his concern. She smiled and again confirmed that she was all right and they continued hiking down this hidden twisting trail that literally cut through the mountain. They truly didn't know how long they had been following this trail but suddenly it made a sharp left, and like the entrance from the other canyon, suddenly dumping them into a very beautiful valley – a valley that appeared to be completely enclosed. And the trail – the one that they had used to enter the valley – giving the appearance of being the only access, although a well-hidden one as they had found out, had to be the one used by their ancestors. Since, like the other side, this point appeared to be as well hidden, they quickly built another cairn to insure that they could find their way back out. The suns were well towards late in the day when they exited into this hidden valley, so removing their packs and taking a quick break they decided that they would make the trip back. There was no time left to do any exploring at all. On the morrow they'd pack everything and move into this valley to explore it and see what hidden secrets would be here. At this moment they really didn't know if this hidden valley was the legendary Valley of the Gods or not. As twisted and broken as the land was here, this could just be another of the hundreds. Kal, watching Jura carefully, couldn't see anything that reflected that illness she had earlier in the morn so was at a loss as to what had happened. So with dusk not far off they headed back out the trail, pushing so that it wouldn't be completely dark by the time they reached their camp.

Yet when they awakened next morning she again was ill. Just what was going on with her? It seemed like her stomach couldn't handle anything in the mornings, well at least the last two anyway. And again, like yesterday, after a short period of time and eating of the travel bread, things settled down, and they made their move, packing up everything and moving deeper into the broken land. With their pack beast they reached their destination just a little earlier, set up their camp close to the pathway in and out of this canyon. And in the distance they could see some wild herd beasts grazing, and every once in a while staring at them as if they had never seen the likes of them before. They could hear falls, although, because it was cross canyon from them, it was muted somewhat, and not too far from where they had set up their camp, the stream worked its way across the valley and disappeared somewhere towards the herd beasts. And as the suns set, it was on a beautiful, peaceful, tranquil setting. It would be another day before the true exploring would begin, and with the seasons slipping away as they were this would be close to the end of the search for another cycle of the seasons.

Marking off on their calendar the end of another 9-day, they sat around their campfire enjoying the peace that seemed to permeate this place. Slowly as the heat of the day dissipated and the chill of the night arrived, with its soft down canyon breezes, they moved closer to the fire saying nothing and enjoying what was being offered. Finally Kal spoke saying, "If this place isn't the Valley of the Gods, it surely could be. I can't remember feeling this free of worries or having to think about ways to keep the predators away from our pack beast.

It's like we're away from the worries of this world, and such things aren't allowed here. I know that it's just an illusion, but at this moment that's the way it feels to me."

Jura thought a moment, and nodded her head in agreement. Yet there was that nagging worry as to what was causing her to be sick in the mornings, and yet feel okay the rest of the day. Just what was going on anyway? Still, he had a point; this place seemed to emanate a quiet and peace that they hadn't felt anywhere else. She sighed, for some reason she felt that all was right with the world and that didn't make sense. Maybe it had something to do with the atmosphere here in this hidden place – one of so many in this area. "Yes, I feel it too. But I don't know why. And maybe it's not important to know why, but to just accept it and leave it at that."

* * *

This is getting old, she thought as she was again behind their portable shelter heaving her guts out. *What is happening to me? And whatever it is, why is this only happening in the morning, and I feel normal the rest of the day? And why is it that that really bland, travel bread seems to be the only thing that settles this down and I'm fine the rest of the day?* She had no answers to these questions and she knew that Kal didn't. She could see the worry on his face since this was the third day in a row that this was taking place. They were far from anyone who could help if this turned out to be more than a nasty inconvenience. Yet, at the moment that's all it seemed to be. She had never liked throwing up, and hated the taste it left in one's mouth, but just couldn't keep it from happening. Well, maybe it would go away in a few days – although, she had to admit, if today was the day it went away it wasn't soon enough. Once this bout was finished she headed for the fire and the bread that he handed her. There was little else he could do. Again like the other two days once she had gone through the episode, had eaten that bread, her stomach would settle down, even though certain smells would make her queasy, but once past this point she'd be okay.

With the suns rising over the walls that surrounded this valley, they viewed an idyllic scene making both want to sit and watch as the day came alive. It was time to explore the valley and see what was really here. So they started by doing a circuit around by going from right to left as one looked to the center of the valley. As they headed this way they could hear the sounds of the waterfall getting louder, and as they turned a small corner, they could see the full falls in front of them. They could see that as time had passed that it had cut back creating this deeper indentation in the cliff walls. And that's exactly what you would have called them – walls. As they looked around the valley it appeared that all the walls were almost vertical. Climbing them would be next to impossible. As they approached the falls, the mist off them cooled the area and created small rainbows as the sunlight filtered through the mist. The beauty almost took their breath away. Still standing here they began to chill and moved on back into the sunlight to get warm once again.

On this first time around they carried nothing but some water and food for a zenith meal if they were out and away from their camp that long. Later when they began their serious exploration of this valley they'd bring their noting materials so that they could write down their first impressions, and what they discovered here. Once they had warmed, they continued their trek around the perimeter, and soon discovered a number of caves in one of the faces, and what appeared to have been a possible exit that had long been closed from what looked to be a landslide. Guessing at the location of this closed exit they could see that it might have led to the desolation. They knew that they had to be close and this one seemed to point west. And as the suns continued to climb into the sky they found that this place was actually much larger than they first thought. It was nearing the zenith and they guessed that they were less than half way around the perimeter. Soon they'd break eat their midday meal and finish the circuit.

The valley had many areas that formed offshoots from the main area, enlarging its size tremendously, and it was close to dusk by the time they had made the initial circuit getting a feel for the size and shape. This valley seemed to be a world untouched by any. There seemed to be a peace that lay over the area – one that they could more sense than feel. So when they finally reached their basecamp, they were relaxed. It seemed more like an outing than them exploring a hidden valley deep in the badlands. They thought that most likely they had located what could have been originally exits to west out of this valley. Exits that probably emptied into the desolation, but so much time had passed since these routes existed that it was difficult to tell whether it was their imagination or what they surmised was correct. The only way they truly would know would be to locate, from the desolation, the other side where these blocked trails exited. But that would be for a later time, if they felt the need to confirm what they had concluded.

So with night they watched as the major moon rose over the cliffs and lit the area with a soft ghost like light that made the valley even more magical. They could almost see spirits move through the grass and trees, crossing the small stream. But all they truly heard were the night crawlers as they sounded off looking for a mate. And since the sound was unbroken they knew that nothing was out there. If there had been a danger, then they would have fallen silent – silent until that danger or perceived danger had disappeared. So, with this music in their ears they fell asleep in each other's arms, knowing that on the morrow they would begin to search the center of this hidden paradise, and soon, and very soon, be heading back to their home.

* * *

As had become the norm for Jura, she went through her normal bout of throwing up, but instead of grumbling about it came back from behind the shelter smiling. Kal looked at her questioningly as she sat down next to him and put her arms around him and laid a big kiss on his mouth. "What was that for?" He asked, quite surprised by her actions.

"Well, mate of mine I have to say I have been a little slow to recognize what this is all about." Here she laughed

"All about?" He looked around and asked, "Are you meaning what we are doing? I thought we knew all about that."

Again she smiled and just shook her head. "I see you're just about as dense as I've been. Haven't you figured this out yet?"

Still at loss at the point she was trying to make, all he could do was shake his head – again not sure where she was leading him – although, as far as he was concerned, she could lead him wherever she wanted.

"Okay . . . look, and think about it. What would cause a female to be sick in the morning and then get better as the day goes on?"

He got this look in his eyes and suddenly realized what she had been trying to tell him. "Are you saying that you think you are carrying?"

With that she laughed again and threw her arms around him and said, "Yes!"

He sat there stunned. It was the last thing he expected. Although he couldn't deny that they had been quite physical out here. But it was the very last thing he expected. "Wow", was all he could say. He then hugged her back, completely at loss for any words. He whispered once again, "wow."

With that news it changed the atmosphere for both of them but they were close to returning anyway, and this early in the carrying would only mean the morning sickness and very little else. It would be later that problems could develop and that would be under the care of the females that helped other females through this time in their lives.

As they worked their way to the center of the valley, and in an area filled with tall grass they found it. The alter they all had read and studied back in the learning centers. It was facing the section of the cliffs that the waterfall bordered. In front of the altar was a wall, which was built of stone but was only about knee high. They saw that its shape was such that it formed a "V" and the point of that "V" pointed in the direction of the same cliffs where the altar faced. So, it had been here in this very valley, so very long ago in the past that their ancient ancestors had met their gods face to face, changing the name forever to the Valley of the Gods. Although how that truly came about and what had happened here still was an unknown, a mystery that may never have a true answer. They knew that such gods did not exist, and that there were natural laws at play, for which no gods controlled. There was one creator who had created everything, as they saw and understood it, and laid the laws of this world down, and would not have appeared as their ancestors had insisted that their gods had.

So understanding and solving this part would come to others. While they had yet to accomplish everything they had set their sights upon, with the carrying that Jura was now doing, it would have to wait for another time. And who really knew if that other time would arrive? Their desire to search the Sacred Mountains would now be on hold, for who knew how long. And maybe in the end it would fall to one of their ancestors to discover those hidden secrets, those other mysteries that lay deep in those mountains. They had accomplished what they had set out to do – changing myth to fact – proving the family writings to be accurate and it was enough. Now they had their true lives ahead of them and it was very promising – yes, very promising indeed. Much of their past had been what they had searched and discovered, but it was another generation's past. Yet, with the knowledge gained, changing myth to fact, they now knew much of their true past and the influences on their world. Now was the time to create their own history from their present, and with the changes that this had wrought, their future appeared to be truly strong – strong indeed.

EPILOGUE

With the suns rising it promised to be another hot and humid day. He was alone on this island and how he had arrived here was a blur and how he would find a way off an unknown. At least there was fresh water and plenty of food – although his choices were few. He looked to the east once again as he had done every day since arriving here. It had been difficult at the beginning and the passage of time hard to track. There only appeared to be two seasons here – wet and dry. So he guessed that he must have been here for approximately three cycles of the seasons, but he had no way to track the passage of time accurately. The island was large enough to provide support for a small population, at which he laughed bitterly, since at the moment, it was a population of one. His clothes were rags, a remnant of their former selves.

He cursed his lack of control over his anger for what was probably the thousandth time. Had he controlled it that night then he wouldn't be here now. But that was the past, and again he laughed bitterly since the past was his specialty. But no more, no, he was stuck. He couldn't see the mainland that was just over the horizon, so he paced his prison. After all that's what it really was. At least it might as well have been. He knew that there were small boats that worked the large sea, but rarely came to these islands. There was nothing to attract them here. Someday that could change, or maybe some sailor would get brave and want to see what was out here, but for now here he was. He truly missed the game, the fencing between his rivals and himself. He wondered what had happened to those two and if they had been successful in what they were trying to accomplish. But here there were only the winds, the island, the sandy beaches, and the squawking of the feathered fliers.

He remembered that night, when his anger drove him into the wrong part of the village, the fight that had followed – the collapsing of that old dock after he had received that wound. Yet, even as he recounted this he smiled. Before that knife wound he had taken four of the bastards out. He still had it. But then that dock collapsed and into that rain gorged river he went with the rest of them. He had been lucky that he had found a major piece of that dock and had clung to it as it tore down that river trying to shake him off as a beast shook water off its back. Yet somehow he had remained with it. Eventually exhausted he had passed out, only to find that it was broad daylight and he was now in the sea when he had awakened. And at that time panic had risen as there was no land in sight. And in whatever water flow he was in, it continued to push him west. Somewhere during this time he passed out again only to awaken when he found himself beached on this island and that had been a long time ago.

Sabohl paced the eastern shore walking the beaches looking east. *Someday, yes someday I'll get off this island. Then all of you had better watch out – because, when I return, and this will happen, I will reclaim what I have lost.* He smiled as his thoughts reached out for that distant hidden shore. Yes someday he'd leave this prison, this island, and the world better be ready.

F.D. Brant always wanted to write, but life got in the way. Finally after retiring he got his chance.

Storytelling and writing has always been F.D. Brant's passion, but responsibilities took preference. And because of those responsibilities it took retiring to allow those passions to come to fruition. Since retiring he has written nine books, and maintains a weekly eclectic blog, Words in the Wind.

Growing up in the backcountry he learned the appreciation of "doing things for yourself". Because it was impossible to call in someone to repair anything one either did it themselves or went without. This led to the appreciation of the natural world, and the daily struggles that one faced as nature threw problems at the family that had to be overcome, leading to confidence and self-sufficiency. This led to the strong characters that populate his stories and books. And his female protagonists are strong willed and confident – something that he saw in both in his mother and sister.

www.ingramcontent.com/pod-product-compliance
Lightning Source LLC
Chambersburg PA
CBHW050615170726
48283CB00001B/258